# PASSING HIS GUARD

AN AGAINST THE CAGE NOVEL

# ALSO BY MELYNDA PRICE

Against the Cage Series

*Win by Submission*

The Redemption Series

*Until Darkness Comes*
*Shades of Darkness*
*Courting Darkness*
*Braving the Darkness*

# PASSING HIS GUARD

MELYNDA PRICE

AN AGAINST THE CAGE NOVEL

This is a work of fiction. Names, characters, organizations, places, events, and incidents are either products of the author's imagination or are used fictitiously.



Published by Montlake Romance, Seattle

www.apub.com



ISBN-13: 9781503945517
ISBN-10: 1503945510

Cover design by Jason Blackburn

Printed in the United States of America

# PROLOGUE

"Did anyone follow you?" Axel Andrews demanded as he shut the stall door and slid the wobbly lock into place.

"No. I got here early, just like you asked me to. Mind telling me what this is all about? Haven't heard a word from you in ten years, and now you're calling me out of the blue like we're cloak and dagger."

"You're better off if you don't know the details. Let's just say I've fucked up—pissed off the wrong people and I'm trying like hell to make things right before it's too late."

"Seein' as how you and I are in the john talking through a wall, I'd say that ship has already sailed for you, my friend. What kind of trouble are you in?"

"The mob kind."

"Shit . . ." Henry hissed, exhaling a sigh. "What about Ryann? Does she know?"

"No. And I want to keep it that way if I can help it."

"Fair enough. What do you need me to do?"

"Hang on to this." Axel passed a credit-card-sized envelope underneath the divider to his friend. "If something happens to me, I need you to make sure Ryann gets it. I gotta go. I'm pretty sure I'm being followed. Wait here a few more minutes and then go out the back when you leave. Thanks for doing this, Henry. I owe ya one."

"It's nothing you wouldn't do for me. You've helped me out of more than one tight spot back in the day."

A nostalgic chuckle rumbled in Axel's chest as he thought back to the antics of his childhood friend and all the trouble they used to get into running the streets of Brooklyn as kids. Life was simpler back then. It was a tragedy how quickly time seemed to slip away. He was thankful for the bond youth had forged between them, an unbreakable tie that Axel had no choice but to lean on right now. When this was over, once he put the mistakes of his past behind him, they'd have to sit down together at O'Lunney's and have a beer.

"Take care of yourself." Axel unlatched the flimsy lock, anxious to keep moving so as not to arouse suspicion. The hinges squeaked in protest as he opened the door.

"You too, man."

Axel left the bar and headed down the street. Zipping his coat, he tucked his chin into the collar and shoved his hands into the pockets, burrowing in for the six-block walk back to his car. He'd made every attempt to lose his tail before entering the bar, but the man following him was a professional—too good to be seen—but Axel knew he was there . . .

His skin prickled with unease, the fine hairs at the nape of his neck rising. He quickened his steps, the brisk clip accelerating the tempo echoing off the vacant buildings as he ducked down an alley, taking a short-cut back to his car. A fresh coat of snow blanketed the streets—snow was still falling, but not fast enough to cover his tracks. The cold snap had come on fast and hard, driving many of the people who were usually out at this time of night to seek either the shelter of their homes or the transportation of cabs.

How had his life spun so out of control? The question haunted him almost as relentlessly as the man following him. He heard it before he saw it—the roar of the engine, followed by the blinding headlights as the car turned down the alley, its tires grappling for traction as they struggled to meet the demand of the accelerator.

Axel glanced behind him, adrenaline flooding his veins as he broke into a run for the intersection, dashing to the finish line in a life-or-death race. He had nowhere to go, trapped between two brick walls with space barely wide enough to fit the Escalade barreling down on him. It drew closer. He ran faster—legs feeling like they were stuck in quicksand as the vehicle sped toward him. The road ahead was near, yet so far. He swore he could feel the heat of the headlights burning the back of his neck. Oh, God! He wasn't going to make it!

Bracing for impact, Axel squeezed his eyes closed, one thought resonating in his mind: *I'm so sorry, Ryann . . .*

# CHAPTER

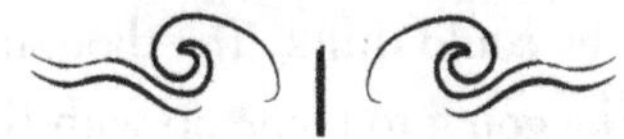

Ms. Andrews?"

"Yes?" Her grip tightened on the receiver at the sound of that all-too-familiar voice. Dread took up residence where her heart used to be, which now beat wildly in her throat.

"Twenty days, Ms. Andrews."

"I'm well aware of how much time I have left," she snapped. "And like I said before, you'll get your damn money."

"All seventy-five-thousand of it."

*Okay, so that could be a problem.* "I umm . . . might be a little short."

"How short?"

"Ten thousand."

He chuckled, that insidious rumble chilling the blood in her veins.

"You're going to have to suck a lot of cock for ten grand, sweetheart."

Revulsion sent a surge of bile burning up her throat. God, she hated this man—this faceless stranger who'd played a starring role in her nightmares for the past month. The calls began the day after her father died. Not a day had gone by since where she wasn't reminded that time was running out.

"You're being unreasonable. This isn't even my debt."

"Sins of the father, Ms. Andrews. It's unfortunate the life insurance policy wasn't large enough to cover what he owed. We've been more than patient with you."

That was debatable. If by *patient* he meant hounding her day after day and threatening her with bodily harm if she didn't pay, then yes, he'd been patient. The line went dead, and she willed her clamoring heart to calm so she could think. Ten thousand dollars . . . How in God's name was she going to come up with that kind of cash? It might as well be a million. There was no way she could earn ten grand in two weeks—not even if she did take that prick up on his less than helpful suggestion, which she'd rather die than do.

Between her father's life insurance and exhausting her credit with the bank, she was still short. The only thing she had left was her father's business, Andrews Private Investigation Services, and now even that was slipping through her fingers. The house, the business—all of it, mortgaged to support her father's secret gambling addiction.

She'd known her dad had a penchant for cards, but he'd hidden his vice well—too well. She had no idea he'd squandered it all, or that he owed seventy-five thousand dollars to Vincent Moralli, the don and patriarch of the infamous Moralli family. Not until a man approached her at her father's funeral last month with a pile of debt notes, all bearing her father's indisputable signature.

She knew the "accident" that claimed her father's life was no accident. She'd spent the last month doing her own investigation because New York's finest certainly weren't trying very hard to find her father's killer. Unfortunately, she'd found little evidence to support what she knew in her heart to be true—Vincent Moralli had murdered her father. His enforcer had all but admitted as much, but proving it was another matter entirely, and the police weren't interested in hearing what they called her "conspiracy theories." She'd spent the day at the precinct—again—trying to light a fire under someone's ass and running into roadblock after roadblock.

After an exhausting eight hours of senseless paperwork and being shuffled from one detective to another, it was obvious that Moralli's reach extended deep into the pockets of the police department. Her suspicions were confirmed when an officer pulled her aside as she was leaving today and told her, in no uncertain terms, that unless she wanted to end up like her father, she'd better let it go.

The thought of giving up, of letting her father's killer get away, went against every fiber of her being. But after today, it was glaringly evident the police weren't going to help her. At this point, she saw little alternative than to just pay the debt. Which brought her around full circle to one blatantly obvious problem—she didn't have enough money. What was she going to do? Desperation clawed up her throat, suffocating her as she fought to stave off the rising panic.

"Excuse me."

She startled at the unexpected voice, letting out a surprised yelp. Her head jerked up to meet the impatient scowl of a woman standing in the doorway of her office, flanked by two guys who looked like the Men in Black. Before she could greet the fifty-something brunette, who was dressed in a calf-length fur coat, the woman snapped, "I'm looking for the private detective Ryan Andrews. Is he here?"

Her dangling diamond earrings weighed heavily on her lobes, stretching the skin unnaturally taut. A matching necklace, easily worth the remainder of Ryann's debt, encased the woman's long, slender neck, drawing her gaze to the fine lines and wrinkles apparently no amount of money could erase.

"I'm Ryann," she replied, silently cursing her father for giving her a boy's name. How many times did mistakes like this happen?—every freaking day, it seemed. It might have been cute when she was younger, but now that she was an adult it wasn't funny anymore.

Well, that wasn't exactly true, because the look on this woman's face right now was pretty freaking hilarious.

Disdain oozed from the woman, as potent as her heavy floral perfume. "There must be some mistake."

"I assure you, ma'am, there is no mistake. I am Ryann Andrews—two *n*'s," she added with mirroring crispness.

The woman's disapproving scowl deepened, putting all that Botox to the test.

"What can I do for you?" Ryann asked, forcing a smile and sweetening her tone as she grappled for patience. The office had been closed for well over an hour. Since she'd lost the day getting the run-around at the police station, she'd come in after hours to work on a few cases. She must have forgotten to lock the door behind her. Her assistant usually took care of those things, but since Andrews Private Investigation Services was nearly bankrupt, she'd unfortunately had no choice but to let Joyce go, and now she was running a solo operation here—and apparently not very well.

She held the woman's bold stare as she waited for the aged diva to state her name and business. Something about her pricked Ryann's memory, giving her the distinct feeling she should know who this woman was. She stepped into Ryann's office like she owned the place—which immediately tap-danced on Ryann's last nerve, considering how close she was to losing it.

"I was told Ryan Andrews specializes in missing-persons cases."

The woman spoke her name as if she were still unwilling to accept that "Ryan" had a vagina and was sitting across from her right now.

"Oh, Ryann does," she replied, referring to herself in the third person. "In fact, Ryann is very good at what *she* does. What can I do for you, Ms. . . . ?" Ryann waited for the woman to supply her name, but she declined to answer, and instead glanced back at one of her heavies, as if undecided whether or not to proceed.

Agent J nodded his approval.

"But she's a woman," she hissed under her breath.

"Then perhaps she'll have better luck than the last man you hired," Agent J replied, a mumbled response probably not meant for her to hear. "It's unlikely he'll put this one in the hospital."

And *that* was definitely not for her ears. *Seriously? In the hospital? Oh, hell no!*

"Very well." The woman exhaled an exasperated sigh. She turned back toward Ryann, opened the snap of her Louis Vuitton clutch, and pulled out a photo. "I need you to find my son." She set the photo on Ryann's desk and, with one perfectly manicured nail, slid it toward her.

Ryann picked up the photo and studied the glossy pic. The man appeared to be in his late twenties, maybe early thirties. He was dressed in a dark blue suit that would probably pay her mortgage for a couple of months. His tawny hair was tamed by a product to ensure every strand remained perfectly in place. His square jaw drew her eyes to the grim set of his mouth which appeared to be the masculine version of the pursed one frowning at her right now.

The man was breathtakingly gorgeous. Even from the picture, Ryann could see he exuded discipline and rigidity. He gave off an air of tempered control—except for the eyes. They didn't fit, and damn if that wasn't the most stunning thing about him. Dark amber with flecks of brown and gold, the closest color she could compare it to would be a tigereye stone. How utterly fitting, because the eyes staring back at her held an undercurrent of untamed wildness and caged discontent.

Gauging the man's size in reference to the park bench he stood beside, she'd put him at a few inches over six feet and just shy of two hundred pounds—not exactly the kind of missing-persons case she was expecting.

"If you don't mind me saying"—Ryann handed back the photo—"in my experience, a grown man that looks like this isn't *missing.* If you don't know where he is, it's because he doesn't want to be found. There's a difference."

"Hardly," the woman scoffed with enough disdain to officially put her on Ryann's bitch list.

"How long has he been *missing*?"

"Officially? Fourteen months. But it was going on long before that, disappearing for days, missing important meetings—"

"It sounds like he's on drugs," Ryann interjected. *There, mystery solved. You can go now.*

"It's not drugs," the woman snapped.

She seemed awfully sure of that, giving Ryann the distinct impression there was a hell of a lot more to this story than Ms. Stick-Up-Her-Ass was telling her. Considering what she'd overheard, Ryann wasn't the first person hired to track down this woman's son. And by the sounds of it, he didn't want to be found.

"Listen, Ms. . . . ?" Again Ryann waited for the woman to supply her name.

"Madeline Kruze," she said with all the haughtiness of a woman dressed to the nines and trailing two bodyguards behind her.

*Shit.* Now the face connected with the name. This woman was Senator Kruze's wife. And she was every bit the hell on wheels in person that she appeared to be on camera. So the senator's son was missing, huh? Interesting . . . And she wanted to hire Ryann to find him. Well, this day just kept getting better and better.

"So, do you want the case or not?" she said impatiently.

No. She most certainly did not. But before Ryann could tell her as much, the woman continued: "I'll pay double your fee."

"Why me? There must be plenty of private investigators in Manhattan you could hire."

"Not with your specialty. Your knack for finding missing persons is . . . impressive." The woman spit out the compliment as if it had been distasteful on her tongue. "As I said, I'll pay double your fee, plus a five-thousand-dollar bonus if you can deliver him to me within two weeks."

Wait. What? "Deliver" him? She wasn't the freaking UPS. Her job was locating missing persons, not returning them home like little lost pets—and Ryann had the distinct impression that was what this woman wanted. There were missing children, runaways, desperate parents that needed her help. *This* was definitely not one of those cases, and would no doubt turn out to be a big waste of time. She'd been around this block enough times to know there was a hell of a lot more going on here than that woman was telling her.

But she was offering Ryann a lot of money to retrieve her son—enough money for Ryann to pay off the remainder of her father's debt and get herself out from under Moralli's strong arm. Coming to grips with the fact that she was going to have to take this case, she sighed and leaned back in her chair. She pulled her cheaters off and dropped them on the desk. Closing her eyes, she pressed her fingers into her throbbing temples.

After a moment, she lifted her head and met the woman's determined stare. "Two weeks, you said?" That was a short amount of time to track down someone who obviously didn't want to be found and bring him home—short of kidnapping, that is. And this guy didn't exactly look like the abductable type. "What's the rush? He's been gone more than a year. What is happening in two weeks?"

"His wedding."

"Get up!"

The metal rasp of curtains being yanked open sent a blast of bright Nevada sun beaming onto Aiden's face. He squinted against the unwelcome light and lifted his arm, shielding his eyes from the blinding assault.

"What the fuck, Coach?"

"Don't you 'what the fuck' me, boy. Easton's at the gym waiting for you and he's pissed as hell."

"Aww shit . . ." he muttered under his breath and lifted his head, squinting to see the alarm clock on the nightstand—5:50 a.m. Trapped beneath a tangle of arms and legs, Aiden tried to wrest himself free without waking the women on both sides of him.

Marcus, his surly coach, wasn't nearly as considerate. "Come on, ladies," he announced, kicking the foot of Aiden's bed. "Up and at 'em." As he made his way across the bedroom, he swiped up the clothing off the floor and began tossing it at the women. When it began raining bras, panties, shirts, and miniskirts they began to stir, stretching lazily beside Aiden. Bare breasts rubbed against his ribs, long legs dragging over his as they reluctantly untangled with moans of protest.

They didn't seem to care they were no longer alone. Apparently, modesty was a foreign concept to these women. Aiden, on the other hand, would have preferred not having a cranky Marcus glowering at him while the woman on his right slid her hand between his legs to grab his—

"Uh-uh!" Marcus barked, kicking the foot of his bed again when the blonde tried to slip her hand beneath the covers. "This disco stick is done dancing, sweetheart. Get dressed and get out—now."

Damn . . . Coach must really be pissed. It wasn't like him to be so gruff. The man normally had the patience of Job, which was something Aiden always admired about the guy—so opposite his own father. The girls booed and whined about getting tossed, but they were smart enough not to push the old guy, who looked like he was about to lose his shit. They began exchanging bras and sorting out whose clothing belonged to whom as they dressed, making no attempt to cover their nakedness from Marcus's scowling view.

"It's not even six a.m. yet," Aiden complained, scrubbing his hands over his face, trying to wake up.

"Cole's been at the gym since five."

"He still bitchy?"

"As ever. He's the jackass and you're the jack-off. I swear between the two of you, you're gonna force me into early retirement."

Once dressed, the blonde turned and kissed his cheek. "See you later, Disco."

"Call me," the brunette added, planting a lip-lock on his mouth. They took another moment to search the floor for their shoes. The girls held on to each other for balance as they slipped into their stilettos and wobbled precariously toward the door. Marcus stood by the entrance, ushering them out. Whether their instability was from sleep deprivation or intoxication, Aiden wasn't sure. He tipped his head, his gaze following the girls as they walked away, appreciating how that black miniskirt hugged the blonde's barely covered ass.

Once they were out of view, he glanced at a glaring Marcus, whose arms were crossed over his burly chest as he shook his head in disgust.

"What?" Aiden grouched.

"You're better than this, Kruze. Getting trashed every night and crashing in hotel rooms with your latest piece of ass."

Maybe he was better than this—once—but he left that guy back in New York along with the Armani suits and five-thousand-dollar-a-plate dinner parties. "Don't judge me," he growled, throwing back the covers, mindless of his own nakedness. "You're not my father." Swinging his legs over the side of the bed, he stood and then promptly grabbed hold of the nightstand to steady himself against the spins. Fuck, he was still drunk.

"Son of a bitch . . ." Marcus muttered under his breath, dragging his hand over his hairless head.

Once the topsy-turvys slowed down, Aiden made his way to the foot of the bed and snagged his own clothes off the hotel floor.

"You're right," Marcus snapped. "I'm not your dad—thank God. But I am your coach, which means you do *what* I say *when* I say, and right now I'm telling you to get your ass in that shower. Wash those women off and be ready to leave in fifteen minutes. You've got a fight in two days. What the hell were you thinking? I can't believe you, staying out until God knows when, getting shitfaced, and whoring it up."

He wadded his clothes in his hand and had the decency to hold them over his groin as he shuffled toward Marcus, the self-appointed doorkeeper. The old man was tough as nails and hard on his fighters, but that was nothing compared to the bear he'd become since his niece, Katie Miller, had taken a rather abrupt and unexpected departure back home to Wisconsin. Not that Aiden let it stop him from kicking the hornet's nest as he passed the guy, knowing full well he was going to pay for it once they hit the gym.

"Whoring implies there was payment for services rendered. That right there was for free. YOLO . . ."

# CHAPTER

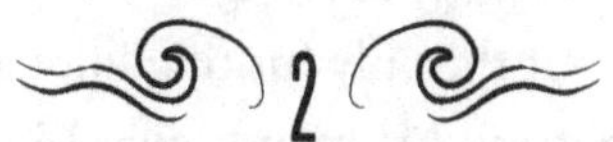

2

*Fff-fff . . . fff-fff . . . fff-fff . . .* Aiden exhaled in succinct time with his punches as they connected with the heavy bag. Cole Easton, aka "the Beast of the East," stood on the other side, holding it steady. The man was an MMA god—and his best friend. It was a damn shame what happened to him. These last seven months had been a living hell for the guy, and just when it seemed like there was finally a light at the end of the tunnel . . .

"You heard from Katie yet?" Aiden asked before laying another round of rapid punches into the bag.

"Nope."

*Fff-fff . . . fff-fff . . . fff-fff . . .* "You gonna call her? Straighten this mess out?"

"Nope."

*Fff-fff . . . fff-fff . . . fff-fff . . .* "You wanna talk about it?"

"Nope."

Aiden didn't envy his friend. Easton was going through some tough shit right now, and it didn't help that he'd fallen for his physical therapist, who just happened to be his coach's niece. What he wouldn't give to know what happened between those two to send that gorgeous woman running back to Wisconsin.

*Fff-fff . . . fff-fff . . . fff-fff . . .* "You know you're a fucking idiot, right?"

"Yep."

"Kruze!" Coach bellowed across the gym. "Warm-up time is over, dickhead! Del Toro is here! Get your ass in the ring!"

"You really pissed Coach off," Cole muttered, unhelpfully stating the obvious.

*Fff-fff . . . fff-fff . . . fff-fff . . .* "Yep."

"Looks like I'm not the only fucking idiot around here."

Del Toro was putting his mouth guard in place when Aiden slipped between the ropes. Heading to the opposite corner, he took a moment to stretch out a cramp in his calf muscle. Shit, he must be dehydrated. So, admittedly it probably hadn't been the best idea to drink a bottle of Jägermeister and then head back to his hotel for a threesome. But what the hell, right? He grabbed his bottle of Gatorade and drained it before tossing it into the trash near the lockers. "You see that, old man? Nothing but net," he proudly proclaimed, raising his arms in the air as if he'd just won the middleweight title.

Marcus rolled his eyes, but the twitch of his top lip told Aiden the cranky-ass was trying really hard to stay mad at him. Not a feat easily accomplished when he turned on his charm.

"Nice shot, Disco," Del Toro called, stepping into the center of the ring and knocking his gloved fists together a couple of times, the universal language for *Get your ass over here and let's do this.* Nikko "the Bull" Del Toro was no fucking joke. The guy could pound—and if you didn't have good stand-up, the Bull would pound your ass into the mat.

"Thanks, man."

"Too bad that's the only shot you're gonna land today." The ex-marine's challenging grin only made him look meaner, the scar on his top lip pulling tight. Stony gray eyes met Aiden's—hard and determined. There was something in that stare, or maybe a lack of something, that put Aiden on edge. The guy always seemed like he was holding his shit together by a thread. He pitied the dumb bastard who ever clipped it.

"We'll see about that," Aiden muttered before slipping in his mouth guard.

Easton took a seat next to Marcus, and they whispered back and forth, their eyes locked on him. "Let's see what you've got," Coach called out, signaling him to get the show on the road. Del Toro wasted no time assuming his fighting stance: knees bent, arms up, and fists clenched. He swung for Aiden, narrowly missing his jaw.

*Motherfucker . . .*

"He's got a long reach!" Easton yelled, "Don't let him range you!"

Del Toro dropped his guard, and Aiden couldn't resist. He shot in as Cole yelled from the sideline, "Dammit, he's baiting you!"

But it was too late. He swung for Del Toro's face as the fighter's arm came up, deflecting the blow, which left Aiden open to take an uppercut. The blow to his jaw was fast and solid. It rocked him back a couple of steps and sent a few stars bursting behind his eyes.

"Fuck!" Easton yelled from the sideline. "Are you still drunk, Kruze?"

*Maybe . . .*

"Because that is the oldest shit in the book and you just fell for it. You do that in the cage two nights from now and you are going to lose this fucking fight!"

Well, that right hook killed the remainder of Aiden's buzz and effectively pissed him the hell off. He tipped his head to the left, then to the right, cracking his neck back into place, and then nodded to Del Toro, silently complimenting his striking. The fighter gave him an arrogant, lopsided grin and relaxed his stance, confidence overruling common sense. Kruze took a step forward and wobbled just enough to incite Del Toro's famed killer instinct. But when the Bull came for him this time, Aiden was ready. He ducked as the powerful fist came at him and brought his leg up, sending a hook kick slamming into Del Toro's ribs. Air whooshed from the guy's lungs, the momentum sending him forward just enough to bring his face in line with Aiden's fist. He slammed an uppercut into the Bull's jaw that took the fighter to his knees.

"Stop, goddammit!" Cole yelled, voice booming off the metal rafters, as he jumped to his feet. "Do either of you two assholes know the meaning of the word *spar*? If you want to kick each other's asses, save it for the cage!" He turned to Del Toro and pointed at Aiden. "He has a fight in two days! I don't want him stepping into that ring with a fucking concussion! And you—" He turned his wrath on Aiden. "Del Toro is training for a rematch with Kennedy, so how about you don't break his fucking ribs? Give me those gloves!"

"Oh, shit . . ." Coach muttered, no doubt wishing he hadn't handed Aiden's training over to the light-heavyweight champion. "Katie is going to have my ass."

Cole pinned Marcus with a steely glare. "Katie isn't here now, is she?"

Aiden didn't miss the accusation in that snarled growl or the guilty grimace on Marcus's face.

Cole climbed into the ring with a surprising amount of agility for a guy who hadn't even been able to walk six months ago. He'd taken an illegal flying side kick to the back after winning the light-heavyweight title, shattering his spine and what they all had thought would be his career. It was nothing short of a miracle the guy was standing in front of him right now—a miracle in the form of a physical therapist named Katie Miller.

Del Toro pulled off his open-mitt gloves and slapped them into Cole's waiting hand. He shot Aiden a *sucks to be you* smirk and rose to his feet.

"Go get those ribs checked out," Easton told the fighter before turning his full attention to Aiden. "Now I don't have a guard in, so if you hit me in the fucking mouth, I'll kill you." That being said, the Beast of the East knocked his gloves together and they squared off.

There had to be some kind of mistake. This could not be the same Aiden Kruze, son of Sen. Bennett Kruze and Lady Madeline Kruze, that Ryann was searching for. Yet the similarities were striking. His eyes, for one—those amber irises flecked with dark brown and gold were unmistakable. Even from across the gym, she could see their unnaturally bright hue that seemed to glow with a predatory glint, reminding her of a giant cat. He was larger than the man in the photo. Perhaps not in height but definitely more muscular, and his hair . . . still the same tawny color, it was considerably longer and disheveled. Not one rebellious strand cooperated with the other.

Aiden stood in the center of the ring as one fighter handed another his gloves and then exited the ring. He moved a little slow, seeming to guard his left side. The two men in the ring began sparring, and watching them fight was like observing a well-choreographed dance. Aiden moved fast and fluidly, ducking and dodging more punches than he was throwing. His opponent seemed stiffer, but what he lacked in footwork he more than made up for in skill and power.

Ryann had never been an MMA fan. She knew of the sport, understood it was a combination of mixed martial arts styles along with boxing and wrestling, but she'd never seen an actual fight. Watching Aiden in the ring sparring with the other man, she had to admit being a bit awed in the basest, most primal way. The Darwin in her stood up and took notice of what was, without a doubt, the most beautifully well-built man she'd ever seen. Heat flooded her veins, centering in all her feminine places as she stood there watching these two men exchange blows. She was so engrossed in the mock-fight playing out before her that she didn't even see the third man approach until he was right beside her.

"You lost?"

"Excuse me?" She startled, taking a step back to put a little more distance between her and the man towering over her.

"This isn't Snap Fitness, lady. Women aren't allowed in here."

*What a sexist jackass.* "Oh . . . I was umm . . . was looking for someone."

The man crossed his beefy arms over his chest, and his dark brows drew tight. Eyes the color of steel, and just as hard, stared her down. The scar slashing through his cheek didn't do the guy any favors. He looked too mean to be called handsome, though she figured some women would find him so—if they were into that *I'm going to eat your liver with fava beans and a bottle of Chianti* sort of thing. Ryann, on the other hand . . . not so much.

"Let me guess," he said, rolling his eyes in disgust. "You're looking for Disco."

"Who?"

Instead of answering her, he made half a turn toward the fighters and yelled, "Hey, Disco, you've got another banger here to see you!"

She looked behind her. Was he talking about her? What the hell was a "banger"?

Aiden turned to look her way. His attention shifted from the brute standing beside her to Ryann. When her eyes briefly locked with those amber jewels, she momentarily forgot to breathe. Something sparked between them, an instant connection held suspended in time—until the man he was sparring with punched him in the face. Ryann gasped, sucking in a giant gulp of air. Aiden stumbled back a step and swiped the back of his gloved hand across his now bleeding lip. He spit out his mouth guard, sending it tumbling across the mat. "Goddammit, Easton! That was a cheap-ass shot and you know it."

"Then keep your eyes on me, asshole—where they belong, instead of on that tail making eyes at you."

Ryann stiffened indignantly. She wasn't making eyes at him, and she sure as hell wasn't anyone's tail. The man beside her chuckled, seeming to take great delight in watching Aiden take one in the mouth. His dark, throaty rumble made the fine hairs on the back of her neck prickle and she shot him a disapproving scowl. "Think that's funny, do you?"

"Immensely. Serves the bastard right for breaking my rib."

She glanced back at Aiden to find him slipping between the ropes. The moment his feet touched the ground, he headed her way at a determined clip that did funny things to her pulse.

"That's enough, Del Toro. Leave the lady alone."

Aiden's attention was fixed on the man standing beside her. It wasn't until the other fighter chuffed and ambled away that the full weight of that imposing stare became centered solely on her—up close and personal. Her heart actually missed a beat, which was so clichéd she might have laughed out loud if her lungs hadn't quit working. As his gaze swept over her, making an unhurried head-to-toe assessment, she swore to the Almighty she could actually feel everywhere those eyes touched. They lingered on her breasts without apology. Her nipples hardened in response, and she prayed they weren't showing through her rayon top, but she suspected her plea had gone unanswered when a crooked grin tipped his mouth.

As that bold stare traveled south, she found herself thankful for those many hours of Pilates that kept her stomach flat and her waist narrow. By the time his eyes met hers again, all trace of seriousness was gone, and in its place was a flirtatious cad.

"Hey, baby girl. What can I do you for?"

It took her a moment to find her voice. "Are you Aiden Kruze?"

His roguish grin faltered for the briefest moment. "That depends."

"On what?"

"On who wants to know, because I'm sure we've never met before."

"Oh, and how's that?" With all the tail this fighter was obviously getting, how could he possibly keep it straight?

"Because I'd remember meeting the most beautiful woman I've ever seen."

Oh, he was good . . . dangerously good . . . "I'm here because—"

"I know why you're here." He cut her off, his voice a husky growl that should not be warming her in all the right places right now.

"You do now?"

He smiled, and she felt that panty-dropping grin all the way to her toes. Oh, boy, this was not good. Not only was Aiden Kruze a breathtakingly handsome handful, he was also engaged to be married, and she would do well to remember that. That thought alone stopped her cold. What kind of a moral-less asshole eye-fucked a woman he just met while he was engaged to marry another? Seriously. It didn't matter how gorgeous this guy was, he was a total douche bag.

Hanging on to that ire, Ryann scowled and folded her arms over her chest, which only seemed to succeed in drawing that arrogant gaze back down to her well-endowed cleavage. She cleared her throat loudly to say *My eyes are up here, buddy*, and arched her brow. "Why is it, exactly, that you think I'm here?" she asked, her tone saccharine sweet.

"You want a ticket to the fight."

"The fight?"

"Yeah, at the Mirage. It's sold out and you want me to get you in. I tell you what, baby girl. I'll do you one better. Go to the ticket office and I'll have a front row seat waiting for you with a pass to the after party."

"But—"

"Now I gotta get back to training," he said, cutting her off again.

The man slipped his arm around her shoulder and guided her toward the door, not caring that he was getting his sweat all over her. She would have corrected his assumption—informing him he was a self-absorbed pompous asshole-cheater, if all rational thought hadn't fled her mind the moment he touched her.

Holy shit . . . every nerve ending inside her lit up with feminine awareness. This was unreal. She'd never had this strong a reaction to a man before. Even the sound of his voice was like sex to her ears.

He pulled her closer, hugging her against his side, and bent his head, whispering, "I'll see you after the fight, and we'll pick up where we left off."

His breath smelled of mint, mixed with the vaporous undertone of alcohol. Was he . . . drunk? The heat of his exhale skated down her neck, sending a shiver of goose bumps prickling over her arms. Her pulse quickened at his wicked promise as he ushered her out the front door. Before Ryann could respond or string two coherent words together, his hand connected solidly with her ass in a parting farewell and the gym doors rattled shut behind her.

And there she was, standing on the sidewalk with wet panties, wearing his sweat all over her, and with a date she never asked for. *What in the hell just happened?*

# CHAPTER

3

Aiden was not exaggerating when he said the Mirage was sold out. The only empty seats she could see were the ones beside her, seats she suspected were reserved for family, and sitting there made her feel a little awkward. People eyed her with a mixture of surprise and curiosity. Some gave her blatant glares—mostly the women—while others stared at her like she was some kind of circus oddity.

A guy from the group of men, presumably Aiden's camp, came over and plopped down in the empty seat beside her. His shirt had *Disco Stick* printed across the front of it and *Take a ride* plastered across the back. How cute. She recognized the man he'd been sparring with the other day, standing among the group. He looked no friendlier now than he had then.

"Don't let those bitches get to you. They're just jealous," Disco Shirt said, bumping her with his shoulder as if they were old friends.

Ryann turned an assessing look on the man. He was lithe and muscular. The scar above his brow and over his cheekbone hinted he was a fellow fighter. The man was handsome, though not in Aiden's league of hotness, but he could definitely hold his own.

"I'm not bothered." A denial neither of them believed. "I just don't like large crowds"—which was absolutely the truth.

He shrugged as if her lie mattered not to him either way. "Suit yourself. I'm Regan, by the way."

"Ryann," she said, accepting his offered hand. His grip was firm, his palm callused—exactly how she had imagined the hands of a fighter would be like.

"You excited about the fight tonight?"

"Curious is more like it. I've never been to something like this before."

Regan laughed. "Well you picked a great one to break your cherry on, sweetheart. Disco puts on one hell of a show. Wicked talented fighter, that guy. So . . . if you don't mind me asking, how do you know our boy?"

"I don't."

Regan shot her a surprised look. "Yet here you are, sitting in a spot reserved for family and close friends." The suspicion in his tone suggested he didn't believe her.

"I assure you I am neither."

"Wow . . . Disco must want in your pants pretty bad to give you a front row seat to this fight."

Ryann's jaw dropped.

"What?" he asked, having the nerve to sound offended. He did a double take, looking between her and the aisle as if expecting "our boy" to come jogging down it any moment. "Why are you looking at me like that?"

"Like what?"

"Like I just told you something you didn't already know."

No comment. This conversation was not happening. Change of subject. "Why do you call him Disco?"

As if on cue, the house lights went out and floodlights clicked on, illuminating the path from the octagon to the doorway where the fighters emerged. Regan leaned closer to be heard above the announcer and yelled over the ramping noise. "You're about to find out." Standing, he laid his hand on her shoulder, giving it a friendly squeeze and said, "Enjoy the show, Ryann. It was nice meeting you."

As the music started up, Regan made his way back to his friends. She immediately recognized the beat coming from the speakers and couldn't hold back the bubble of laughter. *Lady Gaga? You've got to be kidding me . . .* She rolled her eyes, shaking her head as the intro continued to play. *This guy is walking out to "Love Game"? Seriously?*

"Ladies and gentlemen, it's the fight you've been waiting for! Put your hands together for Aiden 'Disco Stick' Kruuuze!"

The crowd went wild and the music boomed louder.

Ryann followed the gaze of the masses and watched as Aiden descended the aisle, pumped up and moving to the beat of the music. Men slapped his back as he passed them and women pawed at him. Fans waved signs proclaiming things like *I love you, Disco!*, *Go Disco!*, and *I'll take a ride!* Once he reached the main floor, his team surrounded him. A short, bald man approached, elbowing his way into the throng. After patting Aiden down, he wiped something greasy on Aiden's face, and the fighter nodded periodically to the questions shouted at him, but she couldn't hear what he said over the noise.

Her stomach knotted with a mixture of anxiety and anticipation—emotions he did not seem to share, because that cocky grin he wore never faltered.

After a few back-slapping hugs from his team, Disco Stick entered the octagon and promptly began parading around the ring as if the fight was already won. Despite herself, Ryann found his confident arrogance a bit charming, the roar of the crowd infectious. They loved him—then again, who wouldn't? He exuded a raw, masculine sex appeal that women went wild over, and as much as Ryann hated to admit it, not even she was immune to his charms. She was finding it very difficult to take her eyes off this stunning man.

What she didn't expect, however, was for the fighter to turn and lock gazes with her. There were easily sixteen thousand people in here, but it was her he stared at, and holy shit if that didn't shoot a heady sensation right into her core. That glam-cam smile softened, taking on a sensual grin that absolutely melted her heart.

He seemed genuinely pleased to find her here, which made zero sense, because he didn't even know her. Yet, the connection they shared, although brief, was absolutely undeniable. Perhaps she wasn't the only one who felt it. But before her heart could gallop away from her head, she sternly reminded herself, *He's engaged, you idiot. Stop looking at him like* you *want to take a spin on that disco stick. He's a paycheck and that's it.*

This wasn't real. It was nothing more than a show for the fans. Unable to hold his amber stare another moment, she broke the connection. Looking into her lap, Ryann took a deep breath, forcing herself to focus on breathing and calming her racing heart. Her cheeks burned with the flush of desire, her body aching in places she'd forgotten existed after such a long dry spell. By the time she rallied the courage to look up again, Aiden was across the octagon and waiting in his respective corner for his opponent to enter. If it wasn't for her heart still rioting in her chest and the undeniable moisture in her panties, she might have convinced herself she'd imagined the whole thing.

Regan hadn't been kidding. Aiden did put on one hell of a show. He was a great fighter, as was his opponent. The brawl wasn't as one-sided as she'd been expecting. The fighters exchanged blows in two rounds of stand-up that had her wincing every time Aiden took a shot, and inwardly cheering every time he gave as good as he got—and then some.

Watching him fight was both exhilarating and captivating, the control and power he exuded, astounding. She'd come tonight expecting to hate MMA, and was only here because this was her job—or so she told herself when she'd taken a painstaking amount of time deciding what to wear tonight. There weren't a lot of colors she could get away with wearing. Her deep, fiery locks looked almost black in this darker lighting, but once she got into a brighter setting, her flaming tresses could really clash with her clothes if she wasn't careful. She'd chosen a dark green sleeveless cowl-neck with a lace-patterned back and a black above the knee pencil skirt. Her matching shoes had a modest one-inch heel. She'd chosen something to give her average five-six height a little boost, but not tall enough to scream "I'm easy." A lot could be said about a woman by the shoes she wore, and Ryann did not want to give this fighter the wrong idea—though she suspected from their last interaction that he might have come to that misconception all on his own.

She gasped when Aiden took a hit to his cheek and then found herself cheering as he shook it off and shot for his opponent's hips, taking Mallenger "the Mauler" to the mat. The fighter hit the ground hard, and in a matter of seconds he was past Mallenger's guard, whatever that meant—but it must have been good, judging by the commentator's excited yelling. Aiden rained fists and elbows onto the man's face. The right one apparently connected, because a moment later the Mauler was no longer defending himself. The ref pulled Aiden off his opponent, held his arm in the air, and declared him the victor by KO.

Aiden's team flooded into the octagon, jumping and cheering. They picked him up, spun him around, clasped him in back-slapping hugs. The energy in the room was contagious, and Ryann found herself wanting to join the melee, to congratulate him on an amazing, well-fought fight. A part of her was actually looking forward to seeing him at the after party—until she remembered why she was there.

Not wanting to get caught up in the crowd, Ryann slipped into the aisle and made her way out of the arena. The celebration was supposed to continue on the fourth floor. She'd get there early and hopefully find a few private minutes to speak with Aiden alone.

Where in the hell was she? Aiden searched the crowd for the redheaded beauty and found her seat was empty. The disappointment at discovering her gone resounded solidly in his gut. Ever since she'd walked into that gym two days ago, he'd scarcely thought of anything else. He hadn't been kidding when he'd told her she was the most beautiful woman he'd ever seen, though he'd gotten the distinct feeling she hadn't believed him for a second. That she might not know how gorgeous she was, he found sexy as hell. Her seeming lack of vanity was refreshing. Most women who approached him were ridiculously vain and superficial, and so cosmetically enhanced that if they'd possessed any natural beauty, it was long dead and buried.

But not this woman—there was something special about her. The moment he laid eyes on her he could tell she was nothing like the others. His attraction to the beguiling redhead had surprised him, a swift and guttural response that just about took him out at the knees. She'd caught him so off guard that, rather than stand there staring at her like a complete dumbass, he'd donned his famed Disco persona and treated her just like every other cage banger that walked into his gym—except this one he wanted to see again.

She intrigued him. Not only was she stunning, but intelligence lit those verdant eyes that reminded him of brilliant emeralds. Brains and beauty—a rare combination found in the circles he ran. When he'd glanced over and found Del Toro talking to her, a wave of irrational jealousy had surged up inside him and grabbed him by the balls—and it had yet to let go.

Wanting to see her again, Aiden had impulsively given the woman front row tickets to the fight and a pass to his after party. He had the spare seats, the ones reserved for family he would never invite—not that they'd ever come, even if he did. Sen. Bennett Kruze and Lady Madeline wouldn't be caught dead in a place like this. If you didn't own at least three lake homes and vacation on a monthly basis, they wanted nothing to do with you. It was a lifestyle Aiden didn't miss. He'd learned the hard way a long time ago that money didn't buy happiness.

"What's the matter, Disco? You look like your puppy died."

By the shit-eating grin on Regan's face, Aiden was pretty sure the guy knew exactly what was gnawing at him. "Did you talk to her?" he demanded. "Make her feel welcome like I asked?"

Of all his friends he could have turned loose on that woman, Regan had been his best bet. The guy was laid-back, outgoing, and, most important, hopelessly in love with Willow Scott, the baby sister of his best friend and fellow MMA fighter Kyle "the Killer" Scott.

So far, those two had managed to avoid each other in the octagon as they climbed the welterweight ranks, but a matchup was inevitable. Now throw one Willow Scott into the mix and that shit had the potential to turn ugly fast. That fighter had an insane protective streak when it came to his baby sister. Aiden didn't envy Regan one bit. If Kyle ever found out Regan and Willow were sneaking around behind his back, then friend or not, shit was going to get real.

"Of course I made her feel welcome. Man, Disco, that little honey is a sweet piece of ass."

The urge to punch his friend in the mouth rose up swift and hard. Grabbing the front of Regan's shirt, he jerked him close and growled, "You call her that again, and Kill might just find out who's been dippin' in his little sister's honeypot."

"Jeez, Disco, chill." Regan held up his hands in surrender. "You know I didn't mean anything by it, man. What the fuck happened to 'bros before hos,' huh?"

Shit, Regan was right.

"Besides, I wouldn't fuck around on Willow and you know it."

He *did* know it, dammit. So why in the hell was he acting all Neanderthal over this woman he barely knew? Especially when she'd ditched him the minute the fight was over. *Not worth it,* he told himself, pasting on a Disco grin. Aiden slung his arm around the guy's neck. "You're right. I guess Easton must be rubbing off on me. Sorry I bit your head off. I'm gonna hit the shower. See ya upstairs at the party."

"Sounds good, man."

Aiden made his way through the crowd and headed back to his room to get cleaned up before joining the after party. He was just about to step into the elevator when he heard the sharp clap of heels echoing down the hall and a soft, feminine voice call out, "Aiden, wait up!"

He instinctively tensed, assuming a cage banger was cornering him. Glancing over his shoulder, he smiled at the little blonde hustling toward him. He could hardly see her face peeking over the boxes in her arms. "Hey, Willow," he rushed toward her, scooping the burden from her arms. "What are you doing here?"

She gave him a grateful smile, then blew a wayward strand of bangs from her eyes. "Running an errand for Coach. I'm dropping off some promotional CFA stuff for the party tonight."

He grinned and nodded, using his elbow to hit the Up button on the elevator. "Couldn't wrangle yourself an invite to the party, huh?"

A guilty blush stained her cheeks.

"Lookin' kinda fancy for an errand."

Willow bit her bottom lip, and shot him a nervous glance. "Kyle wouldn't bring me," she confessed. "He said the party was twenty-one and older." Smoothing her hands down her shirt, she tossed her wavy blonde hair behind her shoulder and undid the top button of her blouse to expose her cleavage. "You think I'll pass?" She turned to fully face him, presenting herself for his inspection.

Aiden shifted the boxes beneath his arm and scowled down at her. Hell yeah, she'd pass. Willow Scott was a gorgeous woman that did *not* look twenty years old. "Jesus, Will, button your shirt back up. For crissake . . ."

Willow sighed and rolled her eyes. "Come on, Aiden, you sound just like Kyle," she complained, refastening the button. "'Button your shirt, Willow.' 'Your skirt's too short, Willow,'" she mocked. "I tell you, if you boys had your way, I'd be wearing a gunny sack."

"Gunny sacks are good," he grumbled. "Bulky is in."

She snorted and crossed her arms over her chest, arching her brow.

Ho-ly shit, Kyle had his hands full with this one. He didn't blame the guy for not wanting his baby sister at the party. No doubt the fighter was going to be spending the entire night cock-blocking. But if Aiden knew Willow, and he did, there wasn't going to be any way of keeping her from that party, especially since Regan would be there. If she was going to insist on going, she'd be safest with him—until he could hand her off to her brother. "I tell you what, you can come with me and I'll get you into the party."

"Really?" she asked excitedly, bouncing up and down and cheering her victory.

Aiden shook his head and averted his gaze to the ceiling. "Really, but only if you promise not to do *that* anymore, and you stay right by Kyle's side the whole time. There's going to be a lot of people here, not just our camp. It's a big press night for the Cage Fighting Association—sponsors, fans, paparazzi, you name it." If he thought he could convince her not to go, he'd have tried, but when that woman put her mind to something, there wasn't going to be any changing it.

"I promise," she vowed, placing her hands together like she was praying, all sweet and innocent.

Damn, looks were deceiving . . .

# CHAPTER

# 4

Ryann's plans to get to the party early and talk with Aiden privately were dashed the moment he arrived with his entourage. Women hung on him, men congratulated him, and paparazzi took so many pictures the room was aglow with flashing lights. The music was loud, the booze was flowing freely, and people were partying like it was 1999. Prince would have been impressed.

Everyone was having one hell of a time, except for her and the guy sitting two tables kitty-corner from her. She recognized him as Aiden's sparring partner from the gym. Grabbing her Bacardi Limon from the bar, she swiveled in her seat just enough to watch the women approach the fighter who seemed solely interested in consuming his whiskey. One by one they sauntered over and practically threw themselves at the fighter, only to be shot down time and time again. Each time he sent one packing, the broody scowl on his handsome face grew darker. It was actually pretty entertaining, considering her alternative—watching women throw themselves at Aiden.

He'd arrived fashionably late with a stunning blonde at his side, though she didn't appear very interested in staying there. When she'd tried to take off, he'd caught hold of her arm and dragged her back to him. His brows wrinkled in frustration as he bent close and whispered something in her ear. All the while, her gaze scanned the room as she nodded impatiently, agreeing to whatever he was telling her. Their interaction, although very familiar, appeared platonic. If she didn't know better, she'd think the woman was his sister, but Aiden was an only child.

As soon as he released her, she was off like a shot, and then it was game on for Aiden's attention. Women approached one after the other, hanging on him and posing for pictures. Ryann knew it shouldn't bother her as much as it did. She told herself her misplaced ire was merely vicarious pity for the poor woman who happened to have the misfortune of being engaged to the flagrant playboy. Nearly an hour into the festivities and Aiden had yet to spot her at the bar or make any movement in her direction.

Even Regan ignored her, though she suspected that had more to do with the pale-haired beauty Aiden had arrived with than anything else. He was standing beside another guy Ryann recognized from the fight tonight, pretending not to notice the woman. As the small group chatted away like old friends, drinks in hand, the girl cast Regan an occasional glance from beneath the protective arm of the man standing on the other side of her. There was something in the way her bright blue eyes watched Regan that seemed . . . intimate, but the guy who was hanging on to her didn't seem to notice as he kept talking to his friend.

Turning her gaze back to Aiden, she found him standing in a larger crowd, peeling off a woman who'd locked her arms around his neck as he tried to back away from the group. His infamous smile was devastating—flirtatious and gregarious. What woman could be expected to resist those charms? Well she, for one, intended to be the first. This was ridiculous. She had better things to do than sit here all night watching women grope him. They were just going to have to talk tomorrow—perhaps when he wasn't so . . . indisposed.

Finishing her drink, she sat the glass down with a temperamental clap and was about to hop down from the stool when she saw him finally break away and walk toward her. He'd yet to make eye contact, but that didn't stop her pulse from quickening at the sight of him. He moved with a fluidity not often seen in a man his size. She felt a sharp sting of disappointment when he veered left and slid into a seat opposite his surly sparring partner. Aiden waved the waitress over, and a few minutes later they each had a glass of whiskey in their hands.

Between the music and the crowd, it was too loud for her to hear what Aiden said to him. Whatever it was, though, the guy must not have appreciated hearing it. His scowl deepened and he drained his glass, then slammed it down on the table. Someone took their picture, and the fighter looked like he wanted to leap across the table and ram the camera up that paparazzo's ass. Aiden finished his whiskey and held the ice-filled glass to his cheek as they continued to talk. The bruise looked sore, a bit red and swollen, but not even the wounds earned from his fight could detract from that man's raw, masculine appeal.

He waved his drink-holding hand across the crowd, indicating the scores of people there, and she saw the glint of metal reflecting in the light. Holy shit, was that a piercing through his bottom lip? She squinted, trying to get a better look. It was . . . and another in his brow, too. *Huh.* The Aiden Kruze she'd seen in the photo didn't exactly strike her as the kind of guy who'd pierce his face and ink his arms. But apparently he was that guy, and damn, it looked good on him—as if he wasn't already hot enough. *God have mercy . . .*

As his gaze swept the room, his amber eyes locked on her—bold and unflinching. She felt the heat of that stare all the way to her toes, those stunning eyes holding her so transfixed she couldn't look away if she tried. Keeping his gaze on her, as if he thought she might disappear if he looked away, Aiden gave his friend a parting comment and a friendly slap on the back. He rose from his seat with the fluid grace of a predator and moved toward her. By the time he approached, she felt thoroughly eye-fucked. How was it possible that a look across a room could be so devastating? Aiden slipped into the empty seat beside her and promptly ordered another whiskey and "whatever she's having."

"Did you enjoy the fight?" he asked in the way of a greeting.

The bartender handed her a fourth Bacardi. She probably should have stopped at her second, but Ryann accepted the glass and took a sip of her drink.

She couldn't tell if he was fishing for praise or if he genuinely cared to hear her answer. At any rate, it was difficult to hold a conversation amid all the noise, and this was not the place for what they needed to discuss. Leaning closer to be heard over the thrumming bass, she asked, "Is there someplace more . . . private we could go?"

A look that seemed a lot like surprise and oddly, disappointment, briefly flashed across his face. The emotion didn't make sense, and it was gone so fast, she couldn't be sure she didn't imagine it. In its place was that self-assured, arrogant, cocky grin. It was the same smile he'd given the crowd in the octagon tonight. Not the smile he'd given Ryann at finding her filling one of those empty seats, and not the genuine smile he'd gifted her with just a moment ago—not the smile that melted her heart, and damn her for wanting it again now.

No, this was a Disco grin, and although he was absolutely gorgeous wearing it, there was vacancy—a disconnect—in his eyes that left her cold. But before she could think any harder on it, Aiden grabbed her hand and pulled her off her stool.

"Sure there is, baby girl. I just figured you'd want a drink first." He didn't look back as he led her through the crowd at a determined clip that bordered on rude. She nearly had to jog to keep up with him, his grip on her hand firm and unrelenting. If she didn't know better, she'd swear she'd offended him.

*Un. Fucking. Believable.* Had he honestly thought this woman was any different from the rest of these cage bangers? And to think he nearly busted one of his best friends in the mouth over her. He must be going soft, spending too much time with Easton dealing with his lovesick drama. He hadn't spent sixty seconds with this woman before she was asking him to take her upstairs and fuck her. Cris-sake . . . that must be some sort of a record or something. He should really start carrying a stopwatch.

They reached the elevator and he jammed the Up button with his finger. The muffled sound of the party echoed down the hall. He didn't try to talk to her again. What was the point? She wasn't here for the conversation, so why waste his breath? The doors dinged as they slid open. He stepped inside and pulled her in behind him. There was another couple in the elevator or he would have just done her right here. He could make her come before they'd reach the fortieth floor. Save himself the trouble of getting her back on it. Shit, he hoped she wasn't a clinger. He was tired. He'd fought his heart out tonight and could use a good night's sleep—alone.

She stepped a little closer, looking like she wanted to say something, but she must have thought better of it when he shot her a *not here* scowl. Her movement, although slight, was enough to hit him with an earthy, floral scent that teased his nostrils. His cock began to swell at the sensory foreplay, and he ground his teeth in defiance to his body's willingness to toss away his self-respect for the chance to get inside this woman who, in truth, turned out to be nothing more than a flagrant fan. The muscle in his jaw twitched.

"Is something wrong?" she whispered discreetly.

He arched his brow, glancing down at her, and then promptly

discovered what a mistake that was. She was too beautiful, too innocent looking, to be such a whore. Because, yeah, Coach was right, that was exactly what these women were. He may not be paying them in coin, but they were getting plenty of compensation between the sheets.

"Why would anything be wrong?" He answered her question with a question—straight up lawyer style.

She shrugged. "You just seem—"

The elevator jerked to a halt, cutting her off. They exited the elevator before the other couple. Keeping his firm grip on her hand, he led the little cage banger to his suite.

Aiden didn't give her a chance to speak. The moment the hotel door closed, he had her pressed up against it, his mouth coming down on hers with all the finesse of a hurricane—powerful, consuming, and destructive to her defenses. His tongue pushed past her lips, and the first contact of warm metal surprised her. Seriously? His tongue was pierced, too? How many more surprises did this enigmatic man have secreted away?

He tasted more intoxicating than she'd imagined—the dark burn of whiskey, a sinful bite as his tongue teased across hers, playful at first and then plundering. He shifted his mouth, adjusting his kiss as his hand fisted into her hair, angling her head so he could fully claim her lips. Every inch of Aiden's impossibly hard body molded against hers, pinning her between the door and a wall of hard, unyielding muscle. His erection, grinding into the flat of her stomach, was impressively large and equally demanding. His hips rocked against hers, and his low growl sounded a mix of frustration and pleasure, as if he couldn't get close enough fast enough. But their kiss seemed to be a pressure valve tempering his flagging restraint.

He consumed her. Every thought fled from her mind, completely shutting down to everything except the feeling of him against her, his spicy masculine scent, the taste of his tongue. Despite herself, she melted against him, and for a brief moment, he was just a man and she was just a woman, partaking in the most primal, ageless dance of passion.

"Fuck, you feel so amazing," he growled against her mouth as he grasped her breast, squeezing to the point where pleasure and pain blurred. "So . . . real. So fucking perfect . . ."

For feeling so amazing, he certainly didn't sound very happy about it. He took her mouth again, diving in for another breathtaking kiss as he trapped her nipple between his thumb and forefinger. Exhaling a soft moan she was helpless to hold back, Ryann arched into his hand, pressing her tender nipple into his palm for more delicious torture.

Lord help her, he felt incredible. His energy was like a drug, his touch infusing her with an electrical current that lit up her nerve endings, all centering to the little bundle between her thighs. Oh, to have him there—touching her, filling her . . .

As if he'd read her mind, Aiden untangled his hand from her hair and slipped it down between her thighs. Rucking up her skirt past her hips, he groaned, his husky voice full of regret. "Why did you have to be like them?"

*Wait. What? Be like who?*

His hand slipped into her panties. Bold, skillful fingers parted the slick folds of her flesh, teasing over the bundle of nerves that had her crying out and bucking her hips against his hand.

"Damn, baby girl, I can't wait to make you come," he growled, fastening his mouth over hers again.

Still rocked from his confusing question, and now hearing him calling her that generic pet name, was like a cold bucket of reality on her Aiden inferno. No doubt, every woman he met was his "baby girl," which slammed home the undeniable truth, that as much as this was new to her—because she did not make out with random men—she was nothing more to him than a quick fuck. And more than she wanted to admit, that hurt. Which really cooled her jets, because she had zero business getting close enough to this guy that he would have the power to emotionally affect her one way or another.

His fingers teased near her opening, but before they could enter and become Ryann's final undoing, she reached between her legs and caught hold of his wrist. She tore her mouth from his, panting for air, but he didn't miss a beat, dipping his head to the sensitive spot on her neck just below her ear.

"What's my name, Aiden?" Ryann hated herself for the broken, throaty pant in her voice, giving away just how deep down the path of rapture he'd taken her.

Aiden tensed against her, as if just now sensing this was heading somewhere he might not want to go. But oh, he was good, and he wasn't a quitter. No, not this fighter. Slipping a finger deep inside her, he teased her clit with his thumb. A helpless moan escaped her lips, so close to defeat, so close to coming . . . He sucked the flesh of her throat covering her traitorous, thundering pulse that gave away just how close she was to saying *Fuck it* and letting him take her to the moon.

Through her lust-filled haze, she realized he'd yet to answer her question, and that was all the push she needed to steel her resolve. "Aiden, stop. This isn't why I'm here."

Slowly, with deliberate ease, he pulled his hand from beneath her panties and she nearly cried out at the loss of his touch. Never before had a man made her feel like this. Never before had a man so masterfully played her body like he knew it better than she did. His lips hovered beside her ear, his breath hot, ragged exhales.

"Then why are you here?" His seductive growl held a hint of suspicion and was laced with an undertone of unease that sent a prickle of goose bumps racing up her arms.

Perhaps this was not the smartest thing she'd ever done, locking herself away with a fighter she truly knew nothing about. There was no one to hear her scream—in pleasure or in terror. But now that she had his attention, there was no going back. This was why she was here. She had a job to do, and the sooner she got it done, the better for the both of them. "Your mother sent me."

He tensed against her. When his head snapped up, sparks of golden fury shone in his eyes, boring into hers with nothing short of cold, hard rage. "Get out," he snarled.

Her heart missed a beat as it dropped into her stomach and then promptly began thundering wildly, making her nauseous. He couldn't be serious. But Aiden didn't even give her a chance to explain as she stood there frozen in shock at the complete one-eighty this man had pulled on her in a matter of seconds. With the speed of a striking viper, he slammed his fist into the door beside her head. She closed her eyes and flinched, knowing her first moment of true fear since meeting this cage fighter.

"I'm serious, Ryann! Get the fuck out. Now!"

He knew her name. The realization was so irrelevant in light of his outburst, and yet it resonated somewhere deep inside her. But how . . . ? He hadn't asked her, and she certainly hadn't offered, yet he'd taken the time to discover it. *Regan*, she realized. Had Aiden sent him over to talk to her tonight? What had his friend told him and why had Aiden cared enough to find out?

Before she could think on it any longer, he reached for her skirt, still bunched around her hips, and jerked it back into place before grabbing her arm. Ryann winced at his biting grip, sure she'd be wearing the evidence of his anger tomorrow. Without another word, Aiden dragged her away from the door's path, ripped it open, and shoved her out into the hall, slamming it behind her.

Seconds passed and then something crashed inside his room as Aiden roared. "Fuck!"

Ryann stood there a moment, stunned, trying to process what the hell just happened. Going from sixty to zero in that man's arms in the space of a heartbeat left her dazed and confused. She'd figured he wouldn't be pleased to discover the truth, but not once did she imagine he'd respond so violently. His rejection gnawed at her, which was ridiculous, because he didn't mean anything to her, and she certainly didn't mean anything to him. Why should it matter to her what he thought? The unsettling emotions were just the low after being brought so high—a natural response to the endorphins released by his touch and now leaving her system.

As the shock began to fade, a prominent emotion quickly began to take root deep in her gut—indignant anger. How dare that presumptuous prick bring her up here and just assume she was going to sleep with him? That took a lot of fucking nerve. Maybe she should have reminded him he was engaged while she was at it. As Ryann stomped toward the elevator, she grabbed her cell from the purse that miraculously still clung to her shoulder. Selecting her contact, she hit the Call button just as the elevator chimed and the doors slid open.

"I found him," she announced, forgoing a greeting.

"And?" Madeline responded impatiently.

"You were right. He isn't going to cooperate. Send me the package."

Ryann rattled off the address of the hotel she was staying at and hung up. Shaking her head in disgust, she rode the elevator to the main floor lobby, hoping she didn't look like the whore she felt.

Damn Aiden Kruze and his witch of a mother. Because of those two, she was about to commit her first felony.

# CHAPTER

# 5

That lying, manipulative bitch! His gut had been right. Ryann wasn't a cage banger after all—she was worse! And he was the fucking idiot who almost slept with her. Rage tore through his veins like a firestorm. Spinning away from the door, he grabbed the first thing he could get his hands on and hurled it across the room. The vase of flowers shattered against the wall, sending glass shrapnel ricocheting back at him. A shard sliced into his arm.

"Fuck!"

He slapped his hand over the wound, but the blood oozed between his fingers, running down his arm. Shit, this was going to need stitches. Aiden reached over his shoulder and tugged his T-shirt off. He wrapped the stretchy cotton around his bicep and used his teeth to tie a knot, then fished his cell out of his pocket and dialed Marcus's number. Flopping onto the couch, he raised his arm above his head, waiting while the phone rang.

"What's wrong?" Coach demanded in way of a greeting.

"Who said anything was wrong?"

"I know you, Aiden, and if you're calling me instead of being buried balls deep in some cage banger, something's wrong."

"Shit . . ." He sighed, dragging his hand through his hair. "She sent another one, Coach. This time it was a woman."

Silence—then, "Oh, Jesus . . . Aiden, what did you do? The last one spent two weeks in the hospital."

Yeah, he kinda felt bad about that, but he'd warned the man to keep his hands off him. Dammit, that woman just would not give it a rest. He was past the point of hoping she'd quit doing his father's bidding. Did she have any idea how deep his father's treachery ran? What he was involved in? He doubted it would matter at this point. The closer they got to the wedding, the more tenacious his bitch of a mother became. He wouldn't put anything past her, or her hired whore.

"I, uhh . . . need a ride to the hospital. I've been drinking too much to drive myself."

"What happened?"

"I cut my arm on a piece of glass."

Marcus cursed under his breath, and Aiden could hear the click of a bedside lamp and the rustling of bed covers.

"How bad?"

"Bad enough that it needs stitches, but it'll be fine."

"All right, son. Hang tight and I'll be there as soon as I can."

As Aiden paced the floor, waiting for Marcus to arrive, guilt assailed him when he thought of the argument he'd had with the old man a few days ago. He'd told Coach he wasn't his father, but the truth of it was, that man had been a better dad to him than his own ladder-climbing, turncoat of a father had ever been. The only time that man had shown any interest in him was when it suited his agenda to do so.

He'd done everything for that man, trying to earn his love and respect. He'd become a lawyer because his father wanted him to. He'd taken over the family business because his father wanted him to. It didn't matter what he did or how hard he tried, nothing could ever please that man. Now he wanted him to marry a woman he'd never met in some fucked-up twelfth-century archaic union. And that, my friend, was where he drew the line. Fuck you—sayonara—go to hell. That shit was not happening.

But of course, his father hadn't listened to him. Instead, the asshole signed Aiden's name to a marriage contract for a shitload of money being funneled into his father's senatorial campaign—a marriage that was due to take place in, oh, about a week. *Ha, good fucking luck with that.* Aiden had zero interest in getting married—ever—let alone to a complete stranger. He was done doing his father's bidding. He'd always known the guy was a shrewd businessman—he'd just never thought the bastard would sell his own son for a profit.

So fourteen months ago, when Aiden accidentally and luckily discovered what his father had done, he up and walked away from his rich-bitch life and moved out to Vegas to pursue his own dream of fighting in the CFA. Aiden had been brawling his whole life. He boxed throughout high school, and once he'd graduated and started attending Harvard, he moved into mixed martial arts. When he wasn't buried in law books, he was training in the gym. He'd been fortunate to meet Cole Easton shortly after moving to Vegas. Cole had introduced him to Marcus, and the rest was history.

Cole and Aiden had hit it off, becoming fast friends and sparring partners until his recent injury. Del Toro was newer to the Cage Fighting Association and had stepped in as his partner to replace Easton. It was no secret Del Toro was having trouble adjusting to civilian life. No one knew the specific deets about what got him discharged from the military, and he wasn't talking. But as far as sparring partners went, Aiden couldn't complain. The guy was out of his weight class, but in truth, there weren't a lot of fighters willing to pound with the guy for fun.

Life was good, his career was taking off, and he had all the pussy he wanted. And then, just like a bad fucking penny, his parents started showing up. Well, by proxy anyway, because heaven forbid they inconvenience themselves enough to deal with him directly. This latest stunt had topped them all, though. Seriously? Sending a woman to hunt him down? Like she could possibly accomplish what two full-grown men before her had failed to do. Did this woman think she possessed a magical vagina that would enslave him and turn him into her mindless minion? That after one dip in that tight, wet cunny, he'd drop to his knees, bow before the almighty vag, and follow her back to New York?—not fucking likely.

It didn't matter that those few stolen minutes with Ryann tonight had been the hottest moments of his life. The way she'd kissed him, touched him, he'd sensed a wholesome, unpracticed honesty in her desire that caught him off guard, hitting him below the belt. For the briefest moment, he'd almost believed she wanted *him*, not Disco Stick Kruze the famed MMA fighter. He couldn't explain it, but the way she felt in his arms and responded to his touch . . . No woman had ever affected him like that.

It'd come as a staggering blow when in minutes, that woman had driven him mindless with need. And then to discover just as quickly, it was all a lie . . . Fuck, he hadn't been that furious since he'd uncovered his family's plot to betray him. Even now, the memory of her kiss haunted him. Thinking of her body pressed so perfectly against his made him hard all over again. His balls ached with the need for release. He'd never felt breasts so soft, tasted lips so sweet, or touched a pussy so tight and wet . . .

Her scent still lingered on him, and despite himself, he occasionally drew a deep breath, relishing the rush of breathing her in all over again. He really should go shower, but damn, he wasn't ready to part with her yet. As pathetic as that seemed and as pissed off as he was, he couldn't stop thinking about the woman who, for the first time in his life, had truly made him feel alive.

Huh . . . maybe she did have a magical vag, after all.

Ryann felt like shit. Perhaps it was the two hours of sleep she'd gotten last night, or the gnawing ache of unsatisfied need that had left her restless and cranky. She'd tried to take the edge off herself, but it was a poor substitute for Aiden's touch. Or . . . maybe it was guilt over what she was about to do to him that rode her so hard. Perhaps it was a combination of the two, but whatever the reason, Ryann was pretty sure she'd hit an all-time low when she got out of bed this morning—until her phone rang with her daily countdown.

There was no point in ignoring the call that had become as predictable as the rising sun. He would just call again, and again, and again until she answered. It did no good to change her number. The calls always came in on her business number, and unless she wanted to put herself out of a job, she had to keep herself available for people to contact her.

Some days he was more courteous than others, but the message was always the same—pay up or else. Exhaling a sigh, Ryann disconnected the call and tossed her phone onto the bed before heading to the shower. A part of her wanted so badly to be mad at her father, to blame him for leaving her alone and putting her in this situation. But the anger just couldn't come. She was too tired and it was buried beneath too much grief.

Years of suffering from the loss of her mother had eaten away at the man who had once been her hero—her rock. Axel Andrews had been an honorable man in whose footsteps she'd wanted to walk. It was why she'd become a private investigator and her father's business partner. If she'd only known how easily her world would fall apart. She'd seen how quickly a life could unravel at the clipping of just one key thread—her mother had been that catalyst for her father, and Ryann often blamed herself for not doing more to help her dad. The changes had been subtle at first—the drinking, the gambling, the unaccounted business expenses. He'd hidden them well, and they'd been easy enough to ignore as she struggled to tread the waters of her own grief.

By the time she realized just how badly things had gotten, it was too late. Andrews Private Investigation Services was nearly bankrupt, and her father was drunk more than he was sober. In the last months prior to his death, he'd spent his days and most of his nights gambling at the Lion's Den, one of a chain of clubs owned by Vincent Moralli. It was no secret Moralli was Mafia. While doing a missing-person investigation last year, she'd discovered he was also the proprietor of an illegal fighting circuit as well as being heavily involved with drugs and prostitution.

She'd reported her findings to the police back then, and she had never heard another word from them. So should she really have been surprised when she couldn't get the police to look into her father's death? She'd suspected at the time the police were being paid to turn a blind eye to Moralli's dealings, and after being warned off by the officer last week, she was sure of it. Ryann had enough on her plate without painting a target on her back. A man as powerful as Moralli would be well connected and heavily protected.

The only thing whistle-blowing would accomplish at this point would be getting herself killed, which wasn't entirely off the table.

If she didn't get Aiden delivered to his mother and collect her payment before Moralli's deadline, death was a very real possibility—or worse. His enforcer made it clear they'd get their money out of her one way or another. She didn't even want to consider what the other way could be.

So on that happy note, Ryann finished rinsing the suds from her hair. With renewed conviction—because facing off with Aiden Kruze was still the lesser of the two evils in this shit sandwich she called a life—Ryann stepped out of the shower. Wrapping a towel around her hair and one around her body, she headed back to the bedroom to get dressed. As she passed the mirror above the bathroom sink, something caught the corner of her eye and she stopped. Turning her head, she studied the line of dark purple bruises lining her bicep.

*Shit*... She raised her arm, checking the underside, and found the fifth—a thumbprint. Did she really just think Aiden a lesser of anything? Sighing, she kept on walking. There was no denying it, she was royally fucked—and not in a good way.

When Ryann reached the downstairs lobby, she stopped at the courtesy desk to inform the attendant she was expecting a package to arrive. To her surprise, the man behind the counter reached down and retrieved a small, brown, paper-wrapped box. Her stomach knotted at the sight of it, her pulse quickening with anxiety. Saying a quick prayer for forgiveness, she thanked the man and grabbed the package, stuffing it into her purse before rushing out the door.

God help her, she was going to hell for this.

# CHAPTER 6

You lost again, Gingersnap?"

If anyone could make an endearment sound derogatory, it was this man—of all the fucking luck. Ryann knew she was taking a chance showing back up at the gym, considering the whole "no girls allowed" thing. But when she'd gone back to the Mirage this morning to look for Aiden, the woman at the front desk had informed her he'd already checked out—in the middle of the night—which made zero sense. The chatty woman had gone on to confide in her that his room had sustained several thousand dollars' worth of damages, and they'd had to hire a cleaning crew to remove bloodstains from the carpet and the furniture.

What the hell had he done? At the thought that he might have hurt himself, a band of guilt tightened around her chest. She needed to see him, to apologize for their misunderstanding and try one final time to reason with the man before he forced her to do something they'd both regret.

The fighter Aiden had called Del Toro turned from the heavy bag he'd been beating the shit out of and ambled over to her. He moved with a fighter's powerful grace that reminded her a lot of Aiden. The fight-or-flight instinct kicking adrenaline into her bloodstream was telling her to run. She forced herself to stay, holding her ground. But when the fighter finally stopped, he was much too close for comfort—so close she could smell that salty tang of clean male sweat and feel the heat radiating off his body like an inferno.

Propping his forearm on the doorway, he leaned closer and inhaled deeply. Was he . . . smelling her? Ryann took a reflexive step back, and the man smiled—if that was what you'd call that flash of straight white teeth. Again, the thought hit her that this man might be handsome, but her self-preservation instincts prevented her from seeing past his scars or those silver-gray eyes that effectively hid any and all emotion, making him look more animal than man.

Clearing her throat, she notched her chin in defiance to her railing nerve and forced the air from her lungs to speak. "I'm looking for Aiden. Is he here?"

"Nope. Disco left town last night."

*He what?* "Do you know where he went?"

"If I did, I sure as hell wouldn't tell you, sweetheart. I hate to break it to you, but you're not the first cage banger to come chasing after that one."

*Cage banger? This guy thinks . . . that I . . . that we . . . God, how embarrassing . . .*

"Disco doesn't do long-term. Save yourself a lot of trouble and go find another cock to rock, huh?"

Okay, now she was pissed. Ryann crossed her arms over her chest, holding her ground and raised a brow defiantly. "And I suppose you're offering, is that it?"

The man actually smiled, a hint of humor lighting his eyes that, on closer inspection, held little flecks of silver and sapphire. She'd been right, he was handsome. Not in the in-your-face, panty-dropping way Aiden was, but in a very rough, primal, testosterone-charged way. This man exuded masculine prowess like she couldn't believe.

"Sorry, babe, I don't do clingy any more than Disco does, though I have always had a thing for redheads."

"You're a pig." The rebuttal was out of her mouth before she had a chance to call it back or consider the wisdom of baiting a man twice her size.

He laughed. The asshole actually laughed!

"You keep sweet-talking me, and I might just reconsider. With a mouth like that, I bet you could suck some c—"

She reacted. Instantaneous and reflexive, Ryann swung for his face. But the man was fast, catching her arm before her palm could connect with his cheek. He'd been baiting her this whole time, she realized, when the anger she'd expected to shadow his face didn't come. Why was he testing her?

Before she could think too hard on it, the fighter's eyes dropped to her bicep. All humor left his face as he stretched out her arm and rotated her wrist. "Did Disco do this to you?" The fighter's deep voice took on a gravelly edge that sent the fine hairs on the back of her neck prickling.

"Why would you think he did?" Was she wrong about Aiden? Did he make a habit of taking his temper out on woman?

"Because I saw you leave with him last night, and because he spent two hours in the ER this morning before hopping on a fucking plane. What in the hell went down between you two?"

She couldn't tell if he was angry *at* her or *for* her.

"Listen, Ryann, let's cut the shit, huh? I know you're not what you appear to be. Tell me what you want with Disco and I might consider telling you where he is."

For real? This guy knew her name, too? Good thing she hadn't told that magpie Regan anything more personal about herself. Ryann considered the fighter's request and calculated the risk of how much to say in good faith that he'd give her the answers she was looking for. After all, she was a PI. She could find Aiden on her own—problem was she was running out of time. The sooner she found him and dealt with this mess, the better.

"I was sent here to give him a message from his family. I just want to talk to him."

"You didn't speak last night?" Then he laughed at the absurdity of his own question. "Of course you didn't—it's Disco we're talking about."

Her cheeks heated with embarrassment at the fighter's assumption, and just how close he'd come to guessing the truth. Oh, they'd spoken all right—eventually. "So will you tell me where he is?"

He studied her another minute, seeming contemplative.

"Somerset, Wisconsin, that's all I know. He left with Coach early this morning. When you see him, tell him I said that's for the busted rib."

Seriously? She was Aiden's punishment? Resisting the urge to stomp her foot and tell this guy what an asshole he was, she painted a false smile on her face and sweetly said, "Thank you. I'm sorry to take up your time."

He grunted in acknowledgment, but when she turned to leave, he called after her. "Hey, Ryann?"

She stopped and glanced back at the fighter.

"Don't let that pretty face fool you. Disco isn't harmless. Then again, by the looks of that arm, you probably already figured that out. You want some friendly advice? Go back home to wherever you came from and forget you ever met him."

That was probably some good, sound advice. Unfortunately, she couldn't take it.

# CHAPTER 7

Aiden exited the Lakeview Hospital in Somerset and headed for the parking lot. He chalked up the prickling feeling of being watched to the fact that it was twenty fucking degrees below zero. His goose bumps had goose bumps, for crissake. Why in the hell anyone would voluntarily live in this frozen wasteland was beyond him—and he'd thought New York was cold.

That Easton was actually considering leaving Vegas to move here and freeze his balls off proved either (a) he'd taken one too many shots to the head, or (b) he was so head over heels for Katie, he couldn't think straight. Considering what those two had been through in the last thirty-six hours, he'd be willing to bet the Kruze fortune it was the latter.

After donning his lawyer cap and spending the better part of the day at the Somerset Police Department, he'd made sure no criminal charges would be filed against Cole for what had gone down here. Now that all was in the clear, and his buddy was due to be discharged from the hospital, Aiden was anxious to get back home. It'd probably take a good solid day to thaw his frozen ass out.

Not only was he craving the desert heat, but Dean Nelson, the president of the CFA, should be announcing any day now if he was in contention for the middleweight title. Thanks to Easton and Coach prepping him for his last fight, it couldn't have gone better.

His mixture of stand-up and jujitsu had given him an opportunity to showcase his diverse skill set. He hadn't been fighting for the CFA very long, but Aiden was undefeated in his circuit, which put a title shot within his grasp.

Yeah, he was definitely antsy to get home, and his restlessness had absolutely nothing to do with a certain redhead he'd tossed from his room two nights ago. More than he was willing to admit, Ryann plagued his thoughts over these past few days, and try as he might, Aiden couldn't seem to block out the memory of that woman melting in his arms.

How far would she have let things go to get what she wanted from him? To what lengths would she have gone, trying to convince him to return with her?—all questions that plagued him, robbing him of sleep. Of all the people his sadistic mother could have hired to track him down . . . Then again, he shouldn't have been surprised. Madeline Kruze was as manipulative and crafty as they came. Of course she'd try to blindside him, and it had almost worked.

He had to give Ryann credit, she'd managed to get closer to him than the two PIs hired before her—excluding the very brief encounter that had landed the last guy in the hospital. He thought that would have sent a clear enough message to his parents to leave him the hell alone. Obviously not, since they'd sent Ryann, the seductive sacrificial lamb, into the lion's den. How they thought a woman half his size was going to get him to go anywhere against his will was beyond him. Sheer physics doomed this mission from the start.

He did regret not fucking her before throwing her out, though. Without a doubt, that woman was the sweetest piece of ass he'd ever had his hands on. She'd caught him completely off guard with her confession, and admittedly, he hadn't reacted well. Not one of his finer moments, that was for sure, and he had seventeen stitches in his bicep to prove it. He didn't condone violence against women—for any reason—but Aiden was pretty sure Ryann was wearing the evidence of his temper on her arm right now. Yet, despite her deception, and as much as his wrath may have been justified, he felt bad about hurting her. Only a jackass coward would ever touch a woman in anger.

For the countless time today, Aiden shoved the beguiling ginger from his mind as he hopped into the driver's seat and fired up the rental. He promptly shut off the heater when it began blasting him in the face with freezing air, and muttered a curse as foul as his mood. He had twelve hours to kill before his flight back to Vegas, and Marcus wasn't coming with him. His brother had suffered a stroke this week and was still in the hospital, so he was staying in Somerset a little while longer.

There wasn't a lot to do in the small town whose welcome sign proudly displayed the population at 2,656. Aiden preferred big-city lights, crowded bars, and loose women—the no-strings-attached kind that wanted nothing from him other than the satisfaction of a quick bump-and-grind. After the severe case of blue balls Ryann had left him with, he seriously considered getting the hell out of Dodge early and spending the night in Minneapolis. Tension ran through him like a live wire thrumming through his veins. If he didn't blow off some steam soon, that shit was going to find another release—which usually involved his fists.

If he left now, he'd be that much closer to the airport to catch his seven a.m. flight. Yeah, that sounded like a grand idea, heading into the city and getting totally shit-faced. He'd hook up with a redheaded honey and fuck Ryann out of his system. Aiden shifted into reverse, and began backing out of the parking lot when a flash of movement caught his eye.

*What the hell?* He hit the brakes and shifted the Yukon into park. Someone was running up behind him, but he couldn't make out a face through the fogged-up window. He swiped his hand over the freezing glass and cleared a swath. Recognizing the beautiful blonde bundled in a gray plaid pea coat and furry gray Uggs, he dropped the driver's-side window as she jogged up beside him.

"Hey, Katie Bug. What's up?"

"Aiden, I'm glad I caught you." Her quickened breaths billowed steam into the cold evening air, filling the cab of his SUV. The tip of her pixie nose was already pinched by the cold, her cheeks a becoming rosy red. Fucking Easton, lucky bastard . . . Hell, he'd have taken a bullet for her, too, if it meant earning the doting affection of this woman. Katrina Miller was the whole package—brains, beauty, and hot little body. Not that he was macking on his best friend's chick or anything, but he'd have to be a blind eunuch not to notice that girl's swag.

"I know you're probably anxious to get going, but I was wondering if you would mind taking me back to the house so I could get a change of clothes for Cole. I haven't been back there since . . . well, you know, and I didn't really want to go alone. Uncle Marcus is visiting Dad right now, and I didn't want to bother him."

Well, so much for his plans to get ridiculously drunk and tap a little Minnesota ass. "Sure, Bug." He gave her a no-worries Disco grin. "Hop on in."

She skirted around to the front of the SUV and climbed into the passenger side. "You sure you don't mind?" Katie caught her bottom lip between her teeth, casting him an anxious glance.

Aiden put the vehicle in reverse and began backing out. "I'm sure. Besides, we can't have our boy going home in his underwear, right? A guy's likely to freeze his balls off here."

She laughed, some of the tension easing from her slender shoulders as she relaxed against the seat. "He may not admit it, but he's lucky to have you, Aiden. We both are."

"Yeah, well, ditto."

Except for giving him directions, they spent most of the ride to her house in silence, each seemingly caught up in their own thoughts. The closer they got to their destination, the more white-knuckled Katie's little hands became. By the time they turned down her road, anxiety reverberated from her like a force field, and when they pulled into the driveway, his own nerves were strung tight as a drum.

"Hey." He shifted into park and laid his hand over hers. "You all right?"

Katie's gaze darted to his as if she'd momentarily forgotten he was here. She shook her head. "No. But I will be."

Aiden wasn't sure if she was fronting or if she really believed what she said. "I know what happened here, Bug. You don't have to go in, you know. I can grab Easton's stuff."

She appeared to consider it a moment. This was fucked up. When he thought about what had gone down here, the terror Katie must have endured . . . This woman had been through hell.

"No, I have to go in. If I don't do it now . . ."

"All right. I'll come in with you." He admired this woman's strength. The fighter in him recognized a kindred spirit, and he respected the hell out of her for it. Getting out of the SUV, Aiden came around the passenger side and opened her door. Taking her hand, he led her up the steps and stopped in front of the door. "You sure we're doing this?" he asked again. "Last chance to change your mind."

"I'm sure."

As she dug through her purse, looking for the key, Aiden glanced behind him, taking notice of his surroundings. A bare patch of ground marked the front yard where the snow had been removed. Curiosity tempted him to ask her about it, but when he glanced back, Katie's hands were shaking so badly, she nearly failed to fit the key in the lock, and he decided right then and there to table any questions. This shit was hard enough on her the way it was, he wouldn't risk saying anything that could make it worse.

The lock snicked and she opened the front door, hesitating a moment before stepping inside. He followed her in and closed it behind them. Turning back around, he nearly ran into her as she stood there, frozen in the entryway.

"I can't believe it . . ." she whispered more to herself than to him. "It's like it never happened." Katie looked around as she slowly stepped forward, entering the living room. "If I didn't know better, I'd swear it was just a nightmare."

Aiden stepped up beside her and wrapped his arm around her shoulders, pulling her in for a brotherly hug. "It's over now, Katie Bug. My boy won't let anything happen to you."

"I know." She looked up at him with those tear-filled eyes, and his heart lodged in his throat. "He saved my life, Aiden." She sniffed and swiped at the tears spilling down her cheeks.

*Aww hell* . . . He hugged her tight against him, giving her a moment to pull herself together. "I can't pretend to know what you're going through, bug, but I can promise you won't have to do it alone. Cole's got you in this."

She nodded against his chest. They stood there another minute before her back stiffened, shoulders tensing. He knew she was rallying her nerve, battling back more tears. This woman was a fighter. He smiled to himself as the memory of the first time they'd met came to mind. Cole was teaching her hapkido, and she'd just put the light-heavyweight champion on his ass. Yeah . . . this girl was going to be just fine.

"I won't be very long," she murmured, stepping out of his embrace to walk across the living room, her steps quickening with determined purpose. Aiden kept his eyes locked on her until she disappeared down the hall and into one of the bedrooms.

He entered the living room, his gaze canvassing the open floor plan. The faint scent of latex paint still hung in the air, the last remaining evidence that something bad had happened here. The eggshell walls added a modicum of coolness that bristled his nerves. The brown suede couch and matching love seat still bore the price tags hanging from the arms, as did the end table sitting between the furniture.

Refurbishing this house must have cost Easton a small fortune, not that he couldn't afford it. The place was immaculate with a Parade of Homes, don't-touch-anything elegance that reminded Aiden far too much of his parents' house in Manhattan, only on a much more micro level.

Shoving his mental baggage aside, Aiden wandered into the kitchen, contemplating what kind of a sick fuck would want to hurt someone as sweet as Katrina Miller. Katie was the kind of woman that made you want to be a better man. What he wouldn't give to have a woman look at him the way she looked at Easton. What would it be like to have someone see *him* for once and not Disco—not Sen. Bennett Kruze's son—not the heir of the Kruze fortune—just *him* . . .

For a fraction of a moment the other night, he'd thought he might have had a chance at that with Ryann. She'd melted in his arms so sweetly. Her response to him had been so honest, so uninhibited . . .

"Okay, I'm ready."

Katie stepped into the hallway with the strap of a CFA duffel bag slung over her shoulder. He smiled at the sight of her little self, touting Easton's overstuffed gym bag. He had one just like it in the back seat of his rental. "Here, let me . . ." Aiden walked toward her, holding out his hand to take her burden.

"It's all right. I got it."

She made a beeline for the front door like the devil himself was hot on her heels.

"Why don't you head out and I'll lock up?"

Katie shot him a grateful half smile and didn't hesitate to take him up on his offer. By the time he quickly checked the other door and secured the front, she was already in the Yukon and the engine was running. He hopped into the driver's seat and backed out of the driveway. It wasn't until they'd braked for the stop sign that Aiden noticed the silver Escape parked along the shoulder, pulling out and heading his direction. A niggling of unease crawled over his flesh as the feeling of being watched returned—just like at the hospital. What the hell? Was someone following him? Or worse, was someone following Katie?

Not wanting to alarm her, he took his time heading back to the hospital. "You mind if I fill up before I take you back?"

"No. Of course not."

Aiden took a sharp left, pulling into the gas station, and parked beside the farthest pump from the road. Hopping out, he rounded the SUV and waited for the Escape to declare itself—which it did a moment later when it drove right on by without as much as a braking hesitation.

Hmm . . . his instincts were usually dead-on. Though it was entirely possible that the last stunt Mommy Dearest pulled was making him a touch paranoid. His thoughts jumped to Ryann, and a twinge of guilt pricked his conscience at the thought of the wrath that woman had probably endured when she'd returned to Manhattan empty-handed. Hell hath no fury like a displeased Madeline Kruze. Nine more days and counting . . .

Bennett Kruze had stuck a lot of start-up costs into his Harvard graduate, and Aiden wasn't naïve enough to think for one minute that man wouldn't demand a return on said investment. No, he wasn't being paranoid. Ditching Ryann in Vegas had been too easy. No way was this the last he'd hear from his parents. Question was, just how far would they go to get what they wanted? Knowing Bennett Kruze?—to any length. He'd been at the helm of his father's law firm long enough to know that man wasn't afraid to get his hands dirty. Aiden's mistake was being dumb enough to think just being Bennett Kruze's son would somehow make him exempt from his treachery. Everyone was a price tag to that man, including his own flesh and blood.

Now that he was righteously good and pissed off, Aiden ripped the fuel pump free from its holder and shoved the nozzle into the gas tank. He locked the trigger and when the gas began pouring into the Yukon, he came around to the passenger side of the vehicle. When Katie didn't see him standing there, he rapped the back of his knuckles against the window to get her attention. She let out a startled yelp and jumped, her hand flying up to her throat. Shit. That was real smooth. *Give your bro's girl a heart attack, why don't you?*

She smiled at his winced apology.

"I'm running inside. Do you want anything?"

She shook her head. "No, I'm good," she called through the glass.

"Be right back."

She nodded.

He hurried into the station, grabbing a grape Powerade and vanilla Frappuccino. After settling up with the clerk, he tucked the bottles under his arm and headed back to the SUV. Aiden was pulling the nozzle free from the tank when he glanced up just as a silver Escape passed by. It was coming from the opposite direction this time. Mother. Fuck. Was that the same vehicle? Those things were a dime a dozen and hard as hell to tell apart. Unless you were specifically looking for one, you'd never notice them, they blended in so well.

He stalled another minute, washing the rear window and giving the vehicle some time to pass. When no more silver Escapes made an appearance, he got back into the Yukon. "Here you go." He handed Katie the Frappuccino.

"What's this for?" She took the bottle from him and grinned so big it was easy to see how his friend lost his heart to this woman.

Aiden shrugged. "You were drinking them in the hospital. I thought you might change your mind."

"Thank you. I was just thinking about how tired I was. I haven't rested well these past few days. This will help give me a boost." She held up the bottle and shook it before popping the cap.

After taking a healthy swig of his Powerade, he refastened the cap and tossed it into the cup holder. As he pulled forward, heading back to the road, Aiden glanced left, then right, and discovered Katie watching him with a thoughtful expression on her beautiful face.

"What?"

"I don't get it." She shook her head as if in disbelief.

His top lip curled in a lopsided grin. "Don't get what?"

"I don't understand why a guy like you doesn't have a woman. I mean, beneath all that Disco bullshit, you're a really good guy."

"'Disco bullshit'?" he laughed. See, now this was the problem with having women for friends—they meddled in your shit. "What are you talking about? I have women—lots of them—sometimes two or three at a time."

Katie gasped in shock, reaching over and slapping him in the chest.

"Oww . . ." he complained, leaning away from her assault and laughing. "What'd you do that for?"

"You are hopeless, you know that? Mark my words, Disco Stick, someday you're going to meet a woman that's going to rock your world, and that player guise you hide behind ain't going to hold up for shit."

He chuckled. "You think you know me so well, do you, Katie Bug?"

"As a matter of fact, I do," she said, folding her arms across her chest and giving him a look of cool confidence. "Because you and Cole are a lot alike."

"Is that so?" he grunted, not sure he liked where this conversation was going. Casting Katie a raised-brow glance, he turned his attention back to the road. That she thought he and Easton were alike proved just how much this woman didn't know him. Cole was disciplined, rigid and tough as nails, while Aiden was . . . well, not. If there was a party going on, he was there—booze to drink, he was your guy—ass to tap, he was on it. Wild, unruly, and undisciplined had been Coach's specific words, if he recalled his last ass chewing correctly.

"Yep, all it's going to take is the right woman to come along and you're going to be putty in her hands."

"But you're already taken, sweetheart."

She blushed and gave his shoulder a playful shove. "You're such a flirt," she laughed. "And your smooth-talking distractions will not work on me. Besides, you wouldn't want me, I'm a mess. For some crazy reason, I've yet to scare Cole off. I figure if taking a bullet for me didn't do it, nothing will."

"Yeah, I'm afraid you're stuck with him," he teased, giving her a playful wink. "Just so you know, he was a wreck when you left him. Don't ever do that again."

The smile fell from her face and was replaced by a concerned frown. "That's what Uncle Marcus said."

"Yeah, well, Coach is a smart man."

Her smile returned, but this time it held a touch of nostalgia. "That he is, Aiden."

# CHAPTER

8

It was nearly midnight by the time Aiden reached the Embassy Suites near the MSP airport and checked in for the night. Before heading to his room, he took a detour to the Corner Bar, not yet ready to abandon his plan of getting shit-faced and laid—not necessarily in that order. On his way to an empty table, he stopped at the bar and ordered a tequila shot with a beer chaser. As he waited for the bartender to load him up, a redhead two stools down shot him a flirty grin.

"Do I know you?" she asked over the music. It was a classic pick-up line, but in his case, most people who asked genuinely meant it. Sports bars usually televised MMA fights, and a lot of the people who frequented these places were fans.

"Sorry, sweetheart, this is my first night in Minneapolis. Just killing time before my flight leaves."

"Oh . . ."

Her duck-lipped pout accentuated the fullness of a mouth that instantly sent his mind to other places he'd like to have those lips right about now. She was a beautiful woman. Not as gorgeous as another redhead he'd been finger deep in a few nights ago, but she was totally fuckable, and he was all for getting Ryann out of his system. The woman's breasts were smaller, her hair more orangish than fiery deep red. Come to think of it, the eye color was wrong, too, but hey, he was still game.

"Now, don't look so disappointed, baby girl. I'm not leaving until tomorrow morning. I've got all night."

At his open invitation, she smiled like she'd won the lottery. And by the time he was done with her, she'd be believing it, too. The bartender came back over with Aiden's drinks. "Thanks. Can you get her another of whatever she's having?" He nodded toward the woman.

"Cosmopolitan," she told the bartender, handing him her empty glass.

The man refilled her drink and she slid off the stool, sauntering up to him. That's when he noticed how petite she was—a few inches shorter than Ryann. She just might have to keep those heels on.

He turned to find an empty table, and the woman followed him as he weaved through the crowd. Finding a quiet spot in the corner, he slipped into a chair and she sat across from him.

"My name is Mandy."

"Aiden."

She reached across the table and offered her hand. "Are you sure we've never met?" He took her outstretched hand and shook it. She beamed at him with a flirtatious grin. "I swear . . . you look so familiar."

"Are you a fan of MMA?"

"Are you kidding? I love MMA! There's nothing sexier than watching two hot men get into a ring and beat the shit out of each other. Did you see the last CFA fight? I—"

*Ding, ding, ding.* There . . . now she got it. A little slow on the uptake, but his dick wasn't too picky about IQ scores.

"Nooo . . . seriously?"

His top lip curled in a crooked grin and he tipped back his tequila while he waited for all her synapses to start firing.

"Oh, my gosh! It *is* you! Disco Stick Kruze! Oh, man, I gotta tell you, you're way hotter in person. Not that you aren't hot on TV but . . . Wow . . . You're like a freaking celebrity!"

And there it was, signed, sealed, and delivered in one neat little take-me-home-and-fuck-my-brains-out package. It was too easy, really. And for the first time since Aiden could remember, he found the simplicity of it—dull. There was no thrill of the hunt, no excitement, no making him work for it. It was just there, thrown at his feet. All the pussy he could want—easy and effortless. Not like . . . No. He wouldn't go there. This was what he wanted. It didn't matter that Mandy hadn't shut up since she sat down. There were many ways to occupy that yappy trap of hers. A couple more shots and he should be ready to go.

Four tequila shooters later, Aiden was starting to rethink his decision to bag this babe. He'd met women who could talk, but holy fuck, this one would not shut up. Seriously, he was starting to get a headache. This woman was killing his buzz. "You want to go upstairs?" he interrupted.

She gave him a knowing smile full of promise. "Sure. Just let me grab one more drink first. I'll get you another shot."

Normally, he would have objected to a woman buying him booze, but considering the fine line of sobriety he was walking, another shot was definitely in order. She slipped from her chair before he could offer to go, leaning forward to give him a perfect titty shot.

"Be right back," she promised, planting a wet kiss on his cheek before heading to the bar. She smelled of coconut tanning lotion—light and tropical. Not bad, but it was a far cry from the lavender scent of the woman who shan't be named, searing his senses with her feminine essence.

Redirecting his thoughts that seemed to have taken on a will of their own, he watched Mandy go, appreciating the sway of her gently flared hips and the rounded curve of her skirt-hugging ass as she weaved through the crowd. Once she disappeared, he turned his attention back to his beer and downed it before retrieving his phone and checking his messages. He had an itinerary alert, notifying him that his flight was leaving an hour early due to an impending snowstorm they were trying to avoid.

*Shit.* Aiden checked his watch. It was almost one. He shot an antsy glance toward the bar, but couldn't see Mandy through all the people. Returning his attention to his phone, he was verifying his flight details when a flash of red hair caught his peripherals and Mandy sat back down, sliding another shot of tequila his direction. "If we're going to do this, baby girl, we gotta go. My flight's been rescheduled."

"Wow, that's a shame."

The familiar voice held a feminine huskiness that put Aiden's cock on notice. His head snapped up and he locked eyes with the redhead sitting across from him—not Mandy. No fucking way . . . His initial surprise and—goddammit—pleasure at seeing Ryann again quickly gave way to anger as a melee of emotions rocketed through him. It didn't matter whether he was glad to see her or royally pissed, amid his warring emotions there was one common denominator that couldn't be denied—hard-core lust. Holy hell, Aiden couldn't decide what he wanted to do more, fuck her or strangle her. He couldn't believe it. That tenacious little ginger just wouldn't give up. She'd actually followed him halfway across the US.

Masking his surprise, his brows drew tight and he arrowed her with a glare that had cowed many a man in the cage, but not his gutsy little PI. She arched an unimpressed brow, looking dutifully bored, and took a sip of her drink before fishing the speared olive from her martini glass. With her stare locked on him, a triumphant gleam shining in those mischievous emerald eyes, she trapped the green ball between her teeth and smiled. Pulling the toothpick free, she closed those lush lips around it and bit down.

A tortured groan unfurled deep in his chest that ended in a snarled growl when his cock shot hard as granite. The rush of blood heading south made his head feel light, or perhaps the tequila was finally catching up with him.

"Where's Mandy?" There were oh so many other things he wanted to say to this woman right now, none of which were fitting for the public ear.

"Oh, her?" Ryann asked innocently, flippantly waving her hand. "I don't think she'll be back." She flashed him a sexy grin and nudged the shot closer, holding his chaser hostage.

"Why not?" Suspicion threaded his husky voice made raw from four tequila shots, soon to be five. He lifted the small glass to his lips and tipped his head back, swallowing the booze in one searing gulp.

The hot amber burn was on its way down his throat when she casually replied, "I told her you had crabs."

Aiden inhaled, choking on the fire searing a path into his lungs and sending him into a coughing fit. Mother. Fuck. "You did what?" he wheezed.

The corner of Ryann's mouth twitched, and he swore to God, he'd never been more close to throttling a woman in his life.

"I. Told. Her. You. Had. Crabs." she repeated slowly, enunciating each word more clearly than the last.

Like he really needed to hear her say it twice. "That shit's not funny, Ryann!"

"It's funny to me." She shrugged and took another sip of her drink, giggling into the glass.

"What the hell are you doing here?" he growled.

"I think you know why I'm here." Growing serious, she set the beer chaser on the table and slid it toward him.

"How did you find me?"

"It wasn't very hard. I *am* a private investigator—kind of my job to find people. Oh, by the way, Del Toro said to tell you that's for his broken rib." She shrugged as if the message meant nothing to her, though he knew damn well that wasn't true.

*Fuck. Me.* He grabbed the chaser and slammed it down. "So what are you going to do, baby girl?—cock-block me until I leave with you? Cuz I can tell you right now, I'm not going back to Manhattan. I don't give a shit what you say or what you do, it ain't happening."

"I just want you to listen to me, Aiden. Hear me out." She shot a quick glance at her watch before locking gazes with him, and if they weren't the most entrancing green eyes he'd ever seen. "Your parents are worried about you."

His harsh bark of laughter drew the attention of the people sitting at the tables nearby, but at this point, he didn't give a shit if he was making a scene. His buzz was burning through his veins like liquid fire making him reckless and edgy. "Is that what my mother told you? That she was worried about me? Because that's a big-ass lie. She might be worried all right, but I guarantee you, it ain't about me."

Ryann scowled in concentration, like she was having a hard time understanding what he was saying. No clue why, because he had a Harvard fucking degree that claimed he knew English quite well.

Exhaling a frustrated sigh, she tried again. "Look, Aiden, you can't keep running forever. Between you and me, your mom doesn't actually strike me as the type to give up easily. What would be the harm in coming back with me and just talking to her?"

"That you can sit there with a straight face and ask me that tells me you have no clue who you're dealing with." Another wave of dizziness crashed over him and he grabbed the corner of the table to steady himself.

"Are you all right?" Ryann reached for him, laying her hand over his.

At her slightest touch, heat rushed up his arm, sending his pulse hammering inside his chest. That his cock didn't seem to notice should have been his first clue something was seriously wrong here. He never got whiskey dick—ever.

"I'm fine," he growled, ripping his hand out from under hers.

"How much have you had to drink?" Concern tightened her brows in the most gorgeous frown. Damn, she was beautiful . . .

"Obviously too much," he grumbled. Even to his own ears, his words sounded slurred. He needed to get to bed. Sleep this shit off and forget he'd ever met this beguiling redhead. Aiden shoved back his seat and tried to stand, but the lead weight in his ass kept him grounded, sending him listing to the side. Holy shit, this tequila was really nailing him. The room was spinning, his arms and legs felt cement heavy, uncoordinated, and reluctant to move.

"Aiden!" Ryann shot out of her chair and rushed to his side, using her delectable body to brace him up as she slipped an arm around his waist. "Here, let me help you."

"Don't want your help," he slurred, but contrary to his words, his arm came around her, holding her tight against him. Holy hell, he felt like he'd spent the last half hour on a Tilt-a-Whirl.

"Maybe not, but I'm helping you anyway."

She pulled him up and he stood this time. Sweet. Progress.

"Can you walk?"

"Of course I can walk," he snapped with all the arrogant confidence of any drunk worth his salt, but the feat took a hell of a lot more effort than it should have. Crissake, he couldn't remember the last time he'd been this wasted. Ryann guided him out of the bar, and though he'd never admit it to her, he was glad for the help. His vision was going from clear to blurry and spending a lot of time in the blurry. If he could just get to bed, he'd be fine in the morning.

"Key. Grab my pocket," he told her.

At least that was what he thought he said until Ryann huffed impatiently, "I'm not grabbing your rocket, Aiden."

Another round of dizziness rolled through him. This time his knees buckled and his vision went from fuzzy to black. Ryann cursed and stumbled under his weight as she half-walked, half-dragged him across the lobby.

"Damn, Aiden, you weigh a ton," she complained.

He did his best to help her, but his body was simply refusing to obey commands at this point. What the hell was wrong with him? He'd never been this sauced before. Not even when he and Cole rented out the penthouse of the Mirage and threw the largest after-fight party in CFA history after he'd won his first televised fight. Aiden was busy making a mental note never to drink tequila again when a serious bout of light-headedness rolled through him, and this time when the darkness came, it didn't let him go.

# CHAPTER

Shit! Shit . . . shit . . . shit!" Ryann sat in the driver's seat, arms outstretched, hands gripping the steering wheel. "I'm going to hell. No, first I'm going to prison. Then, I'm going to hell."

She shot a quick glance at Aiden, slumped against the passenger door. He was fully unconscious now. Thank God he hadn't gone down sooner or there was no way she would have gotten him into her rental. This guy was a beast. She continued to watch him, waiting for the reassuring rise and fall of his shoulders. When she saw no movement, she slapped two fingers against his neck. Feeling the slow bounding pulse, she grabbed a fistful of his hair and tipped his head back. As she unkinked his airway, Ryann startled at the sudden gasp of breath resonating in the cab.

"Aiden." She shook his shoulder and his head slumped forward again. "Frick!" Ryann repositioned his head and grabbed her sweatshirt from the back seat, stuffing it along the window between his shoulder and his jaw to help hold his head up. Satisfied he wouldn't asphyxiate, she fastened her seat belt and fired up the Escape.

Anxious to get on the road, she typed her address into Google Maps on her cell. Great, eighteen hours to Brooklyn. Glancing at the unconscious man beside her, Ryann wondered how many of those hours would pass before Aiden woke up and raised holy hell.

"Take a right onto Thirty-Fourth Avenue South," the computerized voice politely instructed.

Ryann shot one last quick look at Aiden, just to make sure he was all right, before following the directions coming from her phone. She was responsible for this man, especially now, and although his mother hadn't specifically said as much, she was pretty sure the woman expected her to deliver her son back to her alive.

Of all the many questions surrounding this man, one thing was for certain—this was going to be one hell of a long road trip.

Holy. Hell. His head hurt. Every beat of Aiden's heart drove the invisible spike deeper into his brain. A cloud of disorientation fogged his mind. This wasn't a hangover. It was so much worse. Nausea rolled his stomach, threatening to revolt as the cacophony of his heartbeat thundered in his ears. His shoulders ached, arms bent at an awkward angle. Why were his arms behind his back?

Aiden shifted his weight and tried to pull them out from behind him. He only got an inch or two before he heard a metal *chink* and something sharp bit into his wrists. What the fuck? Was he . . . restrained? Where was he? Straining to hear over his crashing heartbeat, the hum of road noise told him nowhere good. Thinking back, he tried to recall the last thing he could remember before passing out, but processing thoughts was like trying to run through quicksand. That shit just wasn't happening.

Cracking open an eye, his blurry vision met the green glow of dash lights. A car. Okay, he was in a car. And it was still dark out, so less than eight hours had passed. He tried once again to remember where he'd been before he passed out, but the effort intensified the pain. Exhaling a groan, he forced open his other eye and rolled his head to the left. The sight of the fiery-haired beauty sitting beside him flipped the switch of his memories and they all came crashing back with the speed of a tsunami—a tsunami named Ryann. The woman who'd tracked him halfway across the United States. The woman who'd chased off his lay by telling her he had an STD, the woman who'd given him tequila and beer—beer that carried a bitter after bite . . . *That fucking bitch!*

She shot him a nervous glance from the driver's seat, guilt written all over her beautiful face. "You're awake."

*No shit.*

Directing her eyes back to the road, she mumbled to herself, "Well, that was fast."

Despite the truth staring him in the face, he still didn't want to believe it—didn't want to believe this sweet, innocent-looking woman would be capable of doing something so underhanded, so manipulative, so . . . fucking illegal. This he would have expected from Madeline, but Ryann? Until this moment, he'd still held out hope. Oh, how wrong he'd been. Hell, she was no better than his mother after all, just in a prettier package. How could he have been so stupid to think she was different? What a joke!

Shoving his shoulder against the door, he used the momentum to force himself upright, biting back a pained groan. The adrenaline flooding his veins quickly muted the pounding in his head. In a burst of Herculean rage, he yanked against the bonds shackling his wrists. The chain rattled, and the edge of his cuffs bit deeper into his flesh. He welcomed the pain that helped ground him, clearing the foggy haze that blanketed his mind.

"What the fuck did you give me, Ryann?" His raw throat felt like he'd been drinking broken glass instead of tequila, and the sound of his raspy voice mirrored the sentiment.

She shot him a nervous glance, trapping that full, lush bottom lip between her teeth. He would not notice how beautiful she looked with that blush of shame and guilt staining her cheeks, nor would he think about the sweet flavor of those lips or how perfect they once felt against his. No, this woman was a wolf in sheep's clothing—a viper coiled and waiting for the perfect opportunity to strike. He'd underestimated Ryann, and for that he was furious with himself. He should have known better. His mother wouldn't send some flighty waif to do a job two grown men had failed to do.

"Answer me," he growled.

"Rohypnol . . ." Her whispered response was spoken so softly, he barely heard her.

"Are you serious? You fucking roofied me?"

"Well, when you say it like that, you make it sound so bad."

*Unbelievable.* "That's because it is! Do you have any idea how many laws you've broken?" He yanked on his cuffs, rattling the chain to prove his point. "Kidnapping is a class A-1 felony, Ryann, violating federal criminal code 18 U.S.C. 1201, punishable by up to twenty years in prison."

Eyes wide, she looked at him as if he was speaking a foreign language. "How do you know that?" Suspicion threaded into her voice.

"Because I'm a fucking lawyer!"

"Oh, Jesus, help me . . ." she mumbled the plea, reaching up and pressing her palm against her forehead.

"Doubt *that's* gonna happen. Didn't think that one through too well, did ya?"

"But you're an MMA fighter . . ."

"Yeah, and I'm also one of the best damn attorneys in Manhattan. Hope you like prison food, baby."

She gasped, having the nerve to look at *him* aghast! "You wouldn't!"

"Oh, I fucking would!"

"Bullshit." She shook her head in denial.

He wondered who she was trying to convince, herself or him.

"You're bluffing. There's no way in hell anyone's going to believe a six-foot-two, hundred-and-eighty-five-pound MMA fighter got abducted by a five-foot-six, hundred-and-twenty-pound woman. Good luck proving that, jackass. You'll be the laughing stock of MMA."

"Goddammit!" He slammed his shoulder into the seat, rage boiling through him and turning his veins to ash. She jumped, startling at his outburst. "You're such a manipulative bitch!"

She hit him with a surprised scowl that just as quickly morphed into a crestfallen frown. And fuck him if that hurt look on her beautiful face didn't make him feel like a total asshole—which was absolutely absurd considering *he* was the one in the handcuffs. The sudden urge to apologize rose up swift and unbidden, which pissed him off even more. How dare she make him into the bad guy here!

"That wasn't very nice, Aiden."

"This from the woman that roofied me, put me in handcuffs, and is hauling me, against my will, to . . . where in the hell are we, anyway?"

"Wisconsin."

"Great." He glanced at the dash—2:30. "I'm going to miss my flight. I've had enough of your and my mother's tricks, Ryann. Pull over and take these cuffs off me—now."

"I'm sorry, I can't do that."

"Sweetheart, I think you're under the impression that I'm giving you a choice. You've already pointed out the glaring differences between our sizes and strength. I don't need my hands free to get away from you. You've been driving all night, and I'd be willing to bet you were up all day. There is no way in hell you're going to get this vehicle from Minneapolis to Manhattan without stopping. And just to make things interesting, I gotta piss."

This was crazy. Had she honestly thought this insane plan was going to work? The man was impossible to argue with. From what she'd seen so far, she suspected he'd prove equally impossible to reason with. And what would she say anyway? *I'm sorry your mother hired me to abduct you and haul your stubborn ass back to Manhattan, but if I don't do this job, I'm as good as dead.* Yeah, not likely . . .

She'd given up any hope of gaining Aiden's cooperation about the time she slipped a Mickey into his beer. He probably didn't even have to pee—tricky bastard.

"So what's it going to be, baby girl?"

She knew the instant those walls of his came up and he donned that arrogant Disco persona, hiding behind an image of the sexy, don't-give-a-shit fighter. She liked the real Aiden so much better than this cocky playboy. A part of her wondered what he'd been like before—in his other life when he'd been a suit-wearing, slick-haired lawyer.

If she hadn't seen Madeline's picture, combined with the confession from his own mouth, she would never, in a million years, have believed this tattooed, pierced, messy-haired MMA fighter was the same man spewing legal jargon at her like it was his native language. One thing Ryann knew for certain: Aiden Kruze was a highly complex, intelligent man, and not to be fucked with.

*Well, that ship has definitely sailed . . .* Hell, that freightliner was so far across the Pacific, it was nearing Maui.

"Well . . . ?" Aiden raised a taunting brow. "Now that I think on it, I'm kinda diggin' these cuffs, sweetheart. You think when you're down there, before you unlock me, you could suck my—"

"All right! That's enough!" Ryann jerked the wheel hard to the right, taking the off ramp at the last possible second.

The momentum sent Aiden's shoulder slamming into the passenger door. He growled a foul curse.

"Oh, did that hurt?" She grinned innocently. "Silly me, I was so busy listening to your tempting offer to blow you, I nearly drove right past our exit. I can see why the ladies have a hard time resisting you with that silver tongue of yours. I mean, I'm so wet right now, I'm practically sliding off my seat." *Boom. Roasted. Fuck you. Asshole.*

And the look of shock on that man's face was absolutely worth every dirty, embarrassing word spewed from her mouth. Ryann was quickly learning there was one way, and one way only, to deal with this man—head-on and swinging, because Aiden Kruze didn't pull his punches. If he couldn't bully and intimidate her into letting him go, he'd just be an obnoxious ass and sexually harass her until she was so freaking miserable, she wouldn't be able to stand riding in the car with him.

Unfortunately, her victory was a small one. Before she could high-five her inner self, that arrogant and, blast it all, sexy Disco grin tugged his top lip into a crooked smile and he drawled, "Damn, baby girl, that was hot. You know this silver tongue is good for more than just talking. Why don't you pull over and unlock these cuffs and I'll be more than happy to show you. Give me thirty seconds between those sweet thighs of yours and I'll make you come so hard—"

And just like that he won with a KO. Ryann slammed on the brakes, locking the tires up and sending Aiden into the dash. Without his hands to protect himself, his chest and shoulder took the brunt of the hit. "Fuck!" he snarled, slamming back into his seat and pinning her with a glare so feral, his amber eyes nearly glowed in the darkness. She felt the heat of his wrath burning into her, searing her flesh and firing up all the sensitive spots his lurid offer ignited.

Ryann had never, in the history of ever, had a guy talk to her so bluntly, so crudely, or so . . . freaking hot. Dammit, she didn't want to want this man! For one, he was engaged to marry another woman—poor thing. And second, the guy was a total man-whore. She swore to God if he *baby-girl*ed her one more time . . .

And what pissed her off all the more was the knowledge that every word he said was absolutely true. She'd felt those hands on her body, tasted those lips as his tongue made wicked promises to her mouth of better things yet to come. He'd barely touched her that night, and it shamed her to admit how quickly he'd shattered her resolve. But that didn't mean she needed to act on those feelings. She wasn't some sex-crazed—what had Del Toro called her . . . a cage banger?

Pinching the bridge of her nose, she tipped her head forward and closed her eyes. "I cannot do this with you, Aiden. Not for the next fourteen hours."

"Well, that's good to know, because I can go all night long, baby girl."

*That's it.* Ryann's head snapped up, she balled her fist, and socked him in the arm as hard as she could.

"Ouch, goddammit! What'd you do that for?"

"If you call me 'baby girl' one more time, Aiden Kruze, the next blow is going to be below the belt! I am not one of your cage-banging whores whose bra size is larger than her IQ. For your information, I don't want to be here any more than you want me here. But I don't have a choice—hence *you* don't have a choice. Believe it or not, I've got bigger problems to deal with than tracking down some spoiled, self-entitled rich boy who's run away from home because he had a spat with his mommy and daddy. Seriously! Grow the fuck up!"

Every muscle in his body turned to stone. That cute-as-hell smile on his handsome face was instantly replaced with lines of tension bracketing his mouth. His amber eyes were so golden, they looked almost otherworldly, extinguishing any softness and leaving him with a deadpan glare of serious badassness. *This* was the face of the man in that picture, the lawyer—hard, unbending, merciless, and intimidating as hell. She pitied any attorney going against him in a courtroom. For a moment she knew a brief twinge of guilt at being the one to flip his switch, snuffing out that irresistible light that attracted his fans, men and women alike. It was as if there was a stranger sitting in the seat beside her—and she didn't like it. Flirty and cocky she knew, that she could handle, but this . . . ? Lord help her, if she could call back those hurtful words, she'd do it in a heartbeat.

"You don't know the first thing about me, Ryann." His growl was low, so feral it sent a prickle of goose bumps trekking up her arms. "So don't you dare sit there and judge me. And for the record, being rich is not an entitlement, it's an indenturement. There's a big fucking difference. Now it's twenty degrees below zero and I am not exposing my dick to frostbite, so find a fucking gas station so I can take a piss."

# CHAPTER

# 10

Wow. That took a lot of goddamn nerve. At the brief flash of regret in her eyes, he'd wondered, for a moment, if she was going to apologize—as she well should. But then she turned her attention back to driving, checking behind her before pulling onto the road. He had no clue where they were, and combined with the roofie hangover he was sporting, the effects were pretty disorientating.

As Ryann followed the signs to the closest gas station, her hastily spoken, brutally honest words played over in his mind on an endless loop—particularly the part about her having bigger problems than him. Was it possible that Ryann wasn't the enemy here? Could she just be another casualty of Hurricane Madeline? Not that it excused what she'd done to him, but it did cue Aiden into the level of desperation this woman must be feeling to do something as dangerous as tangling with a middleweight MMA fighter and think that was a better option.

No, he decided, watching her from the passenger seat. Ryann wasn't his enemy. She deserved his pity, not his wrath. She was doing her job, a job she admittedly didn't want, and he'd done everything in his power to make it an impossible task. Shame washed over him when he thought of the vulgar way he'd provoked her—definitely not his finest moment. His cheeks flamed with embarrassment, which cooled a measure of his anger. It wasn't like him to be so crass and offensive. Talking it up in the bedroom was one thing, but sexually harassing a woman who was not into him was quite another. He owed her an apology. Then again, she had her own list of shit she needed to be apologizing for. And she could start with roofie-ing him.

Ryann hadn't uttered a word since her outburst, keeping her attention fixed solely on the road. She had to be exhausted after driving all night. From the slump of her shoulders and the dullness of her usually bright verdant eyes, he'd guess she was close to hitting a wall. And she wasn't the only one. The lingering effects of the Rohypnol still dogged his system, and exhaustion blanketed him. His head felt fuzzy, his limbs heavy. He needed fluids and lots of them to flush out his kidneys.

Up ahead, he spotted a truck stop and, miraculously, it was still open. The parking lot was empty, except for a few semis parked at the far end and two cars, one by the door and one in the employee section by the side of the building. As she cut the engine, he leaned forward and turned, presenting her with his cuffed wrists, anxious to get these things off and stretch his arms. He'd hyperextended his right shoulder in the fight last week and this position wasn't doing it any favors.

"I don't think so, Aiden. I'm sorry. You're going to have to step through those cuffs to get your hands in front of you."

*Bloody hell . . .* He shot her a dark look over his shoulder. "You can't seriously plan on keeping me bound the entire trip back to New York. Listen, I'll make you a deal. You uncuff me, and I promise I won't ditch you. How's that? Besides, where the hell would I go? It's freezing outside, I don't have a coat, and we're in the middle of bumfucknowhere. Where could I possibly run?"

"You could overpower me—"

*A tempting thought, that.* "Sweetheart, I'm a submissions artist. Like I said before, if I wanted to take you down, I wouldn't need my hands free to do it." Okay, did that sound as hot to her as it did to him?

Because he was imagining so many ways he could pin this woman right now. "You're operating on a false sense of security here, baby gi—" He stopped short and cleared his throat. "Umm . . . Ryann."

At his correction, her triumphant grin hit him harder than that punch she'd laid on him earlier. He wasn't cowing to her demands, per se, he just didn't see how it'd be beneficial at this time to antagonize the woman who held the key to his freedom. "The only reason we're even having this conversation right now is because I don't want to hurt you, Ryann. But I'm telling you right now, I am not riding all the way to Manhattan with my arms tied behind my back, and you will not deliver me to Madeline Kruze trussed up like a Thanksgiving turkey. It'll be a lot easier on the both of us if you just take these off. A little good faith would go a long way here, and trust me, sweetheart, you're going to need it."

She stared at him, unmoving, as if she couldn't quite make up her mind what to do. But he was a lawyer, a pro at convincing people to do what he wanted, so he wasn't sweating it. She just needed one more nudge in the right direction. So he did what any good, self-respecting lawyer would do in his case: He lied his motherfucking ass off.

"Look, I've been thinking about what you said—about how I need to man up and face my parents. And you're right, about everything. If you take these cuffs off and if you promise not to roofie me again—and by the way, I'm still pissed about that—I'll go back to Manhattan with you, Ryann, but on my own free will, not because you've forced me." A twinge of guilt pinched his chest as the lie rolled off his tongue like warm honey. There was a lot of road between here and Manhattan—plenty of time to ditch the woman. As much as she might actually be right, he was not ready to see either of his parents, and no amount of forcing the issue was going to change that.

The hope blooming in her emerald eyes killed him. This woman was too beautiful for her own good. He could feel his will bending to hers; the unexplainable desire to ease the burden she carried on her slight shoulders was now weighing heavy on him. What was her story? How had she gotten mixed up with his mother? All questions Aiden was bound and determined to get answers to before reaching New York, and none he would discover if he couldn't gain this woman's trust.

Despite his wish otherwise, Aiden's attraction to this woman was fucking with his good judgment. If he had a brain in his head, he'd bail on Ryann the first chance he got. He'd purloin her ride and haul ass back to Vegas without looking back. But the gentleman in him refused to leave her stranded and defenseless, and if he wasn't careful, his attraction for this intriguing woman might ultimately prove to be his Achilles' heel. But, first things first: He wasn't going anywhere with these handcuffs on.

"Really?" she asked, doubt and suspicion lacing her voice. "You'll come with me? Just like that?"

This woman wasn't dumb. Then again, he already knew that. Single-handedly, she'd managed to accomplish what two grown men twice her size had failed to do. If he wasn't so pissed at her, he'd have to admit his grudging respect.

"What can I say? You give a convincing argument." He wiggled his fingers at her, prompting her to remove the cuffs.

After another moment of hesitation, she exhaled a sigh of surrender and grabbed the connecting chain. "Don't make me regret this," she warned. With her free hand, she clicked on the cab light and pulled the keys from the ignition. Without the heater running, a chill instantly began seeping into the SUV, making him acutely aware of his missing coat. His injured shoulder protested the movement when she lifted the cuffs toward the light, extending his arms as she worked to fit the key in the lock.

He held his breath, biting back a pained groan, but a different groan entirely escaped his throat when her fingertips skated over his wrist. How such a simple touch could light him up with need was beyond him. But there was something about this woman that did it for him. Maybe it was her fiery spirit, maybe it was the memory of how good she felt in his arms, how delicious she tasted. Maybe it was that challenge of finding a woman who saw past his bullshit and wasn't afraid to call him out on it. But whatever it was, Aiden wanted her—bad—and the idea of working Ryann out of his system as they made their way to New York and parted ways sounded like a bravo idea to him.

"I'm sorry," she apologized, struggling with the lock. "I can't see the hole. Can you move closer this way?"

Her small hand gripped Aiden's waist as she attempted to guide him closer to the light. Not a small feat, considering he filled over half the cab, leaving Ryann little room to maneuver. The cusps of her nails bit into his flesh, sending a jolt of awareness straight into his cock, his response to her immediate and maddening.

Exhaling a frustrated growl, he attempted to turn in the seat, knees wedging against the door as she fumbled with the lock. "Good thing you weren't Houdini's assistant," he grouched, bending forward. He had his face in the dash, legs tangled, one shoulder pressed against the freezing window, arms twisted back—and a partridge in a pear tree.

She laughed, which did nothing to give credence to the sincerity of her apology. The airy, feminine sound lit up his nerve endings, sending every pounding pulse point straight into his groin. Despite the pain in his shoulder and throbbing of his crimped hard-on, he found himself desperately wanting to hear that laugh again, and he was willing to endure this sick version of Twister to get it.

"I'm almost there . . ."

*Oh, good Lord . . .*

"Can you just . . . ? Yeah, that's it. A little higher . . ."

Aiden bit his bottom lip to hold back his tortured groan. Seriously, could she not hear herself speaking?

"Wow, you're flexible . . ."

"I think that's my line, sweetheart," he murmured, unable to help himself. He chuckled at her startled gasp. "Oh, come on, you really didn't think I was going to pass that up, did ya?"

"You're an ass."

But her insult was only half-hearted and just breathy enough to let him know he wasn't the only one feeling the heat. A moment later, the cuffs sprang free. "Thank God," he grumbled, wincing as he brought his arms forward and began rubbing the circulation back into his wrists. "I'll be right back." Anxious to stretch his legs and put a little distance between him and his hot redheaded abductor, Aiden bailed out of the SUV and double-timed it into the station.

Ryann prayed she wouldn't regret letting Aiden go. He'd made a convincing argument, though, and it wasn't like she could keep him bound the entire trip back to New York. She'd done the right thing, she told herself, giving him the benefit of the doubt. She just prayed he didn't prove her wrong. She had a lot riding on this, and if Aiden decided to screw her over, it'd likely be a mistake she might not live long enough to regret.

With eyes heavy-lidded from fatigue, Ryann struggled to keep her gaze fixed on the storefront window as she waited for Aiden to return. She yawned, battling the exhaustion riding her hard. She wasn't sure how much longer she could keep going without some rest. Perhaps an energy drink would help. Getting out of the SUV, Ryann entered the store and headed to the coolers. It took her a moment to find the Monster she was looking for. Of course, it would have to be the one on the top shelf. Standing on her tiptoes, she was reaching for the can when an arm stretched over her head and plucked the soda from the rack.

Startled, she stepped backed, stumbling into a wall of muscle. "Shit, you scared me," she said, pressing her hand over her thundering heart as she turned to face Aiden. Only, it wasn't Aiden trapping her between his body and the cooler. The man standing over her was a few inches shorter but just as definably muscled. The tattoos sleeving his arms ran up the sides of his neck, disappearing into a beard that twined into matching braids hanging several inches from his chin. How was it possible that the ink Aiden wore could look so hot on his muscle-roped arms and so terrifying on this man? Perhaps it was the grim images of death trekking up his arms, or maybe the *Welcome to hell* sign collaring his throat. Not a great selling point there. If this guy was going for panty-dropping tats, this one was a swing and a miss. He had more piercings than she did—the bullring looping through his septum was especially lovely, but it was hard to beat that spike poking out of his bottom lip.

"Excuse me." Ryann stepped to the side, no longer caring about her Monster when she had a real-life version standing in front of her. But Sons of Anarchy followed her step for step.

"Hey, baby, what's the rush?" His arm shot out, blocking her retreat as he planted his palm on the glass door. "Don't you want this?" Anarchy held up the Monster and waved it at her.

"Keep it." She ducked beneath his arm, but the one holding the can caught her around the waist. He pulled back, jerking her against him.

"Where you goin', sweetheart?" he purred next to her ear.

She cringed as his breath blasted her neck, the stale scent of cigarette smoke assaulting her nostrils. "Let me go," she demanded with more bravado than she felt. Ryann's heart crashed inside her chest, her thoughts stuttered with surreality as adrenaline flooded her veins. This wasn't happening . . . And yet, there was no denying the tattooed arm banded across her stomach, wedged high beneath her breasts, squeezing the air from her lungs.

The malevolent chuckle rumbling behind her sent a surge of bile coursing up her throat. He growled something, but she couldn't hear it over the thundering of her heartbeat. Her panicked gaze darted around the convenience store, searching for someone, anyone, who might help her. Where was the clerk? Better yet, where was Aiden?

She spotted two men that looked a lot like the one who had ahold of her standing off in the corner, amusement dancing in their insidious stares as they watched their friend manhandle her, and she knew the only assistance they'd be giving would be to hold her down. The post behind the cash register was vacant. Where was that attendant? Shouldn't someone be here?

"Let me go!" Ryann hissed as she began struggling in earnest, which only seemed to excite the man behind her more.

"Ooo . . . you are a feisty one," he growled in her ear. "Must be that red hair. I can't wait to find out if you're just as fiery down here." Anarchy's hand slipped between her legs and grabbed her crotch, jerking up so hard her feet left the ground. The mocking laughter of his friends filled the store. A moment later, it was cut short by a feral growl. Her assailant tensed behind her.

"Get your fucking hands off her."

Anarchy didn't even have a chance to comply before Ryann found herself torn free of the man and stumbling forward. The can of Monster hit the ground and popped, sending a fluorescent green geyser shooting in the air, spraying energizing soda all over. She turned around just in time to see Aiden slam Anarchy into the cooler—head first. His knee came up at the same time, nailing the bastard in the ribs and dropping him to the ground. The guy hit the floor and curled in a ball, moaning just as his buddies decided to join the fray.

They dove for Aiden at the same time. She slammed her hand over her mouth to hold back the scream threatening to tear from her throat. Ryann stood there in shock as she watched this MMA fighter take on two men. Not a flicker of fear or hesitancy crossed his handsome face. Despite the terrifying situation, she couldn't help but notice the fluidity in the way he moved, and the skill in which he fought, timing his strikes and dodging their blows.

When a flash of steel caught her eye, true terror froze the blood coursing through her veins. Before a warning could pass her lips, Aiden sent out an impressive hook kick that caught the guy in the wrist. The sickening crunch of bone accompanied his pained cry as the knife clattered to the ground and skidded out of sight.

She had to do something! *Call the police!* The still rational part of her brain screamed at her nonfunctioning limbs. Ryann reached for the cell in her back pocket and her hand connected with her ass. Shit. She must have left her phone in the car. Forcing her feet into motion, she ran for the counter, praying they'd have a phone at the register. As she rounded the corner, her foot hit something wet and she slipped. Ryann clutched the counter to keep from going down as her foot went out from under her. Scrambling to regain her balance, she looked down and locked gazes with a man lying on the floor, his sightless eyes staring back at her. A crimson stain saturated his chest, and his life's blood was seeping out in a large pool beneath him, ending in a skid mark beneath her foot.

*Oh, God!*

It all clicked together—what she and Aiden had walked in on. She reached for the phone to dial 911. A deafening gunshot startled her, and she dropped the receiver.

# CHAPTER

As the third guy hit the floor, knocked out by a solid uppercut to the jaw, the first man—the one who'd had his hands on Ryann—got his bearings. He staggered to his feet, and it wasn't until he pulled his hand out from behind his back that Aiden realized the bastard was armed. Fuck. He dove for the guy, catching his wrist, forcing his arm toward the ceiling just as a shrill scream shattered his senses. Aiden's focus shifted, centering wholly on Ryann as bone-deep fear rocketed through him. The gun went off, the explosion so close to his head that the ringing temporarily deafened him.

*Oh, God, Ryann!*

As they hit the floor, Aiden turned, making sure the asshole took the brunt of the fall. He slammed the guy's gun hand onto the ground—once—twice—before knocking the nine-millimeter from his grip. The weapon skidded under a stack of metal shelving.

He hit the man with another solid blow that slammed the back of his head into the floor. This one knocked him out, and Aiden was on his feet, running in the direction from which he'd heard Ryann scream. As he came around the corner of an aisle, she was hanging up the phone. Her vibrant emerald eyes were wide with shock, her pallor washing out the pink flush of her lips as she clamped them together with the effort not to cry.

"Ryann . . ." He rushed over, taking her face in his hands and tipping it to meet his searching stare. "You're bleeding. Where are you hurt?" he demanded, inspecting the crimson along her jaw. Her appearance alarmed him. When she didn't answer right away, he began patting her down, hands sliding along the slender column of her neck, onto her shoulders, then down her arms. Shit, she was so small, so fragile . . . Just the thought of that bastard's hands on her sent another rush of fury flooding his veins. The possessive surge was a wholly unwelcome feeling, but one he wouldn't take the time to consider right now. His hands circled her ribs beneath her breasts and slid down her waist, his eyes searching her face for any sign of pain.

"It's . . . it's not mine," she stuttered, grabbing his wrists and halting his inspection. "It's him." She pointed behind the counter. "I dropped the phone. There was blood on it."

Stepping around her, Aiden peered over the counter and found the source of Ryann's scream. Muttering a curse, he turned toward Ryann and pulled her into his arms, holding her tight against his chest. Holy hell . . . they'd blindly walked right into a robbery. What horrible fucking luck! He hadn't even noticed the guys when he'd come in here and beelined it to the head.

Ryann's arms wrapped around him and he moved her away from the crime scene. Each step she took left a crimson stain on the floor behind her. "Did you call the police?"

She nodded.

One of the guys moaned and Ryann flinched. "Hey . . . you're all right. He's not going to hurt you. Why don't you go wait in the car? I'll stay in here until the police arrive."

"I thought . . . when that gun went off . . . I thought you'd been shot."

Her concern for him made something in his chest tighten. Uncomfortable with the foreign sensation, Aiden cracked a joke, playing off the feeling as posttraumatic stress. "Worried about me, were you? Not looking forward to explaining to my mom that I got shot on your watch?"

She let out a half-hearted laugh—poor attempt that it was. And honestly, there was nothing humorous about this situation. An innocent man was dead, and if he hadn't gotten to Ryann when he did . . . Unconsciously, his grip on her tightened, pulling her petite, curvy frame tight against him. What was it about this woman that moved him so deeply? Whether it be his passion, his anger, or his protective instincts, every emotion seemed heightened with her.

"That's not funny, Aiden," she chided, making no effort to move out of his embrace.

"I know, Madeline Kruze is a scary woman, huh . . ."

This time her laugh didn't sound quite so forced. Given the choice between serious or joking, Aiden would choose the latter every time. The defense mechanism worked beautifully at keeping people from getting too close without realizing he was maneuvering them—always the jovial smartass.

"That's not what I meant and you know it," she chided. "I was referring to you being shot. But now that you mention it, she is pretty terrifying."

She glanced at him beneath her long, dark lashes. Her top lip twitched as if a small smile were threatening to make an appearance. Was she seriously teasing him back? Honestly, if Ryann wasn't working for his mother, if they'd met under different circumstances, he could seriously dig her. She was so different from the women he was used to hanging with. Ryann was gorgeous, smart, and tenacious. How such a tiny thing could have nerves of steel was beyond him, but any woman who could walk in on a robbery and not lose her shit deserved tons of respect in his book.

Did that mean when this was all said and done, he wasn't going to fuck her over? No, but he wasn't going to enjoy it half as much as he'd planned to when he'd been handcuffed in her car. Bottom line, he wasn't going back. And he sure as hell wasn't going to marry Cynthia Moralli.

The distant whir of sirens grew louder. "I think the police are here." It was with more reluctance than Aiden wanted to admit that he let her go and took a step back. "You don't have to stay in here," he told her again, knowing that in about two minutes this place was going to explode into chaos. He wanted to protect her from any further trauma, but in stubborn Ryann fashion, she shook her head.

"I want to stay with you."

The siren outside abruptly cut off, and red, white, and blue lights strobed through the store window. Several car doors slammed outside, and before he could warn her, the front door flew open and four officers stormed inside.

"Get on the ground! Get on the ground!"

Aiden raised his hands and locked them behind his head as he knelt on the ground. An overzealous cop charged over to him and helped him the rest of the way by slamming his chest into the floor. And for the second time in as many hours, Aiden found himself in cuffs again.

"What are you doing?" Ryann cried, looking shocked and outraged.

It wasn't anything Aiden didn't expect to happen. He didn't exactly look like he was out selling Girl Scout cookies. And these officers had no idea what they were walking into. For all they knew, he was the shooter. But if Quick Draw McGraw here didn't get his booted heel off Aiden's spine in the next two seconds, he was going to get pissed.

The three other officers swept the aisles, guns drawn, calling out their findings. "Clear! Clear! Clear! Three men down! All clear! Medic!"

Ryann was in Quick Draw's face. "Get off him!" she yelled. "He's not the guy! It's them!" She pointed down the aisle where the three men each had an officer checking them out. "The man they shot is behind the counter."

Apparently, Ryann had a trusting face because the cop removed his foot from Aiden's back and holstered his gun. A medic appeared in the doorway and the officer waved him over. They both left to check behind the counter and Ryann knelt on the floor beside him.

"Are you all right?"

He craned his neck to look up at her. Her brows were drawn tight with concern. "I'm swell. I get off on being cuffed, so this is actually working for me."

Ryann let out an unladylike snort and rolled her eyes. "Get up here." She grabbed his arm and tugged him to his feet. "Are you always such a smartass?" she grumbled.

"Always."

The cops had the other three men on their feet, each shoved against a section of the cooler as they were cuffed and read their Miranda rights. Quick Draw called out that their victim was DOA. When he came back over, the officer began hammering Aiden and Ryann with questions.

"You mean to tell me you took all three of these men down, by yourself?" The officer asked Aiden, looking skeptical.

"He's an MMA fighter," Ryann interjected.

If he didn't know better, he'd swear there was a hint of pride in her voice. Could it be possible that this woman actually approved of what he did for a living? And why did the idea of Ryann's approval give him so much pleasure? He'd stopped caring a long time ago what other people thought of him. He was done trying to please people in what would ultimately result in one more failed attempt to earn love and acceptance.

"Is that right?" Quick Draw asked. His assessing gaze held no such appreciation for the sport. He'd yet to remove the cuffs, and thanks to Ryann's unhelpful defense, it might be quite some time before that happened now. Not that he totally blamed the cop for being cautious. There was a dead man behind the counter and Aiden didn't exactly look like the take-you-home-to-mother kind of guy.

His arms were sleeved in gray-wash tats, his ears were pierced, and his brow was studded. He wore a steel hoop through his bottom lip, and a balled bar through his tongue. The first thing he'd done after moving to Vegas was wipe away any remnant of Sen. Bennett Kruze's son. If anything, he looked like he belonged with those jackasses by the cooler, not with this stunning redhead with the peaches-and-cream complexion and expressive vibrant eyes. If it weren't for Ryann, he'd probably be getting booked with them right now. These cops had walked into a dangerous situation. They would arrest now and ask forgiveness later.

"Yes, that's so," she answered for him.

Both he and the officer shot her an annoyed scowl. He could speak for himself, for crissake, and the officer obviously wanted to hear what he had to say. But Ryann wasn't having any of it.

"Would you please remove these cuffs from my boyfriend?"

She'd gotten pissed at the officer's less than gentle treatment of him and apparently wasn't going to be happy until they uncuffed him. What spurred her sudden protective streak he couldn't know, but it was certainly an unexpected response. Aiden wasn't used to having anyone fight for him—ever. And seeing this adorable pixie standing up to a room full of officers and making demands she had no business tossing about was not only charming but it made something in his chest cramp and his heart warm uncomfortably.

The officer's brow shot up at her demand. As if to prove her claim on him, Ryann moved closer and slipped her arms around his waist. Despite the inappropriateness of the situation, the press of her soft breasts against his side uncomfortably heated his blood.

"Ryann . . ." He was about to ask her to step back. Her effect on him was swift and uncontrollable. The last thing he needed if this cop decided to pat him down was for the guy to come in contact with his rock-hard cock. He'd be arrested for intent with a deadly weapon for sure.

"Do you have any ID on you?" Quick Draw cut in impatiently.

"My back pocket."

Ryann helpfully obliged by slipping her hand into the back of his jeans. She removed his wallet and handed it to the officer. He flipped it open and a condom hit the floor. The cop shot him a *Really?* eye roll and slipped his license from the clear plastic jacket. He handed the wallet back to Ryann, who did not retrieve his rubber before shoving it back in his jeans.

"Long way from Vegas," the officer commented. "Where did you say you were going?"

"I didn't."

Ryann nudged him in the ribs for being difficult and added impatiently, "We're on our way to Manhattan. Aiden has family there."

The officer nodded. "I'll be right back." He turned and headed out to his car to run Aiden's license.

"Why are you being so difficult?" she hissed under her breath.

"Why did you tell him I was your boyfriend?" he asked, ignoring her question.

Ryann's cheeks reddened, her gaze darting nervously to the floor. "I thought it'd be easier that way, give you more credibility—"

"You think my credibility is lacking?" he asked, arching his pierced brow, half teasing, half serious.

Her eyes shot up to his, uncertainty pinching her brows as she studied him. "Of course not. *I* don't, but you'll probably have a little more trouble convincing *them*." She nodded toward the officers by the cooler. "Besides, what do you think I'm going to tell them?—that I abducted you from the Embassy Suites in Minneapolis and dragged you against your will halfway across Wisconsin?"

"You left out the Rohypnol part." His top lip twitched at her slack-jawed look, all color draining from her beautiful face.

"You're not going to tell them, are you?" she demanded in a harsh whisper.

"That's depends . . ."

"On what?"

He gave her his signature sexy Disco grin. Her eyes went wide with understanding, but before he could barter for his silence, one of the other officers came over.

"Are you the one who called 911, ma'am?"

She nodded.

"Would you come with me, please? I have a few questions for you." At first, she looked hesitant to leave Aiden's side, as if she didn't trust him not to rat her out. "Don't worry, ma'am. It'll only take a few minutes."

# CHAPTER

12

A few minutes felt like forever. She was fairly certain Aiden was only joking about the roofies, but this being her first felony and all, she couldn't help but feel a little nervous letting him out of her sight. In as much detail as she could remember, Ryann quickly explained what happened. The officer wrote everything down and sent his partner to retrieve the weapons. By the time he escorted her back to Aiden, the one who'd taken his license was removing the cuffs from his wrists.

"I appreciate you being so understanding, Mr. Kruze. Under the circumstances, we had to take every precaution."

The officer even picked the foil package up from the floor and handed it back to Aiden. What the hell? He took it back and shoved his hand in his front pocket, looking more pissed off than ever. Why? They were letting him go and with an apology at that.

"Like I said, it's not a problem." Aiden's clipped tone belayed his annoyance.

"Is everything all right?" she asked, looking between him and the officer.

"It's fine. They ran my ID. They know who I am."

*And that's a bad thing?*

"Apparently, it doesn't look very good on your record when you rough up a senator's son," he grumbled.

Ryann didn't think he could have said *senator's son* with more distain. Was Aiden actually mad about getting preferential treatment because of who he was? And the fact that this officer looked ready to shit himself told her there was a hell of a lot more to Aiden Kruze than she realized.

"We're free to go, then?" she asked.

"Well, not exactly," the officer who'd spoken with her chimed in as he approached. "We're going to need you to stay close."

*What? This can't be happening.* "How close?"

"In town close."

"But why? For how long?" Quickly, she did the mental math, counting down the days to her deadline—seven. She had seven days to get Aiden to Manhattan.

"A couple of days. You're witnesses in a murder investigation, ma'am. We'll need you to come down to the station and give official statements tomorrow and answer any other questions. You'll have to officially identify the suspects."

"Identify the suspects? They're right there!" She pointed to the three men as they were being led past her single file.

"I realize that. It's just a formality, ma'am."

"Can they do that?" she asked, turning to Aiden. "Can they keep us here?"

"Not without a court order. But given the circumstances, getting one wouldn't be difficult."

*Shit.* "I don't even know where we are."

"Portage, ma'am."

"And where exactly is that?"

"Not quite an hour past Madison."

"My girlfriend's tired," Aiden cut in, seeming anxious to be done with the whole thing. "And she's had quite a shock. Can you point me to the closest motel around here?"

"That'd be the Shady Lawn."

"Thank you, we'll GPS it. If you'll give me your card, I'll call later today to schedule a time to come in and give our statements."

The officer handed him his card and Aiden placed his hand on the small of her back, guiding her to the exit. They were nearly out the door when the officer called, "Mr. Kruze . . ." Aiden stopped, but didn't bother to turn back. "On behalf of the Portage Police Department, we apologize for any inconvenience this has caused—"

"Don't." Aiden cut him off. "You're just doing your job. I'm not my father." He grumbled that last part under his breath, his heavy undertone of resentment not lost on Ryann. She couldn't help but wonder what they'd discovered about Aiden that would make these officers so skittish. Before she could think too hard on it, Aiden grabbed her hand and led her out the door.

"Keys . . ."

He held out his hand expectantly.

Ryann hesitated before pulling them out of her pocket and dropping them into his palm. The guy had just saved her life. She could hardly insult him by denying his request to drive. Yet, somehow, she couldn't help but feel they'd reversed roles. She considered balking about it, but given Aiden's souring mood, she decided now might not be the best time to take her stand. With him, she'd have to pick and choose her battles carefully. Gaining his compliance was her main goal here. All that mattered was getting him to Manhattan, not how they arrived. Perhaps if she surrendered some control, he'd soften a bit, let down his guard, and become more compliant.

Aiden didn't exactly strike her as the kind of guy who took well to not being in charge. He might appear to be a happy-go-lucky, womanizing flirt, but she'd glimpsed enough of his dark side to know that deep down there was a whole hell of a lot more to this fighter than met the eye. And damn if Ryann didn't find herself wanting to solve the puzzle that was Aiden Kruze—which was a really bad idea, considering this guy wasn't her enigma to solve. For the countless time since she'd met him, Ryann reminded herself he was engaged to be married in a week.

The Escape's headlights flashed as he used the remote to unlock it. They broke apart, and she wordlessly rounded the back of the SUV. Without his support, her legs felt shaky and weak. Maybe it was the aftermath of adrenaline finally clearing her system that was messing with her head, making it feel light. By the time she climbed into the passenger seat, she was shaking. It didn't help that she couldn't stop thinking of how different this night would have ended if Aiden hadn't come to her rescue. That easily could have been her lying dead in that store . . .

"Hey, you all right?" he asked, shooting her a sideways glance from the driver's seat.

She nodded, not sure her voice would support the lie. She was just tired, that was all. Once she got some rest, this would all seem less . . . overwhelming.

Aiden didn't look convinced. Turning in his seat, he reached for her, taking her face in his hands and forcing her eyes to meet his. At the intensity of his stare, her pulse quickened, butterflies awakened in her stomach. Never in her life had she seen eyes this color. The unnatural golden tones with darker flecks of brown were a kaleidoscope of design she could get lost in if she wasn't careful. Though firm and unyielding, his touch was gentle—comforting.

Ryann resisted the urge to close her eyes, to relax in his hands, soaking in the strength of this fighter who single-handedly saved her life and stopped a robbery. Because of him, three dangerous men were off the streets and would hopefully remain that way. It was only too bad he hadn't gotten there sooner—before an innocent life was lost.

"You're shaking." His brows drew tight with concern.

She was shaking, worse than before. It definitely wasn't Aiden's touch making her tremble, or the genuine concern in his eyes making her walls of resistance crumble. And she surely didn't want him to pull her into his arms like he had inside that store, holding her against his rock-hard body as he told her everything was going to be all right—even if it wasn't true.

"I'm . . . just cold, that's all," she murmured, finally finding her voice.

He hesitated a moment, his all-too-perceptive eyes taking her in, missing nothing. She felt the heat of his gaze every place they landed, now searing her mouth as it stalled on her lips. Nervously, she wet them with the tip of her tongue. Her pulse beat faster. She swallowed against the lump in her throat, which drew his eyes to the small divot at the base of her neck. Something in the air electrified between them. His expression darkened, and the concern that had been there seconds ago was replaced with another emotion she didn't dare try to name. Whatever it was made him look hungry—predatory.

If Ryann had had half a brain in her head she would have been afraid, for at that moment, she knew any semblance of control she thought she held over this fighter was nothing more than an illusion. Aiden Kruze was a force to be reckoned with—inside the cage and out. This man was an absolute powerhouse, and her feminine instincts told her that he would be no less dominant in the bedroom. She'd gotten a small taste of it just last week, when he'd believed her to be nothing more than a panty-dropping fan.

The memories returned, swift and unbidden—the feel of his barely controlled restraint as he pinned her against the door with his powerful body. The dominance of his mouth as he took what she had to give and demanded more, consuming her as no man had before. His skilled tongue did things to her mouth that made her want to feel that talent in other aching places.

His thumb brushed over her bottom lip, ripping her back into the here and now. Oh, Lord, he was going to kiss her. The rough, callused hands of this fighter lit her nerve endings on fire. Her reaction to him was fierce and irrational—a dangerous combination. A strangled moan escaped her throat as she forced her mind to shut down the memory of his last touch. This was not happening. He wasn't for her. This man was a paycheck, nothing more and nothing less, and she must remember that—before she got hurt.

Clearing her throat to cover the escaped whimpering sound, she pulled away from Aiden's touch and hugged her arms across her chest as if she could somehow contain the desire thrumming through her veins. She rubbed her biceps furiously in an attempt to scrub away the goose bumps prickling her flesh.

"It's freezing in here. Will you please start the car?"

Aiden paused a moment, still watching her, then grunted his consent, tearing his gaze away and turning his attention to the task of getting them the hell out of there.

What the hell was he thinking? Had he really almost kissed Ryann—again? The first time he'd had the excuse of ignorance. He'd thought she was a typical cage banger, but it didn't take spending more than a few minutes with this woman to know there was nothing typical about Ryann Andrews.

And just maybe that was the crux of it. She intrigued him like no other. Obviously, his protective instincts were still running on overdrive and fucking with his common sense. He should not want her like he did, especially after that shit she pulled in Minneapolis. But despite his ire over her drugging him, a part of him couldn't help but respect the hell out of her for having the balls to take him on. And now, after seeing how she handled herself in a crisis, how she kept it together . . . that was some impressive shit.

Aiden stood beneath the motel's hot shower spray, mentally berating himself for softening toward the woman who sat no more than twenty feet from him. There was only one wall separating them, and it wasn't nearly thick enough, as far as he was concerned. This was a mistake—sharing a room with her—but she'd refused his offer to book two rooms, leaving them to share the single-occupancy suite with the queen bed.

She wasn't letting him out of her sight, which wouldn't be such a big deal if he didn't want to fuck her blind. Now *that* was a problem. She still wasn't convinced he wouldn't bolt on her, and to be honest, he vacillated on the idea himself. Hell, he'd be lucky if she didn't cuff him to the bed tonight. Just thinking about it sent a wicked visual flashing through his mind. In response, his cock began to swell with eager anticipation. Growling a ripe curse, he swore at the stiff member and cranked the cold water, letting the tepid spray beat his erection into submission.

This was a mistake—spending any amount of time horizontal with that woman was a really bad idea. Apparently, saving her life hadn't won him enough points in the trust department—or maybe it'd won him too many, if she thought he was going to be able to share a bed with her and keep it platonic.

If all that wasn't bad enough, the shower still smelled like her. The light, feminine scent of her lavender soap tormented his senses. Anxious for this to be over, he grabbed the courtesy bar of soap and did a quick lather. Ryann had left hers in the shower with an innocent offer to share, but he'd be damned if he was going to subject himself to that kind of torture. Come morning, after they'd both gotten some much-needed sleep, he'd hit up the local store to get a change of clothes and some manly soap.

After rinsing off the filmy bubbles, Aiden cut the shower's spray and stepped out of the tub. Grabbing the towel from the rack, he dried off before sliding on his underwear. As he prepared to enter the main room, he sent up a silent prayer Ryann would be asleep.

# CHAPTER

13

What are you doing?"

Ryann didn't even try to disguise the alarm in her voice when Aiden came swaggering out of the bathroom towel drying his hair in nothing but his underwear. The boxer briefs rode low on his waist, clinging to his thighs and hugging his ass. Hanes never looked so good. The black cotton stretched taut over an impressive piece of male flesh hanging between his thighs, the detailed outline leaving nothing to the imagination.

His arms were up, displaying a roadmap of muscled abs and sculpted obliques. Not a spare ounce of flesh adorned this man's body, a body he clearly had no shame in putting on display. Then again, why should he?—he was absolutely gorgeous.

Aiden froze at her alarmed outburst and canted his head, looking at her from beneath the towel. "What's it look like I'm doing? I'm getting ready for bed."

"Wearing that?"

His brows rose, more in amusement than in question she suspected. "What do you propose I wear, Ryann? I don't suppose you happened to grab my duffel bag when you were abducting me."

No. No, she had not.

"I didn't think so," he grumbled, tossing the damp towel on the chair as he walked past her side of the bed. Unable to tear her eyes from his incredibly hard body, she watched as he ambled to his side of the bed and flopped down, hands laced behind his head, long legs crossed at the ankle. The unforgiving mattress bounced like a trampoline, throwing Ryann into him. Her hand shot out to stop her trajectory and landed solidly on his chest. Eyes remaining closed, he chuckled. A low, throaty rumble vibrated beneath her fingers and traveled up her arm like a seductive shock wave.

Aiden cracked open an eye, pinning her with that heart-stopping amber stare. "Not tonight, honey. I have a headache."

She gasped. Shock and outrage made her impulsive and reckless. Without thinking better of it, she grabbed the flat disc of his masculine nipple and pinched him—hard. Aiden flinched, barking out a surprised curse.

"You're going to have a lot more than a headache," she snapped, refusing to let go, and taking sadistic pleasure in wiping that arrogant smirk off his too-handsome face. But her win was a short victory. Perhaps she should have considered the wisdom of taking on an MMA fighter, because in less than two seconds she was on her back, arms pinned above her head as his body pressed her into the hard mattress.

"Not so funny now, is it?" he growled.

She couldn't tell if he was angry or playing—perhaps a little of both. "Let me up," she bucked her hips, a half-assed attempt to displace 185 pounds of hard, muscled fighter.

He didn't budge. She struggled beneath him, trying to work herself free, but his grip only tightened, his body hardening to stone as a low growl tore from his throat. "Fuck, Ryann, quit moving."

"Then let me up!"

"Not until you tap."

"What? You're insane. I'm not tapping for you."

"Then get comfortable, sweetheart, because until you do, I'm not moving."

For good measure, Aiden ground his hips between her parted thighs, letting her feel the full force of his arousal against the sensitive bead of her sex. A jolt of heat arrowed into her core, releasing a flood of desire she'd been fighting like hell to hold back. The thin cotton of her pajama pants provided little barrier to his Hanes-covered cock, and soon her body's moisture would betray her aching need for this man.

Pride and principle warred with self-preservation.

"Tap," he mocked, arching his pierced brow, daring her to push him further.

"Never."

Aiden chuckled, a deep, throaty rumble she felt all the way to her toes. With eyes locked on hers, he lowered his head, stopping just before his lips would brush against hers. Seconds ticked by. Her breath stalled in her lungs. He wouldn't . . . would he?

"Tap," he growled. The moist heat of his minty breath kissed her lips but his flesh did not. He was bluffing . . . right? Did she really know him well enough to take that risk? By the unwavering intensity of his amber stare the answer to that would be a no. Apparently sleep deprivation was skewing her good judgment, because the insane impulse to see how far this fighter was prepared to go in order to win was too tempting to resist.

He thought he had her all figured out, did he?—thought that he could intimidate her with his body, bully her into submission. Well, he had another thing coming. Someone should really teach this guy a lesson, and Ryann was just daring enough to volunteer.

"You want me to tap?" she whispered, smiling sweetly. "You first." She closed the scant distance separating them and kissed him. Aiden froze. For a moment, she thought he was going to pull back. When he didn't, she couldn't help but smile against his lips—another win. He didn't move, nor did he kiss her back, holding himself stone-still, as if he wasn't certain he trusted her motives. Smart man.

What the hell was she doing? Which seemed to be his mirroring thought when he tensed as her tongue traced his bottom lip, teasing over the loop piercing. His breath passed his parted lips in shortened pants. He seemed to be at war with himself, the energy coiled inside him stringing his muscles ripcord tight.

If she was honest, she'd admit to using this game to sate her wicked curiosity. Did he really taste as good as she remembered, did he kiss with enough skill and passion to wipe all reason from her mind? What would it take to break this fighter?—to make *him* tap?

She found her answer when she sucked his bottom lip into her mouth and bit down on his lip ring, gently tugging the metal loop. A tortured growl tore from his throat that sounded more like a harsh curse, and he crushed his mouth to hers. His tongue unapologetically pushed past her lips, invading and conquering. She tried to meet the demanding thrust, the tangled caress, but she quickly found herself drowning in this man. His free hand dove into her hair, fisting in her curls with enough tension to shatter the illusion that she had any semblance of control here.

Nothing about Aiden's kiss was gentle or wooing, nothing about his touch coaxing or courting. He seemed pissed off, almost as if he resented wanting her. Everything about his kiss, his touch, felt punishing and punitive, which only made it more humiliating in the way it excited her, the way her body came alive beneath his. She'd never thought herself the kind of woman that liked to be handled rough, not that she'd had enough experience with bed partners to know what she liked. Every nerve ending tingled with awareness, her core heating until the internal fire raging inside her turned the blood in her veins to molten lava.

God help her, he tasted just as good as she remembered. Aiden released his grip on her wrists and grabbed her hip, anchoring her to the mattress as he ground the steely ridge of his erection against the cotton cloth barring him entrance. Were they not still clothed, he would have been balls deep inside her right now. And that was her first warning as to just how far over her head she was—and Aiden didn't appear to have any intention of stopping.

"Fuck, Ryann," he growled, nipping her bottom lip and then sucking away the sting. "You're so wet . . . I can feel you through your clothes."

He rocked against her again, sending little jolts of pleasure shooting into her core. Her muscles contracted, an empty glove aching to be filled. If he kept touching her like this, grinding his arousal against her sensitive clit, she was going to come. Somewhere in the back of her mind was the nagging thought that this wasn't a good idea, though right now, she was hard pressed to remember why.

"I've never tasted lips as sweet as yours." His hand slid underneath her shirt, capturing her breast, squeezing the sensitive flesh. He groaned—a gravelly, tormented, erotic sound. "So perfect . . . the softest I've ever felt." Though meant as a compliment, being compared to the other women he'd been with was an unwelcome reminder of the one he was promised to. The briefest flare of jealousy fired in her veins at the thought of Aiden kissing another woman like this—touching someone else and showering her with the same praise meant for her alone. Guilt assailed her as flesh warred with conscience. She had no right to feel jealous or possessive over this man. She'd known all along he was engaged, and she should be ashamed of herself for being *that* woman—the one who lacked the self-respect and integrity not to mess around with a taken man. And what did that say about Aiden that he would so willingly crawl between her legs when in a week he'd be walking down the aisle and marrying someone else?

Just the thought of it made her heart cramp and her stomach turn. What was she doing? She had no business wanting him like this, not when he was promised to someone else. Just because he didn't seem to care, that didn't make it right. No question, this was a mistake. There was no scenario in which this ended well for her. But dammit, it wasn't fair . . .

Never in her life had she wanted a man more than this one. Why couldn't things have been different? As if the universe were testing the limits to her control, Aiden rucked up her top and took her breast in his mouth. The hard steel ball of his tongue piercing teased her nipple, sending a direct current of energy right into her core. Oh, God, she had to stop this while she still had the sense to speak. But he felt so good . . .

A broken moan escaped her parted lips as he moved to her other breast, nipping and sucking the sensitive peak until it ached with both pain and pleasure. "Aiden . . ." she panted his name on a breathy plea. "We have to stop this."

Either he wasn't listening or wasn't convinced she meant it, and in truth, neither was she. He released her nipple, dragging the tip through his straight white teeth. His spicy masculine scent filled her senses as she inhaled a surprised gasp. Her sex clenched, a direct connection from her breasts to her core. His mouth was hot and wet against her neck, sucking against her thundering pulse that gave away the truth of her desire.

"Damn, Ryann, you taste so good . . ." The rough growl of his voice was strained. "I can't wait to find out if you're just as delicious down here." His hand slipped past her stomach, boldly entering the front of her pajama pants, and deftly parting her silky folds.

White-hot desire rocketed into her as his finger slipped deep inside her. Ryann's hips arched on their own accord, greedily seeking fulfillment only he could give her. Never in her life had she been more tempted to tell her conscience to go to hell than she was at this moment.

"You're so fucking tight . . ."

When he slipped in a second, her breath caught at the unexpected stretch. Her muscles clenched, quivering on the edge of something magnificent—something magical. "Aiden . . ." She meant his name as a protest, but it came out more like a broken plea. "Stop . . ." But even to her own ears it sounded like a desperate petition for relief from this delicious torture. A shudder wracked her body.

"Shhh . . . don't be scared."

Oh, Lord, he thought she was frightened of him. He mistook her hesitancy for fear.

"I won't hurt you, baby."

Maybe not physically—and by the size of his erection, even that was debatable—but could he make that same promise where her heart were concerned?

"Aiden, this isn't right. What about your fi—"

"Fuck 'em . . ." he growled, claiming her mouth in another soul-searing kiss.

Seriously? That was his answer? Here she was wrestling with her conscience, and all he had to say was *Fuck 'em*?

Now Ryann was pissed. She tore her mouth away from his and shoved against his chest. "Aiden, stop!"

He reared back as if she'd slapped him. The frustrated look on his handsome face was a mixture between surprise and anger. "What the hell is your problem, Ryann?"

"*My* problem? Do I seriously have to spell it out for you?"

"Yeah, I guess you do, because you're sending me a lot of mixed signals here."

"You're engaged, Aiden! Obviously that doesn't mean anything to you, but it does to me, all right? Your mom didn't hire me to fuck you. She hired me to find you."

He laughed, not a ha-ha chuckle but a snarky, humorless bark. "That's what this is all about? You're running hot and cold on me because you think I'm engaged?"

"Are you telling me you're not?" she challenged, and God forgive her for praying he would deny it.

Aiden held her stare, seemingly caught in an internal battle before he exhaled a frustrated sigh and roughly dragged his fingers through his hair. "It's not that simple, Ryann."

Not that simple? Oh, it was very simple. "You either are or you aren't, Aiden. It's not quantum physics we're talking about here. So which one is it?"

"Technically, I *am* engaged."

Oh, my God! She couldn't believe he just admitted it! Ryann saw red. How dare he touch her like she meant something to him, kiss her like his very breath depended on consuming hers, and then in the next moment admit to being bound to another. "You asshole!"

She lunged for him, but Aiden caught her wrist before her palm could connect with his face, robbing her even that small satisfaction. She struggled and flailed as he pinned her down to the mattress, saying nothing as she fought to get free. She didn't want to want him, didn't want to be attracted to him—didn't want to care about him.

Unbidden, the threat of tears burned the back of her eyelids, but she refused to give them quarter. This was ridiculous, she barely knew this man. She would *not* cry over Aiden Kruze, dammit! But lack of sleep and sheer emotional exhaustion was working against her. This was not her proudest moment. Oh, hell . . . who was she kidding? This was fucking embarrassing.

Exhausted, she stopped fighting, hating the way her body responded as her quickened breaths rubbed her chest against his. A tingling current of erotic energy made her sensitive skin feel hot and too tight. As she struggled to quell her unwelcome response, Aiden remained silent, seemingly unaffected as he watched her with that impenetrable glower he gave his opponents in the cage.

After a moment, he bit out a nasty curse. "Are you quite done yet?" When she didn't respond, he growled, "Holy hell, you try my patience. Right now I can't decide what I want to do more, throttle you or fuck you."

The vulgarity of his profanity should have shocked her more, and it definitely should not have rekindled the ache blooming between her thighs. What in the hell was wrong with her? She thought she knew herself better than this. Playing it safe had always been her MO. The kind of guys she gravitated toward were predictable and well . . . boring, though she preferred to think of them as safe. There was nothing predictable about this MMA fighter/lawyer who seemed to be the epitome of contradictions.

"Do you honestly think if I had any intention of getting married next week that I would be in bed with you right now?" The offense in his tone told her the question was rhetorical. "What kind of a piece-of-shit prick do you take me for, Ryann?"

Exhaling a frustrated sigh, he dragged his fingers through his hair again and pinned her with a stare that seemed to be searching for something she didn't dare hope for. This was crazy—the man went through women like toilet paper. How many before her had hoped to be that special one? How many had imagined a connection with him that wasn't there when he held them in his arms and kissed them like they were all he ever wanted? Of course he made them feel special. If he didn't, they wouldn't be clambering into his bed and he wouldn't be Aiden "Disco Stick" Kruze.

"Why are you doing this?" he asked her.

Surprised by his question, she blurted the first answer that came to mind that wouldn't give away her internal struggle. "Because you're insanely hot and apparently I'm an idiot."

He chuffed, a grunt that equated to *Figures*, not looking at all surprised or pleased by the backward compliment. "That's not what I meant. What I want to know is why are you here? Why are you working for my mother?"

*Oh, that . . .* She shrugged, going for nonchalance but failing miserably. "I have my reasons."

"Which are?"

"None of your business," she replied, notching her chin defiantly. "Why are you engaged to someone you have no intention of marrying?"

He scowled. "It's none of your business."

So they were at an impasse. Neither of them willing to show the cards they held so closely guarded. For one insane moment, Ryann considered telling him everything—about her father, his debt, and Vincent Moralli. But then what would that solve? By the sounds of it, this guy had enough of his own problems without Ryann unloading hers on him, too. Besides, there wasn't anything he could do to help her, anyway—except return to his family so she could collect the money she needed to pay off her father's debt.

Time seemed to stand still as he hovered over her. His mesmerizing amber stare, torn and conflicted. Then, as if decided on something, he scrubbed his hand over the back if his neck and muttered a growl that sounded a lot like defeat.

"Eighteen months ago, when my father was running for his second term as US senator, he took a hefty campaign contribution from a very rich, influential family in New York. Large funds are often flagged for investigation, and in order to divert suspicion as to why this man would be supporting my father, the two families conspired to arrange a marriage between myself and their daughter. That way, no one could prove ulterior motives. They could claim it was familial support rather than what it truly was—a buyoff to loosen regulations making certain lucrative and illegal activities easier to get away with."

Ryann couldn't believe what she was hearing. "You're not serious. Aiden, this is the twenty-first century. Arranged marriages are unheard of anymore."

"Not so unheard of when you're worth ten million dollars."

*Holy. Shit.* "Ten *million* dollars?"

He nodded. "That's how much money in illegal campaign contributions my father took over the course of a year. My father drew up the marriage contract and set the wedding date without me even knowing it."

"Are you serious? How did you find out?"

"By accident, I assure you. I was going through some of my father's files, looking for information on a court case he asked me to take over, when I found the contract and discovered what he'd done."

"Oh, my God, Aiden, that's terrible. What did you do?"

"I confronted him about it. We had a huge fight. I told him there was no way I was getting married to some woman I'd never even met. I don't give a shit who she is. He told me I didn't have a choice, and unless I wanted to be disinherited, I was going to marry her. I told him he could go fuck himself. That night I packed up my shit and walked away from it all—all their money and all their bullshit. I haven't spoken to either of my parents since."

She could hardly believe what she was hearing. Ryann felt terrible at discovering she was likely on the wrong side of this family dispute. When she thought of what she'd done to Aiden to get him this far, guilt fisted in her gut. She was hardly better than they were, and the worst part of it was, as much as she didn't agree with what his family was doing, and as much as she hated the idea of working for them, she didn't have any choice. If she didn't get Aiden back to Madeline by Friday, she wouldn't have the money to pay off Moralli.

She was running out of time. There wasn't any other way to earn that much cash this late in the game.

"I'm sorry, Aiden. If I'd known . . ." The apology fell from her lips. Remorse became a vise that tightened around her chest—for what she'd done and what she still had to do. "I had no idea."

He shrugged. "You wouldn't."

"Why are you telling me all of this?" Was there more to Aiden's confession than she dared to hope?

Exhaling a deep sigh, he flopped back on his side of the bed. He fixed his gaze on the ceiling and muttered a nasty curse that belayed nothing of his refined upbringing and everything of the steely, tough-as-nails fighter he'd become. "I don't fucking know. This is crazy, Ryann. I just didn't want you to think I would mess around with you if I was actually getting married."

Did he truly care that much about what she thought of him? If she wasn't careful, this MMA fighter was going to pass her guard and lay some serious ground and pound to her resistance.

Aiden rolled onto his side and propped his head beneath his hand and watched her—a model-gorgeous pose that became a visual seduction of her senses. She tried not to notice he was naked except for a pair of low-riding boxer-briefs. But it was hard not to think about it when only a short while ago that powerful, sexy body had been covering hers, delivering pleasure of the likes she'd never experienced before. She knew, without a doubt, if she'd allowed things to go further, he would have taken her to new heights, surpassing her embarrassingly limited experience.

Her curiosity and undeniable attraction to him were powerful aphrodisiacs. How easy it would be to give herself over to this man's wicked charms. Ryann's only fear was that when it came to Aiden, she wasn't sure she could separate her head from her heart.

The last thing she wanted to do was give it over to a man who would undoubtedly break it.

Holding his stare, the question tumbled from her lips. "What do you want from me, Aiden?"

He blew out a ripe curse. "Fuck, Ryann, I don't know. I don't know what this is any more than you do. I've never met a woman who can stir my anger one moment and my passion the next. All I know is that I haven't been able to stop thinking about you since the day you walked into my gym. And when I saw that guy with his hands on you today . . . Something inside me just came undone, which makes zero sense because I know you're not mine, but—"

She cut him off by throwing herself against him and crushing her lips to his. His surprised *oomph* was a throaty grunt as he rolled onto his back, pulling her on top of him. This was crazy. And no doubt she was going to regret it, but Aiden's blunt honesty proved she wasn't the only one feeling this unexplainable connection, and his confession fractured her last bit of self-control. More than anything, she found herself wanting to know what it felt like to be his.

Despite her position advantage, his hand threaded into her hair, knotting into his fist as he held her exactly where he wanted her, tipping her head at just the right angle so he could take over their kiss. His mouth was demanding, his tongue conquering, proving that just like in the cage, Aiden Kruze was as in control and as dangerous on his back as he was on his feet. His other hand slid over her ass and squeezed a handful of flesh as he jerked her against him.

Through the thin cotton of her pajamas, his heat seared her. Every muscular peak and plane molded against her body. She could feel the pounding of his heart against her sensitive breasts, proving she wasn't the only one coming undone. His hold on her was unrelenting, sending a wild thrill skirting through her veins. The fevered pitch in which he kissed her took her breath away. Never had Ryann felt this much emotion, this much passion, in the arms of a man—he verily vibrated with it.

It was so easy to let go with him and know it was going to be the most amazing sex of her life. Already the knot of tension coiling in the pit of her stomach was driving her to the edge. He broke their kiss, giving her lungs much-needed oxygen. Like a diver bursting from the water, she inhaled sharply as Aiden's mouth moved down the side of her throat. He nipped the sensitive flesh just above her shoulder, the mixture of pain and pleasure ripping a startled gasp from her parted lips. His answering chuckle was a deep, masculine growl vibrating against her pulse point. He knew exactly what he was doing to her, how deeply he affected her and how thoroughly he devastated her.

She knew the moment playtime was over—sensed the shift in the purpose of his touch when it went from teasing and exploring to purposeful and deliberate. One minute she was on top of him, and the next, he rolled her, putting Ryann on her back with swift ease, reminding her this wasn't just any man she was messing with here. She was at the mercy of an MMA fighter trained in all forms of submission.

As he moved down her body, he slipped the straps of her nightshirt off her shoulders, baring her breasts to his assessing gaze. She'd never focused much on her breasts before. Growing up a tomboy and being in a profession that was mostly dominated by men, she'd found the large swells of flesh more a burden than a blessing and often took care to minimize their appearance.

But looking at herself now through Aiden's amber eyes, which seemed to take in every inch of bare flesh and missed nothing, she felt decidedly exposed and knew a moment of self-consciousness trapped beneath his bold stare. Instinctively, she raised an arm to cover herself, but he caught her wrist before she could block his view. "No, don't. Just . . . give me a minute. Let me look at you."

Was that . . . awe in his husky voice? No, that was wishful thinking on her part, and thoughts like that were dangerous ones to have. It wasn't until his grip on her wrist tightened that she realized he wasn't as unaffected as she thought. He was shaking, the subtle tremor a testament to his struggle for control.

"Fuck, you're gorgeous . . ."

His strong, callused hands—a fighter's hands—caged her narrow waist and slowly dragged themselves up her ribs and covered her breasts. Taking his time, he tested their weight in his hands, seeming to appreciate the way they spilled past the tips of his fingers. His grip was firm, yet revering. Little darts of pleasure zinged beneath her skin when his thumbs brushed over her beaded nipples. He trapped them against his index fingers and applied pressure until a gasp of pain and pleasure broke her lips. His eyes greedily consumed her, as if he were studying her reactions, searing them into his mind. Was he testing her?—discovering her threshold?

Unbidden, she arched into his hands as a tingling current of white-hot need shot into her core. Her muscles contracted, aching to be filled, to be stretched by him. At her emptiness, a small whimper escaped her throat. His top lip tugged into a satisfied, lopsided grin at her body's shameless response, but she was too far gone to care about her pride.

"You like that, don't you." It wasn't a question—he knew the answer easily enough. "Hell, Ryann, you're so hot, so ready, your body's like a little firecracker just waiting to go off. I wonder how many times I could make you come."

That thought spoken out loud was a jolt to her senses. She wasn't sure if she should be turned on or offended. This wasn't a game—not to her, anyway—and she didn't want him seeing her as just another conquest. Yet, that was what she was, right? Just another notch on his jujitsu black belt? But then, that was all this could ever be, wasn't it?—a fling. Neither of them was in any position to have a relationship.

*Don't over think it, Ryann, just go with it . . .* Her inner conscience seemed to have no qualms about leading her astray. If she knew the score, he couldn't hurt her, right? This was a purely physical, no-strings-attached thing. A part of her really wanted to experience what this fighter was offering. If her prior experiences were anything to judge by, this was something she might not ever experience again. "Well, you'd be the first . . ."

He froze as the confession passed her lips. Oh, shit, did she really just say that out loud? A look of total shock briefly crossed his face before it was quickly replaced by a cocky Disco grin. If she didn't want him seeing her as a game, that had certainly been the wrong thing to say to a man whose life was built around competition and being the best. But before she could tap out and tell him to get off her, that she'd changed her mind, his arrogant smile was replaced by one of genuine interest. Unguarded, his walls down, it was a glimpse of Aiden she'd briefly seen and one she wasn't so ready to dismiss.

"Really?" he asked her, sounding a bit skeptical and disbelieving. "You've never had an—"

She cut him off before she had to hear him say it out loud. It was too embarrassing. For crying out loud, she was twenty-six years old and she'd never had an orgasm with a man. Sure, Aiden had brought her close the first time that they'd gotten hot and heavy, but close was no O. Just like the others, he'd yet to seal the deal. Maybe there was something wrong with her. None of her friends had ever seemed to have any trouble.

"Of course I have," she snapped. "Just not . . . with anyone." Oh, cripes, it didn't sound any better coming from her mouth than his.

He looked at her as if she were a circus oddity. Okay, sharing time was over. Embarrassment was an excellent mood killer. "You know what, I don't want to do this anymore. Let me up." She tried to sit up but Aiden didn't move, nor did he release his grip on her breasts.

"Hey, what are you getting so defensive about?"

"Let me up, Aiden." That determined furrow of his tawny brows told her she was fighting a losing battle here. Still, she wasn't a quitter. Ryann attempted again. Fail.

"Not letting you go, darlin'. Not until you tell me why you're so upset."

He really didn't get it, did he? Of course not. Exhaling a sigh, she dropped her head back onto the pillow, refusing to meet his penetrating stare. What should she tell him? After a brief moment of deliberation, she opted for the truth. It was her best chance at getting him to let her go. "I'm not mad, Aiden. It's . . . embarrassing. I don't even know why I told you in the first place. I certainly didn't mean to."

Now his handsome face contorted into a confused scowl. "I still don't get it. What's there to be embarrassed about? If anyone should be embarrassed, it should be the guys that failed to do their job."

Well, that was definitely a different way of looking at things. "What if . . ." *Oh, hell . . .* "What if the problem wasn't them? What if it's me?"

He laughed—the asshole actually had the nerve to laugh at her!

"I'm glad you think this is funny," she snapped, renewing her efforts to get away.

But he held her firm, amusement playing on his low husky voice when he said, "Sweetheart, I can guarantee the problem is most definitely not you." All trace of humor left him when those heart-stopping amber eyes locked on her. Reaching up, he tenderly brushed his thumb over her cheek. "It would be my honor to prove it to you."

The sincerity in his husky voice, the unguarded honesty reflecting in his eyes . . . This man right here, right now, was the male she'd sensed behind all those walls, behind all that show. And the culmination of it shattered the last vestiges of her control. In that moment, something inside Ryann shifted, connecting to Aiden on a whole other level that scared the ever-loving hell out of her. She so did not want this man getting under her skin, burrowing inside her heart. And she knew if he did, most assuredly, Aiden Kruze was going to break her heart—some things were just inevitable truths. Yet, despite all her head knowledge and the internal warnings sounding off, her body was past the point of caring. Throwing caution to the wind, she found herself saying, "All right, then. Prove it."

# CHAPTER

## 14

Holy hell . . . She actually said yes, and the power behind those words, the vulnerability and trust in her eyes, hit him in the solar plexus like one of Del Toro's sucker punches. If he let himself think on it too long, he'd read more into her response than was there. He'd made that mistake with Ryann before—multiple times, actually—misinterpreting her thoughts, her intentions, and he wouldn't be played the fool again. This was just sex. She hadn't given him any indication she wanted or expected this to be something more. Why that sent a pang of disappointment rocketing through him, he didn't even want to know.

He did casual sex all the time. Shit, he was the grand master of wham-bam-thank-you-ma'am, so why was his head getting so fucked over this fiery ginger? Just because he was about to give Ryann the first male-induced orgasm of her life, he had no doubt he was up to the task. It wasn't performance anxiety tightening that invisible band around his chest—was it? No, it was something much worse . . .

*God help me, I think I might actually care for her.*

Oh, this was bad. This was really, really, bad . . . Perhaps it wasn't too late to rescind the offer. He tried to reerect his walls that, fuck him, lay in a heap of crumbled rock at her feet. How had this woman so swiftly and so thoroughly laid siege to the impenetrable fortress around his heart? He didn't want to like her, and he sure as hell didn't want to care about her. But there was something about Ryann that got to him. Perhaps it was the vulnerability hidden behind her tough exterior that he knew was nothing more than window dressing. Maybe it was the fresh-faced "girl next door" innocence that stirred his protective instincts to life. Could it be the intelligent and clever, albeit manipulative, mind of hers that intrigued him so? In every way, body, mind and soul, she was so unlike any woman he'd ever met, and she was about to give herself to him. Her first release . . . The thought shot an unwelcome arrow of warmth into his defenseless heart.

Yeah . . . this was definitely a mistake. He needed to get away from her and clear his head, despite the tantrum his body was throwing at the prospect of not having her. His cock was already weeping like a baby. Without a doubt he'd never wanted a woman more than the one beneath him right now, looking up at him with those wide, trusting eyes, shadowed with a hint of nervousness and doubt that he'd be able to deliver all he'd promised. *Fuck.*

He must have hesitated too long, let his mask of confidence slip, because her shy smile faltered and with bravado he knew she didn't feel, she purred, "What's the matter, Disco? Not up for the job, after all? Does the cocky 'Disco Stick' Kruze doubt his ability to make good on his promises?"

Her sassy comment hit him below the belt on so many levels it wasn't even funny. She didn't want *him*, he suddenly realized with a blow that knocked the air from his lungs. She wanted "Disco Stick," the MMA fighter and notorious playboy. And she'd taken a cheap shot at his ego by baiting him with doubts about his prowess. As much as this was a bad idea and as harsh a beating as his heart was going to take for it later, he could not, would not, back down from a challenge. If she wanted Disco so fucking bad, then she could have him.

If Ryann could have turned back time and recanted those words, she would have done it in a heartbeat. She'd only wanted to protect her heart by trying to convince herself this was just sex and nothing more. Her attempt to disguise her fear, which was mounting with each passing second as he hovered over her, staring at her with those entrancing eyes that she would swear could see into her soul, just blew up in her face.

Something flashed across his handsome face a moment before that famous Disco mask slipped into place. If she didn't know better, she'd say it was pain, but the emotion was gone so fast, surely she'd imagined it. Ryann knew a profound feeling of regret, and then loss as their connection flickered out like a candle in the wind. She almost stopped him to apologize and attempt to rekindle that spark—almost—but in that next moment Aiden was on her and Ryann's mind went blank to anything other than the feeling of this powerful male whose sole purpose suddenly became her pleasure.

A low growl rumbled in his chest as his mouth claimed hers—hard and fierce. His tongue, intrusive and dominating, as aggressive as the fighter himself. It stole her breath to be kissed so thoroughly, the only oxygen that gifted her lungs was given by him. The air was marked with his scent, rich and masculine . . . intoxicating.

Before she knew it, she was stripped bare. There was no pause this time for admiration, no sense that Aiden truly *saw* her. Not like before. And despite how amazing it felt to be in is arms, how pleasurable his touch was—and it did feel amazing—something was missing. It was Aiden, she realized with a sharp pang of regret. He was with her, but he wasn't *with* her. And she didn't know how to reach him, how to get him back. Her thoughts were a quagmire of *Let's talk about this. Whoa, wait, slow down!* And *Oh, yes! Right there! Please, don't stop!*

His mouth sucked greedily at her breast, teeth nipping and tongue teasing away the pain. It had been over a year since she'd been intimate with anyone, and her poor, neglected breasts were overly sensitive. They felt swollen and heavy in Aiden's grip, and a direct current of energy seemed to radiate from them right into her core. She was like a live wire, and Aiden was her power source. Every place his hands touched sparks of white-hot desire shot beneath her skin, and when his hand slipped between her legs, his deft fingers parting the slick folds of her flesh, a needy whimper escaped her throat. Her hips shamelessly lifted, encouraging his penetrating touch. The tension knotting low in her stomach was nearly too much to bear.

He played her like a pro, knowing her body better than she did. Stroking, toying, torturing . . . he touched her without seeming hesitation or thought, instinctively knowing how to bring her maximum pleasure, while defiantly denying her ardent, unspoken request to enter her and finally bring relief to this sweet torment. Her core ached so badly, her channel clenched impatiently, begging to be filled. Why wouldn't he take her? It was almost as if he knew he was torturing her—punishing her.

Oh, mercy, was he punishing her? Was he mad at her?—sweet, merciful heaven, if this was Aiden mad, then she had to make a note-to-self to piss him off more often.

She was close! So close! If he'd just . . .

His thumb found the small bundle of nerves at the top of her sex. *Yes!* Her breaths quickened, muscles tensed, hips arching . . . *Almost there!* She wanted him inside her, needed him inside her now.

Unable to put thought to voice and impatient to finally experience release, she reached between them to grab his erection and guide him home. What the hell? Aiden was still wearing his underwear. She'd assumed he'd divested himself of that cumbersome cotton back when he'd stripped her of hers. Was he not planning to have sex with her?—and if no, why the hell not? She knew he had a condom, had seen it when the officer had sent it flying out of his wallet earlier tonight, so that couldn't be what was holding him back.

Not that he would know, but she was on the pill, and being an MMA fighter, she knew they underwent rigorous health screenings all the time, so commando was a-okay with her. Anything to ease this sensual agony.

Seeking to rectify Aiden's oversight and grab the bull by the horn, so to speak, Ryann shed his boxer briefs and hooked the waistband with her toe, dragging them down his impossibly long legs. When she gripped the steel length of his shaft and stroked him a couple of times before guiding him forward, he snarled a surprisingly foul curse and none too gently removed her hand from his very large, very impressive manhood.

"You come on my terms, sweetheart, not yours." There was nothing soft or caring in his term of endearment, and his eyes had long lost their warm amber glow, turning him 100 percent Disco Prick. What was she doing? This wasn't what she wanted. Well, that wasn't exactly true, she wanted him—badly—but she wanted Aiden, not this . . . cocky, arrogant ass who thought he was God's gift to women, even if it probably was true.

Before she could respond, he dipped his head and nipped the fleshy swell of her breast. "Stop." Her command was breathy and lacked authority, but no was still no, right?

His mouth moved lower . . . His hands grabbed her inner thighs, spreading her farther to accommodate the wide breadth of his shoulder as he kissed, licked, and nipped his way down her stomach. Oh, no, he wasn't going to . . . Oh, he was! When Aiden dipped his head and parted her folds with his tongue, a hoarse cry tore from her throat and her hips bucked off the bed. Aiden's hands circled her waist, anchoring her in place as he set in to a full feast of her flesh.

The coil of hot, burning need searing her core was back with a vengeance, wound tighter than before and growing stronger by the second. Not like this! She didn't want to come like this, not with this unspoken rift of tension between them.

"Aiden, wait . . ." she panted, struggling to claw through the haze of drunken lust addling her brain, making it nearly impossible to put two words together.

"Oh, now it's 'Aiden,' is it?" he growled against her sex. "First you want Disco, then it's Aiden. You can't have them both, baby girl, so which is it? What do you want?" The heat of his breath, the rumble of his voice against her sex, made her breath catch in her throat and a whimper pass her lips. The delay in answering, her mewled response that wasn't really a response at all, was all it took for him to draw his own conclusion, which was wrong. His top lip curled in that lopsided grin she was quickly learning was the equivalent to a snarl. "That's what I thought."

*No! Wait!*

Lowering his head those scant few inches, Aiden's hands slid beneath her ass, gripping her so hard she'd surely be bruised from his touch. Ryann briefly registered the pain before his tongue plunged inside her, blurring the lines of pain and heightening her pleasure until all was lost—all thought, all breath . . . all control.

The hard metal ball of his tongue piercing dragged against the top of her opening, then centered on the bead of her sex as he plunged two fingers deep inside her. That was all it took. She couldn't take anymore, and with a broken cry, she shattered. Her core milked his touch, the euphoria crashing over her in rhythmic waves of pure bliss.

Her hands fisted into his hair, holding him against her as she rode out this incredible high. As the last few tremors racked her body, she was mindless with awe. Nothing had ever felt this good. No one had ever kissed her like that, which starkly reminded her how incredibly inexperienced she was—and sadly, inadequate, compared to this magnificent man between her legs.

As she lay there in the afterglow of *Wow, I can't believe that really happened*... She reluctantly uncurled her fingers knotted in his hair and mumbled the first thing that came to her lust-drunk mind. "That was . . . that was . . . amazing."

He shifted out from between her legs, not bothering to meet her starstruck gaze—or even look at her, for that matter—and mumbled, "You're welcome."

He rolled off the bed, his feet hitting the floor before her mind could process the edge in his voice. She was shocked stupid. Ryann's breath caught in her throat, and words failed her as she watched him stride toward the bathroom. She flinched when the door slammed behind him. As the lock clicked into place, the full weight of what just happened slammed into her with the force of a wrecking ball. *He doesn't think I wanted him . . . He thinks I wanted Disco . . .*

And in turn, he'd rejected her, too, holding himself back. She'd practically thrown herself at him and he wouldn't even have sex with her. How humiliating . . . How was it possible for the man who'd taken her so high, made her feel so incredibly good, could in the matter of minutes and with two spoken words drag her so terribly low and make her feel so disgustingly cheap? Her vision swam as she raised her hand to muffle the sob that broke from her throat.

*Oh, God, what have I just done?*

# CHAPTER 15

*What the fuck did I just do?*

Aiden cranked on the faucet, taking his second shower of the night—this time a cold one. With the muffling sound of the water's blast, he let his fist fly against the tile wall. *Bam!*

The small white squares shattered beneath his fist, sending an avalanche of porcelain and grout raining down around his feet. His bloody knuckles and property damage did little to unknot the tension fisting in his gut. His cock was granite hard and pissed off at being left that way. But as jacked in the head as he was when it came to Ryann, there was no way in hell he would dare make a bad situation worse by having sex with her.

His pride already stung at Disco being preferred over him—and damn if that wasn't a messed-up feeling, being jealous of yourself. Women preferring Disco Stick Kruze wasn't anything new; it just had never mattered to him before now, nor had he ever let any woman before Ryann get close enough to know there was even a difference.

It was better this way, he told himself, hoping if he repeated the lie enough times, he'd eventually believe it. He and Ryann would never work. For starters, she was working for the enemy. For all he knew, she was seeing someone back in Manhattan and this was all just another sick game of hers . . . a ploy to fuck him into submission.

Where the dick goes, the man follows, right? Wrong. He was done with her games, done with letting a woman twist him into knots. He was definitely done with giving her the power to make him feel used. Aiden had been with a lot of women in his day—more than his share of women, actually—and not once had he ever left his bed feeling more empty than he did at this very moment.

Never again, he vowed, fisting his cock in his bloody hand, relishing the burn as the frigid water beat upon his raw, torn knuckles. He braced his forearm on the tile, ignoring the pinch in his shoulder. It wasn't the first time he'd taken damage in the octagon and it certainly wouldn't be the last. Resting his head against the roped muscle, he began working his hard length, desperate to give himself some much-needed relief. It didn't take long for his release to come. Just closing his eyes and remembering the sight of Ryann spread out before him, that strip of fiery feminine hair leading the way to the true inferno below . . .

The taste of her still haunted him. Aiden dragged his tongue over his bottom lip. His mouth watered; his hunger was renewed. He muttered a pained groan as his balls tightened up beneath him, the pressure in the base of his cock building . . . He came with a harsh bark, emptying his seed into the drain at his feet as tremor after tremor racked his body. But Ryann's essence would not leave him, nor would his cockstand or his insatiable desire for that woman. After another round of tug and jerk, he came again, just as hard as the first time.

He needed a gym, that was what he needed—a heavy bag, and a good sparring partner to exhaust himself. With neither available, he cut the water and toweled off before yanking on his jeans. The denim abraded his poorly abused flesh. With a frustrated growl, he grabbed his cock and rearranged his lingering semi, taking care with the zipper as he fastened his pants. His underwear was still tangled somewhere in Ryann's bedsheets, and he was not about to go digging for them now. So, commando it was. With any luck, she'd be lights-out by now. The idea of facing that woman again, especially right now, was not on his list of top ten things to do.

After scrubbing a towel over his wet hair and drying his face, he used the complimentary toothbrush that shed more bristles than a porcupine. The chalky, half-assed minty paste made his mouth feel about as clean as a two-bit whore. But what the hell, if he had any hope of lowering his flag and getting some rest, he was going to have to get the taste of Ryann out of his mouth.

Aiden had been in there a really long time. If that shower ran any longer, he was going to run out of hot water. Not that Ryann was complaining about his absence. She needed some more time to regroup, to come to grips with what just happened. She told herself her tears were not for him. Aiden just happened to be the breaking point for the torrent of shit she was dealing with right now. Ryann wasn't a crier, dammit, though no one would believe it to look at her now—worst effing timing ever for her to go all emotional.

She'd heard of women experiencing such profound sexual pleasure that they broke down and lost it. *Please*, she thought, *let this not be the case with me.* First of all, it was horribly unattractive to cry after sex, and second of all, she was an ugly crier. Now that her eyes had finally dried, leaving them red and puffy and her nose snotty, she'd moved into the hyperventilating phase of her emotional meltdown.

Lord, this was a nightmare! How was she ever going to face Aiden after this? Guilt came anew, soiling her memory of the best sex, or nonsex, of her life. No one had ever come close to making her feel the way Aiden did, and it was all him, whether he'd ever believe that or not was debatable. She didn't care about his fame or that infamous Disco persona he wore like a coat of arms. She cared about Aiden the man—the lawyer turned fighter who just wanted to be left alone so he could live his dream—until she came along and ruined it all.

In all honesty, she deserved his anger. In the last week, she'd lied to him, manipulated him, drugged him, and what had he given her in return?—earth-shattering pleasure. Oh, yeah, and he'd saved her life.

She *was* a horrible person. How he must hate her, especially now after she'd led him to believe she was using him for an orgasm. She inhaled a stuttering breath and tugged the blankets up to her chin. Something snagged on her foot. She kicked at the tangled bedding and when it didn't come loose, she reached down to pull it free just as the shower shut off. Her hand closed around the soft cotton bundle and realization made her stomach clench with dread. Oh, no . . . she had Aiden's underwear!

God help her if he came out of that bathroom naked.

A few minutes later, the door opened, shooting a beam of ambient light across the foot of the bed. Not wanting to get caught holding his drawers, she tossed them into the chair across the room and dropped back down on her pillow. Turning away from him, she rolled onto her shoulder and pulled the covers high, burrowing beneath them, and pretended to be asleep.

The light clicked off, ensconcing the room into darkness once again. She held her breath, waiting for him to enter. Silence. Where was he? She didn't want to look and risk wrecking her ruse. *Focus, Ryann! In and out, in and out . . .* Breaths! She corrected herself when wicked images filled her mind. Breathe—in and out, slow and even, but she'd yet to recover from her breakdown, and a shuddering breath wracked her body.

Maybe he hadn't heard her? It was a hopeful thought, until the covers behind her lifted and the mattress caved beneath Aiden's weight. The unforgiving mattress was already starting to make her shoulder ache. She wasn't sure how much longer she could lie like this. Was Aiden naked beneath these covers? Of course he would be. What else would he wear?

She winced as another hitching breath gave her away.

"Are you . . . crying?"

Aiden's husky voice was far too close. His hand touched her shoulder and it took all her willpower not to tense, flinch, or move as those strong, callused fingers closed over her arm, his palm resting solidly on her shoulder. Slow and easy breaths, just like she was sleeping. If she didn't respond, then eventually he'd go away, right? The heat of his presumably naked body warmed her back. She could smell the mint of toothpaste on his breath as it teased the errant tendrils of hair at her temple.

She wasn't ready to face him, not yet—not after . . . Ryann shut down the thought. She couldn't allow herself to go there. Already her pulse quickened with anticipation, the slow burn in her core sparking back to life at his simple touch. Shame and embarrassment burned anew when she thought of how greedily she'd taken the pleasure he offered and given him nothing in return. Just one more thing to add to the list of many ways she'd wronged this man.

No, she couldn't face him now, and there was a strong possibility she might not ever be able to look him in the eyes again. Lord, Manhattan couldn't be close enough for her. And to make matters worse, they were stuck in God knew where, for God knew how long, waiting for the police to give them the okay to leave.

Aiden waited another minute for her to respond. When she said nothing, he exhaled a sigh that could have spoken a thousand words. If she were a better woman, she would have given up her ruse and faced whatever this was between them. Did he regret what happened as much as she did? It wasn't their intimacy, experiencing her first orgasm, that she regretted. Hell, who in their right mind could feel remorse over that? No, it was their disconnect she regretted, the misunderstanding she'd failed to rectify.

When he moved his hand, she thought it was to turn away. But instead, he slowly slid his hand down her arm—up and down, a slow gentle caress. More tenderly than she'd been expecting and certainly more than she deserved. Up and down. She couldn't hold back the shudder that ripped through her at his gentle touch, threatening to give her away. Slow, easy breaths, she reminded herself again. But that was easier said than done, especially when the back of his knuckles gently brushed against her cheek—a whispered touch, light and fleeting as a butterfly kiss.

When he tensed behind her, she knew he'd discovered the dampness on her skin. His muttered oath confirmed it, growled so quietly, she nearly missed the self-damning curse.

Sighing as if the weight of the world rested upon his shoulders, he lifted a lock of hair that had fallen into her face. Slowly, he let it sift through his fingers as he posed the question that must have been weighing so heavily on his mind. "What am I going to do with you, Ryann?" With that parting thought, he pulled his hand away and returned to his side of the bed.

*What indeed . . .* Tears filled her eyes anew and she squeezed them tight, forbidding even one more drop to fall for this man.

# CHAPTER

16

Bzzz . . . *bzzz* . . . *bzzz* . . . What in the hell was that buzzing? It took Aiden a moment to clear his head and orient himself to date, time, place, and situation: Tuesday, who the hell knew, bumfuckno-where, and in bed—with Ryann. All the while, that incessant vibrating would not quit. Well, it stopped, for a whole fifteen sec-onds, before Ryann's phone started right back up again. Who could possibly be that desperate to contact her? Who would be that inces-santly annoying? That bold? That rude? Then the answer came to him with teeth-grinding clarity—Madeline.

He was just about to grab her cell off the nightstand, which just happened to be on his side of the bed, and give his mother the ass chewing she deserved, when Ryann began to stir beside him. It'd been a miracle he'd fallen asleep at all. How long had he lain there, knowing full well she was awake, too, aching to reach across those twelve small inches separating them—it might as well have been twelve feet—and pull her into his arms. It gutted him to know she'd been crying, to feel that telltale moisture on her impossibly soft cheek and know most assuredly he had been the cause to put it there. What he didn't understand was why. She'd gotten what she wanted from him. He'd given her the release he'd promised, what more did she want?

He pondered the question until the early crack of dawn broke the eastern horizon. Then the answer eventually settled solidly in his gut, and it didn't sit well. Ryann was nothing like the other women he'd bedded—and that had been his first fool's mistake, treating her like one. Those women had no expectations of him beyond their own pleasure, which had left him wondering: Was it possible Ryann had wanted something else from him?—something more? In his own anger at feeling cheap and used, had he returned the favor by walking away from her while she'd basked in the sated afterglow of her first orgasm, her cheeks still flushed with the warmth of a woman well and thoroughly fucked? Likely—and as the hours endlessly crawled by this morning, the bigger an asshole he felt for it.

She'd fallen asleep before him—for real this time—keeping her slender back to him. So it surprised Aiden to wake now and find Ryann curled up against his side. Curse that phone and its incessant buzzing to hell. Drawing one of those deep sleepy breaths that made Aiden's own air freeze in his lungs, she stretched beside him, branding him with those soft, incredibly lush curves. He could tell by her easy, languid movements she had yet to fully wake and realize where she—

Yep, there it was. She was awake now. Ryann jerked back and regret slammed into him at the loss of contact like a swift hard kick in the balls. He'd yet to open his eyes, yet to move or acknowledge his awareness of the woman lying beside him. He knew if he saw her in sleep-roughened form, it'd be his final undoing. The buzzing started up again. She startled, bouncing the bed. The mattress dipped beside him as she began to crawl over him, reaching for the phone. Pure fucking torture . . . Bracing her leg on the other side of his hip, her breasts dragged across his chest as her hand stretched for the nightstand. Her silky hair brushed against his shoulder, the fine strands snagging on the stubble of his jaw. His teeth clenched with the effort to bite back his tortured groan. Her scent engulfed him, sending a jolt of white-hot lust burning through his veins.

His hands fisted into the sheets, muscles straining with the force it took to keep from pulling her on top of him and crushing his mouth to hers as he rolled her beneath him and buried himself balls deep inside her tight little glove. No contest, he'd never wanted a woman more than his hot little abductor. Imagery of all the wicked ways he wanted to make her his played through his mind. His body shot so hard, his cock jerked violently, breath stalling in his lungs, unwilling to give up her scent surrounding him.

All too soon she retrieved her vibrating cell and crawled to the side of the bed, taking her scent and tantalizing heat along with her. He watched her scoot off the bed and head to the farthest corner of the room before taking the call.

"Hello?" She whispered the greeting.

Silence.

"Really? Do we have to do this right now? I'm well aware of what day it is."

Yep, that was Madeline Kruze all right—overbearing and micromanaging. *Welcome to my world, baby girl. Working for that woman must be just about as pleasant as being her son.*

"Listen, I told you before these calls have to stop. I'm doing my job and you're making it extremely difficult."

Just when he thought Ryann couldn't offend him anymore, she opened her mouth and it happened all over again. A job? Did she just call him a fucking job? That was what he was to her? How horribly ironic was it that the one woman he wanted more than any other, saw him as a goddamn paycheck? Well, this was a new one. Usually he was Aiden Kruze Attorney at Law, son of Senator Bennett Kruze; or Aiden "Disco Stick" Kruze, MMA fighter and notorious playboy, the guy guaranteed to rock out with his cock out.

He'd been called a lot of things in his life, but a "job" was not one of them, and coming from the woman he had no business giving a shit about, it pained him a hell of a lot more than he cared to admit. Just a job, huh? It didn't feel like just a job when she was coming against his tongue last night. And it sure as hell didn't feel like a job when her little hand was fisting his cock, all but begging him to fuck her.

His jaw clenched, making a little muscle twitch in his cheek as he watched Ryann anxiously pace between the bathroom and the front door, her voice lowered to a hushed whisper. Her free hand cupped the side of her face in a failed attempt to funnel her conversation into the phone. As she restlessly trekked back and forth, Aiden tried not to notice the uninhibited freedom in which her breasts moved beneath her thin cotton nightshirt, or the way the hemline was rucked up her side, exposing a swath of low back and shapely narrow waist every time she passed by. Her bottoms sat low on her hips, so low the pant legs covered her feet and dragged on the worn, royal blue carpet as she walked. The occasional glimpse of her pink-painted toenails gave her a decidedly adorable appeal—but the innocence ended there.

Her sexy-as-hell, sleep-disheveled state was no doubt lost on her as she focused on the conversation with his mother. She sounded upset. No doubt she was getting an ass chewing for taking so long in returning with him. Well, wouldn't Madeline be surprised when he didn't show. Picturing the shocked look on the woman's face brought a sadistic smile of satisfaction to his surly mug.

The tense set of Ryann's small shoulders confirmed what her face could not. Her head was tipped just enough to hide her features behind a blanket of unruly bed head. The vibrant copper streaks caught the rays of sun as she passed through the beams arrowing across the room through the small split in the heavy dark blue curtains.

Conflicting emotions gripped him in various places of his anatomy. Pity tightened the invisible band around his chest. He knew what it was like to deal with Madeline Kruze, and that shit was no picnic. Despite how thoroughly Ryann had fucked him over, he honestly wouldn't wish that woman on his worst enemy—which sparked his possessive streak to life. Why in the hell he found himself wanting to protect his little felon was beyond him. Guilt and anger swarmed in his head like a nest of angry bees. He didn't want to want her. He sure as hell didn't trust her—she was working for his mother, for crissake. Yet, just the sight of her shot his cock so hard with lust, the urge to claim her was nearly overwhelming. And after her confession last night, her uninhibited response to his touch, he couldn't stop thinking about what it would have been like if he had taken her. Perhaps if he'd fucked her out of his system, he wouldn't be in knots over her right now.

Shoulda, woulda, coulda . . . But like everything else about this woman, once again she'd surprised him. Her inexperience put her in a whole other league than the women he was used to bedding. He knew if he took her, he'd likely overwhelm her with his intensity, but he also sensed if he could get her to trust him, to let go, she'd detonate in his arms—and the selfish, carnal bastard inside him wanted to be the one to show her what her body could do.

"Hey, threatening me isn't going to get me there any faster."

Wait a minute . . . Threatening her? And damn if that possessive streak didn't rip through his veins, taking center stage and pushing all that other bullshit into the background. Why would Madeline be threatening her? His mother didn't threaten people, it wasn't her style. Not that she didn't manipulate them, but when that didn't work, she'd throw enough money at them until eventually she'd get her way. Everyone had their price, even him he supposed. Unfortunately, it'd taken Aiden nearly thirty years to realize he couldn't put a price tag on freedom.

Wow, this was a new low, even for Madeline—she must be caving to the pressure. Tick-tock . . . tick-tock . . . Aiden sat up. The squeak of the bedsprings drew Ryann's attention. She froze, and then whipped around to face him. The *oh, shit* on her face was unmistakable. Shooting him an anxious glance, a melee of emotions swirled in those gorgeous eyes. He held out his hand expectantly for the phone. This was going to stop—now. He would not tolerate his mother threatening this woman. Ryann's eyes shot impossibly rounder, like she couldn't believe he actually expected her to give him the cell.

"Give me the phone, Ryann." Just in case there was any question.

Was that fear flashing in her eyes? She slapped her hand over the receiver and violently shook her head, silently mouthing *No.*

Oh, hell no, she did not just shake her head at him. Aiden tossed back the covers and was out of that bed before Ryann could blink. He held out his hand as he marched forward. She countered, stepping back until she connected with the wall. "Now. Give me the phone," he growled.

Again, with that stunned, deer-in-the-headlights look, head swinging back and forth, red locks going airborne—enough of the games. He reached forward and snatched the phone from Ryann's hand and growled into the receiver. "You know what, I expected this shit from Bennett, but just when I think you couldn't sink any lower, you go and surprise me. Get off Ryann's case or you're going to have me to deal with."

The answering growl was decidedly male, which nailed Aiden like a roundhouse kick in the chest.

"Who the fuck is this?" the deep voice barked.

Aiden pinned Ryann with a questioning glower. Jealousy and possessiveness surged anew, both emotions he had no business feeling—especially now. Who in the hell was she talking to?—a boyfriend?—a jealous lover who wasn't so keen on the idea of her and her "job" road-tripping it halfway across the US together, making pit stops in skeezy motels and fucking around behind his back?

Couldn't very well blame the dude. Aiden would be livid, too—poor dumb shmuck. Hell, he'd be doing more than threatening her if he was the sorry sucker stuck back in Manhattan while his hot little PI girlfriend ran her own special Mission: Impossible gig on some other guy. For one, it was dangerous what she was doing. Hell, she'd nearly gotten herself killed just last night.

No wonder she hadn't wanted to give him the phone. Now that look of shock and horror on her lovely face made a whole lot more sense. He knew she was manipulative and underhanded, he just never thought she'd sink so low as to mess around behind another guy's back to get what she wanted from him. That whole sweet and innocent *I've never had an orgasm before* routine had really hooked him. Another fucking lie? he wondered.

He was such an idiot. His heart thundered inside his chest, his face flushed hotly, whether from anger or embarrassment at being screwed over by this woman, yet again, he couldn't know. What could he say?—*Hey, dude, sorry I rocked your girlfriend's world last night. She tastes amazing.*

Hitting Ryann with a glower he reserved for the cage, she flinched, sinking farther back against the wall as if desperate to put some distance between them. Without breaking her wide-eyed stare, he told the guy, "I am so sorry you have to deal with her, man. Good fucking luck . . ."

As he disconnected the call, Ryann gasped. Total shock filled her face, and then quickly morphed into rage as she stared at him like she couldn't believe what he'd just done. The air left his lungs at the look of betrayal in her eyes. His chest constricted, refusing to breathe. Why in the hell was she looking at him like that? If anyone had the right to be pissed off here, it was him.

They stood there a moment in a wordless faceoff as he watched her grapple for control. She must have found her edge because a few seconds later, anger flooded her fine features, twisting her beautiful face into a mask of rage.

"You fucking asshole!" She stepped forward and slammed the heels of her hands against his bare chest. For a slip of a woman, she was surprisingly strong. Unprepared for the force of her strike, he took a step back to catch his balance. The give wasn't very much, but it was enough for Ryann to slide past him. But she wasn't the only one livid, and with the speed of a striking viper, he caught her arm, jerking her back around to face him. This two-timing manipulative chit wasn't getting off that easily.

"What's the matter, Ry? Pissed that your boyfriend found out you were fucking around on him?"

He didn't think it was possible for her to look more furious, but as he blasted her with his cutting question, every male instinct clamoring inside him warned Aiden to protect his groin. *Wham!* Her knee flew up just as he shifted his weight and lifted his leg. Her patella connected solidly with his thigh so hard that had she hit his balls, they would have been lodged in his throat. As it was, his thigh would be wearing the evidence of her wrath for some time to come.

"That's not my boyfriend, you presumptive, arrogant piece of shit!" She lost the battle with her tears and angrily swiped them away. Fuck, every one of those giant drops might as well have been a dagger in his heart. She flailed to get free of his grip—a sob breaking from her throat as she wrenched on her arm, trying to get away. If she kept it up, she was going to hurt herself.

It took 0.6 second for Ryann's revelation to slam into him with the force of a hook kick to the head, and about 0.3 second for his head to catch up with his heart, and 0.1 second to realize he was totally screwed. Still, the fighter in him didn't give up, and the dipshit in him didn't know when to quit while he was ahead, though he suspected *ahead* had passed about the time he told whoever had been on that phone—threatening her—that he felt sorry for him and good luck.

"Ryann, stop." He tried to reason with the enraged woman, regret burning his throat to ash and making his voice raw. Holding on to her was like trying to catch a tiger by the tail. Her claws were out, and she was hell bound and determined to get away from him. But something in his gut told Aiden if he tapped now and let her go, this woman would be lost to him forever. So he held on and weathered the storm of her anger. Dodging blows, and taking others, because dammit, he deserved it after what he'd just done, what he'd accused her of.

His gut told him she was in trouble, which ratcheted his protective instincts off the charts. When her small hand curled up and she hammer-fisted him in the chest, he caught her wrist and tugged her closer, pulling her into his guard and wrapping his arms around her slender frame, holding her tight against his chest.

"I'm sorry . . . Baby, I'm sorry . . ." He'd repeat the words over and over, as long as it took for her to calm down and hear them. But he would not let her go—no matter how hard she fought or how many times she cursed him. And Aiden was surprised to discover that Ryann had a pretty colorful vocabulary.

He had no idea how long he stood there waiting for her to drop her guard enough to shoot in, but it felt like forever. By the time she exhausted herself, his heart was shredded. All he wanted to do was hold this slip of a woman with the temper of a tiger and the courage of a fighter. It didn't take a genius to deduct that things were not as they seemed. And the more he discovered about Ryann, the more she intrigued him. And the hell of it was, he wanted to know her—really know her—to protect her. He genuinely cared about this woman, which was why he'd nearly lost his shit when he'd thought she was seeing someone else.

"Shhh . . ." he whispered.

Her struggles were only half-hearted now, whether from exhaustion or defeat he couldn't know. It didn't matter. All that mattered was that she was in his arms. "I'm sorry . . . Baby, I'm so sorry," he crooned against the top of her head, which barely reached his shoulder—the perfect height to tuck her beneath his chin. She fit against him so perfectly, like she was made just for him.

"I thought . . ." he started to explain, but there were no words to excuse his behavior or his assumptions.

"I know . . . what you . . . thought," she hiccupped against his chest. Her tears scalded him, leaving behind a hot, wet trail of sorrow. Evidence of the pain he caused slipped between his pecs, following the road map of muscles down his chest and across his abdomen. "I don't need to hear you say it. Let me . . . go."

*Never.* His grip on her instinctively tightened. Ryann tensed in his arms, refusing to yield to him, to take the comfort she'd so greedily consumed last night—that was before he'd utterly offended and insulted her. "Come on, Ryann, just let me explain . . ." He wasn't sure what the hell he intended to say if she gave him the chance. He only knew he was desperate to hold on to this woman right now and he didn't want to let her go.

"There's nothing to say, Aiden," she said woodenly.

Fuck, she sounded so distant, so broken. He'd done this to her, reducing her to an unrecognizable woman who was nothing like the strong, independent female he knew, the powerhouse in a small package that never took no for an answer and was a force to be reckoned with. This wasn't the same woman who'd drugged him, abducted him, stumbled onto a robbery, and nearly gotten herself killed. Yet through it all, she'd held it together—not missing a beat. Rock solid—that was his Ryann. Wait . . . his? Since when did he lay any claim to this woman? *Probably about the time you stripped her bare and had your face buried between her legs*, his unhelpful self quickly answered.

"You just told . . . the man who's made my life a living hell . . . for the last month . . . 'good luck.' Then you all but called me a . . . a whore by accusing me of having a boyfriend after we . . . After you . . ."

She tried to wrest free from his grasp. God help him, he was an asshole. Muttering a self-damning curse, he gently framed Ryann's tear-stained face and tipped her head up, forcing her to meet his determined stare. "First of all, I want to know who's doing this to you and why. Because I promise you, that shit's gonna stop. And secondly, I never called you a whore and I don't think it. What happened between us last night was—"

"—a mistake," she cut in, finishing his sentence, which was *not* what he was going to say at all. She took a step back, pulling away, and it took all his strength to let her go. "It can't happen again. It won't happen again. This"—she waved her finger between them—"is a mistake. It would never work."

Why was it a mistake? Just because he'd thought the same thing last night didn't stop him from wanting to know where the hell she thought he was lacking.

"I think it would be best if we just pretended that last night didn't happen."

*The hell it would!* What was she thinking?—that she could just forget her first orgasm? Was she going to pretend *that* didn't happen?

Because he had news for her: That fucking happened, and he wanted it to happen again. In fact, he wanted it to happen again right now. So he'd be damned if he was going to let her forget it. If she thought forgetting him was going to be so easy, she had another thing coming.

He'd been trying to forget this woman since the day she walked into his gym a little over a week ago, and look how well that turned out. Ryann had him twisted in so many knots, his balls permanently ached. But pushing her right now wasn't going to do either of them any favors. Maybe what she needed was a little space to regain a sense of control in the situation that admittedly had blown far from it.

Holding up his hands in surrender, he took a measured step back and nodded his acquiescence. "If that's what you want, Ryann." Was he giving up? Not a chance. But she didn't need to know that, and now was not the time to take the offensive with her. This was the stage in the game where a fighter danced around his opponent, finding his range and testing his skills. To the crowd, this was never an exciting part of the match. On the outside, it didn't look like anything was happening, but in reality, a fight could be won or lost based on what a fighter learned about his rival during those critical moments.

Some of the tension seemed to ease from her shoulders as she perceived this small victory as a win, but he wasn't tapping out. "All right, then. As long as we're clear."

*Crystal.*

"Do you umm . . . want the shower first?" She walked backward toward the bed, keeping her eyes on him the entire time. Smart girl. She stopped by the chair where her suitcase was lying open on the table next to the lounger.

"Nope, I'm good. Had a few of them last night." *Step in. Jab. Move out.*

"So you don't mind if I hop in?"

*Too short.* Ignoring his subtle dig, she turned toward her luggage and began rummaging through her clothes. *Circle. Approach.* "Be my guest. I left my shirt in there. I'll just go grab it." *Arms up. Circle. Step in.* "Hey, Ryann?" he called, stopping in the bathroom doorway.

"Yeah?" She glanced over her shoulder when he didn't answer right away.

*Jab.* "Will you toss me my underwear?" *Contact.*

# CHAPTER

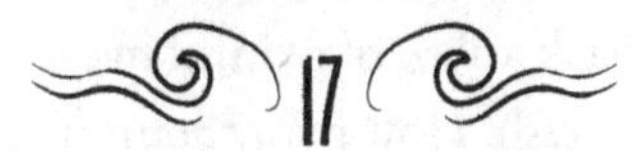

17

You all right?"

Ryann shot him a quick glance from the chair next to her and returned to the restless bouncing of her foot. "Yep." How in the hell could he sit there and look so calm? "Why wouldn't I be?"

Aiden's brow arched in question, but he didn't push her. He turned those uncanny amber eyes forward and appeared to be reading the antidrug posters plastered on the wall across from them. He was stretched out in that lazy sprawl, arms up, fingers laced behind his head, looking as if he hadn't a care in the world and all the time in the day. What did he care if they sat in a police station all afternoon? It wasn't his life on the line, and this morning's phone call had been a blatant reminder hers was precisely that.

She cast him another glance, unable to help noticing how that lax pose put his impressive arms on display. She was bound and determined not to appreciate the ropes of muscle stretching up his forearms, or the defined cut of his biceps and his chiseled triceps. Seriously, who had arms like that?

He wore a simple camo-colored V-neck T-shirt they'd picked up at the local clothing store. Apparently, they didn't grow them that big here in Portage, because XL was all they had and it was still tight on him. And those relaxed-fit jeans didn't look very relaxed, either. They hugged him in all the right places and strained in others, not that he seemed to notice or care. Whether wearing a two-thousand-dollar suit or skintight fight shorts, the man was so comfortable in his own skin, it didn't matter what was covering his body. And considering how much she wanted to jump out of her skin right now, that grated.

She hadn't expected coming here to hit her so hard, but the déjà vu of sitting in the police station waiting for the officer to take her statement brought back a slew of painful memories rising to the surface that were all too fresh. How many hours had she spent waiting in one of these hard plastic chairs, trying to get someone to listen to her?

Sitting in this police station was a good reality check, reminding her why she was here in the first place, and what she had to do. Aiden was proving to be a dangerous distraction she couldn't afford. The more time she spent with him and the better she got to know him, the more she liked the cagey, flirtatious fighter. Getting attached to a client was a really bad idea. It was a rookie mistake and she'd been doing this job long enough to know better.

The longer she delayed in delivering Aiden to Madeline Kruze, the greater the chances of something going terribly wrong. All it would take was for him to change his mind about returning with her, and all this would blow up in her face. There were so many factors out of her control. Although she could always drug him again, she supposed.

"How much longer do you think this is going to take?" Her waspish tone belayed her impatience to have this over with. They needed to get back on the road before anything else happened to derail their course.

Aiden gave a negligent shrug. "These things take time. I suspect this isn't something these guys do every day. Portage doesn't exactly strike me as a high-crime area. If they don't follow everything by the book, all it'd take was a smart lawyer to come in here and get these assholes off on a technicality."

"Is that what you did?"

Those arresting eyes locked on her, making her pulse jump. The blood in her veins heated until she wanted to squirm in her seat under the intensity of his stare. She hated the way her body responded to him. With just a look, he turned her mind to mush and dissolved her will. Despite her claim to forget what happened between them, she knew in her heart that was nothing more than wishful thinking.

"Excuse me?"

"When you practiced law, which side of justice were you on?" She was baiting him, desperately searching for more reasons not to like this man, to think less of him. Unfortunately, she feared his answer would do little to dissuade her heart either way. In the rather small amount of time they'd spent together, she found herself liking him far too much. She liked the white-collar/blue-collar contradictions in him. He was intimidatingly intelligent, yet he spoke with the uncouth vernacular of a hard-knocks fighter. She admired the strength and courage it must have taken him to walk away from an inheritance worth millions of dollars and to forge his way in an industry that chewed up lesser men and spit them out. On the outside he appeared to be nothing more than Disco Stick Kruze, but in her heart, she knew there was so much more. There was a depth to this man that he worked hard at not letting other people see.

"Whichever side they paid me to be on. I told you I was a good attorney, Ryann. I never said I was an honest one."

His gaze swept over her, lingering in all the places that made her blood heat, her skin tingle with anticipation. How could just a look make her hot and achy? But it wasn't just any look. It was Aiden with those unnaturally golden brown eyes that seemed to penetrate her soul.

"What about you?" he challenged. "What makes a half pint of a woman think it'd be a wise decision to become a private investigator?"

His jab hit closer to home than he ever could have known. If she continued to verbally spar with this fighter, she wasn't going to walk away unscathed. She hesitated a moment, not sure how much she wanted to tell him, especially here. Instead, she shrugged. "My father was a PI, and I followed in his footsteps."

In typical lawyer fashion, Aiden latched onto that one word and began his cross examination. "'Was'?" His countenance turned serious and he straightened in the chair, abandoning his lazy sprawl. That too-perceptive stare locked on her, refusing to give her quarter. She immediately regretted telling him even this much. Dear God, she didn't want to do this here, and she didn't think she could talk about her dad and keep her emotions in check.

"Gads, you're such a lawyer," she mocked, trying to turn the conversation back on him, but he wouldn't be deterred.

"You didn't answer my question," he pressed.

It might just be easier to tell him. Maybe then he'd understand why she didn't want to talk about it. Deadpanning her expression, she hoped her emotions would take the hint and follow suit. "My father was killed last month."

Aiden bit out a ripe curse that held more emotion than her own voice. "Jesus, I'm sorry."

And he sincerely meant it. He turned toward her and took her hand in both of his. His grip was firm, more comforting than she wanted to admit. What would it be like to have a man like this in her corner? she wondered. From what Ryann knew of him, she'd bet nothing rattled this fighter who seemed to possess the courage of a lion and the strength of a bull.

She cleared her throat and pulled her hand away from his. Not because she didn't want his touch or like the feeling of his hands on her—but because she liked it too much. He was hell on her defenses, and she was trying like crazy to keep a guard around her heart.

"What about your mother?"

"My mother died seven years ago. Which is exactly how long it took for my dad to ruin his life."

The last part of her confession tumbled out before she could bite it back. Those unnatural eyes skated over her, missing nothing and making her feel emotionally raw as he took in every word with genuine concern and empathy. Weren't lawyers supposed to be heartless?

"I'm very sorry, Ryann. How did you lose her?"

"Cancer. It devastated my dad. He took her to all the specialists he could find. And then the hospital bills began rolling in and he had to start taking a lot of extra cases to pay them. I tried to help him, but he wouldn't let me. Said he didn't want me involved. My mother was a strong woman. She fought so hard. But slowly the cancer began to win. In the end . . ." She couldn't continue. The emotions were still too raw, the memories too fresh—even after all these years. Some wounds never fully healed.

Aiden muttered a curse under his breath. "I'm so sorry you had to go through that. Do you have any other family? Any siblings?"

She shook her head. "There's no one. I'm an only child."

"Me, too."

His confession surprised her, though not as much as what he said next.

"I was always kinda grateful for that. I wouldn't wish my parents on my worst enemy, let alone a brother or sister." But he wouldn't let the conversation remain on him, revealing just enough information about himself to make her want to open up. "How did your father die?"

"Officially? Hit-and-run. But he was murdered."

Aiden's brows pinched into a scowl. "Do you have any idea who did it? Have you gone to the police?"

"Yes and yes. I've been investigating it myself since the police determined it was a hit-and-run. There were no witnesses, at least no one that will talk, so I can't prove who did it and the police aren't interested in solving the case."

"Why the hell not?" he demanded, championing her cause and making her heart melt into a puddle on the floor.

"Because they're paid not to. Vincent Moralli is untouchable."

Aiden muttered a foul curse, the furrow of his brow taking up a full-on scowl. "Vincent Moralli? Ryann, Vincent Moralli is not a man to tangle with."

"How do you know Vincent Moralli?"

"Who do you think kept him out of prison all these years?"

She flinched as if he'd struck her, no longer able to maintain the visage of impassivity. "You work for Moralli?" With each word, her voice hit a new octave. He winced.

"Worked," he clarified. "Moralli is the largest client at my father's firm."

What were the odds of that man being the common denominator between them? Ryann didn't believe in coincidences, but she couldn't find the thread of connection linking them together. Still, something didn't feel right about this. Before she could say as much, the door across the hall opened and an officer she recognized from the night before, the one who'd planted his boot into Aiden's back, stepped into the hall.

"Sorry to keep you waiting, Ms. Andrews, Mr. Kruze." The officer acknowledged Aiden with a nod but only briefly made eye contact. He was clearly uncomfortable around Aiden. Whether it was remorse over his less than gentle treatment of him, or fear that Aiden would use his influence to make trouble for him, she didn't know. "We'll be taking your statements separately. Ms. Andrews, if you'll please come with me."

Separately? A moment of alarm sent Ryann's heart leaping inside her chest. Aiden had to know this was his chance to get rid of her. She had to say something—make him understand why she'd done it. Maybe he would understand. Maybe he would help her. She must have looked as panicked as she felt, because before she could spill her guts and beg Aiden to keep his silence, he glanced at the officer and said, "Will you please give us a moment?"

The cop nodded and stepped back in the examination room. "Whenever you're ready."

Once they were alone again, Aiden grasped her shoulders and turned her to face him. "Are you all right? Ryann, talk to me."

"You can't tell them," she pleaded, no longer caring to disguise the desperation in her voice.

"Tell them what? What the hell are you talking about? Sweetheart, you're not making sense."

"About what I did to you. Aiden, they'll arrest me. You said it yourself, I've committed a felony. If you don't come back with me, if I don't get that money from your mother, Vincent Moralli is going to kill me."

The look of surprise on his face was quickly erased by concern with a healthy dose of pissed-off. Though she couldn't be sure, she suspected the latter emotion wasn't directed at her, even though his grip on her tightened until she winced.

"What the hell kind of trouble are you in, Ryann?"

"I'll tell you. I promise I'll tell you everything. Just please don't tell them what I did to you."

Instead of agreeing, he pulled her into his arms. God help her, he felt so good, so safe. Despite all the promises she'd made to herself and the boundaries she'd tried to erect, Ryann found herself wrapping her arms around him, clinging to him. She tried to ignore the way her curves molded to his unyielding chest, or the strength in those arms that had the power to crush her but offered only comfort.

"It's going to be all right, Ryann. I'm not going to say anything. Actually, the thought never crossed my mind. But you will tell me what this is all about when we get out of here."

His tone brooked no room for argument. Not that she had it in her, anyway. She nodded against his chest and felt his breath stirring her hair as he inhaled deeply. He kissed the top of her head before letting her go, then leaned back and gave her a smile so breathtaking, she momentarily forgot to breathe. This was the man behind the fame, the man she was desperate to know and yearned to spend time with.

Taking her hand, he gave it a reassuring squeeze and said, "Let's just get this over with, huh?"

# CHAPTER

# 18

The following three hours were torture. Aiden could hardly concentrate on answering the officer's questions over the riot of his own slamming around in his head. He'd figured something was up with Ryann after the call she'd gotten this morning, but not once did he imagine it was as bad as the words that spilled from her mouth when she thought he was going to rat her out. It would have been the perfect opportunity to get rid of her, though he was loath to admit a part of him didn't want to. Even if she wouldn't have confessed to being in danger, he never would have said anything. He didn't want to get her in trouble. In truth, he was having far too much fun with her between the sheets to give her up just yet. Although he hadn't intended on this going as far as actually seeing his parents, Aiden suspected that was all about to change.

What kind of trouble could Ryann possibly be in? Whatever the problem, it was serious enough to put her life in danger. And if Vincent Moralli was involved, there was a high likelihood that was true. Of course the thought had briefly crossed Aiden's mind that this could all be a ruse, and she was playing him. They both knew the only way she was getting him to New York would be willingly. And if she hadn't gotten that call this morning, if he hadn't seen the bone-deep fear in her eyes, he'd probably give more credence to the thought that he might be getting played. But something told him Ryann was on the level. If she'd wanted to manipulate him, she'd had plenty of times before now to tell him her story. In fact, he recalled several occasions where she'd purposefully shut down the conversation.

No, this was legit. Ryann was in serious trouble. And what kind of a selfish prick would he be to bail on her? The thought of leaving her alone and vulnerable sent his protective instincts rioting. He wasn't sure at what point he'd come to care so much about her. Admittedly, there were a few hot moments that came to mind, but he'd had a lot of hot moments with a lot of women and he'd never felt any sort of responsibility toward them afterward. But something about Ryann was different. He couldn't explain it, it just . . . was.

"I think that's all we need from you, Mr. Kruze. Thank you for coming down. We appreciate your cooperation."

Aiden recognized the officer interviewing him as the one who'd taken over the lead at the robbery last night. He found the man to be thorough, competent, and direct. He was a straight shooter, and Aiden respected that.

"Not a problem. Are we free to go, then? My girlfriend is anxious to get back to New York."

"That's understandable. I'm sorry to be delaying you, but I'd really appreciate it if you could spend one more night in town. I'll get everything in to the DA today and he'll review the case. If he has any questions or needs clarification, we can have you come back down right away in the morning. If you haven't heard from us by . . . let's say ten a.m. tomorrow, you're free to go."

"That's fair enough." Aiden shoved back his chair and rose, anxious to find Ryann.

"Thank you, again." The officer stood and extended his hand. "For being so understanding about everything."

He shook the guy's hand and made a hasty retreat. When Aiden stepped into the hall, he found the chairs he and Ryann had been waiting in empty. A quick survey of the department revealed no sign of her, and his pulse spiked. Another officer walked by and Aiden stopped him. "Hey, have you seen a redhead walking around here? She's about yea tall." He held his hand up to his collarbone. "Thin, real pretty."

The cop gave him a knowing grin that sent Aiden's hackles up. He wasn't usually so touchy, but he was quickly discovering when it came to Ryann, he didn't know himself nearly as well as he thought he did.

"Oh, her? Yeah, she's kinda hard to miss. Last I saw, she was over by the vending machines down the hall and on the left."

After a curt "Thanks," Aiden spun around and headed in the direction the officer pointed, each step ratcheting the tension inside him. Common sense told him she was safe. She was in a police station, for crissake, and Moralli had no way of knowing she was even here. It didn't matter that his concern for her was irrational, just knowing the threat existed courted the alpha in him to life, and that beast ran on pure testosterone. By the time Aiden reached the break room, there was a healthy dose of it flooding his veins. He entered the doorway and came to an abrupt stop.

The relief at finding Ryann was quickly drowned out by another emotion so foreign to him, he was reluctant to name it. Yet there is was, all the same, spiking his pulse higher, suffusing a rush of adrenaline through his system. His jaw clamped tight to bite back the growl rumbling in his throat. Across the room, Ryann stood in front of the vending machine. Her back was to him, as was the officer's standing beside her. The man was close—too close.

The boy in blue said something Aiden couldn't hear, and she laughed as he shoved his hand in his pocket and pulled out a fistful of change. After dropping several coins in the machine, Ryann pointed to a bag of trail mix through the glass, and the guy entered the code. When a bag dropped into the bottom compartment, the cop retrieved the trail mix and handed it to her. She gave him a smile that set Aiden's teeth on edge. It was a sweet grin he wanted to be the sole recipient of. She thanked the officer, telling him he didn't have to do that and the guy told her it wasn't a problem. When he moved a step closer, Aiden suspected Dudley-Do-Right was about to make his move, and Aiden didn't think twice about cock-blocking the bastard.

"You about ready?"

They both spun around. Ryann looked genuinely pleased to see him, but the other guy . . . not so much.

"Aiden, there you are. I was starting to get worried."

Was it possible this woman completely missed the fact that this guy was hitting on her? There was zero guilt or embarrassment in her eyes, and that beautiful smile she'd given the officer beamed impossibly brighter for him. Holy hell, looking at her was like a sucker punch to the solar plexus.

Pure male instinct sent his feet moving forward. He approached Ryann and her admirer, barely resisting the urge to tell Dudley-Do-Right to back the fuck off. Instead, he opted for the communication that wouldn't get him arrested. Reaching for Ryann, he snaked his arm around her waist and pulled her tight into his side before planting a quick, firm kiss on her lips. She stiffened against him, seeming surprised by his PDA, which was nothing compared to what he wanted to do to her right now. Ignoring her startled response, he shot her a Disco grin that earned him a scowl.

"It looks like we'll be spending one more night here, sweetheart." Then to the officer, Aiden said, "Hey, man, you know of any nice places in town I can take my girl to eat?"

The cop took a measured step back—message delivered loud and clear, but if he was attempting to disguise his disappointment, he was doing a piss-poor job of it. After getting the name of a place to eat, Aiden ushered a contemplatively silent Ryann out the door. Just before they reached the SUV, she pulled away from the hand he'd possessively planted against her lower back and spun around to face him.

"What the hell was that?"

"What do you mean?" he asked innocently.

"You kiss me in front of that cop and call me 'your girl.' And by the way, I'm holding you to that fancy dinner tonight."

Aiden bit the inside of his cheek to hold back his amused grin. She was so damn cute when she was all in a tiff. "I thought you were supposed to be my girlfriend," he said, taking care to keep his expression guileless. "At least that's what you told everyone last night. I'm just playing the part, sweetheart. Wouldn't want them to think you were lying."

"And I suppose none of that had anything to do with the officer talking to me at the vending machine."

"Why would it?"

"Don't give me that lawyer talk, Aiden Kruze. You were jealous. Admit it!"

"I'm not jealous." He was jealous. "I'm just sayin' it doesn't look good when we're supposed to be together and some other guy is panting all over you."

She let out an unladylike snort that somehow managed to sound cute as hell and rolled her eyes. "Please . . . he gave me trail mix."

"That wasn't all he wanted to give you."

"You're being ridiculous," she chided.

"And you're being naïve if you think that guy didn't want to fuck your brains out."

She laughed. She actually laughed at him. "You're right, Aiden. Nothing says 'I want to fuck your brains out' like a bag of trail mix."

Oh, for crissake, when she said it like that, he did sound like a jealous jackass.

"Just admit it, Aiden. You were jealous."

He had no intention of admitting any such thing. But he didn't have to. She gave him a triumphant grin and said, "Well, at least now you know how it feels."

She turned to walk away, but Aiden caught her arm before she could take two steps. "How it feels? What in the hell are you talking about?"

"I'm talking about the night of the after party. Do you think I enjoyed sitting at the bar watching you Disco it up?"

"'Disco it up'? What does that even mean?" He wasn't sure whether he was more amused or more annoyed at this point.

She sighed. "It means have you ever even had a real relationship?"

Whoa, wait, where the hell did that come from? He didn't know, but he sure as hell was going to find out. "Ryann, what do my past relationships have to do with anything?" Again, answering a question with a question. Hopefully, she wouldn't notice. If she did, she let it slide.

"It means that *our* relationship is complicated enough as it is, and I don't think it'd be a good idea to make it worse by getting emotions involved."

"Emotions like lust? Because I think that ship's already sailed for you, sweetheart."

Too far . . . ? His mocking comment earned him a scalding glare. She looked like she wanted nothing more right now than to introduce her knee to his balls. If he wasn't careful, they were going to get into a full-blown domestic right here in the parking lot of the Portage Police Department. But goddammit, her rejection stung more than he wanted to admit.

What the hell happened to that frightened, vulnerable woman

who clung to him so desperately back in there, begging for his help? She shot him one last look before jerking her arm from his grasp and turning away. Oh, she was still in there, he realized, catching a glimpse of hurt reflecting in those emerald eyes as she stomped away. But she was fighting like hell to keep that woman buried. Why? Then the answer came to him like an epiphany. Perhaps it was easier to pick a fight than tell him the truth. The truth she knew full well he was going to demand as soon as they got back to their motel. It was a defense mechanism he'd effectively played many times himself. Oh, this girl was good . . .

"I know what you're doing, and it's not going to work."

Oh, she very much doubted that he did. Aiden fired up the Escape and when a hurricane of cold air blasted Ryann in the face, she reached forward and turned off the fan. As he let the SUV idle, giving the engine time to warm, she felt the heat of his stare burning into her. She avoided his gaze, pulling out her phone to check her messages. Great, one from his mother . . .

"Ryann, look at me."

She didn't want to look at him. She feared if she did, he'd see the truth. The truth of how much that kiss in there affected her. How having him pull her against him and call her his girl melted one more layer of ice she'd been working so hard to build around her heart. Watching him stake his claim as he grappled for control, when she knew he wanted to hit that guy for flirting with her, made Ryann feel wanted—owned. It was a feeling she never would have thought she'd enjoy, but coming from Aiden, it was a heady experience.

If she wasn't careful, she was going to lose her heart to this man. Especially after the kindness and concern he'd shown for her in the station. She no longer had any doubt he would help her. Aiden had his chance to leave her, and he hadn't taken it. Gratitude fractured her last vestiges of control, and the willpower she'd been clinging to in an attempt to keep them from crossing the line she'd redrawn this morning was all but shredded.

So no, he didn't know what she was doing. He had no idea how hard it was for her not to leap across this center console and throw herself at him right now. And to think he might actually have been jealous! The idea warmed her to her very core, because she knew men like Aiden did not get jealous. So if he was, even a little bit, did that mean just maybe he felt something for her, too? The hope that blossomed in her chest had swiftly scared the shit out of her, which in turn had spurred her to lash out in a failed attempt at self-preservation.

"Ryann, look at me."

When his second request got the same result, he reached over and gently but firmly took her chin, turning her head to face him. Damn, he was too gorgeous for words . . .

"You're going to have to talk about it, you know. Fighting with me and pushing me away isn't doing either one of us any favors. You've gotta help me help you, Ryann."

But pushing him away might be her only saving grace. She wasn't sure how much more close-quarters with him she could take. Opening up to Aiden would require her to give him something she wasn't sure she was prepared to part with—her trust. She'd have to tell him everything, about her father and about Moralli. Although in that moment of panic she'd so glibly made the promise to do just that, now that it was time to bare her soul, she wasn't sure she could do that and still keep it.

"And if you must know the truth . . . I was insanely jealous back there."

She gave him a weak smile, returning his boyish grin. A bubble of laughter caught in her throat. How sweet . . . This was his olive branch. For Aiden to admit to any emotion that might be perceived as weakness was a true miracle in itself.

"And that smile . . . Sweetheart, I want to be the only male on the receiving end of that beauty."

Oh, he was good. And she would have told him so if that unguarded honesty in his eyes hadn't rocked her to her very core. That unmistakable spark of connection she'd momentarily experienced last night was back in full force, and she was done for—all defenses obliterated. Meeting his stare, she was helpless to do anything other than nod like a simpering mute. But after the smile she got in return, she was pretty sure she would have agreed to anything at this point.

"So it looks like I owe you one fancy dinner. What do you say we table this talk about Moralli and enjoy the night out together? We'll pick this convo up tomorrow. We've got a lot of miles to kill between here and Manhattan."

Grateful for the reprieve, she thought that sounded like the best idea she'd heard in a long time.

# CHAPTER

Aiden wasn't used to having to make concessions, but where Ryann was concerned, it seemed like that was all he did. Had he really confessed to being jealous? Briefly, his conversation with Katie came back to haunt him like the ghost of Christmas Past. She was so confident he'd meet someone that would turn his world upside down. Well, that pretty much summed up Ryann in a nutshell.

"I feel underdressed," she complained, checking out her backside in the mirror.

Aiden hadn't moved from his spot on the bed. Stretched out, legs crossed at the ankles, hands laced behind his head, he watched Ryann fuss over her appearance. Didn't she know how beautiful she was? If she asked him, he'd have told her all that primping and makeup was completely unnecessary. But she didn't ask, and he didn't offer. He'd already said too much as it was.

"You look fine."

Apparently, *fine* was a cardinal sin, because she shot him a scowl and grumbled, "Gee, thanks."

Deliberately ignoring her snark, he said, "No problem. You about ready to go?"

"Just a minute. Don't rush me. Do you have any idea how long it's been since I've been out on a date?"

Wait, what? Was that what this was? Suddenly, he was the one feeling underdressed, and more than a little anxious. He couldn't remember the last time he'd been on a real date, because he was pretty sure booty calls didn't count. Ryann must have seen the *oh, shit* look on his face because she blushed and quickly stammered, "I didn't mean an actual *date* date. Like you and me."

Yes, she did. Otherwise she wouldn't have said it. And that added a whole other element to this "night out" scenario. He'd wanted to take her out because he didn't think he could stand being cooped up in this tiny room with her all evening and keep his hands to himself. He'd hoped getting her out in public would help him govern his urge to fuck her blind. It never occurred to him that Ryann might have thought this was something more. But if she had, it was probably his fault. He knew he was sending her mixed signals, not that she hadn't been sending a few of her own. Right now, he felt like a pendulum, swinging between his wants and desires and the bone-deep knowledge that it would be a mistake to get physically involved with her—any more than he already had, he amended.

Bottom line, there was something between them, but that didn't mean they should let it go anywhere. If he knew what was good for him, he'd keep Ryann at a distance, and once they got to New York, they would go their separate ways. He'd deal with his parents, Ryann would get her money and do whatever it was she needed to do to get Moralli off her back. Then he would return to Vegas, start some rehab on his shoulder, and pretend this whole fucked-up thing never happened.

And you'd think that all that head knowledge would have caught up with his mouth because in the next two seconds he was asking, "How long has it been? Since you were on a date?" He had to clarify that question because it could have meant so many other things—things he was dying to know but had no business asking.

She shrugged as if the answer were inconsequential and spared him the briefest glance. Mercy, she looked hot in those dark-wash skinny jeans that hugged her curves just right. Her heather-gray sweater was one of those numbers that molded to her. She'd pulled her mass of red, wavy hair into a bun and pinned it on top of her head. With her hair swept up like that, she looked young—too damn young for the thoughts that were running through his mind right now. The touch of makeup aged her just enough that he didn't feel like a total perv.

"How old are you, Ryann?"

She glanced at him through the reflection in the mirror as she skated a sheer gloss over her full, ripe lips. She rubbed them together, smoothing out the gloss, then ran her finger along the border, wiping off the excess. His cock instantly became hard as he watched her apply the finishing touches. It took all his restraint not to go over there and kiss it right off that lush mouth of hers. If she'd sensed the wicked direction of his thoughts, she didn't acknowledge it, which might have been her only saving grace.

"I'm twenty-six. Why?"

Now it was his turn to shrug. "Just wondering. You look younger with your hair pulled up."

She turned toward him, her hand subconsciously lifting to her bun. "You don't like it?"

"I didn't say that."

As if his legs had a mind of their own, they swung over the side of the bed and he was on his feet and advancing on her before he even realized he'd moved. Aiden stopped in front of her and lifted his hands, framing her face. "Ryann, I'm trying really hard to be good here. But you're making it really hard to do the right thing. So

I'm only going to tell you this once, you look absolutely gorgeous. It doesn't matter what you put on, or how you fix your hair, you're stunning no matter what. So unless you want to stay here and let me prove to you just how hot you make me, then we need to go. Now."

But she wasn't heeding his warning. This was him telling her to leave, to go get in that car before he said or did something they'd surely regret—well, she would, anyway, because the one thing he was learning about Ryann was that she did not do casual sex. When she'd let him touch her, it had meant something—he'd felt it in her uninhibited response to his touch.

"Twelve months."

"Excuse me?"

"Twelve months. That's how long it's been since I was on a date. Since my fiancé and I broke up."

He gave her a surprised look. "Fiancé, huh? How long were you together?"

"Four years."

"What happened?" A flash of pain crossed her face that immediately put her ex on Aiden's shit list. He didn't even need to know what happened. All that mattered was that prick had hurt Ryann.

"You don't want to hear about this . . ."

She cast her gaze to the floor and tried to back away, but he wouldn't let her go that easily. "I do. I'm really curious to know what kind of an idiot would be stupid enough to fuck up a four-year relationship with you."

She laughed, the soft and melodic sound hitting him right in the gut. "I'm warning you, it's a pretty ugly story."

"Can't be any uglier than some of mine."

"Oh, trust me, this one's going to win."

"I tell you what, let's get out of here and we'll swap stories on the way to the restaurant. We'll see who has the worst one."

Her delicate brow arched in question. "What will I win?" she asked, her voice dropping a soft, husky octave.

"What do you want?"

She laid her palm against his chest, sending a current of energy straight into his dick. How was it possible that such an innocent touch could pack such a punch? Could she feel his heart hammering against his rib cage?

"Surprise me." Without giving him a backward glance, she dropped her hand and turned away. Grabbing her purse off the chair, she sauntered out the door.

"No way."

"Yep, true story."

"I'll kill him. Do you want me to kill him? Cuz I'll do it."

Ryann laughed, which surprised her, because there was nothing funny about your maid of honor fucking your fiancé a week before you were supposed to walk down the aisle and vow *until death do us part.* She hadn't talked about it since it happened, not to anyone—not her father or her friends—so it surprised her that she was actually doing so now. Aiden was easy to talk to—easier than she'd thought. That he'd championed her throughout her story had made it easier to share the harder parts.

Her tale had taken longer than the car ride to Suzie's Steak and Seafood House. Apparently "fancy restaurant" was a relative term in Portage but, hey, at least she wasn't underdressed. The place was cozy and rustic with knotty pine walls and a large stone fireplace in the center of the restaurant. Aiden had gotten them a table near the roaring fire and it was actually very quaint and, dare she think it . . .

romantic. Her glass of Lambrusco was nearly gone, and she was feeling warm and tingly all over by the time she finished her story.

Aiden was three-quarters of the way through a dark brew from the tap, his attention fixed solely on her. If he noticed the attention he attracted, he paid no mind to it. Then again, he was probably used to that sort of thing. As for her, someone who preferred the shadow to the limelight, it was a bit unsettling. But the wine seemed to take the edge off, and she enthusiastically agreed to another glass when their waiter came by.

Aiden chuckled. "You seem nervous."

"Do I? Well, I suppose that's to be expected after sharing a story like that. To tell you the truth, I'm not really used to all the attention."

His pierced brow quirked in question. "What do you mean?"

"Look around—half the women here are staring at you."

His amber gaze broke away from hers long enough to take a quick glance around the room, before locking back on her, looking entirely unimpressed. "It's not me they're interested in, it's Disco."

"Oh, they're interested."

"Does it bother you? We can leave if you'd like." Aiden drained his glass, set it on the table and scooted his chair back. Before he could rise, Ryann laid her hand on his arm, stopping him.

"No. That's all right. I don't want to leave. I was just making an observation, though I can't promise after I finish this next glass of wine that I won't give them something to talk about."

Aiden laughed, a husky, masculine rumble that sent shivers into all her feminine places, sparking a slow burning fire of need deep in her core—a fire she knew from experience only Aiden could quench.

"Be my guest, sweetheart, though you've got nothing to worry about. Those women have nothing on you."

"How would you know?" she scoffed. "You haven't even looked at them."

"I don't have to. I'm looking at you."

If he kept that up, Ryann was going to drag him into that restroom down the hall and jump him like a pogo stick. Wow, was it getting hot in here or was it just her? Perhaps she could have blamed her flush on the fireplace, but there was no excuse for the moisture in her panties other than raw, hot need.

Gone was that arrogant, cocky fighter that oozed superficial charms. No, this was the man she'd sensed all along and briefly glimpsed now and then when his mask of indifference slipped. He was easy to talk to—maybe too easy, for she'd found herself revealing more about herself than she'd intended. The last thing she wanted from this man was his pity. Was all this flattery his misguided attempt to balm the hurt she'd endured over Tyler's betrayal? God, she hoped not. But just to be sure, she decided to lay the question to rest.

"Aiden, I didn't tell you that story so you'd feel sorry for me. Sure, it sucked and I went through a bad time, but it was a long time ago. Nine months feels like nine years after burying my father. It wasn't easy to lose my fiancé or my best friend, but looking back on it now, I know it was for the best. In a crazy way I'm kinda glad it happened."

"You are?"

"Yeah . . . If Tyler wouldn't have done what he did, I'd be stuck in a loveless, passionless marriage. I mean, not once in four years did he ever come close to making me feel—"

Abruptly, she cut herself off. Her cheeks flushed hotly when she realized what she'd almost said. Holy shit, this wine must really be getting to her. But he wasn't letting her off the hook so easily. Just then, the waiter came by and asked Aiden if he wanted another beer. He barely cast the guy the briefest glance while nodding, because

Aiden's whole attention was solely focused on her. It was a heady feeling, having the full weight of those amber-flecked eyes locked on her.

"Feel what, Ryann? He never made you feel what?"

Picking up her glass, she took another sip of liquid courage and swallowed it down before she said, "The way you do."

His exhale told her he'd been holding his breath as he anxiously waited for her answer. Leaning back in his seat, he scrubbed his hand over the back of his neck and muttered a curse. The waiter came back just then with another beer and took Aiden's empty. He snatched up at the brew and downed a healthy amount of it. When he sat the glass down, there was something in his eyes that lit up every last one of her nerve endings.

"This is a bad idea, Ryann."

What was? Did she miss something here? "What's a bad idea?"

"What I'm thinking about doing to you right now." His rich, smooth voice turned rough and husky.

She shifted in her seat, trying to get comfortable, but the ache was too deep, her flesh too sensitive, and her wiggling only seemed to make it worse. "It doesn't have to be," she found herself rationalizing. "We both know this can't go anywhere, and that in two days it's going to be over. Why not enjoy it while we can? Otherwise, we're both going to be miserable, and what's the point in that?"

Oh, Lord, was she really suggesting what she thought she was suggesting? This was insane. This wasn't her—or was it? Ryann wished she could blame her Indecent Proposal on the wine. But in truth, it only gave her the courage to say what she'd been thinking all afternoon. On paper it made perfect sense. She wanted Aiden, badly, and he wanted her, so why not get each other out of their systems before they got to New York? It seemed the perfect solution, the only solution, and as long as they both knew the score, they could keep their emotions out of it and nobody would get hurt.

"I don't know, Ryann . . ."

What was his deal? Now, all of a sudden the player was getting cold feet? She thought he would have jumped at the no-strings-attached opportunity. The guy was the king of flings.

Looking as if he were fighting an internal battle, he said, "I don't think it's going to be that simple. I've done this sort of thing—a lot—and something about this feels different. Someone could get hurt."

Was he seriously considering refusing her? And by "someone" she was pretty sure he was talking about her. He said it himself—he was a pro at this, the master at not letting his emotions get involved. And she was what, the naïve, foolish, inexperienced little groupie? More than anything she wanted to prove him wrong. She could handle this. People had flings all the time, and she was long due hers.

Giving him her sauciest smile, she asked, "What's the matter, Aiden, afraid you're going to fall in love with me?"

At that taunt, he tensed, sitting a bit straighter, those impossibly wide shoulders thrown back, the fighter in him inherently responding to the challenge. Thoughtfully, his tongue toyed with the loop piercing running through his bottom lip. "What if you fall in love with me?"

Yep, of course it was going to be her. He was afraid she wouldn't be able to handle it. Well, it was sixteen hours from here to Manhattan, two days of driving, less if they could get out of here at a decent time tomorrow. What could possibly happen in two days?

# CHAPTER

Was Ryann seriously suggesting they become fuck buddies during their road trip back to New York? She had no idea what she was saying if she thought they could do this and then just walk away like it never happened. She was fresh—inexperienced—and although he couldn't deny those were qualities he loved about her, they were also an emotional spiderweb just waiting for the unsuspecting fly—i.e., him, or more specifically his dick—to get sucked in.

Emotions were going to get involved; it was inevitable, and she was going to get hurt. But hey, it wasn't like he didn't try to warn her, right? He'd have to be a total idiot not to jump at Ryann's offer to bed and bail. Hell, it was what he did.

Yet, something inside him, some nagging part of his conscience, told him this was a mistake. But that didn't stop him from telling his Jiminy Cricket to shut the fuck up. So why was he hesitating? *Maybe you're afraid you're the one that's going to get hurt, asshole.*

Ryann gave him another saucy grin that made his eager flesh stand up and take notice. She wouldn't have to ask *him* twice. As the seconds ticked by, the unfortunate realization dawned on him: What if he didn't want this to be just about sex? God knew he was getting tired of being used for his cock. Back in New York, he'd had nothing but a string of one-night stands, because that was all he'd had time for. Working sixty-hour weeks and running a law firm didn't leave much time for a social life. And when he did happen to carve out a few precious hours a week, he'd been at the gym.

You couldn't miss what you never had, so relationships had fallen to the bottom of his priority list. Then, when he'd gotten to Vegas, the women he'd encountered never wanted anything more from him than a good time, not that he'd been looking for more, and the hours he'd spent in the firm were now replaced by hours in the gym. But, what if . . . ?

Ryann laughed, pulling him out of his thoughts as she lifted her glass to her lips. He watched as she took a sip of her wine, taking the time to let it sit in her mouth and saturate her taste buds before swallowing it. He knew if he kissed her right now that sweet, potent taste of Lambrusco would be heavy on her tongue. He wasn't a wine drinker, but hell if that woman couldn't turn him into a connoisseur of the fruit of the vine.

"You should see yourself," she teased. "I can't tell if you're about to leap across the table and attack me right here, or bolt out of this place and run for the hills."

Neither could he—hence, the hesitation. She was pretty, with that flirtatious sparkle in her eyes, that wine-kissed flush to her cheeks. In this low lighting, her hair looked almost black, were it not for the fire's glow reflecting against her deep copper strands. Fuck it. Reaching across the small intimate table, Aiden caught Ryann's chin between this thumb and forefinger. Her laughter turned into a startled gasp when he stood, leaned over, and kissed her. It was a kiss just hungry enough to be scandalously indecent. His tongue twined with hers and just like he'd imagined, the Lambrusco flavoring her kiss was spectacular.

A small whimper escaped her throat when he pulled away, but dammit, if he didn't stop now, he might not have the willpower to do so. And the last thing he needed was to wind up back in the Portage Police Department, this time for public indecency.

"You're playing a dangerous game, Ryann, if you think it's going to be that easy to quench this fire," he whispered against her lips before sitting back down. "Don't say I didn't warn you."

Shock and amazement were just about the only words to describe the look on her beautiful face. Aiden gave her a crooked grin that promised all sorts of debauchery. And feeling triumphant, with his point well made, he turned his attention to the waiter approaching with their dinner.

Dinner was delicious, but after that kiss, Ryann was hard-pressed to drum up an appetite for anything other than Aiden. She remained contemplatively silent through their meal, and she suspected Aiden was intentionally letting the warning hang in the air between them. He'd tossed the ball back into her court, and he was an expert player, letting just the right amount of sexual tension simmer between them.

"You feeling all right, Ryann? You've hardly touched your steak."

Aiden took a bite of the medium-rare meat and gave her a closed-lip grin. "I gotta admit, I was skeptical at first. Just goes to show, you can't judge a book by its cover."

She got the feeling he was talking about something other than the restaurant. Not that she could call him out on his enigmatic comment. So Ryann decided to steer the conversation back in his direction. Sending him a sassy grin, she said, "I feel great. I guess I'm just hungry for dessert."

His cocky smile fell, his chewing halted, and she nearly busted out laughing. "You never told me your story. You know, about your worst date ever."

He resumed chewing and relaxed a bit, easing a touch of the tension crackling between them. She tried not to notice the way his throat worked as he swallowed, or the thick ropes of flexing muscles as he lifted his pint of beer and downed another third. When he set his glass down, she saw he was smiling—a genuinely humorous, wholly infectious grin. "You sure you want to hear it? It involves a prostitute, a bar fight, and a rubber chicken," he warned.

"What?" Ryann busted out laughing. "You're kidding!"

"God, I wish I was," he grumbled, but humor laced his voice.

"Of course I want to hear it. You can't preface a story with a rubber chicken and not tell me."

"All right, but I can't promise there were no animals harmed in the making of this story."

She laughed, stabbed her fork in her cranberry walnut salad, and said, "I promise not to report you to PETA."

The rest of the evening settled into an easy, relaxed dinner. Aiden told outrageous stories, and Ryann laughed more than she had in her entire life. She laughed until her sides hurt, until her stomach was stuffed with one of the best dinners she'd had in longer than she could remember, and her head was swimming from too many glasses of wine.

Aiden was utterly charming, impeccably mannered, and to her complete and total surprise, he had the most fabulous sense of humor. She had seen many sides to Aiden Kruze, but this one, without a doubt, stole her heart. She was seeing a side of him she had no doubt he kept very closely guarded, and sharing that level of intimacy with him was more erotic than she ever could have imagined, because she knew this was a part of himself he didn't give other women.

No, it wasn't just about how great the sex would be—and she had no doubt it would be fantastic—or how amazing he made her feel with his skillful touch. There was something else here between them, and she was a fool if she thought she could pretend it didn't exist. He must feel it too, or else he wouldn't have tried to warn her off at her suggestion of a fling.

"I still can't believe that happened to you," she said, coming back to his rubber chicken story. "How could you not know she was a prostitute?"

"It was a Halloween party. Half the women there looked like prostitutes. Besides, it was Easton's fault for slipping her a hundred bucks and telling her I was into that kinky shit."

She broke out laughing again and hugged her aching sides. Aiden joined her, his deep baritone voice like audible foreplay.

"Oh, I can laugh about it now, but I tell you what, it was months before I could step into a Chick-fil-A without my ass getting phantom pains. Fucking Easton . . ." he chuckled, shaking his head. Aiden lifted his beer and drained his glass. "But I got that bastard back. Broke his nose, which then started a bar fight that landed half of Coach's CFA team in the county jail for the weekend. He took his sweetass time bailing us out, too."

"Wait, which one is Easton again?"

"He's the guy I was sparring with at the gym the day you showed up. The one that punched me in the jaw."

Ahh . . . that was the broody guy at the after party Aiden had been talking to. Wow, after everything that had happened, it felt like months since they'd met, rather than days. "So are you two still friends?"

"The best. He's the brother I never had."

"That's who you were visiting at the hospital?"

He tensed. Whether from the serious turn in conversation or the reminder that she'd been following him, she couldn't know. His expression turned slightly guarded, but he wasn't pulling all the walls up yet. She regretted bringing it up, then again they were going to have to talk about it eventually, right? Perhaps easing into it wasn't such a bad idea.

He nodded, offering her no more information.

"Is he all right?"

"He will be."

"And the blonde you were with?" She tried to keep the flicker of jealousy from her tone and realized she'd failed miserably when Aiden gave her a crooked smile.

"That's Easton's girl. Her name is Katie Miller. She's Coach's niece."

"Wow, if that isn't sticking your hand in the cookie jar."

Aiden laughed, seeming to relax once again now that he could see the direction their conversation was going, hovering on the outskirts of personal without getting too deep.

"Does your coach mind? Easton dating his niece?"

Aiden shrugged. "If he did, he's over it now. Which reminds me, I need to call him back. I didn't take his call earlier at the station. God knows he's probably in a fit, and I didn't want to get into it with him there."

"That reminds me, I have some calls to return myself before it gets too late."

Curiosity glinted in his eyes, but he didn't ask and she was grateful for it. She didn't want to lie to him. Not after the wonderful evening they'd shared together. Aiden glanced at his watch. "Shit, I didn't realize how late it was. We should probably get going."

"I'm ready when you are."

Aiden waved the waiter over, stood to grab his wallet from his pocket, and handed the man his credit card.

"This was a really great evening," she told him. "Thank you." Draining her glass of the last few swallows of Lambrusco, she went to stand, but her legs had other ideas. Her knees buckled, but before she could steady herself on the table, Aiden's hand was on her arm and he was pulling her into his side.

"Whoa, there, you all right?" he asked, putting a steadying hand on each of her shoulders so he could get a better look at her.

Her cheeks heated with embarrassment. "I'm fine. I just got up a little fast, is all. I'm not used to drinking so much. Usually two glasses is my limit."

His top lip curled in a crooked grin that revealed those perfect, straight teeth. "I think you might've tripled that, sweetheart."

"Hence, the tripping over my own feet," she added, unable to contain her intoxicated giggle. Out of nowhere, the waiter returned with Aiden's card. Keeping one steadying hand on her arm, he scribbled his signature on the paper and handed it back to the man who thanked him and skirted away. As she watched him maneuver the plastic into his wallet one-handed, her gaze fell on the edge of a foil wrapper poking out the other side.

The sight of it sent a flutter of butterflies erupting in her stomach. They battered all the way to her chest, making it tight with excitement. Nervous energy hummed through her veins. She couldn't believe she was going to do this—she was going to have sex with Aiden Kruze tonight.

# CHAPTER

21

She was not having sex with Aiden Kruze tonight. At least that was what he informed her when she suggested they stop by the gas station on the way back to their motel room. From what she'd seen, he only had one condom in that wallet, and they were definitely doing it more times than that. Or so she'd thought, until he took her face in his hands and placed a chaste, patronizing kiss on her cheek and said, "You, sweetheart, by no means fit the legal definition of *consenting adult* right now."

"Uhhh . . ." she huffed, flopping back against the passenger seat. "You're kidding me, right?"

"Baby, you're trashed."

"I am not trashed, I'm tipsy." As if that somehow made it better.

He chuckled. "Yes, you are. And you nearly tipsied ass over teakettle in that restaurant." He fired up the Escape and turned the defroster on.

"Why do you have to be such a lawyer?" she complained. "I tell you what: you make me come, and I promise not to sue you."

She gave him a saucy wink when his head whiplashed back around to look at her. He dragged his hand through his hair and muttered a nasty curse to which she responded, "That's what I'm trying to do, but you're clam-jamming me."

He busted out laughing, which had not been what she was going for—at all. "I'm what?" he asked incredulously.

"Clam-jamming me. It's the female version of cock-blocking," she snipped. "It's a real thing. You can Google it."

"Oh, I believe you," he said, still laughing like she was Gabriel Freaking Iglesias or something. "I just never thought I'd hear those words come out of your sweet little mouth."

"Well, that makes two of us, cuz I never thought I'd hear the word *no* come out of yours."

His smile morphed into a scowl that suggested she might have dealt him an unintentional low blow. To which he responded, "Guess I'm full of surprises then, aren't I, baby girl?"

Yep, she'd offended him. If she couldn't tell by his cutting tone, then the use of that hated pet name left no doubt in her mind. She might be drunk, but she wasn't drunk enough not to care if she pissed him off and ruined their night. They'd had an amazing evening together, the last thing she wanted to do was be the spark that sent it up in flames.

"Look, Aiden, I'm sorry . . ."

He turned his attention back to the road, shifted the Escape into drive, and mumbled, "It's fine, Ryann. Don't worry about it. I'm used to it."

*Excuse me? What the hell did he mean by that?* She sat up in her seat and grabbed Aiden's wrist before he could move his hand off the shifter. "What is that supposed to mean?"

He looked at her, but his expression belayed none of his emotion. "It means I had a really great evening with you, Ryann. And it isn't very often that I can spend time with a woman and not have it revolve around sex. I thought we might have had that tonight." He shrugged. "I was wrong. Like I said, don't worry about it."

Ryann wasn't sure she could have felt like a bigger ass. Just when she thought she'd figured Aiden out, he went and threw a curveball at her. It didn't make sense, he didn't make sense. *If you don't want me, then why were you flirting with me all night?*

"Of course I want you."

Shit, did she just say that out loud? Oh, man . . . she really was drunk.

"I mean, look at you, you're hotter than hell. But I'm not doing this if there's a chance you're going to wake up in the morning with regrets. And to tell you the truth, I had just as much fun talking to you."

"Hey . . ." She pulled his hand into her lap and laced their fingers together. Struggling to push back her guilt, she forced herself to meet his eyes and said. "I had a really great time with you, too. This night *has* been perfect, Aiden, and I don't have a single regret."

"No regrets, eh, champ?"

Aiden trapped his lips between his teeth to bite back a grin as Ryann sent him a scathing glare from her post in front of the porcelain throne.

"Shut up," she moaned before hurling into the toilet.

With one hand fisted into her hair, holding it up, Aiden used his free hand to grab a washrag off the rack and run it under the sink of cold water. Squeezing out the excess, he draped it over the back of her neck.

"Uhhh . . ." she moaned after her stomach finished rebelling. "Just let me die." She flopped a dramatic arm over the seat and rested her cheek on her forearm.

"Not a chance. You're going to be all right," he reassured her, bringing the cool rag around to her forehead. "Though I suspect you're going to have one hell of a hangover in the morning."

"What time is it?" she mumbled, not bothering to lift her head or open her eyes.

"It's about three."

Ryann had fallen asleep—or more accurately, passed out—before they'd gotten back to the motel. Aiden had tucked her into bed before returning Coach's call. After getting his ass chewed for scaring the shit out of him and for taking five years off his life when he didn't have that many to squander, the old guy wished him luck in New York and told him if there was anything he needed, he was only a phone call away. The thing was, he knew Coach meant every last word. Damn, he loved that man. The guy was a freaking saint.

After hanging up with him, Aiden had taken a quick shower and then hit the sack himself, sleeping the sleep of the dead. At least until Ryann had jumped out of bed and bolted for the bathroom. The night had passed so quickly, and the alcohol had flowed so freely, that before he knew it, it was time to leave, and Ryann was completely inebriated.

"Why are you in here?" she groaned. "To gloat over my shame?"

She was pathetic, and still cute as hell. How that was even possible, he had no idea. "Nah . . . I can't tell you how many times someone's held my head out of a toilet after partying too much. Shit, sweetheart, I'm just paying it forward." He let go of the rag and tucked a few errant strands of sweat-dampened hair behind her ear. "I didn't realize how much you were drinking."

"Neither did I," she moaned. "I don't usually drink."

"You don't say . . ."

She popped open an eye to give him a miserable glower, but her top lip twitched into the faintest hint of a smile.

"I couldn't tell," he teased. "You hold your liquor so well."

"I think you're enjoying this far too much," she grumbled.

"No way." He rinsed the rag with cold water and handed it back to her so she could wash her face while he kept his hold on her hair. Just in case.

She sat back on her knees and ran the cloth over her face. "God, how horribly unattractive is this," she complained into the washrag.

"Yeah, you'd think so, wouldn't ya?" Taking the rag from her, he tossed it into the sink and handed her a cup of water to swish her mouth out. As she spit into the toilet, he said, "Yet, somehow you're still doing it for me."

She gave a pitiful laugh and elbowed him in the thigh. He chuckled and let go of her hair so she could stand, then swept her up into his arms. His shoulder bitched about the movement, but he ignored the burn in his rotator cuff. When she wrapped her arms around his neck and tucked her face into his shoulder, his body stirred at the sheer nearness of her—at having her slight weight in his arms, her fragile frame tucked tight against his bare chest.

Yep, hard as a rock. How fucking pathetic was that?

Now that he was wide awake, he was restless and edgy. It'd been days since he'd trained, and when a guy was used to spending eight-plus hours a day at the gym, that left a lot of bottled up energy with no good outlet. Being trapped in here with Ryann certainly wasn't doing him any favors. He needed to get out of here.

Aiden tucked her back into bed and pulled the covers over her shoulder. "How ya feeling, sweetheart?"

"Oh, splendid. If I could just manage not to hurl, I should be good to go. "

"What a trooper," he teased, smiling as he brushed her hair back from her face. When he turned and grabbed his shirt off the chair, Ryann's hand shot out and latched on to his wrist.

"Wait, where are you going?"

"To the store for some ginger ale and Gatorade. If we don't get you hydrated, you're going to feel pretty rough come morning."

Her bravado fell and that grip on his wrist tightened. "Don't leave me," she pleaded miserably.

Fuck, how could three little words shred him like that? Exhaling a defeated sigh, he dropped his shirt back into the chair and lifted the covers. "Scoot over."

She inched into the middle of the bed. As soon as he sat down, reclining against the headboard, she snuggled into his side and wrapped a slender arm around his waist, hugging him close. He tensed at the contact, his heart clenching inside his chest, his lungs refusing to breathe.

Having her this close to him, drawing comfort from him as if it were the most natural thing in the world, made something inside his chest shift. It was as if one of the key puzzle pieces in his life had finally fit into place—and it scared the ever-loving hell out of him. Had he really thought the risk laid in having sex with her? Fucking her probably would have been the safest thing he could have done, because this—the visiting with her, laughing with her, holding her—was far more dangerous than anything else he could have done.

He wasn't sure how long he lay there, not breathing, not moving. Surely she was asleep by now. Just when he was about to slip his arm out from under her and make his escape, her arm around his waist tightened and she said, "You really are a great guy, you know that?"

*Aww hell . . .* "Yeah, well, don't tell anyone else, okay?"

"Is it hard?"

Oh, man, it was so damn hard his balls ached. "Is what hard?" he asked, his voice rough as gravel.

"Pretending to be someone you're not. I think it would be very tiring after a while, showing the world one thing when you're really something else."

His hand slipped into her hair, running through her long silky tresses while he thought about her question a moment. "When you've been doing something your whole life, after a while it just becomes natural. And eventually, even you begin to believe the lie."

"Well, I think it's sad."

"What's sad, sweetheart?"

Her hand slid to his stomach and her fingers began tracing the path of muscles across his abs. Little jolts of electricity arrowed into the base of his cock, making the member strain toward her touch. He closed his eyes and tried to concentrate on his breathing. Thank God he'd decided to sleep in his jeans. The denim barrier wasn't much, but it was better than his Hanes.

"That the world doesn't really know you. Can I tell you a secret?"

"That depends. Are you still drunk and will you remember it in the morning?" he teased.

"I'm pretty sure I am and probably not."

"Okay, then go ahead," he chuckled.

"I think I'm falling for you."

# CHAPTER

"Oh, God, Aiden, will you please stop that pounding?"

But he didn't answer. It took Ryann a moment to realize the pounding was occurring inside her skull. She was pretty sure her heart was playing bongo with her brain. Exhaling a pain-filled moan, she tried to open her eyes against the sunlight beaming in on her through the break in the curtains and failed.

"Aiden . . ." she called, curling in a ball and pulling the covers over her head. When seconds ticked by without a response, panic slammed into her, drowning out her hangover migraine. Ryann threw the covers back and bolted out of bed. Which was a horrible mistake, because her world tilted and her stomach immediately flopped, sending waves of nausea crashing over her. She had to force back the urge to vomit as she stumbled toward the window overlooking the parking lot. Bracing a hand against the sill, she ripped back the drapes and became instantly blinded.

"Shit!" she hissed and lifted her hand, shielding her eyes as she shrank back from the light like some vampire in a B movie. It took a moment for her eyes to adjust. All the while panic ratcheted her pulse until she was sure she'd died of an aneurysm. Maybe she was just a sucker for punishment, because she knew what she was going to find when she looked out that window. Steeling her resolve, Ryann stepped back into the light and forced open an eye.

Betrayal hit her like a sucker punch, the air leaving her lungs in a *whoosh* of defeat.

*He's gone . . . I can't believe he left me.*

Had that been his plan all along? Get her to trust him, to lower her guard, and then steal away in the middle of the night? She was such an idiot! Numbly, she staggered back to the bed, plopped down on the mattress, and put her head between her legs as she tried to take deep breaths into lungs that refused to cooperate. "I'm such an idiot," she moaned miserably.

Through the veil of her hangover, the night came crashing back to her in flashes of bits and pieces. The dinner, the drinking, the laughing, the vomiting . . . *Oh, Dear God, I told him I was falling for him!* Right now, he was probably laughing his ass off at how gloriously he'd played the naïve little girl. Hell, he could be halfway back to Minneapolis by now, getting ready to catch the quickest plane to Vegas—and there wasn't a damn thing she could do to stop him.

"It's over," she said in defeat, shaking her head as the world of shit she was in slammed into her with the force of wrecking ball. "I can't believe I fell for it. I fell for Aiden Kruze . . . and he left me." Heartache warred with rage, both emotions rocking her already tumultuous stomach. Oh, God, she was going to puke. Dropping her head between her knees, she took a few slow deep breaths, trying to push back the nausea.

Ryann wasn't sure who she was more furious with: Aiden for leaving her, or herself for being dumb enough to trust him. *I'm such a fool . . .* As she sat there berating herself for letting her guard down and allowing herself to care about him, the key fob beeped outside, the lock released, and the door pushed open.

Before she could lift her pounding head, that familiar deep voice bit out a sharp curse. There was a rustle of a plastic bag and something heavy hit the ground. And then he was there, kneeling before her, her face gently framed in those strong, callused hands. He tipped her head up to meet his amber eyes, and he searched hers with concern and dare she hope something more . . .

Relief flooded her at the sight of him, the feel of those hands, that comforting strength. As a part of her rejoiced at discovering she'd overreacted, another part warned her she'd traveled into dangerous territory where this man was concerned. Her total lack of keep-your-shit-together proved it. Faced with the prospect that he might have left her, there was no more lying to herself or trying to deny it. She was hopelessly head over heels for this man. *"I think I'm falling for you" . . . ?* Shit, she had fallen and was down for the count. *"The winner by KO goes to Aiden 'Disco Stick' Kruuuuze!"* the mocking announcer's voice proclaimed in her head.

"Hey, Ryann, talk to me. Are you all right?"

All right? Hell no, she wasn't all right. She just realized she was in love with the big jerk! "Where were you?" she demanded, taking a page out of his lawyer playbook.

His brow arched in question, as if that clearly was not the response he was expecting. A measure of concern lifted from his handsome face and was replaced by . . . humor? Oh, no, he didn't . . .

"Looks like someone woke up on the wrong side of the bed."

He brushed a chunk of hair away from her wet cheeks and tucked it behind her ear.

"Wrong side of the bed? Aiden, I thought you'd left me."

His brows pulled tight into a scowl, all trace of humor fleeing his face. "You think I'd do that to you?"

"Well, what was I supposed to think when I wake up to find you gone? You didn't leave a note, and after last night . . ." There was no way she was going to finish that sentence. But Aiden wasn't going to let it rest—of course.

"What about last night?"

Shit. She could tell by the determination in that bold stare, he wasn't going to let it rest. "After puking up my toenails and then telling you I was falling for you, I'm not sure I would have blamed you for running off."

His top lip twitched into a crooked grin that, holy hell, had the power to make her instantly weak in the knees. "Don't worry about it, sweetheart. I don't scare that easily. We all say stuff we don't mean when we're wasted."

What was that? Was Aiden giving her an out?—giving her the opportunity to save face and retain a scrap of dignity? Or was this his way of asking her if she meant what she'd said? Did he want to hear her admit it now that she was sober? And what if she did? How would that possibly be a good idea considering their situation? But something in the way he watched her, the subtle tension in his jaw, told her he was waiting for an answer.

Shit. "I don't know what you want me to say."

What he wanted her to say? Hell, he'd spent the last six hours in knots over what she'd said before promptly passing out on him, leaving him trapped against her with nothing but time to meditate on her confession. For the most part, he'd convinced himself she hadn't meant it. How many women had told him in a lull of drunkenness or the throes of passion that they loved him? Too many to count. And he hadn't once given a second thought to their declaration—until Ryann.

"Until Ryann" was pretty much turning into his damn mantra. He'd never wanted a woman to truly know him—until Ryann. He'd never known a woman who challenged him, excited him, and stirred him—until Ryann. And he'd never met a woman he'd considered opening himself up to—until Ryann.

He'd mulled on that epiphany for the next several hours as she lay passed out in his arms, wondering what in the hell he was going to do about it. Would she even remember what she'd said? And did he want her to? He didn't need this complication—and this would most assuredly be one big complication. He wasn't looking to fall in love. He liked his life footloose and fancy free and wanted to keep it that way—didn't he?

Right now, his course was set. Ryann's situation had been eating at him ever since she'd gotten that call from Moralli's man. After discovering just how much trouble she was in, and what was at stake for her if he didn't go back so she could get that reward money and pay off Moralli, he didn't see how he had a lot of options.

Bottom line, he liked Ryann. Hell, he cared for her, even, and he had the means to help her out. Truthfully, he was her only hope. It was as simple as that, and he'd have to be a special kind of selfish bastard to abandon Ryann now and make her face Moralli alone.

He wasn't excited about doing it, but it was a little easier pill to swallow when he knew he was making the sacrifice for her. He never thought he'd find himself agreeing to do this, but he'd meet with his parents. Ryann would get paid, and Moralli would get off her back. Then, Aiden could return to Vegas with a clear conscience and no worse for the wear. It was a good plan, a solid plan, so why was she rocking the boat now with talk of emotions? Why was he giving her the opportunity to tell him he meant something to her? Ryann was a smart woman. She had to see this couldn't go anywhere. *Or could it?*—his Jiminy chimed in at the worst possible time.

Aiden knelt before her, staring into eyes that held a gut-wrenching amount of conflicting emotions, and he found himself holding his breath as he waited for her to respond. Something soul deep inside him flickered to life, burning slow and warming him from the inside out. It took him several moments before he recognized the emotion. God help him, it was hope. He wanted to hear Ryann tell him she'd meant what she said.

"Aiden, I—"

Her phone abruptly began buzzing on the nightstand, cutting her off. She tensed, a flicker of apprehension shadowing those jewel-colored eyes. He glanced at his watch, recognizing this was the same time she'd gotten the call yesterday. Before she could reach for the phone, he snatched it off the table and stood. Tension snapped through him like a whip, straining his sore, tired muscles. The ache in his shoulder intensified as he swiped his thumb across her screen to accept the "Unavailable" call and then lifted the phone to his ear.

"Hello?" He growled the greeting with all the friendliness of a pissed-off lion.

"Aiden?"

"Mother?" That was so not the voice he was expecting on the other end of this phone, though he was no more pleased by it.

"So you are alive after all. After fourteen months, I wasn't so sure."

When would she realize he didn't respond well to sarcasm? He never had and he never would. Unfortunately, it was the woman's main style of communication. Behind him, Ryann whispered, "Oh, shit, I forgot to call your mother back."

His eyes lifted heavenward as if praying for patience. "I can't do this with you right now, Mom. What do you want?"

"Well, I *wanted* to talk to Ms. Andrews. Seems she's just about as good at returning my calls as you are."

Aiden's hackles rose. It was one thing to turn that snarky temper on him, he was used to it, but he drew the line where Ryann was concerned. "Don't start, Mom. Ryann is busy right now. Can I take a message?"

"You can tell *Ms. Andrews* I'm not paying her to ignore my calls. And if I wanted to talk to her receptionist, I'd call him."

"Well, you could try, but he blocked your calls when he left Manhattan over a year ago and he'll be advising *Ms. Andrews* to do the same. I will contact you when I reach New York. Rest assured Ryann has done a spectacular job of doing your bidding."

He regretted the words the minute they left his mouth. He didn't hear what his mother said next, his attention caught on the offended gasp across the room. Fuck, he shouldn't have said that. How was it that several states away, this woman could still manage to bring out the worst in him? As she continued to rattle on in his ear, he turned back toward Ryann to mouth an apology, but she was already off the bed and closing the bathroom door behind her.

"Mom, I gotta go." Without waiting for a response, he ended the call and tossed the cell onto the bed before heading for the bathroom. "Ryann?" he called, rapping his knuckles against the door. She didn't respond. He knew full well she heard him. When the shower started up he tried the knob—locked. Their conversation wasn't over, not by a long shot, and he'd be dammed if he was going to let her get away with avoiding him. What had she been about to say before they'd been interrupted? "Ryann, I know you can hear me. Open the door."

"I'm taking a shower," she called back. "Why don't you get ready to go? Your mother's anxious to get you back, and she isn't paying me to lounge around here all day."

He knew from her brittle remark that he'd offended her with his thoughtless comment. Though spoken in haste, it might not have been such a bad thing to say to Madeline. If she so much as suspected there might be something between him and Ryann, his mother wouldn't hesitate to renege on paying her, and that was a risk Ryann couldn't afford to take. Getting involved with him was a mistake.

Reluctantly, he moved away from the door and began packing up his few belongings. Perhaps it was better this way, he tried to convince himself. Better to pretend this thing between them wasn't happening, because come tomorrow they'd be in New York and this little road trip would be over—along with any reason they would have to see each other again. Best not make this any more complicated than it had to be. Piece of cake, right?

Zipping up his newly purchased duffel, he slung the strap over his shoulder and headed outside to load the car before checking out. Feeling solid about his conviction and ignoring the cramp in his heart that told him he was a bullshit liar, he mumbled to himself, "It's only one more day. What can possibly happen?"

# CHAPTER

# 23

Ryann happened. She happened right out into their connecting rooms wearing nothing but a skimpy towel just as he was walking through the doorway to give her a room key. Certain he couldn't bear the temptation and needing to put some space between them after spending the better part of a day cooped up in an SUV with her, he'd booked them each their own room. At her insistence, he'd gotten ones with a connecting door. The closer they got to New York, the antsier he grew, and he suspected Ryann didn't completely trust him not to flake on her.

They'd been driving all day. She hadn't brought up their conversation in the motel room or his mother. It seemed as if they'd both mutually agreed those two issues were off the table for conversation. She spent most of the car ride sitting in stony silence, leaving him alone with his thoughts—a dangerous place to be. Whether her silence was brought on by the lasting effects of a hellacious hangover or her still being miffed over his comment to his mom, he couldn't know.

True to her promise, she'd answered his questions about her involvement with Vincent Moralli, and he'd needed to bite back a foul curse more than once. Ryann was in danger, for more reasons than she realized. After hearing her story, he had no doubt the man had her father killed and had been banking on the life insurance money to resolve his debt. But knowing Vincent Moralli, it wasn't that simple.

Seventy-five grand wasn't anything to him, but it was a way for him to get his hooks into a beautiful young woman. If Aiden were to venture a guess, he'd wager Moralli wanted her for something a hell of a lot more distasteful than paying off her father's debt. He knew how the bastard thought, he'd been forced to work with him for enough years, seen enough manipulative, underhanded dealings to know he wasn't going to let Ryann just walk away from this.

She was convinced that after she collected her paycheck from his mother and she paid her father's debt, that'd be the end of it and fuck him, he hadn't had the heart to dash her hopes. Time would tell. They'd play it her way and see how it rolled out, but Aiden couldn't shake the feeling that returning was a mistake, and New York was about to deal them each a life-altering hand.

Aiden hissed a curse and abruptly spun around, giving Ryann his back, but it was too late. He was already hard as a rock, his pulse thundering wildly through his veins, centering in the base of his cock. "I'm sorry, I thought you were still in the shower," he said to the wall. "I wanted to give you your keycard."

"Oh . . . umm . . . you can just leave it on the table. Thanks."

He set the keycard down and had to give his legs a firm command to get their ass moving, all the while his dick pitched a fit like a two-year-old who'd gotten his favorite toy taken from him. "Good night, Ryann." Shit, he sounded like he'd been eating gravel.

"Good night, Aiden."

Something in her voice made him pause. Hesitancy? Disappointment? Who the hell knows. All he knew was that this was killing him, being this close to her and wanting to get closer. But he'd done casual enough times to know that with Ryann, he couldn't pretend it was just sex. Ryann was different. And if he crossed that line, he was going to be entering into uncharted territory. He cared about Ryann—more than he ought to—and if he let himself get closer to her, let himself explore what this was between them, there was a good likelihood he wasn't going to be able to let her go.

How many times had he stepped into the cage and faced an opponent without giving it a second thought? And now here he was, backing down from a midge half his size, because she made him afraid of his feelings? Fucking embarrassing was what this was. If Easton was here, he would have been demanding Aiden's man card. With a self-damning curse, he shut the adjoining door with more force than necessary and beelined it to the shower to try and take the edge off.

*You're effing kidding me!* Ryann put a pillow over her head, trying to drown out the moans and sighs coming from the other side of the wall, opposite the room connecting to Aiden's. The rhythmic banging of the headboard made sleeping in this room absolutely impossible. The screams were unbearable—seriously, was someone killing her in there? If he was, the guy wasn't doing a very good job of it because he needed to do it "more" and "harder."

With a frustrated groan, she lifted her pillow and glanced at the alarm clock—three a.m. They'd been going at it for almost two hours. Was that even possible? Who in their right mind could want to do it that long and that many times? Unbidden, an image of Aiden popped into her mind and she answered her own question.

Her pulse quickened at just the thought of him, and the symphony of pleasure playing out in the room next door heated her blood. She couldn't get comfortable. Her skin felt too tight, the bedsheets too rough. Every one of her nerve endings seemed to tingle with awareness—awareness of the man one adjoining door away. She'd thought he would have tried to come over, but sadly that fighter had a will of steel. In the last two days, something had changed between them. Gone was the arrogant Disco Kruze who seemed to have a mind for one thing and one thing only, and in his place was a complex man who, if she didn't know better, she'd swear was avoiding her.

This was ridiculous. Here she was, lying here and listening to this while a man who would rock her world, and undoubtedly put those two to shame, was no more than twenty feet away from her. Maybe he thought he was doing the honorable thing by keeping his distance. Maybe she'd scared the ever-loving hell out of him with her drunken confession. It didn't matter. Tomorrow they'd be going their separate ways, and she was not going to pass up her last chance to be with him. Maybe he'd send her packing, but she'd never know unless she tried—what did she have to lose?

Throwing back the covers, her feet hit the floor just as the woman in the other room agreed with her.

"Yes . . . ! Yes . . . !"

Ryann rolled her eyes and padded across the floor. She didn't bother knocking before turning the knob. It easily gave to the pressure, and she counted it a good sign he hadn't locked her out. Silently, she slipped inside and closed it behind her—blessed silence. Her heart beat wildly as she approached his bed, her breath frozen in her lungs as she crept closer. The room was blanketed in darkness, except for the nimbus breaking out through the crack in the bathroom door, lighting the room just enough to see an outline of Aiden's big body taking up a good portion of the full-sized bed. What should she do? Should she wake him? Take off all her clothes and slip under the covers with him?

She was weighing her options when his voice startled her.

"What are you doing, Ryann?"

"Aiden, you scared me," she whispered, nervously shifting her weight from one foot to the other. "Did I wake you?"

"No. I haven't been able to sleep."

"Me neither. The couple next door is keeping me up."

"You want me to go say something to them?"

"No, they're umm . . . enjoying themselves. I was wondering if I could, you know, maybe sleep in here? With you?" Her courage started to waver when he didn't respond right away.

"Ryann, I don't think that's a very good idea."

"Why not?"

"Because it's killing me to do the right thing here, and if you get into this bed, I'm not going to be able to stop."

"I wasn't suggesting you do."

"If you think you're going to be able to have sex with me and then just walk away tomorrow like it didn't happen, you're either naïve or you're lying to yourself."

"Think you're that good, do you?" she teased, a poor attempt to lighten the mood. It was a fail.

"I know I am, but that's not the point. Ryann, I've done this enough times to know when something doesn't feel right, or maybe in this case feels too right. You're going to get hurt."

"Listen, Aiden, I've played it safe my entire life. Doing all the right things, following all the rules. And look where it's gotten me—the nice guy cheated on me with my best friend a week before my wedding. I'm nearly bankrupt, and one of the most dangerous men in New York is hunting me down. From where I'm standing, safe and responsible doesn't look quite so good."

"Fuck, Ryann, you're killing me."

The raw honesty in his voice sent a shiver of anticipation up her spine. It was all the encouragement she needed. Ryann pulled her nightshirt over her head and slipped her panties over her hips, letting them fall to the floor. "I'm not under any misconception about what this is, Aiden. I'm a big girl, I know what I'm doing," she whispered as she lifted the covers and slipped in beside him.

He tensed. A tortured groan rumbled in his chest when her hand made a slow trek down his abdomen. "I'm not so sure you do, Ryann. But I'll be damned if I'm going to lie here and explain it to you."

Before her fingers could breach the waistband of his boxers, he caught her wrist in a firm grip and pulled her arm up over her head, pinning it to the mattress as he rolled on top of her. His mouth followed, coming down on hers with zero finesse. A raw, masculine sound rumbled in his throat as his tongue thrust past her lips and commandeered her mouth. He filled her senses and she immediately yielded to him, desperate for more. Either the man was a mind reader, or he really was very good at this, because Aiden anticipated her every want, her every need, before it could take root as thought. He consumed her with ravenous hunger, his lips teasing, his teeth nipping, his mouth devouring . . .

The trail he made down her neck would surely bear the evidence of his touch. He was like a starving man, and she was his last meal. When his head dipped and his mouth covered her breast, sucking hard against the turgid peak, she almost lost it right then and there. His touch was electric, his tongue torturing. Oh, mercy, she was so out of her league with this guy. All she could do was hold on and enjoy the ride.

"You have no idea how badly I've wanted to be inside of you," he groaned, his confession a ragged gasp. "How many cold showers I've endured . . ." His mouth blazed a path down her stomach. "How many times I came by my own hand, thinking of you and wishing you were there to relieve the agony."

Oh, Lord, his wicked confession was like injecting lighter fluid into her veins. She burned up with him. The imagery he painted drove her senseless with desire. The tension coiling tight in her core propelled her hips off the mattress. She ceased processing thought beyond the need to be filled by him. The emptiness inside her became an insidious ache bordering on pain.

"Please, Aiden," she panted, needing . . . needing . . . She didn't know what she needed right now, only that he could give it to her.

"Shhh . . ." he crooned. "I'm going to take care of you, sweetheart, just trust me."

His breath brushed over her glossy lips, wringing a desperate moan from her throat. She didn't even recognize this mindless woman begging him to make her come. Ryann had never behaved so wantonly or with such reckless abandon. She was so close—already hovering on the razor edge of bliss. When Aiden slipped between her parted thighs, forcing them farther apart to accommodate the wide breadth of his shoulders, it opened her to him fully. The vulnerability of lying before him completely exposed, entirely at his mercy, was a heady sensation.

He muttered a curse that sounded more like reverent awe. "You're so fucking beautiful. I don't think you could be more perfect."

She was moved beyond words. Reaching for him, she threaded her fingers through his hair, met his worshipful gaze, and warned, "You keep saying things like that and you *will* make me fall in love with you."

But his response rocked her to her very core. "Would that be such a bad thing?"

What was he saying? Was he telling her this wasn't just sex for him? That he *wanted* her to fall for him? No, not now . . . She couldn't have this conversation with him now. That would change everything. But before she could stop him, Aiden dipped his head and ripped the protest out of her mouth in the form of an unintelligible moan.

The hard ball of his tongue piercing teased the bundle of nerves at the top of her sex as he applied rhythmic suction that sent her crashing over the edge in seconds. She cried out, and her fingers curled into his hair, holding him against her as spasm after blissful spasm wracked her body. Her empty core contracted, still yearning to be filled, leaving her both sated and aching for more. The physical contradictions he stirred in her mirrored her emotional turmoil. Did Aiden have any idea how thoroughly he'd just fucked her?—in every sense of the word?

When he pulled away and crawled off the bed, a horrible sense of déjà vu slammed into her. "Where are you going?" she cried, cursing herself for sounding so needy.

"To get my wallet."

The ambient light from the bathroom outlined Aiden's shadowed form. Lord, he was big. She watched him grab his pants off the floor and dig his hand into a pocket. He swore and then shoved it into the other. When he pulled out his wallet, she noted the hastiness in his movements. He lacked his natural grace. Perhaps she affected him as deeply as he did her. Finding what he was looking for, his wallet hit the table with a *thump* and the crisp sound of a tearing wrapper announced Aiden's intent.

Ryann was suddenly seized with a mixture of anticipation and uncertainty. She knew she wanted him. In her whole life, she'd never wanted a man as badly as she wanted this one, but his comment earlier had rattled her, and a part of her was scared that if she did this, come tomorrow she wouldn't be able to let him go. In seconds he was sheathed and coming toward her, proving his deft efficiency at donning protection.

Aiden must have taken her silence for what it was—second thoughts. When he reached the bed and crawled back over her, he took her face in his hands and gifted her with the sweetest kiss. "You don't have to do this, you know. It's not too late to change your mind."

A part of her wondered if he was hoping she'd chicken out. But she'd meant what she'd said. She was tired of playing it safe. Bottom line, she was falling for Aiden, and regardless tomorrow was going to suck. Letting him go was going to be painful no matter what happened between them tonight, and one thing she knew with absolute certainty: She would never regret being with him.

She slipped her arms around his neck and pulled him closer, opening her legs to accommodate his hips as she deepened their kiss. His spicy masculine scent mixed with her light feminine flora, blanketing them in an intoxicating cocoon of lust. She could taste herself on his tongue, and the intimacy sparked feelings of possessiveness that surged up inside her, catching Ryann off guard. No, there was no doubt about it, after tonight she would never be the same, but she was determined that neither would Aiden.

"I haven't changed my mind," she whispered between kisses. "I want you to make love to me."

# CHAPTER 24

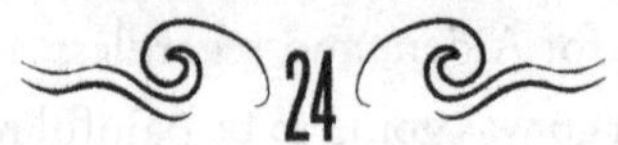

Whoa . . . wait a minute. Is that was she thought this was? *Was* that what this was? It sure as hell didn't feel like just sex, but love?—he wasn't sure. He'd never been in love before. No question he was in lust with her, and he'd be the first to admit he cared about her, but love was crossing a line he wasn't sure he was willing to step over. When he'd asked her if it would be such a bad thing to fall in love with him, it was a question he'd been mulling over ever since she'd told him she was falling for him. They were hastily spoken words he wished he could take back, because the answer had resoundingly been yes.

He needed her to say it, to agree with him that they were a terrible idea. No matter how much the thought might appeal to him, the analytical side of his brain, the side that refused to be ruled by emotion, barraged him with multiple reasons why they shouldn't—couldn't—be together. His life was in Vegas, for one. And Ryann's career was in New York. Aiden would never consider trying a long-distance relationship. Fuck, he didn't even know if he could do a short-distance one. And theirs wasn't exactly the best basis to build a lasting relationship on. This would be one messed-up episode of *How I Met Your Mother.*

But then Ryann tugged him closer and she shimmied beneath him, seating him at her hot, tight entrance. All rational thought fled his mind, and lust rolled through his veins like the backdraft of an inferno. She was wet and ready for him. He'd made sure of that, not wanting to risk hurting her. He wasn't a particularly gentle lover, and she was so damn small, so fragile. Breaking their kiss, he looked down at her, searching her eyes for any hesitation. Reflecting back at him was only trust, and possibly another emotion he couldn't deal with right now. His chest tightened, his heart cramping at the sight of her—so fucking beautiful . . .

There was no doubt or anything else he could cling to in order to convince himself to stop. He wanted her too badly, needed to sink into her too much, to stop now. He nudged his hips forward, pushing himself past her entrance as he kept his gaze locked on her vibrant stare. Though, God's truth, if she changed her mind now, he wasn't sure if he'd have the willpower to stop.

She was so tight, her wet little glove squeezing him unbearably as he inched inside her. He couldn't go faster, not without hurting her, and the pressure building at the base of his spine, the ache of the twin weights between his legs, warned him he wouldn't last long with her this way.

She felt too good—too amazing. Never in his life had taking his pleasure been so . . . perfect. His concern for her comfort forced him to slow down, to savor when he would have plundered and conquered. He gained precious ground with his gentle retreat and advancement. Held captive by her trusting gaze, a well of emotion he wasn't prepared for crashed into him. He wanted this to be as earth-shattering for her as it was for him. If he didn't get a handle on himself, he was going to come like an untried adolescent, and he still had several inches to go.

"Ryann." Her name left his lips on a breathy plea for restraint. "Fuck, I don't want to hurt you, but I'm not sure how much longer I can hold back." Every muscle in his body was strung ripcord tight. His cock throbbed in time with his hammering pulse, each beat building unbearable pressure.

"It's okay," she whispered, wrapping her legs around his hips and inching him farther. Her mouth moved to the thick cords of muscle running down his neck. As she nipped and sucked, kissing her way down his throat, she whispered. "I can take it, Aiden. I promise you won't break me."

"Well, that makes one of us then, sweetheart, because I'm pretty sure you've already broken me."

But he was wrong. It wasn't until she dug her heels into his ass and thrust her hips up, seating him tight against her core, that he truly shattered—into a million fucking pieces. Barking out a sharp curse, he slipped his hands beneath her back, fingertips gripping her slender shoulders as instinct took over. He pulled back and slammed into her once, twice, three times, and then he came harder than he'd come in his entire life. As his cock pulsed against her core, his massive body shuddering over hers, Ryann's orgasm gripped him, squeezing tight and milking every last drop of release from him. Her nails bit into his shoulders, her back arched beneath him, crushing her soft, full breasts against his chest, and her breathy moan broke through the rush of blood pounding in his ears.

As the euphoria slowly began to ebb and Aiden drifted back to reality, one thought resonated in his mind: *Come tomorrow, there is no way in hell I'm going to be able to let this woman go.*

*Oh, Lord, what have I done?* Ryann lay in Aiden's bed, curled in his arms, her back nestled against his solid chest, unable to sleep—which had not been a problem for him. Aiden's slow, rhythmic breaths teased her bare shoulder. How could he sleep at a time like this? Granted it was after four a.m. and they had a long day ahead of them, but in the wake of what they'd just shared, shouldn't they at least have talked about it or something?

Aiden had said precious few words after heading to the bathroom to dispose of the condom and then returned to tuck her against him. She had so many thoughts and questions buzzing through her head, but she kept them all to herself when she sensed an uneasiness about him. Snuggled in his muscular arms, he brushed a kiss against her shoulder and gave her an affectionate squeeze, holding on as if he feared she'd disappear. Was he dreading tomorrow as much as she was?

She tried to sleep but was too wound up to rest. The melee of thoughts running rampant through her mind made her restless and anxious. Just as she'd imagined, sex with Aiden had been amazing. He'd been gentle and considerate, sweet and . . . loving. Though she'd sensed he'd taken a pace with her that had come at great cost to him. It wasn't until the end, when he'd finally let go, that she'd felt a glimpse of what it'd be like to be possessed by this man. He was power and passion all bottled up in a 185-pound package of hard, muscled fighter. Never would she have guessed he would be capable of such tenderness.

Just lying here thinking about it made her want to experience it all over again. She was running out of time, and she felt the tick of each passing second eroding the hole inside her heart. Tomorrow would come soon enough. Snuggling in deeper, she wiggled her bottom against him and felt the instant response of his erection pressing between her thighs. He drew a deep breath behind her and buried his face in her hair as he exhaled a growl. His hand slipped from her breast to travel down her stomach and between her thighs. He parted her folds and slipped a finger deep inside her, his thumb teasing the bead of her sex.

"As much as I want to do this again," he whispered, his voice a throaty rasp against her neck as he nuzzled her shoulder. "I don't have another condom."

Reaching behind her, she took him in hand and stroked his impressive length, forcing her mind to shut down all thought beyond him and her, right here, right now. "I'm on the pill," she offered. "I'm okay with it if you are."

"Are you kidding me? Sweetheart, if I'd known you were good with commando, I would have had you six ways to Sunday by now."

Before her mind could process his movement, she was on her back and being devoured by a soul-searing kiss. Aiden positioned himself between her slick folds and thrust deep, burying himself inside her. The way he filled her, stretching her sheath, was the sweetest blend of pain and pleasure. The pressure of him hitting her core, connecting with her innermost sensitive places, ripped a moan from her throat as a sharp curse tore from his. His oath told her exactly what he intended to do to her.

She arched her back, tipping her hips to put him at just the right angle. Without the latex barrier between them, everything was heightened, stripping away all physical and emotional walls. There was nothing sweet or gentle in the way he took her. And Ryann knew this was going to be a hot, intense ride. A dangerous thrill skittered through her veins as she slipped her hand up to his shoulders, dug her nails into his flesh, and held on for dear life.

Ryann woke to her phone ringing in the next room. When it stopped and promptly started up again, she knew who it was. The sickening feeling of dread settled in her chest like a lead weight, ushering in a slam of reality that wrecked her postorgasmic bliss. Exhaling a groan, she reached behind her for Aiden, wanting to burrow into the safety of his arms and pretend the rest of the world didn't exist—just for a little bit longer. He wasn't there. The place behind her was still warm, his masculine scent clinging to the sheets. A moment of alarm made her pulse leap, and then she heard the shower kick on.

She wasn't ready for it to end, wasn't ready to leave his bed and pretend this hadn't been the most amazing night of her life. Aiden had been every bit as wonderful as she'd thought he would be. He'd been attentive and patient, gentle and wooing at times, and rough and dominant at others. His style in the bedroom was as variable as the aspects of his personality. After making love throughout the night and then this morning, she felt like she knew him better than anyone. And there was no doubt how thoroughly he'd gotten to know her.

With him, she'd discovered things about herself she'd never known. How and where she liked to be touched, how she liked to be handled. She'd lost count of how many times he'd made her come, and was amazed to discover that each time was a unique mind-blowing experience. He was an attentive lover, but a demanding one, as well. His complexity and passion were unlike anything she'd ever experienced before, and something told her she never would again. She loved everything about it—everything about him. *Oh, my God . . .* the thought sent an eruption of butterflies battering abound inside her chest. *I'm in love with Aiden Kruze.*

"Oh, no . . ." she groaned, covering her face with her hands. "This wasn't supposed to happen." She thought she could handle it. Thought she could compartmentalize the sex and keep her emotions out of it. She thought wrong. And it wasn't like she could very well tell him how she felt. No doubt he heard it all the time after taking a woman to his bed. Who wouldn't fall in love with that and become a cling-on? And that was exactly what he'd think of her. He wouldn't believe it was truly him she was professing to love. No, telling him how she felt would be a huge mistake. It'd only further complicate an already touchy relationship.

She knew from experience that Aiden wasn't the kind of guy that wanted to be chased. He didn't respond well to pressure. If Aiden had feelings for her, if he wanted to be with her, to see where this thing could go, he was going to have to do the pursuing. She'd already said too much the other night. Now the ball was in his court. The last thing he needed was her acting like a love-struck cage banger.

The ringing started up again, and she cursed one of Aiden's favorite oaths. Shooting a quick glance at the bathroom door, she offered up a quick prayer of thanks that the shower would likely drown out the noise. The last thing she wanted was for Aiden to get any more involved with her problems. The poor guy had enough of his own without dealing with hers, too. Throwing back the covers, Ryann quickly dressed and returned to her room. She closed the partition door between them just as the ringing ended. With lead in her feet and heaviness in her heart, she drudged over to the bed and grabbed her cell off the nightstand—twelve missed calls.

When the phone began ringing in her hand, she swiped her thumb over the screen and snarked, "What do you want?"

"Good morning, Ms. Andrews. And I think you know full well what I want."

Goose bumps prickled up her arms, revulsion washing away any last vestiges of endorphins flowing through her veins. She feared she did know what he wanted, and decided it'd be best to ignore the innuendo. "I still have four days. You'll have the money."

"Running it down to the wire, are you? Who was the man on the phone the other day?"

When she didn't answer, he pressed, "Do you think taking a lover will keep you safe, Ryann?"

A shiver wracked her spine, dread taking root deep in her gut.

This was the first time he'd used her name, and the familiarity in the way he spoke it made her stomach threaten to revolt.

"I hope you're not trying to run from me, Ryann. Though I do love the thrill of a good hunt."

"I told you, I've been working," she snapped. "Earning the money to pay your boss. You can tell Mr. Moralli he'll have his money. Stop calling me!" She heard the shower in the adjoining room cut off and quickly ended the call. She didn't want to field any more of Aiden's questions. Talking about it wasn't going to change anything. Soon enough, it would all be over, which truly was a bittersweet thought, because saying good-bye to Aiden was going to be one of the toughest things she would ever do.

Tossing her phone on the bed, she grabbed a change of clothes and hurried into her shower. They had another full day of driving ahead of them, and she was already exhausted. The thought of getting home and settling in after almost two weeks on the road held surprisingly little appeal to her. What was there to look forward to?—an empty house full of painful memories that only drove home the direness of her situation. How could she feel safe knowing Moralli had someone watching her? She was behind in her other cases, having had to focus solely on Aiden these past two weeks, and the thought of all the work waiting for her when she got back was overwhelming.

Sighing, she admitted a secret part of her wished they could steal away to Aruba or some remote place where no one would ever find them. *Fuck Moralli, fuck his parents, and FML.*

So on that happy note, Ryann rinsed the shampoo out of her hair, stepped out of the shower, and put on her big-girl panties. No one said it was going to be easy—or even pleasant, for that matter—but she would see this through to the end.

# CHAPTER 25

The knot in Aiden's gut tightened the closer they got to the city. He wasn't sure what bothered him more: parting ways with Ryann or the unpleasant task of dealing with his parents tomorrow, but something wasn't sitting right. The entire time they'd been stuck in this car, she hadn't said a word about last night. And it wasn't like she didn't have plenty of opportunities.

Not a *Last night was amazing* or *I wish it didn't have to end.* Nada. Nor had she tried to get him to talk about his feelings or press him for more of a commitment, something he'd gotten used to women doing after they slept with him, which in part was why he'd made it an unspoken rule never to hit the same hole twice. But something about Ryann was different. Even now, he had a hard time keeping his eyes on the road. His attention kept drifting to that lush mouth of hers, or the pert fullness of her breasts, and his hard-on was depriving his brain of some much-needed blood flow.

Last night *had* been amazing. Hell, he'd say it even if she wouldn't, even if it was to himself and in the silence of his own mind. Everything about Ryann had surprised him—her openness, her passion, her unguarded trust. She'd given herself to him fully, and it'd rocked him to his very core, so why was he having such a hard time telling her? It was ironic, really, because the one woman he wouldn't have minded having that awkward morning-after conversation with hadn't brought it up.

Maybe she hadn't found last night as wow-worthy as he had. Maybe she lacked the experience to know just how once-in-a-lifetime-amazing that sex had been, or maybe she'd never intended for this to be more than a good fuck. Perhaps he was arrogant in thinking that she would be as taken with him as he was with her. She'd dismissed his warnings easily enough—maybe it had been her intention all along to fuck him and forget him.

"You're frowning . . ." she said, watching him from the passenger seat.

"Am I?" he asked noncommittally, glancing at her.

Is there something you want to talk about?"

He shrugged. "Not really. You?" This was her chance. Speak now or forever hold your peace.

"Are you worried about meeting with your parents tomorrow?"

Not the thing he wanted to talk about—Not. At. All. "Not worried as much as just not looking forward to it. But since I'm here, I have some other business to take care of before I head back, so I might as well make the most of it."

"Where are you going to stay?"

Her gaze darted into her lap. Those delicate fingers, with the blunt-tipped nails that had scored his back a few short hours ago, fidgeted nervously.

"I own a condo in Manhattan. I'll stay there."

"Oh . . ."

Was that disappointment he heard in her voice or just wishful thinking? "Why?"

She shrugged. "Just wondering. I didn't want you to have to stay in a hotel while you were here. How long will you be staying in New York?"

"Probably a couple of weeks. Just long enough to list my place and hopefully find a buyer. I'd like to have it sold before I go back. It's my last financial tie here. Where do you live, Ryann?"

"Brooklyn."

He frowned. "Brooklyn?" Holy hell, maybe he should ask *her* to stay with *him*. There weren't a lot of places in Brooklyn he'd deem safe for a woman to live. "And your office?"

"Also Brooklyn."

Now the lawyer in him stood up and took notice, suspicion niggling up his spine as his mind worked to fit the connections together. "Why would my mother, a woman that doesn't set foot outside Manhattan, travel to Brooklyn to hire a private investigator? I'm sure there are plenty of them in Manhattan."

Ryann's shoulders stiffened indignantly. He hadn't meant to offend her, though he obviously had. "Maybe I'm just that good. Have you ever thought of that? I do specialize in missing persons, you know."

"You might be, but unless you found Jimmy Hoffa, you wouldn't have blipped on my mother's radar. There's something going on that either you're not telling me or she's hiding."

"I told you everything I know, Aiden."

The defensive edge in her voice told him either (a) she was telling the truth, or (b) she was a damn good liar. If she was lying to him, her evasiveness today sure would make a whole lot more sense, and it wasn't like she hadn't done it before. And while they were talking about coincidences, what were the chances that they were both connected in some way to Vincent Moralli?

Suspicion seeped into his veins like black, insidious poison. How could he have not seen it before? Was he walking into a trap? It was a brilliant plan, sending a beautiful woman in to snag his attention and then plead for his help to get her out of her bind with

Moralli. How cleverly Ryann had snuck past his defenses and broken down his barriers. If this was a ploy, she would have played him to a tee. And to think he'd been tempted to tell her he had feelings for her. Fuck. But what if he was wrong and Ryann was just as much a victim in all this as he was? Guess only time would tell.

"Why are you looking at me like that?"

"Like what?" he asked gruffly, suddenly ready for this ride to be over and to get some much-needed space between him and his little felon. He couldn't think straight around her. He needed to clear his head.

"Like you don't believe me! You don't, do you? What, you think I'm working for Moralli? Is that it?" she accused.

Seeing as he hadn't suggested it, that was a pretty damn accurate leap not to have a thread of truth wrapped up in it somewhere. Pinning her with his stare, he said, "Are you?"

If looks could kill, the glare she shot him would have stopped his heart cold. "I can't believe you just asked me that. Stop the car."

Was she crazy? They were in rush hour traffic. It was bumper to bumper, and they were moving at a steady twenty-five miles per hour. There was no way in hell he was pulling his car over. Not that he'd have to. Just ahead, brake lights began flashing like a row of falling dominoes, forcing him to hit his own brakes a few seconds later. Just to be sure she didn't do something crazy, he hit the driver's panel power-control button, and not a second too soon. As the SUV ground to a halt, Ryann's hand was on the handle and she was throwing her shoulder into the door. He winced when she slammed her tiny frame into glass.

"Ryann, stop."

She shot him a glare over her shoulder and he'd be damned if she didn't slam into it again. If she was expecting a different result, she'd be sorely disappointed.

"I said stop. You're going to hurt yourself."

"What the hell do you care? If you were worried about me getting hurt, you wouldn't have said what you just did."

"Oh, come on, Ryann, try to see it from my perspective. You gotta admit it doesn't look good. And you've been acting cagey as hell ever since we left that motel this morning. I'd be a fucking idiot not to question it."

"And I was a fucking idiot for ever thinking you could get past my earlier actions and trust me!"

"'Get past it'? Who in the fuck do you think I'm doing this for, Ryann? It sure as hell isn't for my benefit. If I didn't care about what happened to you, I would have left your ass back in Portage! But I swear to God, Ryann, if you're keeping something from me—"

"I'm not! I told you everything I know! Turn right here."

He gave her an arched-brow glance.

"You can take me home and keep the Escape. It's a rental. Just have it returned by Monday."

When they reached the intersection, he turned right. She was throwing off some serious hostility as she navigated him to her place in Brooklyn. Perhaps he was being an asshole, but coming back here, being in this city, was really fucking with his head and giving him a bad case of déjà vu.

He didn't know what to say to make this better. He knew he'd offended her, but dammit, what did she have to be so touchy about? Who could blame him for being suspicious? She could hardly deny something wasn't adding up here. Admittedly, he'd had his mind so focused on getting in her pants that he hadn't given it much of a second thought before now.

"Stop here. It's the first on the left."

He hit the brakes, shifted into park, and the locks automatically unlatched. His pulse quickened, the invisible band around his chest tightening with dread. *Aww shit . . .* What could he possibly say to make this better? Hell if he knew. Relationships were not his forte, not that this was one, but dammit, it was something—something he didn't want to just throw away over a carelessly spoken accusation, whether founded or not.

She turned to leave, and he grabbed her arm. "Ryann, wait—"

"You know what, Aiden, don't bother. I've been dreading this all day. Did you ever stop to think that's why I might not have been myself? I was wondering how I was going to say good-bye to you, especially after last night. But I should actually thank you. You've made it real easy for me. Good-bye."

She jerked her arm out of his grasp and jumped out of the car. There weren't many times in Aiden's life he'd been rendered speechless, and now was a hell of a bad time to have it happen. She yanked open the back door and grabbed her suitcase before slamming it shut and stomping up to her house. Back straight, shoulders stiff, and head held high, she dragged her suitcase on wheels behind her. When it hit the cracked sidewalk, the thing turned and crashed into the back of her leg.

He noted a slight limp in her step and his grip on the steering wheel tightened. It took all his self-control to watch her go and not race after her. *It's for the best*, he told himself. *You don't need this kind of drama in your life. She's just like every other skirt you've crawled up and in a couple of weeks, you won't even remember her name.*

Bullshit—all of it. And if he didn't feel like a complete asshole before, he sure as hell did now.

Ryann let herself into the house and slammed the door behind her. *Don't look back, don't look back*, she chanted, sure if she did, the result would be as disastrous as what happened to Lot's wife. There were far worse things than turning into a pillar of salt, like having your heart torn out and stomped on by the man you'd been foolish enough to fall in love with.

What was she thinking?—clearly, she hadn't been. Foolishly, she'd thought he trusted her, that he'd forgiven her for the manipulation, the lies, and the roofies. Huh . . . when she put it like that, it didn't sound quite as compelling of an argument.

Oddly enough, she'd always prided herself on her honesty, her straight and narrow moral compass. She wasn't proud of what she'd done, nor had she been given much choice. It was in the past, what was done was done, and if Aiden couldn't let it go, then there was nothing more to be said. She didn't know why his mother had hired her. By her obvious surprise in discovering Ryann was a woman, it was clear Madeline Kruze didn't know very much about her. Ryann's and Aiden's connections to Moralli baffled her as much as it did him.

But that suspicion and mistrust in his eyes had come as an unexpected blow. It hadn't been as much what he said but what he didn't say. She knew what he was thinking, could sense the wheels of that clever mind turning. For being such a smart man, he could sure be an idiot sometimes. If he couldn't see how much she cared for him, especially after last night, then he was hopeless and so was a future with him. Better to learn the truth now before she gave any more of her heart to him. It was better like this, she told herself. Make a quick, clean break.

She could still hear the SUV idling on the road. What was he waiting for? Why wouldn't he just go?

It didn't matter. She was done. Flipping the lock on the door, Ryann left her suitcase right where she dropped it and made a beeline up the stairs, straight for the bathroom. What she needed right now was a hot, steamy bath. After pressing the plug into the drain of the antique claw-footed bathtub, she added lavender and rosemary oils to the water and headed back downstairs to pour a tall glass of wine.

Exhaustion blanketed her, and every effort felt like an insurmountable task. After being up all night and traveling all day, the only thing she wanted to think about was soaking away her aches and pains and going to sleep. As she passed the front door, she tried not to look out the side window, refusing to give Aiden another minute of her attention. But the reflection of headlights caught the corner of her eye, giving her pause. She ignored the subtle tug in her heart telling her to stop. She'd be damned if she was going to give Aiden the satisfaction of seeing her staring out the window, pining away for him.

After she got out of the tub, she'd call Madeline Kruze and let her know that Aiden was now in New York. Despite how things were left between them, she had no doubt Aiden would carry through on his agreement to meet with his mother. He knew what was at stake if he didn't. Her job here was done. Dealing with that man was Lady Kruze's problem now.

Ryann shoved the cork back into the bottle of merlot, grabbed her glass, and headed up to her waiting bath. One of the things she loved the most about her family's brownstone was the bathroom. The tub had deep sides, perfect for soaking. It was her number one stress reliever—well, that and a glass of wine—and right now she had 185 pounds of stress to unload. She glanced at her wineglass as she set it on the small table beside the tub, thinking she should have grabbed the whole bottle.

Stripping off her clothes, she eased into the steaming water and sighed. Her muscles were stiff from the long car ride, aching from inactivity, while other places were sore from too much activity. Unbidden, the memory of last night came rushing to the forefront of her mind, ushering in a wave of soul-deep regret—not for what they'd shared together, but for the way things ultimately ended between them.

With a half a glass of merlot warming her insides, and the lavender-rosemary scented bath warming her outside, Ryann sank deeper into the tub and closed her eyes. She thought again of her parting conversation with Aiden. The replay stung no less the second time around. Bottom line: His mistrust in her, whether founded or not, had wounded her deeply. And she hadn't reacted well. Lashing out wasn't typically her style, but when it came to Aiden Kruze, she didn't know herself nearly as well as she thought she did. If someone would have told her three weeks ago that she was going to meet a man, commit a felony, and fall in love, she would never have believed it. Yet here she was, wallowing in heartache and a healthy dose of self-pity. Draining her glass, she set it on the decorative table beside the tub and slipped beneath the water. Well, shit . . . What now?

*Thump!*

The muffled sound sent Ryann bolting upright, breaking through the water with a startled gasp. What in the hell was that? Wiping her hands across her face, she cleared the water from her eyes and strained to listen, but couldn't hear anything past the thundering of her heartbeat. Had the sound come from inside or outside? Was Aiden at the door? Had he refused to leave things like this between them? The thought of seeing him flooded her with a score of mixed emotions. She was still upset, and justifiably so, but Ryann regretted leaving him like she did. What had he been about to say when he'd tried to stop her from leaving the car? She really should go talk to him.

When the knock came again, it spurred her into action. Ryann stood and quickly dried before grabbing the bathrobe hanging on the hook behind her. She slipped into the terry-cloth wrap and rushed across the hall to her bedroom to pull on a sweatshirt and yoga pants. As she descended the stairs, another round of knocking was starting again. When she reached the landing, she peeked outside but could only see the silhouette of his shadow behind the door. Grabbing the knob, she turned the lock and opened the door. "Aiden, I'm—"

Her apology died in her throat when her eyes connected with a man she didn't recognize. Wait, that wasn't true. He looked familiar, she just couldn't place where she'd seen him before. The man was tall, not quite as tall as Aiden, but what he lacked in height, he more than made up for in width. He wore a three-piece suit and a deadpan expression that faltered as his dark brown gaze took a sweeping assessment of her. His top lip curled in wry amusement, not quite passing for a grin.

A shiver of unease needled up her spine, her grip on the door tightening. "Can I help you?"

"Good evening, Ms. Andrews."

That voice . . . Oh, God help her, it was him. Instant dawning registered, the connection clicked into place, sending a surge of adrenaline flooding into her veins. Her father's funeral, that was where she'd seen him before. Ryann pushed the door shut, but the toe of his shoe slipped inside and kept it from closing. With brute strength, the man forced the door open and pushed his way inside. Ryann let out a startled yelp and stumbled back. Turning, she dashed for the stairs, hell-bent on reaching her father's gun, which she kept in the top drawer of her nightstand.

If she could just get to it . . .

A few steps from the top stair, a beefy hand clamped around her ankle and the man jerked her feet out from under her. A terrified scream tore from her throat as Ryann fell—hard. Air exploded from her lungs when her chest slammed into the stairs. Her head cracked against the top lip of the staircase and blackness swamped her vision, stars bursting behind her eyelids as a tidal wave of dizziness crashed into her and dragged her into a sea of oblivion.

# CHAPTER 26

Welcome home, Mr. Kruze."

Aiden froze. The delay in translation from English to understanding left him standing there a moment, staring at the doorman like a complete idiot. God, he was a wreck. Unable to get his mind off Ryann, and how royally he'd fucked things up with her, left him feeling and no doubt looking like a cast member of *The Walking Dead*.

"Thank you, Fredrick," Aiden mumbled in passing. "Wish I could say it was nice to be back."

Forcing one foot in front of the other, he felt like he was walking toward a prison cell instead of approaching his four-million-dollar pad. Stopping in front of the elevator, he hit the Up button, and when the doors slid open he shuffled inside. Turning to the keypad, he entered the six-digit code to his penthouse and stood there numbly waiting for the elevator to take him to the thirty-second floor.

He should call Ryann. See how she was doing and tell her he was sorry for what he'd said. Since leaving her place, he'd been wracking his brain, trying to decide his best course of action. How could he make things right with her? She deserved a hell of a lot more than an apology for doubting her. He'd been hoping he could continue seeing her while he was in town, but before he'd gotten around to asking her, he'd let his suspicions get the best of him. *Note to self: Don't accuse your girl of lying to you without hard-core proof. And whatever you do, don't bring up her past mistakes. That shit's the curse of death right there.*

"Fuck . . ." he groaned, dragging his hand through his hair and looking up at the ceiling. His gaze caught the red light of the camera in the corner. "Hey, that you, Roz?"

"Good evening, Mr. Kruze," the feminine voice called over the intercom. "Is everything all right?"

"Just peachy."

"If you don't mind me saying, sir, I hardly recognized you. I see you've done some redecorating."

He grunted a humorless laugh and subconsciously tongued the hoop through his bottom lip. No doubt he was a sight: piercings through his brow, his lip, his ears, and sleeved in tattoos exposed by an ill-fitting, grungy V-neck. His reflection in the steel doors proved his hair was a wild mess after he'd dragged his hand through it a hundred fucking times since dropping Ryann off. Unless he was heading to the gym, hardly a day had gone by that he hadn't stepped onto this elevator without wearing a suit and looking anything less than 100 percent put together. Right about now, he'd be lucky to hit 30 percent.

"Is this not working for you, Roz?"

"I umm . . . Well, it's just . . ."

Aiden chuckled, a half-hearted rumble in his chest at the woman's shock and obvious discomfort. The elevator came to a stop and the doors slid open. "See ya later, sweetheart." He gave the camera a saluting wave and stepped into the hall.

"Good evening, Mr. Kruze," she responded stiffly. "It's good to have you back."

He wasn't back—well, not for long, anyway. Aiden entered the code to his front door and stepped inside. Kicking off his shoes, he walked into the dining room and emptied his pockets into the decorative bowl in the center of the table—keys, wallet, cell phone . . . Shit, he should really call Ryann. Later, he decided, because yeah, he was pussying out and hoped a little time might help her cool off a bit. Moving on, he took an assessing lap around the place. Everything was just how he left it—still spotless. Good to know the monthly cleaning fees weren't going to waste. The penthouse was so immaculate, there was a do-not-touch vibe all over it, not that the place was warm and welcoming on its best day.

Pristine white walls with an occasional abstract painting placed here and there by his interior designer, adding a splash of color to the otherwise cool and impersonal dwelling. He wouldn't call it a home. There were no family pictures lining the mantel of his fireplace, no personal effects lying scattered around. Aiden stopped as he passed the glass wall in the living room, pausing a moment to take in the Manhattan skyline.

It was one of the few things he loved about this place, and it was the sole reason he'd purchased it three years ago. It was an impressive sight to behold, and one that resonated someplace deep inside him. It was times like this, late at night, where he would stare out the window at the towering buildings, the lighted bridge stretching across the water, and imagine how easy it would be to just disappear. This beautiful view was the one thing he would miss . . .

The phone rang, fracturing the first moment of blessed peace he'd had in days. Muttering a nasty curse, he turned from the window and crossed over to the couch and dropped into a lazy sprawl before lifting the receiver from the docking station on the end table. Caller ID confirmed what he already knew. "Hi, Mom."

"Aiden, you're home. So nice of you to let me know you'd arrived."

Ignoring the barb, he closed his eyes and pinched the bridge of his nose. Damn, he was tired. Right now, he wanted nothing more than to curl up next to Ryann in his king-sized bed and sleep the next two days away. The thought of her sent a pang of regret arrowing into his heart. He really needed to call her. This was ridiculous.

"I just got back. Whatever you want, can it wait until tomorrow?"

"I was calling to let you know the reservation for Pret was moved to ten a.m. Your father has an early meeting—"

"Of course he does." Good to know some things never changed.

"Well then, I'll see you at ten."

"Yep."

She hesitated a moment, giving him the sense she wanted to say something more. She must have thought better of it, because after a long pause, she said, "Good-bye, Aiden." And the line went dead before he could respond.

When Aiden's alarm went off the next morning, he glared at the piece of shit and sandwiched his head in between two pillows. He hadn't slept more than a few hours all night, and at this point, he felt like he was running on pure adrenaline. Ryann was refusing to take his calls. He knew she was pissed, and rightfully so, but there was a part of him that hadn't actually believed this was really the end when she'd said good-bye. Apparently, she was a woman of her word, because four phone calls, two voice mails, and three text messages all yielded the same result—nada. She wouldn't talk to him.

He wasn't used to being on this side of the coin. Usually he was the one doing the avoiding. Fuck, he'd become the clinger. Exhaling a frustrated sigh, he tossed back the covers and planted his feet on the floor. Well, not anymore, he didn't have time for relationship drama bullshit. He had a day chock-full of unpleasantness as it was. He certainly didn't need to add to his shit list of things to do. He planned to meet his parents for brunch, and have a meeting with

Vincent Moralli where he'd settle up Ryann's debt once and for all. Whether she cared about him or not, Aiden wasn't about to let her drive herself into bankruptcy to pay her dead father's debt. Once he squared things away with Moralli, he'd make it clear Ryann was hands off. With her issues put to rest, he could clear his conscience of any last remnant of guilt. Then he could focus on dealing with his own fucked-up mess, and Ryann could get back to her life. If she preferred to pretend he didn't have a place in it, then that was her prerogative. He didn't need a woman complicating his life any more than it already was—no matter how attractive, or beguiling, or utterly amazing she might be.

Aiden stood before the full-length mirror and tugged the slipknot of his tie into place, thinking he might possibly puke. Leave it to Madeline to choose a restaurant he'd have to wear a suit to get in. He snagged the Armani charcoal gray pinstripe coat off the foot of the bed and shrugged it on over his shoulders. At one time, the suit had fit him like a glove—like the thing had been tailored especially for him. Oh, wait, it *had* been. But just like life here, it didn't fit anymore. It was too tight—too confining. His movement was restricted, and the silk cloth around his neck was choking the hell out of him.

Muttering a curse, he reached up and yanked at the collar, gaining another inch of breathing room. Fuck, this sucked. Fastening the jacket button, Aiden stepped back and surveyed the results. His ink might be covered, but he refused to remove his piercings. It might sound crazy, but he felt as if the metal somehow anchored him to his new life when his old one was threatening to drag him back under. His ink and piercings signified who he was and what he'd become. It was bad enough he was back in a monkey suit, but after spending the last fourteen months breaking free of his parents' control, he refused to let his actions be dictated by their approval again.

Dragging his hand through his hair, he let the short, dark strands poke out wildly and took one last look in the mirror. He rubbed his thumb over the red mark on the side of his neck, riding just above the collar of his shirt, courtesy of Ryann. Maybe his mother would be so distracted by all the metal in his face, she wouldn't notice it. It wasn't that he cared what she thought of him; he just didn't want to sit there and have to listen to her carry on.

It pissed him off how much he was dreading this meeting. For crissake, he was a grown man—a middleweight MMA fighter who didn't fear anyone. And here he was, looking at his reflection in the mirror and seeing that ten-year-old little boy all over again, who wanted nothing more than his father's approval and to hear his mother tell him, just once, that she loved him. This was so fucked up. Exhaling a snort of disgust, Aiden turned away from his reflection and told the little boy to quit being such a pussy.

The drive to Pret should have taken less than a half hour, but by the time he navigated traffic, parked, and got inside, he was fashionably late. Before he could tell the waitress his name and which party he was looking for, the woman told him to follow her and led him toward the back of the restaurant. His mother was sitting at a small table for two, her security guards flanking her from behind. She was on the phone as he walked over, her gaze darting up and locking on his. She would be a beautiful woman were it not for that perpetually perturbed expression on her face. His mother didn't crack so much as a smile as he approached. Without removing the cell from her ear, she lifted her wrist and made a point of checking the time before arching her brow at him.

Aiden thanked the waitress and seated himself across from his mother. The woman looked as impeccable as ever. Hair twisted in a tight coif, not a strand out of place. She wore a form-fitting white business suit with silver buttons and matching silver jewelry. As she sat on the phone, eyes that looked like his made a sweeping perusal of his face and a flicker of surprise registered in those dark amber depths before narrowing in disapproval.

"He's here right now. At least I think it's him."

He rolled his eyes at her jab. *Really?* The waitress appeared out of nowhere and set a glass of lemon water in front of him. She offered him a menu but he waved it away. If he ate right now, he was pretty sure he'd puke. Besides, he wouldn't be here that long.

"I will tell him." Madeline disconnected the call and dropped her cell into her Louis Vuitton handbag. "Your father sends his regrets he could not be here. His meeting is running late."

"Of course it is." Was that bitterness souring his voice? Huh . . . he'd thought he was past this pettiness, past the stinging disappointment in having a father who cared more about his career than his son.

"I have good news for you, Aiden," she continued, ignoring his bristling comment. "The wedding is off."

"You say that as if you actually believed it was on. But pray tell, why is it now suddenly 'off'?"

"Cynthia Moralli disappeared three days ago and has yet to return. Apparently, the willful chit wasn't any more excited about the idea of an arranged marriage than you were. Seems she fancied herself in love and eloped. Of course Vincent is furious."

"I'm sure he is. Do you honestly think he's just going to walk away from a ten-million-dollar campaign contribution?"

"He won't have a choice. The dowry is nonrefundable. His daughter breached the contract. Not you."

Aiden didn't bother pointing out that in approximately seventy-two hours he would have done just that. Madeline leaned a little closer and dropped her voice to a hushed whisper. "Rumor has it she was secretly seeing someone from the Lion's Den. Not only is his daughter gone, but he's lost his best fighter. He has a lot more than ten million dollars at stake. He's so furious, he's got his people looking for them everywhere."

*Un-fucking-believable* . . . But the sad thing was, you just couldn't make this shit up. It was like he'd walked into a scene from *The Untouchables.* The Moralli name had roots in this city as far back as the Sicilian immigration in the late nineteenth century. Men like Vincent believed they were above the law, because people like Aiden and his father made them that way. They tied the hands of the legal system, making it damn near impossible for the courts to get a conviction on any charge, and that was assuming they could find a judge not on Moralli's payroll to try their case.

"How do you know all this?"

"Your father has a man working for Moralli who keeps him apprised of certain business. Just because Bennett works with the man, it doesn't mean he trusts him."

"Father shouldn't be working with him at all. The man's a criminal."

She rolled her eyes. "Please, Aiden, don't be daft. You cannot hold the position your father has and wield that kind of power without brushing shoulders with the Cosa Nostra."

"Is that the defense you plan to use in court, Mom? Listen to me. Vincent Moralli is doing things you don't even know about. There is such a thing as guilt by association, and if Moralli ever goes down, do not think for one second he isn't going to take Dad with him. Moralli may like to think so, but he isn't invincible. All it would take is for him to fuck with the wrong person who knows just enough to ruin him."

He let the threat hang in the air. She was a smart woman and her shrewd gaze narrowed on him. "Do not even think about it, Aiden."

He gave a negligent shrug and raised his wrist, pulling back his sleeve to check the time and exposing several inches of ink. Ignoring her surprised gasp, he said, "I have a meeting with Moralli in an hour. It didn't take long for him to discover I was back in town—imagine that. I won't ask you how he found that out. Which brings me to the subject of Ryann. How did you come to hire her?"

Madeline sat back in her chair and busied herself with the napkin in her lap. "She was referred to me."

"By whom?" Her delay in response was all the answer he needed. *Fuck.* It gave him no pleasure to discover he was right. Moralli was behind this. Question is, just how deep did this deception run? "You owe her payment for services rendered."

Reaching across the table, she took hold of his chin and angled his head to the side. It was the first time she'd touched him in as long as he could remember and the unexpected contact surprised him, catching him off guard and rendering him momentarily speechless.

Unfortunately, the same effect wasn't true for her. That hawkish gaze zeroed in on his neck, making him feel all of sixteen again. "That's funny, I don't recall servicing my son to be part of the deal," she snapped, her voice rank with disapproval. It shouldn't have bothered him as much as it did. Hell, he thought he'd be used to it by now. "Just look at you, Aiden. What in God's name have you done to yourself?"

He jerked away from her touch as if she'd burned him. "You'll pay her because she did the job that no one else could do, and she needs the money. Then again, you probably already knew that. And as for this . . ." He pointed to his face. "This is who I am. And for the first time in my life, I was finally happy."

She looked at him as if he was speaking a foreign language. "I don't know who you think you are. But this—" she swept her disdainful gaze over him "—is not my son."

Wow, that hurt a hell of a lot more than he'd expected it to. Pushing back his chair, he cleared his throat, trying to dislodge the swelling lump, and stood. "I'm sorry you feel that way, Mom."

As he turned to leave, she sighed. "Aiden, wait . . ."

But his steps didn't falter, nor did he cast her the briefest parting glance as he walked away. There was nothing left to say.

# CHAPTER

As Aiden headed across town to Vincent Moralli's office, he tried once again to contact Ryann. This time her cell rolled right over to voice mail, which meant either she'd shut the thing off or it was dead. *Shit . . .*

"Hey, Ryann, I umm . . . Fuck, I don't want to do this over a message, but it doesn't look like you're going to give me any other option here. Listen, sweetheart, I'm sorry about yesterday. I was out of line. I shouldn't have said what I did, and umm . . . I'd like to see you. I'm about to head into a meeting with Moralli so . . . I'll stop by when I'm done here."

He disconnected the call just as he was pulling into the parking ramp. Whoever said crime didn't pay obviously wasn't doing it right, because this place was swank. Moralli lived in the penthouse and ran his business in the offices below. The guy had his hands in so much shit, he'd practically turned the Cosa Nostra into an enterprise. Some of his businesses were truly legit, which helped front for his more lucrative and illegal ventures. After years of working for the man, Aiden was confident there was a hell of a lot more going on than even he knew about. But back then, he preferred to keep it that way—deniability was key.

As Aiden pushed the button and the elevator doors slid closed, he forced aside all thoughts of his meeting with his mother, his issues with Ryann, and focused solely on preparing for his meeting with Vincent Moralli. He was a pro at blocking out shit—he'd been doing it all his life. Stepping into this elevator was the same as stepping into the octagon. Over the months, he'd honed the skill of becoming singularly focused on nothing but the opponent in front of him, and he'd be a fool if he didn't count Moralli as his most dangerous one yet.

In fact, he was safer in the cage than he was with this man. At least in the cage they had rules, and a ref and judges. When preparing for a fight, Aiden had the chance to study his opponent's moves and learn his weaknesses. But walking into Moralli Enterprises after being out of this game for over a year, Aiden couldn't shake the feeling he was about to be blindsided. He hadn't been home for even an hour last night before he'd gotten the call from Frank Luciana, Moralli's enforcer, requesting a meeting. He had no clue what this guy could possibly want, but whatever it was, Aiden was pretty sure it wasn't to offer him his old job back. Were it not for settling up Ryann's debt, he wouldn't have agreed to come. Whatever this bastard wanted with him, it wasn't good.

The elevator chimed its destination and the doors slid open. Tension strung his muscles tight; restless energy hummed beneath his flesh with the familiar prickle of anticipation. He was ready to get this meeting over with and was anxious to see Ryann. As he stepped into the hallway and turned left, the industrial carpet absorbed the sound of his brisk, determined steps, though he had no doubt Moralli was aware of his presence the moment he set foot in the building.

Aiden gave the receptionist a curt nod as he walked past, heading for Moralli's office. "Mr. Kruze!" she cried, jumping up from her desk. "Wait!" She chased after him, shuffling on her high-heels. What did she think she could do to stop him? "You can't just walk in th—"

His hand was on the knob and he was halfway through the door when the woman finally caught up to him. Aiden had never treaded lightly around Moralli and he wasn't about to start now. Vincent was sitting behind his desk. At the intrusion, his head snapped up and the scowl darkening his face eased ever so slightly when his eyes locked on Aiden.

"It's all right, Ms. Porter, Mr. Kruze has an appointment." The woman faded into the background and Aiden closed the door behind him. Vincent's gaze darted to the clock on the wall. "You're early. I wasn't expecting you for another twenty minutes."

Aiden shrugged. "My other meeting didn't last as long as I was expecting."

"Please," Vincent said, sweeping his hand toward the empty chair across his desk. "Have a seat." The man's grin was more a showing of his teeth than a smile. Zero warmth filled his eyes as he attempted to appear amiable, but Aiden knew him well enough to see through the false charm. "How are you?" The chair creaked as the man leaned back, stretching out behind his desk. He folded his hands in his lap, fingers steepled, as he waited for Aiden to answer.

He fought the instinct to tense under the man's watchful gaze. Guys like Moralli got off on power and intimidation, and Aiden refused to cow before anyone. Keeping his posture at ease, he returned the man's assessing stare. The light gray suit matched the silver streaks in his dark brown hair. He'd lost weight in the past months, making his custom-fit Fioravanti not so custom anymore. He'd almost wondered if the man was ill, but the dangerous spark in those eyes hadn't dimmed a bit.

"I've been better," Aiden told him in all honesty. If there was one thing the man detested, it was being lied to. He wasn't here to make an enemy, he was here to settle Ryann's debt and be on his way. Aiden reached into his pocket and pulled out a check, setting it on the desk and sliding it forward.

The man's brow rose curiously. "What is this?" he asked, unfolding his hands to pick up the check.

"It's Ryann Andrews's debt. I'm paying it in full. In exchange, I want you to call off your dogs and leave her alone."

The smile that twisted the man's mouth sent Aiden's instincts firing, adrenaline flooding his veins.

Taking great care, and with deliberate, purposeful movements, Vincent held up the check and slowly tore the paper in half. Placing the two pieces together, he ripped it again, and again, and again before letting the small squares flitter to his desktop like pieces of confetti.

"You really have no idea, do you? For an honors Harvard Law grad, you sure are stupid."

Aiden's jaw clenched with the effort to remain in his seat when every impulse inside him was clamoring to slam his fist into this bastard's jaw. "Excuse me?"

"What makes you think this is about her? That any of this was ever about her? I don't give a fuck about seventy-five grand. I wipe my ass with seventy-five grand. Ryann is a pawn. Her dad was a pawn. Sure, the guy liked his booze and gambled a bit too much, but he was a good PI. Found a lot of people for me, and since you're here now, it looks like the apple didn't fall far from the tree."

"How did you know she'd get me to come back?"

He shrugged. "I didn't. But I'm a gambling man, and given the chance to tap that ass, there isn't any place *I* wouldn't follow that pussy. You and I, we're not so different, Aiden."

Rage boiled up inside him. Was it true? Had Ryann been working for Moralli the whole time? Manipulating him, using him to get what she wanted? Fuck! The armrest creaked under the pressure of his tightening grip. Tension strung every muscle in his body ripcord tight, and he waged an inner battle to control the fury coursing through his veins. Never in his life had he wanted to wrap his hands around a man's neck and squeeze the life out of him more than he did right now.

"I don't know what lies she's told you, but this isn't about her. It's about you. I've been grooming you for this business for too fucking long to just let you walk away. I expect a return on my investment. If you thought it was going to be that easy to turn your back on the family, then someone obviously didn't explain the rules to you very well."

"What do you want?" he growled.

"What do I want?" he barked, the already loose rein on that notorious Moralli temper slipping. "Let's start with what I *did* want, Aiden. I have no sons—just one willful, unappreciative daughter. But I loved you like a son, and you betrayed me." He spread his arms wide. "All this could have been yours. But instead you turned your back on me. You refused my offer to join the family, and my bitch of a daughter has just signed the death warrant of my best fighter.

"But fear not!" Vincent proclaimed, pointing to the ceiling as if stuck by a sudden epiphany. "I am a resourceful man. You have made quite a name for yourself in Vegas, my friend."

Tension rocketed through Aiden like a hurricane. *Oh, hell no.* He knew where this was going and planned to nip that idea before the seed could even begin to take root. "I'm not fighting for you," Aiden interrupted. Sitting across from this man was like staring down the barrel of a loaded gun, waiting for him to pull the trigger.

"Ryann's in love with you. Did you know that? Yeah, I can tell by the look on your face this is news to you. Came as quite a shocker to me, too. Looks like my little pawn just became a whole lot more valuable."

And there it was—the metaphorical blast that deafened him, piercing his chest and tearing his heart to shreds. *Fuck* . . . Whether or not he spoke true, it didn't matter. The pain tightening the invisible band around his chest, making it impossible to breathe, forced Aiden to admit his own feelings. He was in love with a woman who had quite possibly betrayed him to Moralli, and the sick fuck was watching his reaction with a predator's glee.

"You will fight for me and you will win. You don't need me to tell you how much money is on the line with these fights—how much money I personally stand to lose if they don't happen. You will take over Broden Hayes's fight roster."

This guy was out of his mind. "No fucking way. I'm not fighting for you."

The sadistic chuckle echoing in the room cemented Aiden with cold, hard dread. "I thought you might say that." Vincent reached over, pressed the intercom button on his desk, and spoke into the small black box. "Bring her in."

A moment later the door flew open, and Ryann was thrust inside by a man easily twice her size. Aiden immediately recognized the bastard and muttered a foul oath under his breath—Frank Luciana—Vincent Moralli's right-hand man. He was the puppet master who pulled the strings for Moralli, doing the bastard's dirty work. If Moralli wanted someone dead, this was the guy who would see it done.

"Watch it!" Ryann snapped, stumbling forward. She shot a scathing glare over her shoulder at Luciana, who looked wholly amused by her anger. The only thing keeping her upright as he dragged her farther into the room was his big, meaty hand clamped tightly around her bicep. She didn't see Aiden standing across from Moralli, her fury focused solely on the bastard manhandling her.

Rage detonated inside Aiden like an atomic bomb. "You motherfucker!" He exploded from his chair, launching himself across the desk.

"Aiden!" Ryann cried, her bravado slipping, voice cracking with desperation.

Papers scattered and the computer crashed to the floor, but before he could get his hands around that fucker's throat, the distinct snick of a gun stopped Aiden dead, and Ryann's startled yelp sent icy shards of fear lancing into his heart.

"I don't think you want to do this," Vincent sneered with the calm of a man who held every fucking card in the deck. "Not unless you want your beautiful girlfriend's brains splattered all over that wall." He nodded to the left.

"Let her go." The feral snarl tearing from his throat made him sound more animal than man. His mind raced with options, his terror for Ryann threatening to paralyze him. He knew Moralli wouldn't kill him—he needed him to fight—but Ryann was another story. She was Aiden's weakness, and the bastard knew it. What had Ryann told him? His heart rioted in his chest, muscles straining with the instinct to protect what was his, even when the bitter sting of Ryann's betrayal was like poison running through his veins.

"I'll let her go . . . once you sign this." Vincent opened the top desk drawer and pulled out a stack of papers, slapping them onto the desk.

"What is it?" he demanded, snatching up the document.

"A contract. It basically says that I own you. You now fight for me."

The man was insane if he thought Aiden would ever work for him again—especially now. They both knew a contract signed under duress was worthless, but he also knew it was Moralli's way of cowing him. The symbolism behind it was the same as forcing a submission in the cage. Moralli was making him tap. And if he didn't, Ryann was going to pay the price. He didn't have a choice but to do it, not when Luciana had a fucking gun pressed into Ryann's temple. The only thing that mattered right now was Ryann and getting her the hell out of here. And if he had to sign a piece of paper to make that happen, then so be it. That bastard didn't realize who he was fucking with, and in that moment, Aiden made a vow that if it was the last thing he ever did, he was taking Vincent Moralli down.

"Give me a goddamn pen," Aiden barked, holding out his hand.

The triumphant grin on Vincent's face would have made the Cheshire Cat jealous.

As soon as the Bic found his hand, Aiden scribbled his signature on the back page and slapped the document into Moralli's chest. The man caught it and nodded to Luciana to let Ryann go. The moment he released her arm, she ran toward Aiden and threw herself into his arms.

"I'm so sorry! Aiden, I didn't know . . ."

Whether that was true or not, it hardly mattered now. And this wasn't the place to discuss it. With a death glare shot over his shoulder at his new employer, he ushered Ryann toward the door. As they passed Frank, Aiden paused long enough to growl, "You touch her again and I'll fucking kill you."

When they reached the door, Vincent's voice rang out loud and taunting. "And just so you know, your first fight is tomorrow night. If you don't show for a fight, we will find Ryann and kill her. This is your only warning. Stop by my secretary's desk on the way out. She has a copy of the contract and a fight schedule waiting for you. See you in the cage."

# CHAPTER

28

*Oh, God . . . oh, God . . . oh, God . . .* she repeated the panicked plea over and over. Aiden must hate her . . . How could he not? Whether intentionally complicit or not, she'd done that devil's bidding. It was her fault for bringing Aiden here, her fault he was being forced to fight for Moralli. She knew how bad it looked. There was no way she could ever convince him of her innocence now.

Ryann sat in the passenger seat and tried not to throw up. In all the time she'd known Aiden, she'd never seen him look as murderous as he did right now. Silence was never so loud. She snuck a quick glance at him as he navigated the streets of Manhattan. She would have asked him where he was going but didn't dare speak. He had a white-knuckled grip on the steering wheel. His jaw was clenched so tight it made the little muscle in his cheek tick. Fine lines bracketed his mouth, and his lips were thin with barely suppressed rage. She desperately wished he would say something—anything. It was the silence that was killing her.

Everything about this man screamed Do Not Touch! Yet all she wanted to do was throw herself in the shelter of his arms as she tried to block out the past eighteen hours.

She'd been so sure she was going to die. If the head injury she'd gotten from the man called Frank didn't kill her first, surely that massive brute still would have. Ryann had no way of knowing how long she'd been out. She'd woken in a modestly supplied bedroom with the door locked. Shortly after regaining consciousness, Vincent had arrived and begun questioning her about Aiden, and oddly about her father—where he'd kept his records and his client lists. None of which she knew the answer to. Her father had always kept his work confidential. And now she knew why.

Her mind was still reeling. She couldn't believe it . . . her father had been working for Vincent Moralli. Why? Why would he do something like that?

Of course . . . the gambling debt. And now Moralli was using her father's debt to manipulate her, too. *Oh, my God . . .* She realized with horrifying clarity that he never wanted the debt paid! He was just using the deadline as a bargaining chip. It was the only way she would have agreed to take Aiden's case—and he knew it. Moralli was banking on her ability to convince Aiden to come back with her. Since the two men before her had tried and failed, he'd had to switch tactics.

Oh, Lord, she was going to be sick. A wave of nausea surged up inside her, her stomach clenched, and the bitter sting of bile burned her throat. Moralli was right, she really was nothing but a pawn—a pawn to be used against Aiden.

She wouldn't blame Aiden if he never wanted to see her again, never wanted to speak to her again. The thought sent a sharp pang of regret piercing her heart, her breath catching in her throat. The sudden hitch of movement didn't escape Aiden's notice. His hard amber gaze briefly darted her way before returning to the road. "Are you all right?"

No. No, she was not. Her head was killing her and the knot along her temple was throbbing in time with her heart, which happened to be shattering more and more with each passing minute that Aiden refused to speak to her.

"I'm fine," she lied, not wanting to draw any more attention to herself. She couldn't possibly feel more horrible about what happened.

The muscle in Aiden's jaw ticked. She was coming to realize it was his tell for *I'm about to lose my shit.* He turned the full strength of that amber stare on her and she never wanted to be a shrinking violet more in her life. It was a good thing they'd hit the highway taking them toward Brooklyn and it was a light traffic day, because that man's attention was not on the road.

"When are you going to start being honest with me, Ryann? For fuck's sake, I see you're not all right. I'm not all right. Nothing about this goddamn mess is all right!"

She lifted her shaky hand to cover her mouth, holding back the sob that threatened to break free. "I'm sorry . . . You're right. I'm so sorry, Aiden! I had no idea this was going to happen or I never would have brought you here, I swear. And I know how bad this looks. I wouldn't believe me either, but I swear to God I didn't know. I didn't find out the truth until today!"

"What truth is that? That your debt is unpayable? That your father worked for Moralli? Or that you work for the bastard, too? You're a smart woman, Ryann. I find it hard to believe that you didn't know this!"

He'd never yelled at her before. Of all the things she'd done to him, all the lying, the manipulation, even drugging him, Aiden had never been this angry. "Just answer me this, was it the plan all along to get me to fall in love with you?"

A broken sob escaped her throat at his question. It fractured her on so many levels, all she could do was force air in and out of her lungs. That he could believe she would be capable of such manipulation, such deceit, broke what was left of her heart. Telling her he loved her was a bittersweet confession that rendered her speechless.

A small flicker of hope bloomed inside her, flickering like a candle trying to stay lit in the torrential storm of his rage.

But he mistook her shocked silence for guilt and snarled, "You can't even give me that, can you?"

"No!" she cried. "You don't understand, there was no plan! I wasn't trying to manipulate you to love me. I had no idea you even felt that way until two seconds ago! And I don't expect you to believe me, but I love you, too. I fell in love with you the night you took me out to dinner and let me see who you really are. I fell in love with you when you refused to sleep with me because you didn't want me to think you were taking advantage of me. I fell in love with you when you held my head out of the toilet because I drank two bottles of wine. I love you so much and I'm terrified I'm going to lose you because I *know* how bad this looks!"

She didn't realize they were stopped until the cars passing by began rocking the SUV. Aiden's amber stare was locked on her, his expression giving nothing away as to what was going on in his mind. But she was seconds from losing it. She rushed to say her piece before she dissolved into a sobbing mess. "Your mother hired me to find you and bring you back to New York. I didn't know Moralli was behind this. I'm sorry . . ." The last part was lost as she finally broke down, mourning for the loss of her father and the illusion of a hero he never was. She resented the mess he left behind, and the helpless situation she was now stuck in with Vincent Moralli. She regretted like hell the mistakes she'd made with Aiden and for ruining what could have been the best thing in her life.

It took her several minutes to realize she was caged in the strength of arms. Her fists were gripping the lapels of his suit as she soaked his black silk shirt with her tears. Her forehead rested against the solid plane of his chest. Each shuddering breath dragged his scent deeper into her lungs until it seemed his very essence infused her soul, giving her his calming strength.

"Shhh," he whispered. "Sweetheart, don't cry. We're going to figure this out. I promise. Just trust me . . . Can you do that?"

She nodded against his chest, unable to speak past the lump in her throat. His head dipped and his lips brushed against her cheek . . . her forehead . . . When they grazed her temple she winced and Aiden growled a nasty oath. His hands cupped her face, tipping it up for inspection. His brows drew tight in a pinched scowl as his fingers slipped into the hair at her temple, carefully probing.

*Ouch!*

She shrank back from his touch, but he persisted, gently parting her hair for a closer look. His scowl deepened. "You're hurt. What in the hell happened, Ryann?"

Wow . . . and she'd thought he looked angry before. There was Aiden mad at *her*, and then there was Aiden mad at the *world*. The severity in him was like night and day.

"How did you get hurt?"

Suddenly, his hands were all over her—in her hair, checking her scalp for any other bumps or bruises, feeling along the back of her neck, the sides of her throat, his thumbs tracing the curvature of her clavicles. He touched her with the deft efficiency of a fighter who'd performed more than one quick exam on an injured partner.

"Aiden, stop. I'm fine," she said, reaching up to grab his wrist before his hands-on inspection could go past her shoulders. It didn't matter that he didn't intend for it to happen, his touch was turning her on, and this was not the time to get those emotions involved.

"Who did this to you?" he demanded.

"The man Moralli called Frank. He came to my house last night. I opened the door when he knocked. I thought . . . I thought he was you." She shrugged. "He wasn't. I tried to run upstairs to get my father's gun, but he caught my ankle and I fell. I hit my head on the stairs. That was the last thing I remember until Vincent came to the room they locked me in and questioned me about you and my dad."

"Fuck . . ."

Yeah, that pretty much summed it up, all right.

"You sure you're okay? Head injuries can be serious."

"I'm fine. The spot is tender and I have a headache, but it's manageable. I'd just really like to go home. It's been an exhausting day."

"I'm taking you home so you can pack your bags. It's not safe for you to stay there, Ryann. You're coming back with me. My place isn't impenetrable, but it's a hell of a lot safer than where you're living right now."

"Wow, you make the offer sound so romantic. How can a girl refuse?" It was a pitiful attempt at humor, but it was all she had to give.

Aiden did his part by giving her a lopsided grin and shrugging. "What can I say, I *am* Disco Kruze. I do have a way with the ladies."

A bubble of laughter burst out at his comeback, and, man, did she need that. It gave her hope she didn't have thirty minutes ago, and a sense that although their situation looked pretty hopeless right now, they were in this together and they were going to get through this—together.

"Wow . . . Aiden, the view from here is amazing! You can see Ellis Island!" Ryann's voice echoed through the penthouse. The open floor plan made the already spacious place feel huge. From where she stood in the living room, she could see the kitchen, the dining room, the foyer and the hallway that led to his office, the bathroom, and three bedrooms. The last room was a master suite he'd converted into a gym. Which, knowing Aiden, actually didn't surprise her at all.

After giving her a brief tour, he deposited her bags in the spare bedroom across from his. She wasn't expecting him to try to move her into his room and told herself not to let it sting that he hadn't offered. She liked the idea of having her own space, but she liked the idea of spending her nights in Aiden's bed even more.

She wasn't naïve enough to think that one heartfelt confession of love blurted in the middle of an emotional breakdown was going to repair the damage done to his trust. She'd have to earn that, and although she was innocent of much, she was guilty of plenty, and Aiden wasn't the kind of man that was ruled by his heart. He was intellectual and calculated in both his thoughts and his actions. He wasn't a man to give his feelings a vote. Though she had no doubt that he cared for her, he was a master at building walls, and she feared the progress she'd made during their journey to New York had been completely undone by Moralli—just one more thing that bastard had taken from her . . .

After showing her around, he headed to his room, shedding his suit on the way as if he couldn't get out of the thing quick enough. She wouldn't think about how gorgeous he looked in that charcoal-gray pinstripe with the black silk shirt. That he'd left his piercings in added an element of badass to the contradictions that were Aiden Kruze. She loved his complexity, she loved his depth—she loved . . . him.

Sighing, she turned away from the wall of glass and did another slow take of his home. Plush rugs broke up the dark marble flooring that appeared to be variegated shades of maroon and black. The place was sparsely yet elegantly decorated. It was nothing like she pictured Aiden's home would be. She found herself smiling as she thought of the first time she'd seen him at the gym. If someone would have told her then that this place belonged to that man, she never would have believed it.

The cool feel of the place didn't surprise her, or the lack of personal effects. In fact, she'd yet to find so much as a degree on the wall or a photo on a shelf. The most personal thing she could find was the floor-to-ceiling bookshelf lining one of the living room walls, opposite the stone wall fireplace. Slowly, she made her way to the mahogany case and ran her finger along the wooden shelves as she scanned the titles. Most of them were law books, but then she found the shelf she was looking for—his leisure reading. *The Catcher in the Rye*, by J. D. Salinger. She pulled the book from the shelf and turned it over. Interesting . . .

She slid the book back into its home and pulled out the one beside it. *East of Eden*, by John Steinbeck. Deep and dark . . . she wasn't surprised this would appeal to him. Ryann replaced the classic novel and pulled out a third. *The Art of War*, by Sun Tzu . . . Hmm . . . *"Conflict is an inevitable part of life, but everything necessary to deal with conflict wisely, honorably, and victoriously, is already present within us."*

"Ryann . . . ?"

She startled at the sound of Aiden's voice, much closer than she was expecting. How long had he been standing there watching her? She hadn't even heard him approach.

"Cripes, you scared the crap out of me!" she exclaimed, putting the book back before turning to face him. Now she knew what had taken him so long. He was freshly showered, the dampness in his hair turning the dark spiky strands black. The gray graphic T he wore was threadbare and had a faded yellow Batman emblem across the chest. It was so classic male and yet it had such a boyish charm, she bit the inside of her lip to hold back her grin.

What was not boyish, however, was the way said T-shirt clung to all those chiseled contours and hard muscles. That was all man—100 percent pure male fighter, to be exact—and Ryann found it difficult not to stare. It was such a sharp contrast to the couple-thousand-dollar suit he'd had on less than an hour ago. His loose-leg black sweats hung low on his hips, the bottom hem brushing over the tops of his bare feet.

Ryann couldn't decide which was hotter, the suited-up lawyer or the dressed-down fighter. One thing was for certain: Aiden couldn't look more out of place in his own home if he tried. She felt like she needed to get dressed up just to sit on the couch. Perhaps the transparency of her thoughts was a bit too obvious, because Aiden gave her a crooked grin and said, "I know it's a lot to take in, but you'll get used to it."

*What?* She stared at him a moment, dumbstruck. And then her brain reengaged and she started laughing. "Oh, you mean the penthouse. Yeah, it is . . . impressive."

The wicked grin he gave her sent a rush of heat into all her feminine places. "What did you think I was talking about?"

"Never you mind. Your ego doesn't need any more stroking." She tried to move past him, planning to get unpacked and then head into his office to try and get some work done, but Aiden caught her arm before she could get away and gently dragged her back to stand in front of him.

"My ego isn't what I want you stroking."

Butterflies battered around inside her chest, making it difficult to breathe as his amber gaze raked over her. Under the scrutiny of his gaze she felt naked and exposed, both physically and emotionally. She wasn't sure she could handle any more of him, not after the day she'd had. A part of her wanted to throw herself at him like a shameless wanton, while another part wanted to run for the hills and try to protect the last vestiges of her raw, exposed heart.

Aiden dipped his head, coming close enough she could smell his spicy, masculine scent. The olfactory foreplay teased her senses, heightening all the others—the feel of his touch on her arm, the husky sound of his voice, ignited a slow burn of desire, making her core ache to be filled. She knew how good it could be, knew how easily he could make her come apart for him. Yet, something was holding her back. Fear? Self-preservation? She didn't know. All she knew was that everything between them had changed. And if she gave herself to Aiden again, there would be no holding back and this man would own her—body and soul. She wasn't ready to give him that kind of power, especially when she wasn't sure he was capable of giving it in return. Not if he couldn't fully trust her.

Perhaps he sensed her hesitation. Maybe he had reservations of his own, because he didn't give her a chance to respond before releasing her arm and heading down the hall. A moment later, the door shut behind him, and she heard the dull, rhythmic thud of the heavy bag start up.

# CHAPTER

Aiden always did his best thinking with his fists, and he was counting on this time being no different. *Fff-fff . . . fff-fff . . .* He concentrated on his breathing as he let his fists fly, connecting with his bag in one-two combos, high kick, low kick, spinning backfist. He ignored the persistent ache in his shoulder and laid into another round of striking. It was just one more thing he didn't need to deal with right now.

One goddamn day . . . That was how long he had before stepping back into the cage. He knew nothing about his opponent or fighting in the underground circuit, except there weren't a lot of rules. It was no-holds-barred shit, and if he got caught fighting unsanctioned, his career with the Cage Fighting Association was going to be over. *Fuuuck . . .* How in the hell was he going to prepare for a fight so quickly? When the answer came to him, he forcibly dismissed it and tabled that problem to move onto another.

Ryann . . . Just the thought of her made his chest cramp. Despite everything Ryann had been through today, she was holding herself together remarkably well. The fighter in him recognized a kindred spirit when he saw it, connecting them on a level that quite honestly scared the shit out of him. He wasn't someone ruled by his will or his emotions, yet since Ryann burst into his life, he felt like he'd been stuck on one never-ending emotional roller coaster.

She was his number one priority—his first and foremost concern. Bottom line: Despite how bad it looked, Aiden believed she was telling him the truth. Her dad hadn't been the man she'd thought, and to learn the truth—that he'd been working for the Mafia—had to have been a devastating blow to take. Aiden remembered how shitty he'd felt when he discovered how deep his own father was in with Moralli, and that Bennett expected Aiden to take over his client base as he pursued his career in politics.

Aiden had no idea what Ryann's father had done to piss Vincent off so royally, but the consequences had been severe. Keeping Ryann safe and away from Moralli wasn't going to be easy, and neither was taking Vincent Moralli down. But make no mistake, that bastard was going to pay. That arrogant son of a bitch had finally fucked with the wrong guy, and Aiden would be damned if he was going to spend the rest of his life constantly watching over his shoulder.

No, this was going to end—for his and for Ryann's sake. She deserved a shot at happiness, a chance at having the life she wanted. Whether or not that included him in it, they'd have to figure that out later, he guessed. But right now, the question was how in the hell he was going to accomplish watching over Ryann, prepare for a fight, and still figure out how to destroy Moralli.

When the answer returned, as persistent as before, Aiden muttered a nasty curse and slammed his fist into the heavy bag.

"Hey, man, how's our little cage banger?"

"Real funny, asshole. How's your ribs?"

"Not too bad. So where the fuck are you? Sparring these pansies is boring as hell." Metal weights clanked loudly in the background and someone yelled "Fuck off, Nikko." But he kept on talking. "I was starting to wonder if Gingersnap didn't pull some *Silence of the Lambs* shit on you. You know, 'It puts the lotion on its skin.'"

Despite himself, Aiden laughed. What in the hell was he thinking? It wasn't too late to change his mind and say sayonara to this prick, but as much as Aiden hated to admit it, he needed Nikko Del Toro. They hadn't known each other very long, but in the months Easton had been out on medical, they'd become sparring partners. Aiden figured he knew the guy about as good as that surly bastard let anyone know him, so yeah, they were friends—he guessed.

"Listen, I'm in Manhattan and I really could use your help."

Silence.

*Ah hell* . . . "You there, man? Fuck, I knew this was a mis—"

"What kind of help are we talkin' about?"

All trace of humor was gone from the fighter's voice. With the flip of a switch, Nikko could turn stone-cold, emotionless—ruthless. Aiden had witnessed it more than once and been on the receiving end of it in the cage when shit got too real. But he'd never asked and he didn't judge. Sure, he'd heard the rumors, the talk going on behind the fighter's back, and a whole lot of speculation about how he got those scars, but Aiden had stayed clear of it.

"The kind of help only you can give me, I suspect."

"What the hell is it you think I do, man?"

Aiden could hear the tension in the fighter's voice, the defensive edge a sharp, warning growl to tread lightly. *Fuck it . . . in for a dime, in for a dollar, right?* "MARSOC stuff."

Nikko snarled an oath and Aiden tensed, preparing to get an earful. "First of all, I ain't into that shit anymore. I left the Special Forces two years ago. Second of all, I don't talk about MARSOC. You assholes do enough of it around here for me—"

"Hey, don't you dare lump me in with that group of vaginas. Your shit is your shit, man, and I don't need the deets. But Ryann is in trouble and I need your help. Believe me, I wouldn't ask if I had any other choice, but you're my sparring partner, so partner the fuck up."

"Wait, hold up. What do you mean Ryann is in trouble?"

"I mean someone snagged her yesterday and I'm damn lucky I got her back. I'm about to go toe to toe with some really bad guys here. I can't be with her all the time, and until this shit gets resolved, I don't want her alone. I need you to come out to Manhattan and help me watch out for her. If these guys discover what I'm up to, shit is going to get ugly fast. Oh, and did I mention I'm fighting tomorrow night and I need someone I can trust to corner me?"

"The fuck you say? That shoulder of yours is in no condition to fight, and if you get caught brawling outside the CFA, you can kiss your career good-bye."

Aiden closed his eyes and pinched the bridge of his nose. There wasn't anything Nikko could say that he didn't already know. "My shoulder will hold. And I don't have a choice. These guys are the real deal, man. Told me they'd kill her if I don't fight, and I have zero doubt that bastard would carry through."

"What the fuck are you still doing in New York, man? This is crazy. Get her the hell out of there!"

"I can't. It isn't that easy. My family is involved, and this is the goddamn mob we're talking about, man. If I screw this guy over, he won't quit until he finds her and me. We'll constantly be looking over our shoulders, and I'm not running. This shit stops here. I'm going to take that bastard down. But until I do, I have to play his game by his rules, which means I fight. I can't do this if I'm worried about her. I need you to help me keep Ryann safe. But here's the thing—if she finds out you're here watching out for her she's going to be furious. Right now, she's agreed to stay with me until this is over, so try to keep a low profile, huh?"

"How are you going to explain why I'm there?"

"I'm going to tell her you're here to corner me for my fights. Which is true—I need someone I can trust in my corner."

"Whatever you say, man. She won't hear it from me. Give me your address. I'm on my way."

Ryann sat at Aiden's desk and flipped to the last page of papers he'd haphazardly tossed into his office. Her eyes stung, tears blurring her vision as she raced to finish the contract before they fell. She lost. A giant drop splattered on Aiden's hastily scrawled name, smearing the black ink.

"Shit . . ." She pulled off her cheaters and dropped them onto the desk. Closing her eyes, she pressed the heels of her palms against them, hoping that would somehow dam the moisture determined to fall. When another landed on his paper, she grabbed a tissue from the desk and dried her eyes before blotting at the contract.

"What are you doing?"

A startled "Oh . . ." escaped her lips. Ryann's head snapped up to find Aiden leaning his shoulder against the doorjamb, arms folded across his chest. How long had he been standing there watching her? By the accelerated tempo of his breathing, she'd guess not very long. She hadn't noticed when the muffled cadence of the heavy bag had stopped. He'd been in there for hours, giving her more than enough time to begin researching the fighter Aiden was up against and read through his contract.

Ryann quickly tossed the wadded tissue into the trash beside her knees, hoping he hadn't caught her crying. "I was just reading your contract. Did you know that according to this schedule, you fight every two weeks? And this man you fight tomorrow, Joe

Paskel, he's really bad news. He just got out of prison last year for aggravated assault and robbery—"

"I'm not surprised. How do you know all this?"

She rolled her eyes. "Because that's what I do for a living. I find people. I investigate them. I study and gather information. I don't want you fighting this guy."

"I don't have a choice, and arguing about it won't do me any favors. Just because the guy's an asshole doesn't mean he's a good fighter, Ryann."

"No, it doesn't. But his sixteen-and-two fight record might."

Aiden shouldered off the doorway and strolled into the office, moving with that undeniable grace that defied his size. "I can take care of myself in the cage. I'm not worried about it. What I am worried about is you, and I'll do whatever it takes to keep you safe. If that means I have to fight, then I'll fight." Aiden shrugged as if it was no big deal. "Moralli needs to believe he's won."

"Why? What are you going to do?"

Planting his palms on his desk, he lowered himself until they were eye level. The knot in her gut dissolved into a battering of butterflies. God help her, this man was gorgeous. His amber-flecked eyes bore into her with the intensity of the sun, scorching her to her very core.

"What I should have done a long time ago. Listen, I have a friend coming to stay with me for a while. He's going to corner me when I fight. I don't trust any of Moralli's men to do it."

"Okay . . . Is there anything I can do to help you? I feel terrible you're in this mess because of me."

A measure of tension eased from his shoulders. "It's not your fault. I should have known that bastard wasn't going to let me go. If you really want to help, you could put together a dossier on every guy I'm scheduled to fight. I want to know everything you can find out about them. If you can get me videos of their fights, that's even better. I always study my opponents before I get into the cage with them, and by the looks of things, I'm going to be short on time."

"Of course I'll do it. Anything you need, just ask . . ."

Aiden cocked his brow in question at her open-ended offer. It wasn't how she'd meant it, but his panty-dropping smile told her exactly how he'd taken it. The hum of nervous energy skittered through her veins. She wanted him so badly but was afraid to let him get too close. At this point, she was clinging to self-preservation. As much as his doubt and mistrust in her might have been deserved, it still hurt—badly—and she wasn't sure she wanted to open that door again. Did she love him?—absolutely. Was she still holding a part of herself back?—most definitely, and some niggling of doubt told her he was doing the same.

Aiden's spicy scent mixed with the seductive lure of clean male sweat. She nervously wet her lips with the tip of her tongue. His gaze dropped to her mouth, and the low growl rumbling in his throat called to every feminine instinct inside her. She had zero doubt that if this desk wasn't between them, he'd be on top of her right now.

The chemistry between them sparked, making her all too aware of her heart hammering inside her chest. Her skin felt too tight for her body. Feeling fidgety, she reached up to tuck a stray curl behind her ear. "It's umm . . . getting late. If you want to get cleaned up, I can go see about throwing something together for supper."

"There's nothing here. I haven't had a chance to shop yet. We can order in or I can take you out," he offered.

She'd had a long day and the thought of getting ready to go out wasn't nearly as appealing as the idea of staying in with him. "If it's all right with you, I'd like to stay here. I'll order something while you're showering. What are you hungry for?"

The intensity in his eyes surged brighter, igniting her own slow burn deep in her core. With the fluid grace of a predator, Aiden came around the desk. Towering over her, he leaned so close the heat of his breath brushed against the shell of her ear as he whispered, "Sweetheart, what I want to eat is not on any menu you're going to find around here."

*Oh, merciful heaven . . .* Ryann's breath caught in her throat as that slow burn erupted into a full-blown raging inferno. The memory of Aiden's all-consuming kiss returned, swift and unbidden, and with it came a wave of lust so intense, a soft, helpless whimper escaped her throat. Just the thought of his mouth against her intimate flesh, his tongue teasing her clit, slipping inside her . . .

She couldn't resist him. She was too weak, the power he held over her too strong. With just his words and erotic promises, he could bring her to the brink of release. Her breaths quickened as her eyes fluttered closed, waiting in anticipation for him to close the scant distance—waiting for his lips to graze her neck. What was he waiting for? She was helpless to deny him, lust casting out all fears, all rational thought. She knew how good it would be. How good they were in bed together. Question was, did Aiden want more than a fuck buddy? He obviously cared about her, but his outburst in the car was hardly a declaration of undying love and commitment. In fact, she'd gotten the feeling he'd shocked himself as much as he had her with that little admission. Was his love strong enough to go the distance? She guessed only time would tell . . .

Aiden could sense Ryann's hesitation, and it was with great effort he pulled away and let the offer hang in the air between them. They were on new ground here, uncharted territory since their postlove declaration. Aiden had to admit, the many times he'd tried to picture himself actually saying those words to someone, none of them had been in the heat of a fight. For crissake, did it even count when you yelled it at someone? It was the first time in his life he'd ever said the L word to a woman. Half-assed as that confession might have been, he'd have been lying if he said it didn't spook him a little.

He felt vulnerable in a way he'd never been before, exposed and raw, and he didn't like it. But none of that changed how rock hard he was for her, how much he wanted her, or how much he cared for her. Fuck, he was all over the board when it came to this woman. Right now, what he craved was what he knew—sex. He wanted to get his feet back on solid ground again, or rather get himself between Ryann's.

As he pulled back, her lids fluttered open, the vibrant green reflecting back at him a mixture of desire and uncertainty. He knew she'd been expecting him to kiss her, but in truth if he did, he wouldn't have been able to stop. He'd had a long, hard workout and he was drenched in sweat. It was probably best for the both of them if they tabled this for later. Whatever was holding Ryann back, whatever was bothering her, they were going to have to talk about it sooner than later. But considering the emotion-packed day they'd both had, now was probably not the best time.

"Whatever you decide to order is fine. There's cash in my wallet on my dresser. Help yourself."

# CHAPTER

# 30

"Mr. Kruze, we have a man down here from Artichoke Basille's. He said you ordered a pizza. Should I let him up?"

Ryann leapt from the chair where she'd been sitting at the dining room table, working on the dossier Aiden requested, when a woman's voice intruded into her thoughts. The voice sounded like it was coming from an intercom. She turned a circle, looking for a speaker mounted on the wall somewhere, and made a note to herself to have Aiden explain the penthouse security to her a little better.

"Aiden," she called. "Someone's talking to you."

He didn't respond. Crap, he was probably still in the shower.

"Mr. Kruze?"

Ryann followed the sound into the foyer and found a speaker with a silver intercom button beside the door.

She leaned forward, getting ready to speak, finger outstretched to press the button when: "Mr. Kruze? Is everything all right?"

Ryann jumped back and let out a startled yelp, then laughed at how ridiculous she must look. Pressing the button, she spoke into the wall. "I ordered the pizza, please send him up."

A few minutes later, Ryann handed the delivery guy a fifty-dollar bill and took the box from him. She closed the door with her foot and heard the automatic snick of the lock behind her as she carried the pizza to the table. It smelled heavenly. As she went into the kitchen to grab plates and napkins, she checked the fridge for something to drink. Wow, Aiden hadn't been joking—there really wasn't anything in here. She closed the door and spotted three bottles in his wine rack.

*Score!* She searched the cupboards until she found the glasses. After peeling the red foil off the bottle, she began opening and closing drawers, looking for a wine opener. Ryann found one in the last drawer and bumped it shut with her hip. She wrapped her arm around the bottle to hold it steady and screwed the metal curlicue into the cork. Once it was buried, she folded the wings down and forced the cork up. It got stuck halfway. Grabbing the opener, she pulled up, trying to free the cork from the bottle, but it wouldn't budge. Shit . . . she needed better leverage.

Ryann set the wine bottle on the ground and steadied it with her feet. She bent down, gripping the neck with one hand and the corkscrew with the other. She was about to give it a hard yank when she felt something bump into her from behind. Every inch of hard male body folded over her back, Aiden's tattooed arms reaching around her, plucking the wine bottle up from her feet.

"What are you doing?" he chuckled. His deep husky voice was like sex to her ears, all throaty and rumbling. His clean, spicy scent drugged her senses, making her feel like she'd already had a few glasses of the wine she was trying to open.

"What does it look like?" She turned her head to the side, finding his face very close to hers, amusement sparkling in those entrancing eyes. "I'm trying to open this bottle."

He straightened, taking the wine bottle with him and regrettably breaking contact with her backside. She bit her bottom lip to stifle the groan of disappointment.

"I see that. Looks like you're doing a stellar job of it."

"Hey." She turned to face him, propping her hip against the counter and giving him a saucy grin. "I was managing just"—*pop*—"fine."

Aiden sprang the cork loose with zero effort. He raised that sexy pierced brow of his and handed the bottle back to her. "You sure you shouldn't be drinking water?" he teased.

"Ha-ha. You're really funny." She turned and poured two glasses. Setting the bottle on the granite countertop, she lifted the glasses and handed him one. "Come on, your pizza's getting cold." She grabbed the plates and napkins and headed to the dining room, Aiden following her out with the bottle of wine. Ryann moved her laptop and pile of papers over to another spot and made room for him to sit across from her.

"The pizza smells great, what kind did you get?"

"Garbage. Hope you like it." She slid the pizza between them and lifted the lid on the box.

"Are you kidding me? Garbage pizza is my favorite, and Artichoke Basille's is the best. I haven't had a good pizza since . . ."

Ryann glanced up at him when he didn't finish his thought. Something hardened in his expression. "Since when?" she prompted, keeping her query light-hearted when she sensed the subtle shift in his mood. She grabbed a slice and dragged it over to her plate. Strings of connecting cheese followed, and she twirled her finger in the mozzarella, breaking it free.

"Since I left New York." He grabbed his own slice from the box, but instead of digging into the masterpiece, he reached for the wine and downed a good portion of the glass.

"I'm sorry you had to come back."

Guilt assailed her. Maybe Aiden could see the depth of her remorse, because he said, "It's not your fault. I never should have left."

*What?* She almost choked on her bite of pizza. "You can't mean that."

"Oh, I do. If there's one thing I've learned from all this, it's that you can't run away from your problems. Eventually, they'll find you and when they do, they're going to be a hell of a lot worse than before.

I'm done running, Ryann, and by the time I'm finished with Moralli, he's going to wish to God he'd let me go when he had the chance."

"Aiden, what are you going to do?" Her pulse spiked with the familiar rush of panic. If the last twenty-four hours taught her anything, it was that Vincent Moralli was a merciless, cold-blooded killer. Nothing drove that point home more than having the muzzle of a gun shoved against your temple.

Aiden took a bite of his pizza and thoughtfully chewed. The man radiated cold, hard determination. Looking at him now, he appeared every bit the hardened fighter and the ruthless lawyer she suspected he could be. Perhaps it was his Kruze bloodline that gave him the air of power and untouchability it would take to face Vincent Moralli. God knew no one else would do it, and apparently her father had died trying.

Aiden's gaze locked on her—unwavering and decided. "I'm going to collapse his empire. I'm going to do the one thing the feds have tried and failed to do for the last ten years. I'm going to build an airtight case against Vincent Moralli and I'm going to deliver it to the DA with a red fucking bow wrapped around it."

*Ho-ly shit . . .* "You think it will work? That you can do it?"

He drained his glass and refilled it before answering. The depth of raw anger, of unmerciful determination she saw staring back at her, chilled Ryann to the bone. This was a side of Aiden Kruze she'd never seen before, a side that quite frankly was scary as shit.

"Oh, I know I can."

"Why haven't you done it before now?"

He was thoughtful for a moment. Perhaps he was trying to decide whether or not to tell her the truth because his response shocked the hell out of her. "Because when Moralli falls, I will have single-handedly ruined my father."

Ryann pushed her plate aside, her appetite long gone. Reaching across the table, she clutched Aiden's hand. "You can't be serious. Aiden, how is that possible? He's your father, a freaking US senator!"

"The how of it doesn't matter. My parents have made their bed, Ryann. After today, I'm done worrying about them and I'm done covering up for their involvement with Moralli. None of us are going to come out of this unscathed and I'll likely be disbarred. But whatever the consequences, they're worth it to see that man behind bars, to get you out of his clutches. Fuck . . ." Aiden dragged his hand through his hair. "When that bastard had you dragged into that office today and I saw the terror in your eyes . . . I swear to God I could have killed him right then and there."

The tempest of emotion reflecting back at Ryann broke her heart. She could see the anger raging, the helplessness crashing in a sea of desperation, the love anchoring him to her like a lifeline stretched to its limit on a fraying rope. He needed her. He needed her more than he'd ever admit—needed her to support him, to stand by him, to love him through this, no matter the outcome. He was doing this for them. He was fighting for her . . .

Rising from her chair, she came around the table and climbed across his lap. Taking his face in her hands, she admired his strong stubborn square jaw, his noble aristocratic nose that hinted at generations of fine breeding. And his eyes . . . she could drown in the dark rich amber color, so unlike anything she'd ever seen. But when her gaze landed on his mouth, lips that held a masculine fullness she craved to taste, ached to feel in all the places that tingled with awareness of him, she was done for.

"I never thanked you for saving my life today." And there was no doubt in her mind that he had. When that gun cocked and the cold press of metal had bitten into her temple . . . The thought sent a shudder rippling through her body. Aiden must have felt it because his hands came to rest low on her back, just above the fleshy curve of her bottom. "Vincent would have killed me if you hadn't signed that contract. You're not fighting for him, Aiden, you're fighting for me." She leaned forward until her mouth nearly touched his and whispered, "Remember that when you step into the cage tomorrow night."

Of all the things Ryann could have said to him, this was the one that could have brought him to his knees. Holy hell . . . he loved this woman. The tether of his control snapped, and all the emotion he'd bottled up inside him came rushing out. He closed the scant distance separating them, kissing her with a possessive savageness that shocked even him, yet he was helpless to temper the raw, primitive domination in which his mouth claimed hers. She was his. And by the end of the night, he vowed she'd have no doubt who she belonged to.

Ryann met the sweep of his tongue with her own, twisting and tangling with his. Her small fingers gripped his shoulders, little nails biting into his flesh as she ground her hot cunny against his erection, leaving him to wonder if Ryann wasn't just as determined to stake her claim on him.

The hours he'd spent in the gym left an excess of testosterone burning through his veins like octane. He was sick of thinking, tired of planning and plotting. All he wanted right now was to shut it all down and focus on feeling—the feeling of Ryann's hot mouth on his, the feeling of her soft breasts and pebbled nipples crushed against his chest. His arms wrapped around her, jerking her up tight against his cock. His flesh strained to be inside her; his balls ached with the need for release.

He worried he'd hurt her if he didn't get a rein on himself soon. But taking it slow and easy was not on Ryann's agenda. It seemed as if she were just as desperate to forget this FUBAR day as he was.

Her hands were rucking up his shirt, and he broke contact with her mouth long enough for their clothing to go flying. He reached behind her and with the flick of his wrist, her baby-blue lace bra unlatched, and she couldn't seem to wiggle out of it fast enough. The metal hooks tinked against the marble floor somewhere behind him as her breasts filled his hands. Glorious pink nipples beaded against his palms. She was so stunning, so gorgeous, so . . . his.

As he broke their kiss to feast on her perfection, Ryann's head dropped back to rest on the table, an erotic feminine groan escaping her throat that he felt all the way to the base of his cock. He had to have her—now. She let out a surprised squeak when he slipped an arm beneath her ass and stood. As he carried her toward his room, she closed guard, wrapping her legs around his waist and hooking her ankles.

He beat feet to his bedroom and hastily deposited her on the mattress. Hooking his hands into the waistband of her yoga pants, he stripped her with the finesse of an overeager adolescent about to experience his first lay. In fact, he wasn't sure he'd ever felt this frenzied, this anxious, to get between a woman's thighs. Dropping his sweats, Ryann's gaze swept over him as he crawled onto the bed. Everywhere her appreciative eyes touched, his skin felt hot and tight.

Aiden grabbed her ankles and pulled her closer. The movement splayed her hair across his pillow like a fiery halo. *Fucking beautiful* . . . He lowered himself over her and took her mouth in a branding kiss that spoke the words failing him. His muscles shook with the force of his restraint. Fear of hurting her was the only thing holding him back from plunging deep inside her and chasing his release. It wouldn't be much of a race. Already the tightening low in his groin, the tingling at the base of his spine, warned him he was close. The moisture beading at the head of his cock wept for mercy.

Ryann impatiently lifted her hips, inching her wet sex closer, and it beckoned to him like a siren's call he was helpless to resist. Her last little nudge seated him against her opening, and Aiden hesitated one more flagging second before burying himself deep inside her. Her broken cry of pleasure shattered him, his resolve dissolving into nothingness. Her tight glove squeezed him perfectly, her appetite as ravenous as his. She gripped his ass, her nails scoring into his flesh as she arched into his thrusts, meeting his demands with an urgency of her own.

Nothing in his life felt as right as this moment. His world might be crumbling down around him, but as long as he had Ryann, she would be his anchor through this storm. It was as if she were made especially and perfectly for him. The shattering clarity of how much he loved this woman rocked him to his core.

His name was a broken plea on her lips as her release gripped him tight, sending them both over the edge. He came hard, the harsh bark of rapture ripping from his throat as a violent torrent of pleasure shuddered through him, each wracking spasm of her body milking his release until he collapsed over her, utterly spent and deliciously sated in a way he'd never felt before.

Not yet ready to leave her, he rolled onto his back, bringing Ryann with him. Her hair cascaded around her, spilling onto his chest. She lifted her head to look down at him and those luminous green eyes stopped his heart. The wondrous look of a woman well and thoroughly pleasured shone on her beautiful face, stroking his male pride, making him feel ten feet tall—invincible—and yet at the same time he'd never felt more powerless.

He'd faced countless opponents in the cage. He was about to take on one of the most dangerous men in New York, and yet no one could make him feel as weak and vulnerable as this midge of a woman grinning at him right now.

# CHAPTER 31

The muffled sound of voices coming from the other room woke Ryann from her languid sleep. She yawned, breathing Aiden's masculine scent deep into her lungs. The glide of satin sheets kissing her bare skin as she stretched made her wish it was Aiden's lips on her instead. The harsh bark of laughter in the other room, more sarcastic than humorous, piqued her curiosity. Who was Aiden talking to? She glanced at the alarm clock on the nightstand beside the bed. It wasn't even seven a.m. yet.

She climbed out of bed and found her yoga pants and panties in a pile on the floor. After pulling them on, she stood there a moment looking for her shirt and bra until she remembered where they were. *Shit* . . . Lord, she hoped Aiden had picked up their clothes before letting in whoever was out there. Having little choice, she crossed the room to his dresser and pulled open the top drawer. *Socks and boxers—not gonna help.* Closing it, she moved down to the second and found what she was looking for—T-shirts. She grabbed the top one and pulled it on. The thing hung on her like a gunnysack. Glancing up at her reflection in the mirror, she stifled a giggle. Across the chest was a large red *S*. What was it with this guy and graphic superhero T-shirts?

Her flaming, Medusa-like hair wasn't doing the look any favors. Ryann shuffled into Aiden's bathroom and washed her face, removing her makeup smudges, and ran her damp fingers through her hair trying to tame the wavy mess. She'd have to wait until she got into her bathroom to brush her teeth unless . . . Ryann pulled open the top drawer and found a stockpile of spare toothbrushes. She plucked one out, opened the package, and in a few minutes she was minty fresh and just about as presentable as she could be for a braless woman wearing an oversized Superman T-shirt. She opened the door and slipped into the hallway, about to make her walk of shame into the guest bedroom to get properly dressed, when that voice stopped her cold.

"Morning, Gingersnap . . ."

*Oh, merciful God in Heaven, please no* . . . Ryann closed her eyes as she sent up the quick prayer. This was the guy cornering Aiden for his fights? Unable to hide her grimace, she slowly opened one eye at a time and tipped her head to the side, giving her a clearer view of the dining room table and the two men sitting at it. She wasn't sure what shocked her more: seeing the fighter who had given her such a hard time back at the gym—the one with the cold steel-gray eyes and the scar slashing across his cheek—or Aiden. Holy shit, he was dressed in a black suit straight off the cover of a *GQ* magazine. But that wasn't all that caught her notice. His piercings were gone—the lip, the brow, his ears—all of them, and his unruly dark hair was tamed into submission by gel that left his tawny locks several shades darker.

Controlled and sophisticated, his appearance hinted at nothing of the man seething beneath all that refinement—until he flashed her that devilish grin over his cup of coffee. And just like that, the butterflies woke, battering their way into her chest. He was breathtakingly handsome, but not in that badass, panty-dropping way she was used to. No, this version of Aiden was untouchably rich and powerfully intimidating—their differences in class made all the more acute by her disheveled appearance and braless state, wearing a T-shirt that hung down her thighs.

"Ryann, come here. I want you to meet Nikko Del Toro."

"We've met," she said drily, stepping forward.

"Not officially . . ." the fighter chimed in. A smug, amused grin tugged at the scar on his cheek.

Yep, her shirt, bra, and his T-shirt were still scattered on the dining room floor. He could have at least picked them up before his friend came over, but hey, if he wanted to flaunt their sexcapade, then that was his prerogative. She refused to be embarrassed about it. As she moved through the living room and Aiden got a good look at her, his amber eyes sparkled with mischievous humor. Then that smile split into a full-on heart-stopping grin. "I like the shirt," he said into his mug before taking a sip.

"Thanks." Standing up straight with her head held high, Ryann walked into the dining room as if she were royalty, knowing damn well her breasts swayed on proud display. The soft cotton of his T-shirt folded into the deep valley of her cleavage. She knew the exact moment Aiden realized his mistake of calling her over because those rich golden-amber eyes dropped to her chest and he seemed to have a little trouble getting his coffee down. She shot him a saucy, *Didn't think that one through too well, did ya?* smile, and walked over to Nikko, who looked a mixture of shocked and wildly entertained, his gaze darting from her to Aiden then back to her breasts.

"It's nice to *officially* meet you," she said with saccharine sweetness, holding out her hand.

He took hers in his firm grip. "Likewise."

"So, you're going to corner Aiden, huh?"

Nikko's gaze flickered to Aiden before landing back on her. "Yep."

"Have you ever coached before?"

His indulging smile rankled her nerves. "Didn't realize this was a job interview."

Did he think this was a joke? Aiden was stepping into an underground fight club tonight. What he was doing was dangerous, and these guys didn't mess around. She felt responsible enough as it was. If he got hurt because of her . . .

"Nikko and I are sparring partners," Aiden interjected. "He's more than qualified, Ryann."

"Don't worry, Gingersnap. I'll keep our boy in one piece."

She bristled at the nickname, but kept the impeccable smile on her wooden face. She wouldn't let him see how much he rattled her or how much she hated that name. "See that you do," she grumbled. Maybe it wasn't fair for her to take her fears and frustration out on Aiden's friend, but she hated the idea of him fighting for Moralli, and it twisted the knife to know she was the reason he was doing it. She felt powerless to help him and that loss of control made her downright waspish.

"Retract your claws, kitten," Aiden teased, snagging her wrist and pulling her onto his lap. "Everything is going to be just fine."

Aiden was right, this wasn't Nikko's fault. He was here to help. She could cut him a little slack. "I appreciate you coming here to help him."

Nikko nodded his acknowledgment, and she turned her attention back to Aiden and slipped her arm around his neck, not caring if she put wrinkles in his fancy suit. All she wanted right now was to be close to him, to feel his reassuring strength enveloping her. She wiggled in a little tighter, and he tensed, another part of him growing hard beneath her. The low growl rumbling deep in his throat warned her she was playing with fire. She smiled innocently and took his mug from his hand, sipping at his coffee.

"You look very handsome in your suit," she commented, smoothing out his collar. "You took out all your metal."

"Not all of it." He flashed her his tongue and the metal bar sticking through it. "I left your favorite one."

*Rogue!* Her cheeks heated at his teasing. Trying her best to ignore the wicked imagery his tongue presented, she took another drink of his coffee and asked, "Where are you going?"

"The firm."

His voice was strained, whether from his raging erection pressed against her bottom or the unpleasantness of the day ahead, she couldn't know. But the thought of Aiden walking out that door worried her more than she wanted to admit. What if Moralli discovered what he was planning?

"How long will you be gone?" she asked, all carefree pretenses gone.

He reached up and smoothed his thumb between her wrinkled brows. "It's hard to say. I'm not sure what kind of a reception to expect at the firm after being away for so long. Getting security clearance and access to my old files might take a while. I have a lunch meeting with the DA at noon, but I'll be back as soon as I can."

She nodded. "I'm almost finished with that dossier on Joe Paskel. I'll have it ready for you when you get back."

He gave her a teasing grin she was sure was purely for the benefit of belaying her fears. "Wow, I'm impressed. You work fast, Ms. Andrews. I might just have to hire you."

She set his coffee cup on the table and leaned close, whispering, "You'd be surprised how fast I can work." She nipped the lobe of his ear and slipped off his lap, letting the invitation hang in the air as she sauntered toward the bedroom, bending down to swipe her bra and T-shirt off the floor along the way.

A throaty chuckle echoed behind her and she heard Nikko taunt, "Man, you've got your hands full with that one."

"Fuck me," Aiden groaned. "You don't even know the half of it."

No sooner did Ryann close her bedroom door than she heard it open behind her, shut, and the lock click into place. She didn't turn around or acknowledge him as she walked toward the dresser, a mischievous smile playing on her lips. Pretending she didn't know he was there, she slipped off her bottoms and tossed them into the hamper along with the clothes she picked up off the dining room floor. Standing there in nothing but his T-shirt, she was about to pull open the top drawer and grab a change of clothes to bring into the shower when Aiden came up behind her, pressing his erection against her bottom.

His unyielding body fit tightly against her back, setting her off balance. Ryann splayed her hands against the top of the dresser to steady herself as Aiden's hands dropped to her thighs and rode up her hips, bringing his T-shirt with him. "You look so fucking hot in my clothes," he growled beside her ear. Hands spanning her waist, he slid them up her ribs and gripped her breasts. He squeezed, pinching her nipples until pleasure blurred with pain. It was just how she liked it, riding that thin edge with him. He always seemed to know just when to pull back. A wanton moan escaped her throat, and she tipped her head to the side, giving him full access to her neck.

"You're killing me, you know that?" He gripped her tighter, pulling her against him roughly. A thrill of excitement shot through her, the shiver centering between her legs. You might dress a man in expensive, sophisticated suits, but that didn't make him a gentleman. He was still her Aiden, still the same man who'd made passionate love to her last night. It didn't matter how refined he might appear on the outside, on the inside he was still her wild, reckless fighter.

"You're going to wrinkle your suit," she teased, her statement ending with a moan when his hand slid down her belly to dip between her thighs.

His mouth halted on her neck and he glanced up, locking his gaze with hers in the dresser mirror. Holy shit, the erotic scene they made nearly made her come right then and there. Here she stood braced against the dresser, sleep-disheveled in an old, worn-out T-shirt hiked up her front, exposing a wealth of smooth pale flesh. One of Aiden's hands cupped her breast, while his other played between her parted legs. He towered over her, wearing his *GQ* suit, looking all prim and proper, except the sleeves of his jacket had worked up just enough to reveal a glimpse of his tattoos. Mercy, he was stunning—and those eyes . . . dark amber with deep flecks of brown. So intense, so possessive . . . so passionate.

"Aiden . . ." she breathed the plea as he bit out a sharp curse that was exactly what she wanted him to do to her right now.

In seconds his suit jacket was gone, buttons were pinging off the hardwood floor as he ripped his gray shirt off his shoulders and shucked it like the thing was on fire. His hands were at his waist, unfastening his belt. The *riiiiip* of metal friction as his zipper gave way sent Ryann's heart racing with anticipation. She could see a flash of Aiden's bare hip in the mirror as his black trousers dropped to his knees. His foot wedged between hers and knocked them farther apart. The hard length of his erection slipped between her legs as one hand fisted into her dark red curls, pulling her mass of wild hair over to one side, baring her neck.

His mouth was back on her throat, kissing, sucking, nipping the flesh just above her shoulder when he thrust into her, bringing her to her tiptoes. Ryann scrambled for purchase. She locked her elbows, nails digging into his oak dresser as he gripped her hip to steady her. Aiden's hand slammed down on the dresser, his arm crossing over hers for balance. She bit her lip to keep from crying out in pleasure.

His fast, unyielding pace quickly chased her to the pinnacle of release. She was hovering on the edge when his hand slipped from her hip down to her sex. He trapped her clit between his thumb and his cock, pressing the bundle of nerves against his steel shaft. She shattered. A million times over she shattered, coming so hard she turned her head and sank her teeth into Aiden's bicep to keep from crying out. He cursed an erotic "Oh, fuck . . ." and slammed into her one final time before an explosion of hot seed jetted against her core.

As the last pulses of Aiden's release shuddered through his powerful body, Ryann struggled to catch her breath. "You were right, you do work fast," he teased, his breathless confession proving he was just as wrung out as Ryann was. "To hell with the gym, sweetheart, you're the only cardio I need."

She laughed, elbowing him in the ribs. "I came in here to shower and get dressed, you know."

Aiden stepped back and grabbed her by his T-shirt, turning her to face him. "No you didn't. You made me an offer I couldn't refuse." He tugged her closer and planted a solid kiss on her mouth. "I hate to bang and bail, but I really gotta go." He hiked up his slacks and made quick work of tucking everything back in place.

"It's all right." Ryann crossed her arms over her chest, savoring the feel of snuggling into Aiden's shirt. The hem line brushed against her thighs as she leaned her bottom against the dresser, enjoying the view of watching him get dressed. Still naked from the waist up, he was a feast for the eyes. All hard planes and rippling muscle . . . She could feel the heat blooming anew in her core just watching him.

He crossed the room to the closet where he kept his overflow of clothes and grabbed a new shirt from the hanger. Shrugging it over his wide shoulders, he quickly began fastening the buttons as he walked toward her. "Do you mind moving your stuff into my room so I can put Nikko in the spare room?"

"No, not at all. I'd just started to unpack anyway. It's not a big deal."

"Thanks, babe." He scooped his jacket off the floor and attempted to shake the wrinkles out before slipping it back on. As he fastened the two buttons, he bent down and gave her one last kiss. "I'll be back as soon as I can." He flashed her a sexy grin and grabbed the front of his T-shirt, giving it a playful tug. "You look good in my clothes, Ryann."

# CHAPTER

Good morning, Mr. Kruze."

"Good morning," Aiden responded for the umpteenth time, ignoring the double takes and surprised greetings as he made his way toward his office. He walked into the firm with the same cool, determined purpose with which he'd walked out of it fourteen months ago.

In all honesty, there was a part of him that was surprised to see his name was still on the office door. Then again, his father was all about image. Heaven forbid all may not be well within the Kruze Kingdom. The man would do just about anything to save face, and scraping your kid's name off the office door with an X-Acto knife didn't exactly say *all is well.* And it was exactly that prideful arrogance Aiden was counting on to get him the clearance he needed to access his files.

His father believed it was only a matter of time before Aiden came to his senses and came crawling back home with his tail between his legs. The man had said as much the night Aiden stormed out of his parents' mansion and said *fuck it all.* He stopped at his secretary's desk as he passed by and said, "Shirley, would you mind getting IT on the phone to reactivate my security clearance?"

The woman glanced at him, did a double take, and choked on her coffee. "Right away, Mr. Kruze," she sputtered.

Aiden was banking on his office key still working and shook his head at his father's predictability when the metal slid home and the lock opened. It was too easy, really. And that thought lasted for a whole thirty minutes. He was on the phone with IT when his office door swung open then slammed shut. So much for not wanting to make a scene . . .

"Can I call you back?"

"Not a problem, Mr. Kruze. And what about the archived files? They require a special password clearance. Will you want me to reset that as well?"

"Yes, please. I appreciate your help."

"Call me if you need anything else."

Aiden hung up the phone and turned his attention to the pissed-off man towering over his desk.

"What the hell do you think you're doing?" he demanded.

"Hey, Dad. Missed you at the family reunion yesterday morning. Good times . . . What does it look like I'm doing? I'm coming to work. That's what you wanted, isn't it? You and Mom practically moved heaven and earth to get me back here. Did you think I was going to sit at home and eat bonbons all day?"

His dad sat in the chair across from his desk and eyed him skeptically. "You expect me to believe that just like that you're coming home and all is good?"

Aiden shrugged. "Mom said Cynthia Moralli broke the engagement. As long as you don't go trying to marry me off to anyone else, why wouldn't it be?"

"Quit lawyering me, Aiden."

"All right, you want me to be real with you?" He pushed back from his desk and crossed his arms, facing off with the man who might as well be a stranger. Bennett Kruze mirrored his stubborn pose. Thirty years Aiden's senior, the man had lost little of his imposing stature and none of his stubborn arrogance. Those ice-blue eyes cut into him from across the desk. It was a look that would cow a lesser man, but Aiden was immune to that intimidating glower. "I was perfectly content to remain in Vegas. I had a great fighting career and one I'm not just a little pissed about losing. If you want me here so bad, then you can sure as hell give me my job back. I want the Moralli account, too, which means whatever clearance you need to sign off on with IT, I expect you to do it."

Bennett watched him with that same impassive stare Aiden had come to despise over the years. "What are you doing, Aiden? You and I both know you hated working for Moralli. Why in the hell would you want that case back now? Unless . . ."

His dad was smart—too fucking smart.

"What the hell are you planning to do?"

*Something I should have done a long time ago.*

Aiden's father leaned forward, narrowed his gaze, and lowered his voice to a low warning growl. "Need I remind you of what is at stake here?—my career, my reputation, the reputation of this firm! And you, sitting there so self-righteous, are not innocent of any wrongdoing yourself. Whatever you're thinking, let it go."

At this moment, the man sitting across from him looked every bit as ruthless as Moralli, and just as formidable. Too bad the show of force was lost on him. Aiden wasn't a man to be bullied or intimidated. When he was pushed, he pushed back harder. His father should have known that by now—he was Bennett Kruze's son, after all.

Aiden's computer screen flashed, prompting his password reset. He wouldn't need long to get the information he'd come here for, but it certainly would have been easier to accomplish without his father's eyes of suspicion on him. "You think I don't know that? Do you think I would do something that would compromise you or this firm? Do you think I'd disbar myself?"

"In a word . . . yes." Bennett stood and straightened his navy blue suit. "I don't think I'll be handing the Moralli account back over to you. At least not right now. We have many other cases that could use your attention. Feel free to pick up the ones from Shirley that interest you."

"Whatcha doin', Gingersnap?"

Ryann shot Nikko a sharp scowl as he plopped down beside her. "You know I hate it when you call me that, right?"

The grin he gave her was pure wickedness, transforming that severe face into a startling handsome gleam. God help the poor woman who got snared by this wolf.

"Why do you think I do it?" he asked, his answer in the question. Turning his attention to the computer screen on her lap, his steel-gray eyes watched the YouTube video playing on her laptop. All hint of playfulness vanished as his expression became tense and guarded. There was a lot going on behind those eyes. His square jaw was set in grim determination, his brows pulled tight in an assessing scowl that seemed to be permanently etched on his face. Her eyes strayed to the scar slashing from high on his cheekbone down through his top lip. She couldn't help but wonder what had happened to cause what should be a disfiguring injury, yet it only seemed to add to the guy's dangerous good looks. This was the fourth time she'd seen Nikko Del Toro, and she had to admit he was very handsome in a very rugged, ruthless way. If he was self-conscious about his scar, he gave no indication of it. Ryann forced her attention back to the screen when she caught herself staring too long, her cheeks heating with embarrassment. She didn't want to be rude or give him the wrong idea.

"What are you watching?"

"It's a YouTube video of an MMA fight with Joe Paskel."

"Paskel?—never heard of him."

Nikko's eyes never left the screen as he spoke, his attention wholly fixed on the fight playing out before him.

"This is the man Aiden's going to fight tonight."

"No shit? May I?" he asked, reaching over and plucking the laptop off her knees before she could answer either way.

As the fight went on, Nikko's scowl deepened. Yeah, he'd be a gorgeous man if he wasn't so terrifying. They watched as Paskel shot in and slammed his opponent onto the mat. "You see that?" he said, pointing to the screen. "Paskel is passing his guard."

It kinda just looked like two men rolling around on a mat to her. "What's 'passing his guard'?"

"It's when a fighter takes a more advantageous position over his opponent."

They watched as Paskel jumped in for the win, repeatedly driving his knee into the felled fighter's face. She grimaced as a spray of blood shot across the mat and Nikko muttered a foul curse. "That shit's illegal."

Ryann wasn't sure to which "shit" he was referring. It all looked pretty terrible if you asked her.

"This is who Disco's fighting?"

"I've been pulling together fight reels for Aiden so he can study his opponent before the fight tonight. I gotta confess, I don't know what I'm watching."

"You're watching unsanctioned fighting. No-holds-barred kind of shit. This guy here is a grappler. See how he shoots in for the takedown? Knees are illegal when your opponent is on the ground like this. Disco's gonna have to keep this fight on his feet."

Hearing Nikko's fight assessment wasn't doing anything to calm her nerves. "Can he do that? Keep the fight on his feet?"

Nikko took his attention off the fight long enough to shoot her a lopsided, *are you kidding me?* grin. "Disco has amazing stand-up. He's a way better fighter than either of these two. This guy's just a brawler. He's got shitty technique, but that doesn't mean the bastard's not dangerous. The trick with fighters like this is not accidentally getting tagged. Anyone can get lucky. What else you got on this Joe guy?"

Ryann reached for the manila folder sitting beside her and set the dossier in his waiting hands. Nikko shot her a surprised glance. "Damn, Gingersnap, I'm impressed. That's awesome work . . ."

Ryann couldn't help but smile at his compliment. For the first time since Nikko arrived, she let herself entertain the possibility that she might have judged the cagey fighter a bit too harshly. Obviously, Aiden liked and trusted the guy or he never would have asked him to corner his fights. No question Nikko was a total ball-busting hardass, but something about the guy told Ryann she could trust him, and people she could count on were hard to come by these days. It comforted her to know this man had Aiden's back and that he wouldn't be walking into the Lion's Den alone tonight.

"Thank you," she found herself saying.

Nikko froze, the tension he always carried in his shoulders tightening a touch more. He canted his head just enough to look at her, a puzzled frown drawing his brows tight. "For what?"

He genuinely didn't seem to know.

"For this . . . for helping Aiden."

Nikko grunted and turned his attention back to the file. "It's nothing Disco wouldn't do for me."

And she knew that was probably true. Aiden might not have many people in his life he allowed to get very close to him, but he truly cared about the ones he did, and he'd move heaven and earth for them if it was in his power.

"How many other videos do you have?" Nikko asked, turning the conversation back to neutral ground.

"Four. Here . . ." She showed him the links she'd pulled up, and together they began watching the videos from the beginning. As the fights went on, Nikko pointed out flaws and weaknesses in the fighter, and by the end of the afternoon, Ryann knew more about MMA than she ever wanted to learn. But she was also a lot less fearful and fully confident that Aiden had this fight.

# CHAPTER

# 33

Aiden . . . how the hell are you?"

Aiden set his briefcase on the floor beside his feet and reached across the table, taking hold of the outstretched hand. "District Attorney Ike Wilson. It's been a while."

"You could say that." The man released his hand and Aiden slipped into the booth. "I have to say, I was surprised as hell to hear from you. Thought you left town . . ."

"I did."

"Obviously, you're back now?"

His old friend and former law classmate was fishing for details Aiden wasn't sure he wanted to give. He planned to do his best to leave Ryann out of this. Unfortunately, after the meeting with his father, Aiden wasn't sure how long that would remain possible. It also spurred the urgency simmering inside him to start building this case.

"For a while. I have some loose ends I need to tie up."

Ike's dark brow ticked up in question. "I assume that's where I come in?"

Aiden looked around, taking in the view. It wasn't for the topless dancer twirling around on the pole that he chose this place to meet. The high-backed booths discreetly hid them from prying eyes. The bump-and-grind music drowned out their conversation, keeping it from being overheard.

"Interesting choice in restaurants. Probably going to have a little trouble writing this one off as a business expense." Ike saluted Aiden with his beer and laughed. "I see you haven't changed."

Oh, Aiden had changed—more than he wanted to admit. This was the first time he'd ever been in a strip club and felt guilty about it. It was also the first time a half-naked woman dancing with a pole didn't even tempt his gaze.

Ike had gotten here early, just in case Aiden was being watched—a high likelihood, considering what went down yesterday. Anyone who knew Aiden wouldn't think twice about seeing him walk into a strip club. The DA had two empty glasses sitting beside him. "Was that one mine?" Aiden nodded at the empty.

"Maybe."

Aiden chuckled. The waitress came over and took his order. She offered another to Ike but he declined. He still had half a glass left and no doubt had to go back to the office after their meeting.

"As great as it is to see you, why don't we get down to it and you tell me why I'm here?"

Ike had always been a no-bullshit, let's-get-down-to-it kind of guy. That was one of the things Aiden liked about him.

"How close are you to getting an indictment on Moralli?"

Ike choked on his beer and took a moment to clear his throat before narrowing his gaze at him. "You ask that like you think I'm actually going to tell you."

As Moralli's lawyer, it was no secret to him Ike had been working to build a case against him for years. So had the feds.

"What do you want, Aiden? Why am I really here?"

"I want to give you Moralli. I want to hand you a case so airtight there's no lawyer in the country who will be able to get him off."

Ike sat there a moment staring at him, his quizzical frown thoughtful . . . contemplative. "You're serious?"

"As a heart attack."

The waitress dropped off his beer as she passed by on the way to another table. Aiden took a sip and waited for his friend to say something.

"I can't divulge what I have. You know that."

"Well, you can add this to it." Aiden slid the briefcase over to Ike.

"What's this?"

"Proof. Proof of money laundering, illegal gambling, prostitution . . . It should get you started."

"Damn . . ." Ike cursed, reaching down to slide the briefcase beneath his legs. "I can't believe you're doing this, man. You know you're probably going to get disbarred for this, right? And that's just the beginning. When this comes out . . . Shit, I probably shouldn't be telling you this, but Moralli's not the only one we're watching."

"I know. I plan to turn State's evidence for immunity." He gave Ike a sly grin. "You didn't think I'd tip my entire hand, did you?"

His friend laughed. "No, I didn't. And I'll do my damned best to get you through this unscathed. But I wasn't talking about you. I was talking about your father."

"What do you think you're doing?"

Ryann was bent over, shoving her foot into her boot, when she glanced back and found Aiden towering over her. He was wearing a black T-shirt and sweats and had a duffel bag slung over his shoulder. Nikko was in the foyer, a few paces behind him.

"What does it look like? I'm coming with you."

"The hell you are," Aiden and Nikko replied in unison.

Aiden reached for her and turned Ryann to face him. "Listen, sweetheart, I appreciate that you want to be there and support me, but

I don't want you anywhere near the Lion's Den. It's a dangerous place, and I have to be able to focus on this fight. I can't do that if I'm worried about you. This penthouse is the safest place for you to be right now. Promise me you'll stay here and wait for me until I come back."

If he'd put it any other way she would have refused. She wasn't some fragile doll Aiden could keep on a shelf and put away for safekeeping. But her sense of guilt that he was fighting in the first place kept her from arguing. The last thing she wanted was to be a distraction to him. Reluctantly, Ryann acquiesced, trying to hide her disappointment and frustration over being left behind.

"He's going to be fine, Gingersnap. Don't worry. I'll bring him home to you safe and sound."

"You'd better," she grumbled begrudgingly. Exhaling a defeated sigh, she bent to remove her boot, and Aiden caught her arm.

"Hey . . ." Aiden caught her chin and tipped her head so he could meet her eyes. "Thanks for all your hard work on Paskel's dossier. You did a great job on it."

He dipped his head and planted a kiss on her mouth. She stifled a groan of complaint when all too soon, he let her go.

"I'll be back as soon as I can," he promised, walking out the door.

Nikko gave her a passing nod as he strolled by. The door closed behind him and just like that, she was alone.

*Well, shit . . .*

Ryann returned to the living room and stood before the glass wall, taking in the Manhattan skyline as she endeavored to calm her jangling nerves. She had to trust that everything was going to be fine. Aiden was an amazing fighter. She knew that, she'd seen him fight before, and Nikko was in his corner. What could possibly go wrong?

Needing the distraction, Ryann decided to try to get some work done. Since getting back into town, she hadn't been to the office yet.

She'd have to go tomorrow, but for now, she could at least catch up on her e-mails and get a jump-start on Aiden's next dossier.

With a plan in place for the evening, the distraction helped calm her restless anxiety, and a couple glasses of wine wouldn't hurt, either. After changing into her comfy pajamas and pouring herself some Moscato, Ryann dragged the coffee table closer and set up camp in the chair facing the skyline. Deciding to tackle her e-mails first, she began sorting through them by first deleting her spam. As she clicked through the masses, a message titled *Condolences* caught her eye. She didn't recognize the name of the sender, but curiosity prompted her to open the e-mail.

*Dear Ms. Andrews,*

*Please accept my heartfelt condolences on the loss of your father. I regret it has taken me so long to contact you, but I have just recently learned of his passing. We have never met, but I am an old friend of your dad's. I have something he wanted me to give you in the event of his death, and I would like to schedule a meeting at your earliest convenience.*

*Sincerely,*

*Henry*

Ryann's heart hammered in her chest. Was this man serious? Did he truly have something from her father, or was this a ploy of some kind? The vagueness of the e-mail piqued her suspicion, yet hope and curiosity fueled her excitement. What could this man possibly have to give her? Perhaps he held answers to the questions about her father's death.

She checked the date on the message and saw it was sent three days ago. There was no return phone number, no last name; no way to contact the man other than to reply. It felt a little cloak-and-dagger to her, but after what she'd discovered about her father's secret life, maybe it wasn't so out there. She wouldn't go to the meeting alone. Aiden would want to come with her, and Nikko would no doubt insist on going. She would be safe. Decided, Ryann replied to the e-mail and arranged a meeting for the next afternoon.

"How you feelin'?" Nikko asked, wrapping the white fighter's tape around Aiden's knuckles. He circled it around three times, building up a good pad before crisscrossing it up Aiden's wrist.

"Good." Aiden was trying to focus, to block out the noise of the crowd in the underground arena—the screaming, the cheers, the booing. There were six fights on the docket for tonight, and Aiden's was the main event. Broden Hayes, the guy Aiden was standing in for, must be one hell of a fighter to pull in the purse Aiden was fighting for tonight. A bet laid was a bet paid, and Moralli wasn't letting anyone sideline their bets.

As he watched Del Toro wrap his hands with practiced efficiency, he felt frustrated that he was having trouble getting into his zone. The change in atmosphere, the stakes, it all kept him from finding his edge. Thoughts of Ryann distracted him, the confrontation with his father unnerved him, guilt over betraying his family assaulted him. Anger seethed through his veins like a toxic poison, rage building inside him like a pressure cooker. How he wished it was Moralli in that cage tonight. Or Frank Luciana . . . what he wouldn't give for five minutes alone with that fucker.

"Your shoulder still giving you trouble?" Del Toro briefly glanced at him before getting back to business, slipping the wrap through his splayed fingers and circling back around his wrist before repeating the process between each digit.

"It's fine. A little stiff, but it'll hold."

Del Toro secured the Velcro at his wrist and stood. "How's that feel?"

"It's good." He knocked his fists together. "Tight."

"You got this."

"I know." In truth, Aiden was looking forward to expending some pent-up energy. The idea of beating the shit out of someone sounded pretty good right about now. What ate at him was the fact that Moralli was going to make a shit-ton of money off him doing it. He'd be lying if he said he wasn't tempted to throw the fucking fight. But that bastard knew him well, and he'd paid Aiden a little visit just a few minutes ago, adding the caveat *Win or Ryann dies* to ensure his investment paid off.

"Remember to keep the fight on your feet. End it quick. You're not here to entertain, you're here to win. Get in and get out. The longer you let this play out, the more likely you'll take damage."

Aiden nodded, finally feeling that familiar heat of adrenaline coursing through his veins as his body and mind prepared to step into the cage. Knocking sounded on the door, and a gruff voice barked, "You're up."

Aiden stood, taking a deep breath, and held it, forcing all thoughts from his mind except the next thirty minutes. Single-minded purpose came over him, and with it cold, hard determination.

"You ready?" Del Toro asked.

"Yep."

"Then let's do this."

# CHAPTER

34

Stepping into the Lion's Den was like entering chaos. The noise was deafening. The underground arena was built as a small-scale replica of the Roman-style coliseum. As Aiden and Nikko walked through the concrete tunnel leading toward the center ring, Aiden felt Del Toro's tension radiating off him like a live wire. Aiden shot his friend a quick glance.

Nikko was locked down tighter than a drum. His jaw was clenched, and hard lines of tension blanched the scar running down his cheek. The steel gray of his eyes darkened to slate in the shadows of the tunnel. A niggling of unease piqued Aiden's awareness. He'd seen this look before—that far off, "physically here but mentally somewhere else" glower that hinted at the fine razor's-edge of control his friend walked.

It was what made the other CFA fighters wary of him, what spawned all the talk and speculation as to what the hell had happened to give this guy such a hair trigger. Whatever it was, now couldn't be a worse time for it to make an appearance.

"Hey." Aiden stopped and grabbed Del Toro's arm, turning his friend to face him. "You all right, man?" His voice echoed through the concrete dome. He probably shouldn't have touched the guy, because Nikko's reaction was reflexive. He yanked his arm out of Aiden's grip but thankfully he had the clarity not to launch on the offensive.

"I'll be fine once I get out of this fucking rat-hole tunnel," he growled.

Fair enough. Aiden held up his hands in surrender and proceeded to follow his friend down the concrete tube. Everyone had their demons, and Del Toro sure as hell had his share, but when push came to shove, Aiden wouldn't want anyone else in his corner.

True to the guy's word, as they exited the tunnel, the tension ebbed from Nikko's face. That determined focus returned, once again centering solely on Aiden and this fight. As they made their way to the ring, Del Toro glanced left, then right, at the tiers of people surrounding them. "Fuck, I feel like they should have dressed you in gladiator get-up and put a sword in your hand. Can you get a load of this shit?"

Aiden chuckled. "It is a bit theatrical, huh?"

"I'd say. That Moralli?"

Del Toro canted his head toward the elevated imperial box. The platform had stairs on each side and was raised above the podium on a dais supported by four columns. It was obvious Vincent had gone to great lengths to replicate the Roman stadium, and judging by the looks of the fighter KO'd on the mat, he had a feeling the battles that took place here would be just as brutal.

New York was the only state in the country where MMA was illegal. In 1997 the acting governor labeled the sport "barbaric" and urged state legislators to outlaw it. Since then, the UCL, or Underground Combat League, had promoted twenty-three cards in and around Manhattan. There were no weight classes between divisions here, and the UCL's "anything goes" branding would be put to the test here tonight.

"That's him," Aiden growled, glaring up at the bastard who sat in one of the two front seats, watching with bored interest as the ref dragged a bloody, unconscious fighter from the cage. Moralli's arrogant air of untouchability grated Aiden's nerves, making him want to charge up those steps and pummel the shit out of him.

*Soon* . . . Soon this son of a bitch would get what was coming to him. Until then, Aiden would play the game and do his damnedest to stay above suspicion.

"You ever see anything like this before, Disco?" Del Toro asked, grabbing each of Aiden's hands and taking one last look at his wraps. Satisfied, he pulled a roll of fighter's tape from his pocket and began wrapping it over the Velcro to keep it from coming loose during the fight. This would be the first time Aiden had ever fought in just wraps, and he wondered how well they'd hold up.

"Nope. You?"

"In the corps. We used to bare-knuckle it all the time. It was kind of a rite of passage for all who went recon. Then again, we did a lot of crazy shit I wouldn't advise."

This was the first time Nikko had ever voluntarily mentioned the Marine Corps. Aiden wondered if he'd done it to distract him from the chaos mounting around them. The natives were getting restless, yelling and jeering at the ref to hurry up as the guy attempted to mop the blood off the soiled mat, but succeeded in just smearing it around.

"Underground fighting is big in this city, and assholes like Moralli are making money hand over fist. Because MMA is illegal here, there is zero competition with sanctioned fighting. They've cornered the market."

"I meant what I said earlier," Del Toro said, ripping a strip of tape from the roll. "You got this. Just keep your guard up and go for the KO."

It was good advice and the last he'd get as Aiden knocked fists with Nikko and stepped into the cage, ready to get this over with and anxious to get home to Ryann.

At the sound of the lock disengaging, Ryann put her laptop aside and leapt up. By the time she reached the foyer, Aiden was coming inside. Relief flooded her veins in a surge of emotion that lifted an invisible weight from her shoulders. She could finally breathe again.

"Aiden!" She rushed toward him, perhaps with a bit too much zeal, because he bit out a low, pained groan when she threw herself against him and wrapped her arms around his neck. "Oh, gosh, I'm so sorry. Are you all right?" When she tried to pull back, his arm slipped around her waist, hugging her tight.

"He fucked up his shoulder," Nikko offered, closing the door and stepping past them.

"It's fine," Aiden interjected, shooting his friend a *thanks for ratting me out* glower. "I'm fine," he told her, cupping her jaw and tipping her face so he could look into her eyes. That he'd yet to move his right arm wasn't lost on her. "I just need a hot shower, that's all."

"What happened? How did the fight go?"

"He was fucking amazing!" Nikko answered from the dining room. "Just like I knew he would be. Paskel didn't stand a chance. KO'd him in the first round with a right hook."

Since her MMA crash course with Nikko this afternoon, she knew that meant Aiden had knocked Paskel out in the first round. The right hook punch allowed the fighter to use the momentum of his whole body, throwing torque and momentum into the blow, making it one of the most popular and effective knockout punches used in MMA.

"That's how you hurt your shoulder?"

"No, he injured his shoulder in the Vegas fight. This just pissed it off more," Nikko offered. Aiden shot his friend a *shut up* scowl. A worried frown pulled her brows tight; she hadn't realized he'd gotten injured during that fight.

"Come with me." Taking Aiden's uninjured arm, she led him through the dining room and toward his bedroom.

Nikko chuckled as they passed by. "Looks like you're in good hands, Disco. Since I'm officially off duty, I think I'm gonna head out and explore Manhattan a bit. See ya in the morning, Gingersnap."

"Good night, Nikko," she called behind her.

Ryann didn't let go of Aiden's hand until they were in his bathroom and standing beside the Jacuzzi. She bent over the side and turned on the water, testing the temperature with her wrist. "Wait here," she told him, returning a moment later with a small bag of essential oils. She sat on the tile ledge of the tub and unzipped the pouch. After sorting through the vials, she found the one she wanted and poured several drops into the water.

"What are you doing?"

She could hear the fatigue in his voice, but the husky undertone of desire was unmistakable. "It's lavender. It will help you relax."

When she turned toward him and lifted the hem of his T-shirt, he quirked his brow, giving her a skeptical, lopsided grin. "You're not going to make me smell like a girl, are you?"

Ryann laughed as she tugged his shirt over his head, taking care with his right shoulder. "Maybe a little. But it'll be worth it, I promise."

Aiden watched her with a mixture of amusement and curiosity. The fatigue etched in his face was quickly disappearing. She dropped his T-shirt on the ground, and her gaze swept over his sculpted chest, down the rigid muscles of his torso. Lower still, she could see the outline of his erection straining against the cloth of his sweats, the waistband riding low on his lean hips.

Aiden hissed, a breath sucked in through clenched teeth. "Fuck, Ryann, you gotta stop lookin' at me like that, or . . ."

She mentally reprimanded herself for the detour her thoughts were taking. She knew where that destination led, and although she really wanted to go there, this wasn't about her. Aiden had fought for her tonight. And she wanted to show him how much that meant to her. How much she supported him. How much she loved him.

He grabbed for her, but she scooted out of reach before he could get ahold of her. "Just be patient," she teased.

"Baby, I've got so much testosterone pumping through my system right now, all I can think about is working it out on you."

The flutter of heat licking at her core burst into a full blown inferno at his confession. This was the first time he called her *baby* that she didn't want to punch him. Gone was that carefree, flippant pet name. This was an endearing plea for mercy that melted her heart.

*Focus!* Ryann stood behind him, hoping he'd be easier to resist from the back than the front. She slipped her thumbs in the waistband of his sweats and worked them over his hips. She was wrong. Oh, so very wrong. The wide span of Aiden's shoulders began the V down his muscular back to the most spectacular ass she'd ever seen.

As the silky material dragged down his legs, he let out a throaty growl. "If your goal here is sadistic torture, I'd say you're spot fucking on."

Her laughter rang out, and she forced herself back on task. She stepped around him, studiously keeping her eyes averted from his front, and turned off the faucet. As she touched the button for the jets, the motor beneath the tub started to life and the water became a turbulent rush of inviting chaos. Fragrant steam rose from the tub, an earthy floral fauna filling the air.

"The water even smells like you . . ." he groaned.

"Go on, get in," she instructed.

Keeping her back to him, she tried to block out the throaty masculine sounds coming from the tub as Aiden sank into the hot whirlpool. Not wanting to get her only pair of pajama pants wet, Ryann slipped them off and took her time folding them before placing them on the towel rack. She brought a towel back with her. Wearing a maroon tank top and shell-pink panties, Ryann knelt on the plush terry-cloth towel and began soaping a loofah. "Come here," she said, motioning him closer.

Aiden scooted in front of where she knelt and presented her with his back. "You don't have to do this, you know."

"I know. I want to."

"You're going to spoil me," he groaned, when she began running the sudsy sponge over his shoulders and up the back of his thick, corded neck. Her hand dipped beneath the water to follow the path of his spine.

"You deserve it," she whispered beside his ear.

Aiden lifted his hand out of the water and threaded his wet fingers into her hair, holding her there as he turned his head and captured her lips. His mouth plundered hers, his kiss so erotically delicious and hungry. She was awash in the taste of him, defenseless to resist the skill with which he drove her senseless. In a sudden move she wasn't expecting, Aiden turned and grabbed her, pulling her into the tub with him. Water splashed over the side as she landed in his lap.

He laughed at her startled yelp, ignoring her protests as he proceeded to remove her soaked tank top. "I'm trying to take care of you, and you're not cooperating," she complained half-heartedly.

"You are taking care of me," he growled, nipping playfully at her throat. "My way . . ."

He ignored her playful objections, ripping the thin elastic straps of her panties, and lifted her to straddle his lap. If his shoulder was hurting him, he wasn't babying it now. When he set her down, he entered her with a well-timed thrust, seating himself against her core. Her pleasured cry was mingled with his lustful growl as his hands dropped to her hips and began working her up and down the hard length of his cock.

"Fuck, Ryann . . . I'd fight every day if it meant coming home to this."

In that moment, as Aiden took command of her body, of their pleasure, she was pretty sure that was the sweetest thing he'd ever said to her.

# CHAPTER

"You never told me how your meeting went yesterday."

Ryann rolled onto her stomach and gathered Aiden's pillow in her arms, drawing his scent deep into her lungs as she propped it beneath her chin. She lay across his bed naked, knees bent, calves intertwined in the air as she watched him dress. The man was a work of art—from the flawless design of his body to the fluid masculine grace of his movements . . . Would she ever tire of staring at him?

She knew she'd caught his notice when his eyes locked on hers in the reflection of the mirror, hands stilling on his tie. He muttered a curse, the flare of lust darkening that deep golden color. She gave him a grin of pure feminine satisfaction as she watched his gaze break away and travel the length of her naked posterior.

"I'm going to have you like this tonight," he growled, cinching his tie into place.

His warning heated the blood in her veins until her toes tingled with anticipation. Lord help her, she loved this man. "I'll be looking forward to it," she teased.

"Minx . . ." Aiden strode over to the chair and grabbed his jacket, slipping it on.

She didn't think she'd ever get used to seeing him in a suit. She knew how much he hated it, how badly the conformity rankled him. "You didn't answer my question," she prompted.

"The meeting went as well as I expected." Was she just being paranoid or did he sound evasive? "I'm not sure if the evidence will be enough. If we had something clear cut—indisputable . . ." He shrugged. "It's a wait-and-see game right now. My father showed up at the office yesterday. He doesn't trust me, not that I blame him, but he's being cautious. With any luck this will all be over soon. Until then, I'll play the game, working for my father during the day, and fighting for Moralli at night. If they think they've won, they're less likely to see what's coming."

Ryann wanted to ask him what he thought was going to happen when this was all over. What did he envision happening with them?—or was she just a temporary diversion while he gutted out his time here in New York? Would he stay? Would he want a life here with her? She couldn't see him walking away from his career with the CFA. Yet, Ryann couldn't help but notice that Aiden had yet to speak of their future.

"Oh, I forgot to tell you last night. I got an e-mail from a man who said he was a friend of my father."

Aiden tensed, hands stilling on the buttons of his jacket. "What did he want?"

"To give me his condolences, and tell me he had something my father wanted him to give me if anything ever happened to him."

"Do you have any idea what it is?"

She shook her head. "I arranged a meeting with him. I was hoping for today, but he's unavailable until Monday. We're meeting in midtown at seven."

"Where in midtown?"

"O'Lunney's."

"Times Square is pretty crowded. Did you pick the location or did he?"

"I did. It was my dad's favorite bar." She could see the skepticism in Aiden's eyes. She'd be lying if she said she didn't share his concern. She'd considered the risks, the possibility that this could be a setup, and she could see Aiden was thinking the same thing. He was worried for her, yet she could tell he was hesitant to say anything that might dash her hopes. If this was legit, then this was her only opportunity to reconnect with her father from the grave, and the possibility was too great a temptation to pass up. What could her father want her to have that he couldn't share with her while he was alive? Ryann couldn't imagine, but she was determined to find out.

"Do you know the man's name?"

"Henry. That's all I know."

"No last name?"

She shook her head.

"Did your father ever speak of him?"

"Not that I can remember. Toward the end, Dad had grown pretty private, though. Obviously, since I had no idea he was working for Moralli."

"Nikko and I will go with you. He can get there early and scout the area. Let this Henry know that I'll be with you so he doesn't get spooked when you don't show up alone."

"All right."

"I gotta go." Aiden bent down and gave her a quick kiss. He started to pull back, then hesitated, slipping his hand behind her head and deepening the kiss. His tongue pushed past her lips, tangling with hers until she was breathless. With a reluctant groan, he broke away, resting his forehead against hers. "I really gotta go."

"You already said that," she teased. "I'll see you tonight."

Giving her a wicked grin, he growled, "You bet your sweet ass." Stepping back, Aiden gave her a playful swat on said ass and walked toward the door.

"Hey," she yelped, laughing, reminding her of the first time she'd met the flirtatious playboy and he'd done the same thing to her. If someone would have told her then that she'd be head over heels in love with the fighter, she would have said not a snowball's chance in hell. Guess it was looking up for snowballs.

"You know you didn't need to come with me," Ryann complained, shooting Nikko a suspicious scowl from the driver's seat as she parked the Escape in the driveway of Andrews Private Investigation Services.

"I know, but I was going stir-crazy in that condo. Besides, I thought it might be cool to see where you worked."

Uh-huh . . . Nikko didn't exactly strike her as the kind of guy who'd be impressed by office supplies. He was tagging along with her. Why? "I don't need a babysitter, Nikko."

"Well that's good, because I don't do diaper duty. I want your car. That's it. How long do you think you'll be? I have some errands I need to run."

"Oh . . ." Her cheeks warmed with the kiss of embarrassment at jumping to conclusions. "I umm . . . I'll be a few hours."

"All right."

He climbed out of the car at the same time she did and met her halfway. She handed him the keys. "Thanks," he said, pocketing them. When she proceeded toward the office and felt him at her heels, she shot him a questioning glance over her shoulder. "Mind if I use the bathroom before I leave?"

"Sure." She gave him an apologetic grin. "You got in late last night," she commented offhandedly, stopping at the door to dig through her purse for her office key.

"I figured you and Disco could use some space."

"I wish I could have seen him fight." She found the key at the bottom of her bag and pulled it out, a wistful smile touching her lips when she saw the mini Statue of Liberty dangling from the keychain. It was funny how some of the cheesiest, most insignificant things could grow to mean so much in the face of loss. Her father had given her the gaudy keychain in a jewelry box for her sixteenth birthday. It'd been attached to the key of her first car.

"You all right, Gingersnap?"

"Yeah," she said sadly, sliding the key into the lock and turning it. "Huh . . ." She tensed, a niggling of alarm shooting through her when the lock didn't click.

"What's wrong?" he demanded.

"The door . . . It isn't locked. I know I— Nikko, what are you doing?"

Before she could blink, Nikko's arm swept in front of her, herding her behind him and backing her up flush against the side of the building. "Wait here," he commanded, reaching behind his back and pulling out a gun she hadn't even known he was carrying. With swift efficiency, he chambered a round and brought the gun up to a ready position. And *that* was her first clue this guy was not your run-of-the-mill MMA fighter.

Her instincts about him had been right. Nikko Del Toro was a lethally dangerous man. He didn't even hesitate as he stepped through the door. By the way he moved through her office, doing a thorough sweep, it was obvious he'd done this sort of thing before. She'd be willing to bet he was ex-law enforcement, or maybe ex-military.

Glass crunched beneath his feet. She waited as long as she could stand it before following him inside. Her horrified gasp broke the silence. Nikko shot her a tense scowl that softened with sympathy as she surveyed the wreckage. The place was destroyed. Papers were scattered everywhere, glass from the office doors was shattered, computers were smashed.

When Nikko entered the last room—her father's office—his curse echoed in the hallway. Her gut clenched, threatening to bring up her breakfast. She'd left her father's office as it was when he'd died, not yet ready to accept the loss of him, all the while harboring the insane hope that at any moment, her father would stroll into work and life would resume right where it left off a little more than a tragic month ago.

But all that was ruined now. Not a possession remained on his old wooden desk. Books were pulled from the shelves and strewn across the floor. File cabinets were overturned, nothing was left untouched—nothing deemed too sacred to destroy. A broken sob escaped her throat. She raised a shaky hand to her mouth in disbelief as her gaze fell on the family picture her father kept on his desk. It was the last one taken before her mother died. The memory now lay face-up on the floor, the glass spider-webbed across their faces. It was the perfect imagery of her life—shattered and in pieces.

Numbly, she shuffled farther into the room, stopping next to the photo. She bent, picking the sacred picture up from the floor. "Ruined . . ." she said, woodenly. "It's all ruined . . ." Tipping the frame upside down, she dumped the glass onto the floor, adding the shards to the mess. Carefully, she slid the picture from the frame and hugged it to her chest. Oh, God, she was going to lose it right here in front of Nikko . . . "Excuse me," she choked out, tossing the frame to the floor and rushing out of the room.

"Ryann, wait . . ."

She fled to the bathroom, the only door that didn't have a window to break, and slammed the door behind her. The moment the lock snicked into place, she let go, crumpling to the floor in a heartbroken heap. Her job was all she had left—this was all that remained of her dad.

Ryann wasn't sure how long she sat there, sobbing inconsolably while she rocked back and forth, clutching her photo. In between her hitching breaths, she heard a soft knock against the door. It was gentle but persistent. Nikko had tried to get her to open it a couple of times, but when she refused to acknowledge him, he'd respectfully retreated.

"Ryann, sweetheart, open the door," the familiar, deep voice beckoned from the other side.

Like a single ray of light breaking through the clouds, so was the sound of Aiden's voice fracturing her grief.

"How long has she been in there?" she heard him ask, concern straining his voice, making it gruff and impatient.

"About an hour. I called you as soon as she locked herself in."

"This wasn't vandalism . . ."

"Nope. But I think someone wanted it to look that way. The whole place is trashed, but none as bad as her dad's office. They needed it to look random, so they hit the rest of the place hard."

"Fuck . . . I don't think it's a question of who did this as much as what did they want and did they find it."

As Ryann sat on the floor beside the plastic potted ficus, listening to Nikko filling Aiden in on his speculations, she struggled to get a grip on her unresolved grief that'd been brought back to the surface by the destruction of the last thing that was her father's. He loved this office, loved being a private investigator. How had things gone so terribly wrong? Memories of better days, when her mom was still alive and her father was the backbone of their small tight-knit family, tore another broken sob from her throat.

"Ryann," Aiden knocked on the door a little louder and a lot more insistently this time. "Let me in." He rattled the knob and swore.

She didn't want to open it. She didn't want him to see her like this—out of control and emotionally broken.

"Can you open this door?" he asked Nikko impatiently. "Or I'm going to break the fucker down."

A moment later, there was a chink of scraping metal and the soft click of the lock. The door opened and Aiden filled the entrance. The determined scowl on his face bore harsh lines of concern. Before she could move or say a word, she was in his arms, pulled into the shelter of his strong embrace. What little control she'd gained over her emotions was lost. Gut-wrenching sobs came from somewhere deep inside her, somewhere she didn't even know existed. "It's over," she cried. "Every last bit of him is gone now, and I've lost everything."

"Shhh," he crooned, tucking her head beneath his chin and hugging her tight against his chest. "I'm sorry, baby. So sorry . . . but you're not alone. You have me, and we're going to get through this. I promise." The weight of his cheek rested against the top of her head as he held her there on the bathroom floor and let her grieve.

# CHAPTER

36

"How close are you to making an indictment?"

Aiden sat across from the DA, hoping and praying the guy was going to have some good news. He'd had a hell of a long weekend and sure could use some good news right about now. Ryann was fighting to keep it together, and the strain of watching her struggle through her grief was chewing him up inside. Every day that passed without their drawing closer to a resolution was one more day he felt like he was failing her.

More than anything he wanted to take Ryann away from all this, get her away from Moralli and away from all the painful memories of her past. He wanted to offer her a new beginning, offer her the chance to start over—with him—but he couldn't do that, not until this was finished. Not until he knew he'd receive immunity for his complicity while working for Moralli. When this was all said and done, if he ended up going to jail, he wouldn't ask Ryann to wait for him. He couldn't do that to her, wouldn't put her through that.

"Any word on the immunity deal?"

"I filed the petition and am still waiting to hear, but it should be any day now. Jeez, Kruze, have a little patience. You know these things take time. I pulled the feds in to help build this case, but it's not a slam dunk. We're working as fast as we can. The problem we're running into is double jeopardy. We can't try the bastard for the same charges you've already gotten him off for."

"Fuck . . ." Aiden growled, dragging his hand through his hair.

"You're just too damn good of a lawyer."

Aiden didn't miss the frustration and hint of accusation in his friend's voice. He stared at Ike over his beer, paused halfway to his mouth, and grumbled "Thanks" with mirroring sarcasm.

"I'm doing what I can, as fast as I can. But unless you've got any new evidence—something rock solid and indisputable . . ."

"Trust me, I'm trying, but my clearance at the firm is restricted. Shit, I don't know how much longer I can put on a suit every day and go into that office pretending I don't hate every fucking second of it. This isn't me anymore."

"I'm sorry, man. If it helps, you know I've always got your back. I'll push the feds some more and get back to you with an update. In the meantime—"

"Yeah, I know . . ." Aiden waved his hand dismissively. "I probably haven't said it enough, but I appreciate you sticking your neck out like this. It's no simple task you've taken on and if Moralli discovers what we're doing here, either one of us could find ourselves chained to a cement block and tossed into the Atlantic."

Ike grunted and lifted his glass, swigging down his beer. "Christ, Kruze, don't bother sugarcoating it."

Aiden chuckled. "Just giving you a little incentive, that's all. We're playing a dangerous game here, and it's only a matter of time before luck isn't on our side anymore."

This was taking too long. A week had come and gone, and they were still no closer to a resolution. His days were spent at the office, his evenings were busy training for his next fight, and his nights were spent making love to Ryann. It was the only time he felt like he was truly connecting with her these days. He was beginning to resent the demands the firm was placing on him, and he could feel that old familiar undercurrent of bitterness rising up inside him.

The one thing he'd always loved, the one place he'd always found solace, was in the gym. Leave it to Moralli to steal that from him, too. Aiden no longer fought because he loved the sport. He fought because that bastard hadn't given him any choice. Ryann's life was on the line if he didn't fight, and the thought of it just about made him sick. More than anything, he didn't want to fail her, and the pressure was beginning to eat away at him like a slow-growing cancer, making him irritable and edgy. He just wanted this to be over.

The only silver lining in this cloud was that Ryann was meeting with Henry tonight. Aiden hoped whatever he had to give her would help provide some of the closure she needed to begin healing. It wasn't easy, discovering your dad wasn't who you thought he was. God knew when it had happened to him, he hadn't taken the news well. All things considered, Ryann was doing an impressive job keeping it together, though he knew it wasn't without a lot of effort and private suffering.

Aiden was almost back to the condo when his cell rang. He glanced down at his caller ID and uttered a foul curse.

"What?" he answered, his voice a strained growl.

"Bored with the lovely Ryann already?"

*Fuck* . . . Well, that didn't take long, further proof he was running out of time. Aiden hoped the tail was on him and not on Ike. The DA arrived early and left well after he did so as not to arouse suspicion. This time, Ike had booked a private room with a personal dancer, limiting the chances of them being seen together. Yet it left Aiden with the unpleasant task of fronting the lie and feeling guilty as hell for not being totally honest with Ryann about where he was having his meetings with Ike.

"Ryann and I are none of your business, nor are my sexual appetites.

I might fight for you, but what I do with my personal time is no concern of yours."

Moralli's answering chuckle grated on his nerves, making him wish he could reach through the phone and choke the life out of the son of a bitch. "Aiden, do you know what I prize above all things?"

*You've got to be fucking kidding me . . .* He closed his eyes, trying to summon his nonexistent patience. "Is this going to take long? Because I got—"

"Loyalty."

"What?"

"The thing I prize above all else. Don't make me test yours, Aiden. You won't like it very much."

With that warning, the line went dead.

"Does this feel too firm to you?"

Nikko's brow arched in question. "I wouldn't know."

"Well, you're not going to know unless you touch it."

"I don't want to touch it."

"Oh, come on, Nikko, quit being so stubborn. Just squeeze it."

"I don't even know what I'm feeling for."

"It should be soft with just a little firmness."

Nikko defiantly crossed his arms, putting a lot of intimidating muscle on display. She smiled sweetly, trying not to laugh at the sight he made. He was all scowl and brawn, pushing a shopping cart through the produce aisle, arguing with Ryann about avocados.

She was nervous about her meeting with Henry tonight and had decided to channel that restless energy into productivity. Aiden's cupboards could use a good stocking. Nikko had insisted on tagging along—again—and if he was going to pretend he wanted to be here shopping, she was going to make sure he got the full grocery experience, complete with fruit squeezing and all.

"Listen, I am thirty years old, and I have gone my entire life not knowing a thing about avocados. And you know what? I'm all right with that."

"You never know . . ." she teased, deriving sadistic pleasure in torturing the tough-as-nails MMA fighter who looked hilariously out of place partaking in such a domestic chore. "What if you meet a girl who loves guacamole?"

"I don't think that's gonna happen."

"What won't happen? That you're not going to meet that special someone or that she won't love guacamole?"

"Both."

"Why not?"

"New topic."

"Oh, come on, Nikko. Are you seriously trying to tell me there's no one special in your life?"

"Look, Ryann."

It wasn't by mistake that he used her given name. He was getting pissed. He leveled her with a defensive scowl, but that look had lost its effect after nearly being joined at the hip for the last few days. A coincidence? She thought not, but Nikko always had more than enough excuses why he wanted or needed to accompany her.

"You hardly know me well enough to be having this conversation."

"On the contrary." She poked him in the chest with her avocado. "I'd be willing to bet that I know you better than just about anyone, except maybe Aiden."

Those silvery-gray eyes stared her down, but she was immune to his intimidation. "I know you act like a hardass, but deep down you're really a sweet guy. You keep your demons closely guarded, but I suspect they torture you more than you let on. You don't like to let people in because you don't want to care about them and you don't want them to care about you. You like your life simple, and the more people in it, the more complicated it becomes, so you work hard to shut people out whenever you can. You hate to talk about yourself, you're rigidly disciplined and extremely intelligent. Oh, and you never leave the toilet seat up, which I very much appreciate, by the way."

He stood there a moment staring at her, the expression on his face giving nothing away. She could be right or way out in left field for all he let on. But she knew she wasn't wrong. There weren't a lot of guys that would put their life on hold to help a friend. No, Nikko gave 100 percent to the few people he did care about.

"You finished with your assessment there, Dr. Phil?"

"I think so," she said, feeling rather pleased with herself.

"Good, then hurry up and finish your shopping. And for the record, I'm not a hero, Ryann. So don't go making me into something I'm not."

"Would you take a bullet for me, Nikko?" It was a hypothetical question, but Ryann was determined to make her point.

"Of course I would." His response was immediate and without hesitation. Nikko was serious. *Huh . . . well there's a twist.*

"Well then, that makes you *my* hero, and *that* is what qualifies me to ask you about your personal life."

"I'd rather squeeze your avocado," he grumbled.

Ryann laughed and tapped him with the fruit again. "I bet you would." She turned then and piled four dark green fruits into the cart before continuing down the produce aisle. Nikko followed behind her, his surly scowl drawing wary looks from the other shoppers around them—except from the one coming from a twenty-something brunette who was actually quite attractive.

"Ooo . . . Nikko," Ryann whispered, nudging him with her elbow. "What about that one over there?" Ryann nodded toward the woman across the aisle, sorting through pineapples. She'd seen the woman's gaze dart to Nikko a couple of times as they'd rounded the produce department.

"What about her?" he grumbled.

Seriously? The man seemed completely impervious to the woman's beauty or her subtle interest. "Is she your type?" she prodded, elbowing him in the ribs.

Nikko's scowl darkened another degree. "Does she look like she's my type?" he grouched, growing crankier by the second.

Ryann stopped in between the leafy greens and the tomatoes and turned toward him, her hands posted on her hips. "You say that like there's something wrong with you."

He looked at her as if she'd lost her ever-loving mind—and maybe she had, because this conversation was just about as safe as poking a giant bear with a stick. Why she felt the sudden urge to play matchmaker was beyond her. Maybe she felt bad for him. She could sense his loneliness despite his adamant insistence he wanted to be that way. It was just that she loved Aiden so much, and since meeting him, her life had been complete in a way she never could have expected. He filled a void in her heart she hadn't even known existed. And she wanted that kind of happiness for Nikko, too.

"That's because there *is* something wrong with me. And I'm not just talking about the damage on the outside."

She winced when he pointed at his face. It was a handsome face, even with the scars. In fact, some women might claim they made him more attractive. In all honesty, she hardly noticed the marks anymore.

"Now let it go, dammit!" Plucking her list from her hand, he brushed past her and began grabbing food off the shelves.

"Nikko . . ." She followed after him with the cart. He only acknowledged her long enough to dump the load into the basket before heading down another aisle to power-shop. "Nikko, stop . . ."

By the time she caught back up with him, his arms were full again and he added the groceries to her cart. "No, Ryann, you need to stop. You do not get to be in my head. I'm not here to make friends and I sure as hell am not here to find love. And speaking of, let's talk about you and Disco, cuz I did *not* see that shit coming. At. All. Do you have any idea how into you that guy is? And Disco doesn't do long-term. Yet, he's doing you. Every. Damn. Night."

Whoa . . . wait a minute. Where was this coming from? "Okay, Nikko." Ryann held up her hands in surrender. "Maybe we should just . . . not talk about this."

"What's the matter, Gingersnap? Don't like me digging into your personal life? Then stay the hell out of mine!"

*Oh, wow . . . Ouch.*

Nikko didn't speak to her for the rest of the drive home. Ryann deeply regretted disturbing the peaceful camaraderie they'd slipped into over the past several days and felt embarrassed she might have mistaken it for friendship—which Nikko had made glaringly clear it was not. Maybe he was right and she had no business prying into his personal life, but she cared about him and considered him a friend, even if he didn't return the sentiment. She only wanted to help. Instead, she ended up opening what she feared were some old, painful wounds. And she wasn't sure what, if anything, she could do to make it better.

Maybe she'd talk to Aiden about it on the drive to O'Lunney's this evening. On second thought, perhaps she shouldn't mention it. Aiden didn't need to mediate her and Nikko's squabbles. He had enough on his plate as it was, working at the firm, searching for evidence that would help wrap up this case—and with another fight looming at the end of the week . . . No, she wouldn't say anything. Lesson learned. Personal conversations with Nikko Del Toro were off limits.

The moment they got back to the penthouse, they retreated to their respective corners. Nikko headed to the gym and she retreated to the office to research the next fighter on Aiden's roster. The moment Aiden returned, Nikko was out the door. He'd planned to arrive at O'Lunney's early to check the place out and get into position just in case this thing with Henry blew up in her face. Ryann suspected he would have left anyway, and she'd have been lying if she'd said that didn't hurt.

"Hey, baby, whatcha doing?" Aiden came up behind her and rested his chin on her shoulder. Wrapping his arms around her waist, he gave her a much-needed hug. A wistful smile touched her lips as his warmth enveloped her.

"Researching Patrick Davis."

"Who's Patrick Davis?" he mumbled, kissing her neck.

Her pulse quickened at his touch, sending little shivers all the way to her toes. "The man you're fighting this week." He stood, and she turned her chair around to face him. Reaching up, she unfastened his suit jacket. "How was your day?" she asked, making small talk as she tugged his shirt loose from his pants and began undoing the buttons from the bottom up.

His brow arched in question. "Shitty. Thanks for asking. But something tells me it's about to get a lot better."

Ryann laughed, giving him a flirty grin as her hands dropped to his belt. She unbuckled the latch, slowly pulling it through the loops. "I think you might be right." When she released the button of his pants, he exhaled a tortured groan and scooped her into his arms.

"I missed you today," he growled, carrying her toward his bedroom.

She slipped her arms around his neck and kissed his throat, nipping at the flesh covering his pounding pulse. "Me, too . . ."

Her feet touched the floor beside the bed. Aiden dipped his head, capturing her mouth in a scorching kiss as he hastily uncuffed his sleeves and yanked off his jacket and shirt.

Ryann broke contact long enough to tug her shirt over her head. Aiden dragged his mouth along her jaw, and she tipped her head to the side, giving him access to her neck as she reached behind her back and unclasped her bra, then tossed it to the side. "Any word from the DA?"

He tensed, his kisses momentarily pausing on her throat before resuming a path toward her cleavage. "Nothing yet," he mumbled, cupping her breasts and taking a hardened bud into his mouth. After a long sucking pull that sent a tingling current of pleasure right into her core, he whispered, "Soon, I hope," and moved to her other breast.

Heat flooded her body as it responded to the man that could so masterfully command her pleasure. An impatient whimper caught in her throat as her desperation for him swiftly mounted. Her heart hammered inside her chest, her breath sawed from her lungs that were working to meet her body's demand for oxygen. Aiden was her safe haven, her shelter in the storm of life, and right now all she wanted, all she needed, was to be anchored to him.

Aiden must have sensed her urgency, must have recognized her desperation for what it was, or just maybe he felt that way, too, because he wasted no time stripping them both and lowering her to the bed. When she felt the scorching heat of his shaft slip between her slick intimate folds and fill her aching channel, she tipped her hips, taking him deeper.

"Yes . . ." she moaned. "Aiden, I love you."

Aiden stilled above. The confession had slipped so easily from her lips. It was the first time she'd told him how she felt since the catastrophe in the car. When he didn't respond, a surge of uncertainty needled up her spine and she opened her eyes, surprised to see a dark amber blaze of emotion staring back at her.

"I love you, too, Ryann. And I want you to know nothing is ever going to change that."

It was a vow spoken between them and consecrated through the most intimate of acts, and one that in the coming days would be put to the test of fire.

# CHAPTER

37

"Sweetheart, I don't think Henry is coming. He's almost an hour late."

Ryann glanced over her shoulder to the vacant area near the front door. As she scanned the bar, her gaze briefly connected with Nikko's before breaking away to continue her search, though it was a fruitless endeavor. She had no idea how to identify Henry. In their correspondence, he said he would find her, which meant he knew what she looked like. It was a disadvantage that made her increasingly wary as the time passed with no arrival of the mysterious man. For all she knew, he could be here watching her right now. Perhaps this was nothing more than a clever trick to get her out in the open.

"I think we should leave." Aiden reached across the table and rested his hand over hers, giving it a sympathetic squeeze. She nodded, struggling to disguise her disappointment. This was her last hope, her last connection to her father, and it'd been nothing but a cruel ruse. Aiden made a subtle hand gesture, signaling to Nikko they were going to leave. He stood and pulled his wallet from his pocket, tossing some cash onto the table. Taking her hand, he helped her slide out of the booth and guided her to the door. Nikko remained several paces behind them as they headed down the street toward the parking lot.

"I'm sorry he didn't show," Aiden offered.

"Yeah, so am I. Thanks for coming down here with me." Just as they stepped into the parking lot, Ryann heard someone shout her name. She turned just in time to see a middle-aged man wearing a tan trench coat racing toward them. It wasn't his approach that startled her as much as the terror on the man's face. He ran like the hounds of hell were at his heels. Just as he stepped into the street, three gunshots rang out in rapid succession and the man hit the ground.

"No!" she screamed, impulsively lunging toward the downed man. But Aiden was faster. In seconds, he was on top of her, shielding her with his body before she could put one foot in front of the other. God, he was heavy. She could hardly breathe, trapped between him and the blacktop.

"Get down!" Nikko yelled at the same time she hit the ground. His gun was drawn and amid the screams and chaos of people scattering for cover, Nikko returned fire. He snarled a nasty curse and then took off after who she could only presume was Henry's shooter.

"Let me up!" Ryann struggled to get up from beneath Aiden, desperate to reach the man. It felt like forever before his solid weight lifted and she scrambled to her feet, bolting into the street. "Call 911!" she told Aiden, dropping to her knees beside the man.

"Henry?" Oh, God, there was so much blood. Ryann pressed her fingers against his neck, feeling for a pulse. It was faint and thready against her fingertips, and she breathed a short-lived sigh of relief he was still alive. "Henry?" she called again. Slowly, the man's eyelids flickered open, searching as if straining to see her through the darkness. "It's me, Ryann. I'm here." She reached for his tightly fisted hand, holding it between both of hers.

He tried to speak, but the effort sent him into a coughing fit. Blood splattered onto his cheek, pooling in the corner of his mouth. Each labored breath brought the undeniable wheeze of death. "Just hang on," she pleaded, gripping his hand tightly in hers. "Help is coming!"

"Ryann?" His glassy eyes seemed unable to focus on her.

His words were wet and raspy, but she could still make out her name. "I'm here . . ." She squeezed his hand as proof.

"Don't. Trust. Anyone." The warning died on his lips as he released his last breath. His tightly fisted hand went limp in hers and something dropped into her palm. She curled her fingers around the slender rectangle and held it tight as her shoulders wracked with mournful sobs. "I'm so sorry . . ." she repeated the apology over and over as she cried for Henry, cried for her dad—so much senseless death.

As she knelt over the man's lifeless body, the solid weight of Aiden's hand came to rest on her shoulder. Sliding down, he gently rubbed her back as she mourned another life taken by the hand of Vincent Moralli.

It was the middle of the night before they got home, having spent several hours at the police station giving their statements. Nikko had gone back to the penthouse after losing the shooter in the crowd. Neither she nor Aiden had given the police Nikko's name when questioned about the identity of the man who'd chased after the gunman.

She could add that to her list of lies, because she told no one about the flash drive she'd gotten from Henry, either—not even Aiden. A man had been killed for this tonight, and his dying words had been a warning to trust no one. She needed to see what was on this stick before she shared it with anyone.

The moment Aiden opened the front door they were greeted by the sound of a gun being cocked. Aiden tensed and yanked Ryann behind him. "Fuck, man, it's just us," Aiden growled.

She could see Nikko past Aiden's shoulder. He was sitting at the dining room table, facing the front door, wearing nothing but a badass scowl and a pair of sweats. He muttered something she couldn't understand and took the gun off them. With the weapon pointed at the ceiling, he released the hammer and set it on the table beside the half-empty bottle of vodka.

"Didn't anybody ever tell you that guns and booze don't mix?" Aiden grouched, walking Ryann past the dining room, careful to keep himself between her and Nikko. "You shoot me and I'm going to be pissed."

Nikko chuckled, or at least that's what she thought it was intended to be, but it came out sounding more like a dark, angry snarl that sent a shiver of goose bumps prickling up her arms. This was the side of Nikko she'd sensed when she'd first met him, the side that put her on guard and made her wary. As they got closer, she noticed the smattering of scars down the side of his chest. Wow, he wasn't kidding when he'd told her he was damaged. This man who watched her with the silvery eyes of a predator made her feel like prey caught in the hunter's snare. Had she really just today been joking with him?—teasing him about avocados? Well, she'd been wrong about one thing: those demons that tormented Nikko were a lot closer to the surface than she ever realized.

She stopped when they entered the living room, and she placed her hand on Aiden's arm. "Why don't you talk to him? Something is obviously wrong. It's late and I've had a horrible night. I think I'm going to take a shower and go to bed."

Aiden frowned, possibly sensing her dismissal for what it truly was. She wanted to be alone. She needed some time to herself to process everything that had happened. He cradled her face in his hands and tipped it up to search her eyes. What was he looking for? The strain of the day was etched in the fine lines of his handsome face. The draw of his brows seemed to be in a perpetual state of tension these past few days. Not that she blamed him. The man was under an incredible amount of stress. Under the circumstances, he was holding up remarkably well.

"Are you sure you're going to be all right?"

She nodded. "I'll be fine. Please tell Nikko I said thank you—for everything."

He bent down and kissed her before letting her go. She headed down the hallway and ducked into his office to retrieve her laptop before going into their bedroom. After a quick shower, she changed into one of Aiden's superhero T-shirts. Tonight it was Green Lantern. A small smile touched her lips at the sight of her reflection. She brushed her fingers over the lantern symbol printed in the center of the bright green shirt and thought of the fallen heroes in her life—first her father and now Henry. When would it end?

All these years her dad had been her Superman, and that kind of worship didn't just go away. Gambling had been his kryptonite and ultimately it had destroyed him. It didn't matter what mistakes he'd made, she would never love him any less. She just wished she knew the truth so she could finally find closure and claim justice for her father—and now for Henry, too.

Turning from the mirror, she piled pillows against the headboard and climbed into bed. She dragged her computer onto her lap, opened the lid, and turned it on. While she waited for it to power up, she uncapped the flash drive and plugged it into the USB port. A menu popped up in the center of the screen, and the first document she saw was titled *Ryann.* At the sight of her name, her heart began to pound with anticipation. This was it. Whatever was in this file was important enough to kill for. Taking a deep breath, she steeled herself against her mounting anxiety and opened the document. At the sight of the letter, she uttered a little gasp, her hand rising to her lips as she read the last words her father would ever say to her.

*My Dearest Ryann,*

*If you are reading this letter, then that means I am no longer with you. I am so sorry for the way things have turned out. I had hoped for a different outcome. By now you probably know the truth, the truth I've worked very hard to shelter you from, and I want to start by telling you how deeply*

*I regret the decisions I have made. My only hope is that it's not too late to correct my wrongs, and my old friend Henry has agreed to help me do that.*

*I want you to know how much I love you and how very proud I am of the woman you've become. You are the only light in the darkness that surrounds me. I have made mistakes, and in trying to undo them, I've made far greater ones. I fear my demons are about to catch up with me. Were I to do it all over again, I would have taken you someplace far away from here and started over somewhere simpler—someplace safer. It is my hope and my desire that you do that now. Leave New York, Ryann. You're not safe here. Please, Ryann, I beg you, begin a new life far away from here and the evils that pollute our city.*

*I've set up an account in your name. All the bank information is in an attached file. It's your mother's life insurance money, and I want you to use it to start over. It was never my wish to drag you into this, but I fear the ramifications of my actions have made that inevitable. But you must leave, Ryann, before it's too late.*

*Again, I want to tell you how sorry I am and how very much I love you.*

*All My Love,*
*Daddy*

As Ryann read the letter, sadness and regret overwhelmed her, grief wrapping around her chest like an invisible band, tightening until her heart ached from the pressure. If she'd only known . . . if he'd only confided in her, they could have left and started over together and he would still be alive. Now she was alone. No, she reminded herself, resisting the temptation to give into self-pity. She wasn't alone. She had Aiden. Unbidden, Henry's warning returned to haunt her. *Don't trust anyone . . .*

This was crazy. She could trust Aiden—couldn't she? He loved her. And he promised they'd get through this together. She would take her father's advice. She would leave New York. But she had to see this through first. She had to see Vincent Moralli get the punishment he deserved. When it was over, then she'd decide where to go, where to begin her new life, because truthfully, it was just too painful to stay here anymore—safe or not.

Ryann exited the file and opened the one below it. Hope bloomed in her chest, her pulse quickening with excitement when she realized what she was reading. This was it!—the file that would put Moralli behind bars for the rest of his life. But as she read on, her joy was short lived, like a shooting star streaking through the night. After reading through the first few pages, Ryann's optimism began to sink like the mighty *Titanic*.

"Oh, no . . ." she whispered as she read on. Each page was more damning than the last. "Oh, Daddy, how could you do this?" By the time she read through the end of the document, despair gripped her heart. What was she going to do? How was she going to tell Aiden the truth? She didn't have long to think, because a moment later the bedroom door opened.

# CHAPTER

# 38

Ryann startled, slamming the lid shut on her computer. He didn't blame her for being jumpy, especially after tonight, but something told him it was more than that. Guilt was written all over her gorgeous face. He'd seen that look before, been on the receiving end of it more than once, and Aiden got the feeling he wasn't going to like it any more now than he had then.

"I thought you were going to sleep," he commented offhandedly as he closed the door behind him and tugged off his shirt.

"I'd planned to, but . . . I guess I'm too restless to sleep."

She moved the computer off her lap and set it on the nightstand beside the bed.

"What are you doing?" He stripped off his jeans, leaving his boxers on as he crossed to his side of the bed. Funny how they'd gravitated to his and her sides already, how easily they'd settled into a relationship more seamlessly than he'd ever expected. Aiden wasn't used to sharing his space with someone. Hell, he wasn't used to sharing his life with someone, yet now he couldn't imagine spending it without her. He needed this thing with Moralli to be over—like yesterday. And he needed to be free before he could talk with Ryann about their future, about their next step—which they would hopefully take together. How would she feel about leaving New York? Because there was no way in hell he was staying here. With any luck,

Ike would get him that immunity plea bargain, and he could get back to Vegas and resume his fighting career before he lost his position as the top contender for the middleweight title.

"I was reading some files. How is Nikko?"

She was trying to change the subject, clever girl. But he was a lawyer, and a damn good one, too. He was trained to read people. It was what made him so effective in the courtroom, and Ryann was keeping something from him. He shifted tactics, attempting to lower her guard by allowing her to believe her diversion worked.

"Nikko's fine. A little caught up in his head, but he gets that way sometimes."

"Do you know why?"

Aiden climbed under the covers and stretched out beside her. "Not really. He doesn't talk about it and I don't ask. It's why we get along so well, when we're not beating the shit out of each other in the cage. I know he's ex-marine recon and ended his career in Afghanistan. I can only assume it has something to do with that."

"Do you think what happened tonight with Henry might have triggered some memories?"

"It's likely. Again, I don't ask and he doesn't tell." He rolled to his side and faced her, propping his head up with his hand. "I like your shirt."

She smiled and stretched it out, looking down at it. "This old thing? It's not mine. It belongs to my boyfriend."

Yeah . . . he liked seeing her in his clothes. It was sexy as hell, especially when she wasn't wearing anything underneath. "Well, he must have impeccable taste in clothing."

She shrugged. "Or perhaps a superhero fetish. I haven't decided yet."

"Come here," Aiden growled and grabbed her waist, dragging her across the sheets and rolling her beneath him. He kissed her softly, a gentle brush of his lips, wooing her to lower the last of her defenses. It didn't take long for Ryann to melt in his arms. Her hands slipped down his back as her lips parted, encouraging him to deepen the kiss, but he knew once he got started, he wasn't going to be able to stop. And this was too important to ignore. If he wasn't careful, *he* was going to become the one distracted. "You scared the hell out of me tonight," he whispered against her lips, growing serious and steering their conversation back on topic. "When those shots rang out and you tried to run toward that guy . . ."

She grew still beneath him. He could feel the tension edging back into her.

Still he pressed her. "Ryann, I've lived my whole life embroiled in lies and secrets. I don't want there to be any between us."

When her gaze reconnected with his, it was full of uncertainty and regret, making something in his chest tighten with an unfamiliar emotion—dread.

"Aiden, I have something to tell you."

He thought so . . . "What is it, Ryann?"

"Can I get up, please?"

Aiden rolled to the side and raised his arm, allowing her to rise. He sat as she crawled across the bed to the nightstand, grabbed something, and then came back over to him. "When Henry died, I was holding his hand and this was in it." She opened her palm and presented him with the flash drive. "I didn't tell you because I wanted to see what was on it first, if what was on this stick was worth dying for."

He ignored the fact that she'd essentially lied to him for the last ten hours. How easy would it be to let those seeds of doubt begin to take root? If she'd keep something as important as this from him, what else could she be hiding from him? "And is it?" Aiden asked, mindful of his tone and careful to guard his expression.

She nodded.

"What's on the stick, Ryann?"

"Moralli's hit list."

"Fuuuck . . ." Aiden roughly dragged his hands though his hair, locking his eyes on her. "Are you sure?"

Ryann was looking more anxious by the second. "Positive. It's a list of all the men Moralli has hired my father to investigate and all the dates they were killed. There are fifteen names here that go back as far as four years."

"Ryann, that's great news. It's exactly what we're looking for. This evidence, combined with what we currently have, should be enough to put Moralli away for life."

So why was she looking at him like his favorite dog just died?

"That's not all that's on this stick, Aiden."

The knot of dread fisting in his gut tightened, making him want to puke, though he wouldn't let it prevent him from asking the question he feared would derail his life, confirming the thoughts that had already been knocking around in his head for the last couple of days. "Why . . . ?"

She hesitated, and for a moment, he thought she wasn't going to tell him. "Before he died, my dad was investigating your dad. It's all in here—his connection to Moralli and all the illegal activities he's been involved in. Not only will this evidence ruin him politically, but if you hand this flash drive over to the DA, there's a good chance you're going to be sending your father to prison. And if you don't do it, then Moralli's going to get away with murder—including my father's . . ."

Ryann wasn't sure what she was expecting from Aiden, but his thoughtful silence was not it. Was he angry at her for not telling him about the flash drive right away? Was he upset to learn the truth about his father? No doubt the answer was yes to both.

Either way, Ryann didn't feel like it was her place to hand over the flash drive to the DA. As much as she wanted her father's killer to pay, as much as Moralli's victims deserved their justice, she wouldn't take it at Aiden's expense. She would not be responsible for sentencing his father to prison. There were just some things a relationship could not survive, and ruining one's parent was one of them. She couldn't handle the guilt, couldn't be responsible for hurting Aiden, even if it was the solution to all their problems.

"Here." Ryann held out the stick. "Take it."

Aiden frowned. Again, not the reaction she was expecting. "Why are you giving this to me, Ryann?"

"Because what's on this stick could destroy your family, and I don't want to be responsible for that, Aiden. I love you too much to let that come between us. And you might not think that it would, but blood is thicker than water, and I know what it's like to have a father taken from you. I won't be the one to do that to you—even if it means Moralli goes free. Whatever you decide to do with the information is up to you. It's yours now."

When she placed the flash drive in his hand, a surprising amount of peace came over her. The closure she felt in knowing the truth was an unexpected burden lifted from her shoulders. She honestly had no idea what Aiden was going to do with the condemning evidence, but she knew, without a shadow of a doubt, that whatever he decided, she would support him. She wouldn't sacrifice her future for her past.

# CHAPTER

39

Aiden stormed into his father's office and slammed the door, the wall-rattling bang resonating throughout the entire fourth floor. His father looked up from the pile of papers on his desk. The placid expression on the man's face fueled Aiden's fire.

"Aiden, what a surprise."

He strode over to the chair across from his father's desk and plopped down.

"Please, have a seat," his father grumbled, droll sarcasm thick on his tongue. "I assume this impromptu visit is not for pleasure, so it must be business. What do you want?"

"How about the truth? Did you think I wouldn't find out?"

His father exhaled an impatient sigh and slammed his pen on the desk with a sharp rap. "And what injustice, pray tell, have I wrought upon you this time?"

"Cut the shit, Dad. I know . . ."

His father let out a derisive snort, full of contempt. "You don't know anything," he growled.

"I know you had Ryann's father killed."

His expression was completely unreadable, except for the fury sparking in his slate-gray eyes. The seconds ticked by as they sat there in a wordless standoff. After a moment that felt eternal, his father's top lip curled into a sneer. "What you know and what you can prove are two different things. I thought you were a lawyer. You should know that."

So the arrogant bastard wasn't even going to try to deny it. This man actually thought himself so far above the law that he could sit here in this office and admit to murder. Aiden's stomach twisted, and he realized a part of him had been hanging on to the slim hope that he was wrong. He'd been struggling with this for days. Guilt had him avoiding Ryann whenever possible for fear she'd see the truth in his eyes. He'd prayed he was wrong. God, how he'd prayed . . . But after carefully reading the files Ryann had lovingly entrusted into his care, and knowing his father like he did, he could no longer deny the man was responsible for Axel Andrews's death.

Aiden wasn't sure how much longer he could do it. He'd been avoiding Ryann since she gave him the evidence, and the distance growing between them was killing him. He knew how bad it looked. God only knew what she was thinking, but he couldn't tell her, not yet. Fuck, he was trying like hell not to lie to her. If she would give him the flash drive for fear that ruining his father would be too great a strain for their relationship to bear, what did he think was going to happen when she found out his father had hers killed?

The what-ifs haunted him, robbing him of sleep at night and torturing him mercilessly during the day. When at home, Aiden sequestered himself in the gym, claiming he needed to train to justify his distance. It was the truth—sort of—but even Nikko was starting to ask questions, pointing out that he hadn't even trained this hard for his fight with Mallenger. His next fight was in two days. With any luck, this problem with Moralli and his father would be over before then, but if not, he needed to be prepared to step into that cage and win.

Every man had his breaking point, and today, Aiden had hit his when he'd slipped out of bed and snuck from his room, avoiding

Ryann like a coward. This wasn't him, dammit. Aiden Kruze faced life's challenges head-on. He couldn't do this anymore. For days he'd pondered his course of action, but the bottom line was he could no longer turn a blind eye to the truth to protect his father—a man who was loyal to nothing but the lure of power. It didn't matter who he hurt or who he betrayed to get it.

Unfortunately, his father was right: He had no proof, just his suspicions—oh, and the confession of a cold-blooded killer. The lawyer in him knew the evidence he had would never stand up in court—it was his word against his father's.

"You know what, Aiden? You were always too smart for your own good. Someday"—his father tapped his temple with his index finger—"all those smarts are going to catch up with you if you aren't careful."

"Are you threatening me?" It took every last bit of restraint not to leap across the desk and shake some sense into his father before it was too late. But truthfully, the man was too far gone into his hole of self-destruction for Aiden to help him climb out of it now. Someone had to stop him before anyone else got hurt. He just wished it didn't have to be him.

"Christ, you're an ungrateful shit, you know that?" Bennett snapped. It was the first true show of emotion, the first crack in his father's impenetrable armor—and the man was furious. "You could have had it all, you know that? But you threw it all away. And for what?—some cunt and a half-assed fighting career?"

Aiden saw red. Every muscle in his body strung ripcord tight as rage suffused every cell of his body. To keep from saying something he'd regret, he bit the inside of his cheek until the coppery tang of blood touched his tongue. As well placed as those verbal jabs were, Aiden refused to take his father's bait.

"I can't believe you did it," Aiden spat with contempt. "By some miracle Ryann still believes Moralli had her father murdered. What the hell am I going to tell her?"

"You'll tell her nothing!" his father yelled, slamming his fist onto the desk. "Axel Andrews was a man with a death wish—one that I granted him."

"Why was he investigating you? Who hired him?"

"No one! The bastard was blackmailing me. He built a case connecting me to Moralli, then demanded a million dollars for his silence. I silenced him, all right. He could have destroyed my career, Aiden. I couldn't take that chance. He owed Moralli money and everyone knew it. When he turned up dead, everyone just assumed it was a mob hit."

*Oh, my God . . .* Aiden stared at the man sitting across from him, realizing for the first time in his life he was in the presence of a monster. What in the hell was he going to do? How was he going to tell Ryann the truth? In that moment, a single thought resonated deep inside him that chilled him more than the knowledge that his father was a cold-blooded murderer.

*I'm going to lose her . . .*

*I'm going to lose him . . .*

This was the only thought that played through Ryann's head as she woke to find herself alone. He was gone again, and there wasn't anything she could do to stop it. For three days she'd barely seen him. He slipped into bed well after midnight, long after she was supposed to be sleeping, and he was gone again before she woke. Had she erred in giving him the flash drive?—in trusting him? In placing his father's future in his hands, had she pushed him beyond the breaking point?

Though there seemed to be no love lost between him and his father, still the decision he faced was monumental. Once decided, it wasn't something he could go back and undo. She refused to ask him about it. When and if he was ready, she hoped he would talk to her about it. But until then, all she could do was support him any way she knew how. Unfortunately, he didn't seem to want comfort from her. He'd withdrawn into himself, falling back into a pattern of coping she suspected had sustained him all these years—physical exhaustion. Even Nikko had tried to talk to him last night, but Aiden had responded by telling him to either spar or get out of his gym. The flurry of activity she heard coming from the gym had gone on well into the night.

"You okay?"

She looked up from her oatmeal, long gone cold, as she stirred random designs in the mush with her spoon. Nikko shuffled past her on the way to the kitchen, wearing nothing but a pair of black sweats with *Cage Fighting Association* running down the leg. She heard the suction break on the fridge, and a minute later he came walking out with a protein bar in one hand and a tall glass of orange juice in the other.

"I think I should be asking you that," she said, nodding at the dark purple bruise over his left cheek. "It sounded pretty intense in there last night."

Nikko shrugged as if it wasn't a big deal. "Disco just needed to blow off some steam."

"Have you noticed he's been acting different these past few days?" she pressed.

"Of course I've noticed, but you gotta understand, Gingersnap, we're guys. This isn't *The Vagina Monologues*. We don't talk about our feelings."

"Well maybe you should."

"Uh-uh. That's what you're here for. I fight with him, you fuck him. That's just the way it works."

"Well, it's not working," she grumbled under her breath. If he heard her complaining, he didn't press it. She was just glad Nikko was talking to her again. At least whatever dark place he'd slipped into had been a short-lived trip. He'd pulled himself out and brushed himself off as she suspected he'd done many times before.

"What are we doing today?" he asked, changing the subject.

"I'm finishing the dossier for Aiden on Lucas Machio. You want to watch some MMA videos with me?"

He gave a wicked smile that would someday melt some lucky lady's panties. "Hell yeah, let's do this."

The afternoon passed uneventfully, and by late evening when Aiden had yet to come home, Ryann was starting to get restless.

"You're pacing."

"Am I?" She halted midstride and glanced at Nikko, stretched out across the couch in a lazy sprawl, his silvery gaze following her as she trekked back and forth in front of the Manhattan skyline. But tonight she was too anxious to appreciate the view. "How can you sit there and be so calm? It's almost ten o'clock and Aiden isn't back yet. He should have been home hours ago, and he's not answering his phone."

"Relax. Disco's a big boy, not to mention a world-class MMA fighter. He can take care of himself."

Nikko's negligent attitude gave her no comfort. It did, however, piss her off. "What if something happened to him?" That was the closest she would come to voicing her truest fears. Nikko didn't know about the flash drive. She and Aiden had agreed that the fewer people who were aware of its existence the better.

"What do you want me to do?"

"I don't know!" She threw up her hands in frustration, never feeling more helpless. "I'm going to go find him," Ryann declared, marching toward her purse. Nikko was off the couch faster than she thought humanly possible and halting her retreat with a firm grip on her arm.

"Sorry, Gingersnap. I can't let you do that."

"Let me? You can't *let* me?! I have news for you, Nikko, you do *not* get to tell me what I can and can't do. If I want to walk out that door I'm going to, and there's nothing you can do to stop me."

His brow rose, the *oh, really?* an unspoken challenge she wasn't sure she wanted to test. There was some serious *I'm not fucking around* determination flashing in those silver-hued eyes. But she'd never been one to back down from a fight, and Ryann was just worried enough about Aiden to test him.

"Let go of me, Nikko."

They stood there a moment, staring at each other in a wordless standoff. After several tense seconds ticked by, he muttered a foul curse and released her arm. "I'll go find him," he grumbled. "As long as you promise to stay put."

"I promise," she agreed. At this point she'd say just about anything to know Aiden was all right. Now whether or not she actually did it was another story.

Nikko pulled his cell from his pocket and pushed a few buttons. As he stared at the screen, his generally disgruntled countenance darkened.

"What's wrong? What are you doing?"

"I'm pinging him on my GPS."

*Un-fucking-believable . . .* "You've known where he was this entire time and you didn't tell me?"

"I didn't know, because I don't check up on him. I'm not his mother, and neither are you. Sometimes people need their space."

*He means from me . . .* Maybe Nikko noticed the glassiness in her eyes, or maybe he realized what he'd said, because he muttered another curse and dragged his hand through his close-cropped hair. "I didn't mean he doesn't want to be with you. That's not what I was saying . . ."

Oh, no? Well, it sure as hell sounded like it. She held up her hand when he took a step toward her. "It's fine." She turned away to face the window, feigning interest in the skylights. It wasn't like her to be this emotional, but with all the stress of the last few days, and Aiden's growing distance . . . "Just please go and make sure he's all right. I think I'd like a little space myself."

Nikko didn't say anything else as he shrugged on his coat and left. Something was wrong. Ryann had good instincts, and the persistent niggling of unease told her Aiden was keeping something from her. She just wished she knew what and why.

*Note to self: Be careful what you wish for.*

# CHAPTER 40

What in the hell are you doing here?"

Aiden didn't need to turn and look at the man taking the seat next to him to know he was fucked. Dammit, he hated lying to his friend almost as much as he hated lying to Ryann. Could he feel like a more miserable prick? Apparently so, because the condemning daggers Del Toro was glaring at him right now made him want to crawl underneath a fucking rock.

"You haven't changed, have you?"

The accusing growl spoken above the bump-and-grind bass coming from the center stage lit the very short fuse of Aiden's even-shorter temper. Never mind that his back was to the topless dancers. Of course Del Toro would believe the worst. It was a believable front for Disco Stick Kruze, and exactly why he'd chosen this place to meet Ike for the last two weeks. Still, it would have been nice if his friend had given him the benefit of the doubt for even one fucking second.

Today had been hell. After confronting his father about Ryann's dad, he'd come here to meet Ike and the federal agent he'd been working with to hand over the recording of his father's confession and Ryann's flash drive. For the last eight hours, Aiden had been sequestered in the back room where he had told his story, confessed to a lot of shit that would more than likely get him disbarred, and probably would have bought him some jail time if not for the immunity deal Ike had negotiated for him beforehand. He'd answered all their questions and helped build an airtight case against his father and Vincent Moralli. By the time they were done, he was tired as hell, but the lead agent was confident they had enough to make their arrests.

He told Aiden it would take roughly twenty-four hours to file the indictments and obtain their warrants. They planned to pick up his father tomorrow as he left the office after work, but since locating Moralli and getting past his security was a concern, the feds planned to move on him after Aiden's fight. With any luck, after tomorrow this nightmare would all be behind them, but until the arrests had been made, Aiden couldn't say shit about what he'd been doing here.

"What in the hell is wrong with you, man? You've been a goddamn ghost for days and this is what you're doing? *This* is where I find you? Do you have any idea what it would do to Ryann if she knew you were here?"

Aiden snapped, and he was just drunk enough to cast caution to the wind. Spinning on his friend, he grabbed Del Toro, twisting his fist in his shirt and jerking him close. "She better not hear it from you," he growled.

"If you don't get your hands off me right now, I'm going to plant my fist in your face and then drag your stupid ass back home and let you explain to Ryann why I knocked you the fuck out."

By the determination in Del Toro's steely glare, he knew his friend wasn't fronting. Aiden might be lit, but he wasn't wasted enough to miss the edge of protectiveness that iced into Nikko's voice when he mentioned Ryann's name. He didn't appreciate having it directed at him, either, and he was tempted to tell the guy to fuck off and mind his own business. Del Toro had no idea what he was doing here, what he was going through, and he'd be damned if he was about to sit here and explain himself to someone who was supposed to be his friend and sure as hell should have a little faith in him.

Sure, he'd stayed here longer than he needed to, and he'd had a lot more whiskey than he should have, but dammit, he needed to decompress after one hell of a bad day. Right or wrong, part of him was desperate to purge the guilt from his conscience. For just a little while he wanted to escape the weight of condemnation pressing down on him. Was that so fucking horrible? Looking at Del Toro's forbidding countenance right now, the answer to that question was most assuredly yes.

After a long pause, he released his friend with a *fuck off* shove and turned back to the bar, draining his glass of whiskey before waving the bartender over for a refill.

"How many of those have you had?"

"Not enough," he growled.

"Too fucking many, by the looks of it. You know, she's not stupid, man. Ryann knows something's up. Do you really want to throw it all away for bad booze and some used-up pussy? Ryann deserves better than this. I thought you'd changed."

Dammit, he *had* changed. And there it was again, that unmistakable icy shard spiking him in the back. "Perhaps you should take care with your concern, friend, that I don't misunderstand your intentions."

"If you're going to fuck around on her, perhaps you haven't."

Well, what do you know . . . the cherry on top of the goddamn cake. Just when he didn't think this day could get any worse. Aiden sat there, statue still, gripping his glass and putting its durability to the test. He kept his gaze locked on the ice cubes floating in his whiskey. He should have seen this fucking coming. "Does Ryann know how you feel about her?" It took every ounce of strength to temper his voice and not smash this glass upside the bastard's head.

"Nope, and neither would you if you weren't such an asshole."

Rage exploded inside him. In all of two seconds, Aiden was out of his chair and in Del Toro's face. "*I'm* the asshole? *I'm* not the prick getting hard for my friend's girl. Let's get something straight here. I am *not* cheating on Ryann. Nor am I about to stand here and explain myself to you. It may not look like it, but I am fighting like hell for her, fighting for a future with her, and if that's going to be a conflict of interest for you, then I think it's time you go back to Vegas, amigo."

"The only problem I have," Del Toro growled, "is seeing how fucking miserable that woman is, worrying about you while you're MIA. I'm sick of her asking me if I know what's going on with you, or why you're avoiding her. Which I don't and you obviously are." He shoved Aiden a step back. "Or is this not a strip club I just found you getting lit at while Ryann's crying at home, rife with fear that something has happened to you? I know how often you come here. GPS doesn't lie, asshole. Maybe you should shut your tracking off."

"Fuck, is she really crying?" The power of Nikko's words hit him in the gut like a sucker punch. He exhaled a defeated sigh and dragged his hand through his hair as he dropped back in his chair. "God, I'm going to lose her," he muttered to himself, pressing the heels of his hands into his eyes until spots dotted his vision.

Seconds passed while Del Toro stared at him as if trying to puzzle out what he'd just said, then chuffed a masculine snort. "What the fuck are you talking about, man? That girl is crazy about you."

"I've been lying to her. And when she finds out the truth . . ."

Nikko's steely glare darkened. "What are you lying to her about?"

Fuck it, he might as well practice the truth on his friend. If he couldn't say it to him, how in the hell was he going to tell Ryann? "My father had Axel Andrews killed." The words tasted like bitter acid on his tongue, and getting them out failed to cleanse his soul of the consuming guilt.

"Ho-ly shit . . ."

Del Toro stared at him like the universe had just imploded.

Well, Aiden's was certainly on the cusp of doing just that, because Ryann was the center of his and there wasn't any scenario, short of lying to her for the rest of his life, where he saw this working out for them. Who in the hell stays with the guy whose dad is responsible for killing theirs?

"Oh, fuck . . ."

"Yeah, that pretty much sums it up. Not terribly helpful, though, but thanks for that."

"Why? Why would a senator want to risk being caught for murder?"

"Ryann's father had a lot of gambling debts. He was into Moralli for seventy-five grand, and apparently he thought the best way out of that was to blackmail my father. He began investigating him and dug up some pretty unsavory shit."

"This is crazy."

"Tell me about it."

"How long have you known?"

"I've suspected it for a few days. I hoped I was wrong, but when I confronted my dad about it, the bastard didn't even try to deny it."

"Oh, wow, man, this is really bad. Poor Ryann . . ."

Aiden shot him an irritated scowl. "You think?"

Del Toro's glare darkened, reminding him of a CFA weigh-in. That protective glint was back in his eyes, sparking Aiden's already raw nerves.

"You want to know what I think?"

Suddenly Aiden wasn't so sure that he did, but by the determined glare in Nikko's eyes, the option was nonnegotiable.

"I think you'd better tell her before she finds out some other way. She's not stupid, Disco, and sooner or later she's going to figure it out. Maybe you're not giving her enough credit. *You* didn't kill her dad, and it's not like your parents are Ward and June Cleaver. Sure, she's going to be upset at first, but I don't think she's going to leave you. Not if you're up front with her. But if you lie to her about this, if you break her trust . . . you *will* lose her."

If only it was that simple. In telling Ryann the truth, he could possibly lose her forever, and Aiden wasn't sure he was willing to take that risk.

Having Nikko gone gave Ryann the freedom to pace without the scrutiny of his all-too-perceptive gaze. Suspicion, regret, and indecision plagued her every waking moment. Had she done the right thing by giving Aiden the flash drive? The realist in her wasn't so convinced. Ever since that night he'd become withdrawn and evasive. Had she made a horrible mistake by ignoring her father's and Henry's warnings? Could she trust Aiden to make the right decision?

And if her doubts weren't bad enough, Nikko's behavior tonight further confirmed that something was definitely wrong. He might think he was hiding his emotions from her, and generally he was pretty stellar at it, but not today. He was being . . . nice. Which could only mean one thing: Nikko pitied her. He knew something he wasn't telling her. Call her paranoid, and maybe she was, but her gut was seldom wrong about these things, and the knot in the pit of her stomach was telling her something was going on.

Now that she was finally alone, she took another pass through the living room before heading into the kitchen to uncork a bottle of Moscato. Maybe a hot, soapy bath would help unwind her nerves. She carried her glass of wine into the bathroom and set it on the tile rim of the Jacuzzi. She was about to turn on the faucet when she heard her phone ring in the other room. Her pulse quickened and hope fluttered alive in her chest as she rushed to answer the call before it rolled over to voice mail. Maybe it was Aiden calling to let her know he was all right. As she checked the caller ID, her hope was quickly replaced by dread, and the sinking feeling in her gut made her nauseous. When would this be over? When would that bastard finally get what was coming to him? Knowing from experience it would do her no good to ignore the call, Ryann swiped her thumb across the screen and raised the phone to her ear.

"Hello."

"Good evening, Ryann."

She recognized the voice, but it wasn't Luciana's gravelly baritone like she'd been expecting. No, this voice was smoother, more aristocratically arrogant . . . "Mr. Moralli . . . What do you want?"

His insidious chuckle made the fine hairs on the back of her neck prickle. Until meeting Vincent Moralli, Ryann hadn't known she possessed the ability to hate another human being as much as she despised this man.

"I want you to come work for me."

*What!?* He was out of his freaking mind if he thought Ryann was going to work for the man who killed her father. "I'm sorry, as tempting as your offer sounds, I'm going to have to decline," she snarked sarcastically. "I'm not working at all right now, since *someone* broke into my office and trashed the agency. Then again, I'm sure you already knew that. Did you find what you were looking for in my father's office?"

There was a long pause.

"I don't know what you're talking about, Ryann. I haven't done anything to your office. Why would I do that? Admittedly, I've used your father's unpaid debt to manipulate you into taking the Kruze case, but despite what you obviously believe, you're wrong. I didn't touch your agency."

"Wow . . . you almost sound convincing. Next, I suppose you're also going to tell me you didn't have my father killed."

"I didn't."

There was no denying the voice of truth this time. Ryann's stomach clenched, sending a surge of bile up the back of her throat.

"Axel Andrews was my employee, Ryann. Sure, he owed me money, but I have a lot of employees that owe me money. A good PI is hard to come by, and it's bad business to start whacking your staff. So, no, I didn't kill your father. But I know who did."

She didn't want to believe him, but his logic made sense. If Vincent Moralli was telling the truth, that would mean he didn't know about her father's hit list, which would mean he didn't know about the flash drive, so he couldn't have killed Henry. Had she been chasing after the wrong killer all this time? Sure Moralli was guilty of many crimes, and no question he was a very dangerous man. Hell, he was using her to threaten Aiden and forcing him to fight. "If you didn't do it, then tell me who did."

"Now, Ryann . . . you don't think I'm actually going to make it that easy for you, do you? You're a smart girl, I'm sure you can figure it out. Once you take a step back and look at the whole picture, the answer will come to you easily enough. And if not, well then . . . I was wrong and you're not half the investigator your father was. But if I were you, I'd start by asking myself who is powerful enough to influence the New York Police Department. As much as I wish it were, it isn't me."

The pieces began fitting together—clicking into place—and Ryann choked on her startled gasp. "Oh, my God," she murmured, raising her hand to cover her mouth. *Oh, please no . . .*

The deep throaty chuckle echoing on the other end was pure evil. The bastard was enjoying this. He was actually taking pleasure in her heartbreak. "Not quite that high up on the food chain, but you're getting closer."

She didn't want to believe it. It wasn't possible. Aiden's father . . . a murderer? But even as she stood there, numbed by shock, trying to convince herself she was wrong, she knew in her heart it was true. It all made too much sense, the evidence was too damning—evidence that was in front of her all this time, but she was too blinded by her love for Aiden to see it.

"And the answer to your next question is yes, Aiden knows. He met with his father just this morning, before heading to a strip club where he seems to enjoy spending most of his time these days."

Each revelation was another dagger in her heart. "Why are you telling me this?" she demanded.

"I already told you why," he snapped impatiently. "Which means you're not listening, Ryann. I want you to work for me. I'm proving to you that Aiden isn't who you think he is. And although loyalty is an admirable trait I demand in my employees—you've misplaced yours. Your father's death has been terribly inconvenient."

"I'm so sorry for your loss . . ." she mocked.

"You will be if I don't get what I want. I'm only going to be nice for so long, Ryann—and just a heads-up, I'm running out of patience."

"Patience? You call this patience? You had me abducted! You threatened to kill me if Aiden didn't fight for you."

"Yes, well, life is a chess game, Ryann. You can either be a pawn or you can be a rook. If I were you right now, I'd castle."

Before she could utter a response, the line went dead. Ryann swore and tossed the phone onto the bed. Like fine grains of sand slipping through an hourglass, the foundation of everything she believed in was crumbling beneath her. All this time she'd been so quick to blame Vincent Moralli for her father's murder. How could she have been so blind?

Again, the warning in her father's letter came back to haunt her: *You're not safe here. Leave New York.* Henry's dying words—*Trust no one*—echoed like a symphony in her mind, running on an endless loop. *Oh, God,* she thought, *how can this be happening?* The feeling of betrayal became a bitter poison drowning out Ryann's rationality. How long had Aiden known the truth? How long had he played her for the fool, letting her believe Moralli was responsible for his father's crimes?

God help her, she was so naïve. On a whim, she'd handed over the evidence her father had been killed for and Henry had died protecting. How could she have done something as stupid as give that flash drive to the son of her father's killer? Looking back now, it all made a horrible, twisted sense. It was no coincidence that she'd been hired by Aiden's mother to find her son. Was this all some big elaborate scheme from the beginning? Had his parents gotten to him before she'd even arrived in Vegas, or had they turned him once he'd arrived home? Was every second they'd been together a lie? Was he working with his parents to get the evidence that would spare his family ruin? Perhaps this was nothing more than a carefully orchestrated plan for Aiden to inject himself so deeply in her life, blinding her with false proclamations of love, so he could woo the evidence from her. If that had been his game, then she lost. Vincent Moralli was right and she was nothing but a pawn. Considering Aiden's odd, avoidant behavior since she'd handed him the prize, she'd be an even bigger fool to believe anything else.

What if Nikko wasn't here just to help corner Aiden? What if he was really here to keep tabs on her—to watch her and keep her from putting the pieces together? Pieces that fit so perfectly into place, she couldn't believe it'd taken her this long and the aid of a man she despised to figure it out.

All these weeks Aiden had been supposedly meeting with the DA and making no progress, when he'd truly been whiling away his days at a strip club. God, she was such a fool! He'd been baiting her, playing her to give up the evidence that would seal his father's fate. If this wasn't what it seemed, then why wouldn't he have told her the truth from the beginning? Why would he keep something as important as the identity of her father's killer from her?

She couldn't do this anymore. This pawn was quitting the game and taking the advice her father had given her days ago. She was leaving—leaving this place—leaving New York and going someplace no one would find her. There truly was nothing left for her here. Clinging to the blessed numbness of her anger, Ryann pulled her suitcase from under Aiden's bed and began emptying her dresser drawers. She didn't have a lot, and there were precious few things she cared about leaving behind, but her laptop happened to be one of them. Time was of the essence. She didn't know when Aiden would be back, and she wanted to be gone long before he returned. She didn't want to see him, didn't want to give him the opportunity to tell more of his lies and make an even bigger fool out of her.

She zipped the suitcase closed and pulled up the handle, setting it on its wheels. The rollers clacked on the floor with a sharp rap of finality that shattered her breaking heart. If she didn't leave now, she feared she'd lose it before she got out the door. Grabbing her cell off the bed, she shoved it into her back pocket and rushed down the hall, dragging her luggage along behind her. Every few steps the thing would twist and turn, smacking into the back of her legs. "Dammit," she cursed, reaching up to swipe away an escaped tear. As she passed the dining room, she paused long enough to snag a pen and paper from the table and scribble a note:

*I know the truth. Good-bye.*

There wasn't anything else to say. She didn't want there to be any confusion as to why she'd left, or for Aiden to feel like he needed to continue the farce by coming to look for her. He got what he wanted. Now it was time to move on. There would be plenty of opportunity to lick her wounds and mourn her broken heart later. Right now, she just needed to go.

Ryann's grip on her suitcase tightened. She started toward the foyer when the buttons on the keypad outside began to beep. Shit. She was too late. Ryann halted midstep as the door opened.

# CHAPTER 41

Aiden's gaze locked on Ryann. As she stared at him, the storm of emotion he saw raging in those emerald eyes scared the hell out of him. Slowly, he dragged his gaze over her, from head to toe, missing nothing—not the glassiness in her eyes or stubborn tilt of her jaw. And certainly not the fucking suitcase clutched in her hand. When his eyes strayed to the luggage, her grip tightened on the handle until her small fingers blanched of color. Tension radiated from her, tactile energy reaching out and snaking around him.

*Fuck* . . . was the only half-intelligible thought resonating in his mind at finding her steps from leaving him. Just then the undeniable truth hit him with the force of a sucker punch in the gut. *She knows* . . .

His abrupt stop in the doorway caused Nikko to bump into him. "What the fuck, man?" he grouched, sidestepping Aiden. Then he took one look at Ryann and halted. "What are you doing, Gingersnap?" Nikko's naturally gruff baritone suddenly turned soft and cautious, like he was trying to talk her off the ledge. And by the cornered, desperate look in Ryann's eyes, he'd say she wasn't far from it.

"So this is it?" Aiden asked. The hard edge in his voice betraying none of the emotions raging inside him—desperation, fear, panic—all weak, pathetic sentiments she'd reduced him to.

"Nikko, will you please give us a minute?" she asked quietly.

Del Toro nodded, moving past Aiden who had yet to take another step. As he walked by her, he heard the guy murmur, "Don't do anything you're going to regret."

Yeah, it was a little late for that advice. Aiden waited until he heard Nikko's door shut before speaking. "I can't believe you weren't even going to give me a chance to explain."

"What is there to explain, Aiden? I know the truth! I know your father had mine killed. What's worse is that you knew about it and you didn't tell me."

Exhaling a frustrated sigh, he closed the door behind him and stepped toward her. It killed him when she countered with one step back. "Fuck, Ryann, it's not that simple."

"It *is* that simple, Aiden. I've given you everything—my trust, my heart, even my father's secrets—and in return you betrayed me!"

"Is that what you really think, Ryann? That I betrayed you?" Anger made his voice sharp. This was so much worse than he'd imagined. He knew she'd be upset to discover the truth about his father, but betrayal? That was a pretty nasty word, and one not to be thrown around lightly.

"I thought . . . I thought you loved me."

"Dammit, Ryann, I do love you." He took a step toward her and wavered, bracing his hand against the wall to steady himself. *Shit.*

"Are you drunk?" Accusation was ripe in her voice.

"No, I'm not drunk." There was a long silent pause. "All right, maybe I am a little bit," he growled, realizing now might not be the best time to lie to her. He moved toward Ryann and she leapt back with all the finesse of a skittish colt.

"Where were you tonight? For that matter, where have you been for the last three days?—or the last two weeks?"

"I can't tell you."

"Can't or won't?"

"Both."

"Then we have nothing left to say to each other."

She started forward, dragging that blasted suitcase behind her—eyes straight ahead, spine rigid, and shoulders back as she marched past him. Aiden wasn't aware how close to the edge he walked until Ryann shoved him over it—and it wasn't pretty.

"Oh, sweetheart, we aren't even close to being finished." He grabbed her arm, jerking her to a stop and bringing her around until she crushed up against him.

She winced and he bit out a sharp curse, loosening his grip when fear flickered in her eyes.

"Aiden, let me go." Her voice wavered in her attempt to sound calm and in control—both were a fucking lie.

"Dammit, Ryann, don't do this . . ." he pleaded.

She jerked back, wresting herself from his grip, only this time he released her. "You say it like I'm the one being unreasonable here. Aiden, you used me. You used me to get my father's evidence and then you brought it to yours. You've been whiling away your days in a strip club while leaving me to believe all this time you've been working with the DA. I trusted you."

Her accusations couldn't have caught him more off guard if he'd been sucker-punched blindfolded. "That's what you honestly think I've been doing all this time? You believe I would do that to you?" He grabbed her shoulders and gave her a shake he wished to God would rattle loose some sense in her. Her doubt, her mistrust, her utter lack of faith in him were like daggers in his heart, but he wouldn't let her see his pain—his weakness. "Clearly, the shock over discovering the truth about your father has addled your brain."

Her outraged gasp was accompanied by the sharp crack of her palm connecting with his face. He saw it coming; hell, a part of him even wanted it—welcoming the sting of her anger. It was better than the agony of her betrayal. That she could believe he'd use her to protect his father was worse than any physical blow she could deal him.

Ryann bolted for the door, uncaring of her luggage now, and darted past him. She was quick, but Aiden was quicker and just pissed off enough to be reckless. Her hand was on the door and she was halfway out when he caught her around the waist and hiked her into the air. She was so light, so fragile. Even holding her like this, made something in his heart painfully constrict. It also made something else constrict, and the knowledge of how acutely aware his body was of hers, of how uncontrollable his response was, felt like salt in an open wound. Even now, he wanted her, as hurt and angry and betrayed as he felt, he wanted more than anything to strip her bare and fuck any doubt of his loyalty from her mind.

She let out a startled yelp, then an *oomph* as he deposited her over his shoulder and kicked the door shut.

"Let me go!"

He ignored her cry, her small fists hitting his back as he carted her through the dining room and then into the living room. He was numb to her pain, because his own was too raw, too severe. He knew his words had cut deep, but she'd backed him into a corner, and the fighter in him had come out swinging.

She was making a lot of racket and putting up one hell of a fight. As they entered the hall, Nikko's bedroom door flew open and the fighter filled the doorway. Aiden wasn't sure he appreciated the look on that guy's face, which toggled between wary and protective with a general undertone of *what the fuck do you think you're doing?*

Hell if he knew. He was acting on pure anger and instinct at this point—not a healthy combination.

"Nikko," Ryann cried, spotting him. "Help me!"

And for a moment, he thought the ex-marine might do just that.

Aiden hated the desperation in her voice, and hated even more that she was enlisting the aid of his friend against him.

"Don't do it, Ryann," Aiden warned with a growl. "Don't you pull him into this. Not unless you want to see this night come to blows."

That simmered her fire a little and she stopped struggling. Aiden shot his friend a *stay the fuck out of this* glare, and thankfully Del Toro let him pass with a warning glower, or things really would have turned ugly. He marched her into his bedroom, kicked the door shut behind him, and unceremoniously dumped her onto his bed.

She shoved her tangle of fiery hair, as hot as her temper, out of her face and glared up at him. "You can't keep me here!"

*Wanna bet?* "Where are you going to go, Ryann? Huh? You think you're safe out there?" He pointed out the bedroom window. "If you think for one minute that my father doesn't have someone watching you, that Moralli isn't tracking your every move, then you're naïve. So like it or not, until this is over, you're stuck with me, sweetheart."

She paled at his verbal assault, but Aiden wasn't done. He had stellar stand-up and wasn't about to tap to this woman—or anyone else for that matter. "You want to know why I've been avoiding you these last three days? It's because every time I look at you, it kills me to know that my father is responsible for taking yours away. And if that's all I can think about when I look at you, how much worse would it be once you knew the truth? I was scared as hell of how you'd react when I told you. But congratulations, Ryann, you've far surpassed my expectations."

And there it was—the confession that shattered the fault line of their relationship, sending it crumbling into the chasm of the great abyss. But he couldn't do it anymore. He couldn't lie to her, couldn't stand here and listen to her false accusations. She'd pushed him too far.

The sob that tore from her throat was horrific. He felt the bone-deep sorrow all the way to his soul as she stared at him as if he were a monster—as if he were his father. It killed him, and in that horrible moment, every last one of his fears was realized, and they were far worse than he'd imagined.

Her tears broke him. And despite his anger, despite his pain, he still wanted nothing more than to take her in his arms and make this all go away. "Ryann . . ." he sighed and reached for her. She flinched away from his touch and rolled to her side, giving him her back as she surrendered to her own grief. He didn't know what else to do. There was nothing he could say. He'd already said too much and far more cruelly than he ever should have.

Sweat poured off Aiden's brow as he timed his punches with the heavy bag. *Fff-fff-fff* . . . *Fff-fff-ffft* . . . Again and again he drove his fist into the bag, on the cusp of exhaustion, but his thoughts would not clear. Fighting had once been his solace, his mental break where he became 100 percent focused—100 percent in control—where his mind would concentrate on nothing but the next combination of strikes, the next sequence of moves that would bring down his opponent. In here, the outside world would fade away. Nothing mattered but the next submission, the next win. But peace would not come—not for him, not tonight, maybe not ever again.

His anger shredded him from the inside out, and no matter how much he pushed and abused his body, nothing could purge his heartache from his soul. It was worse than he'd imagined. When Aiden came home tonight, prepared to tell Ryann the truth about his father, never once had the thought entered his mind that she might already know. And even worse, that she might believe he had anything to do with the conspiracy.

How could she . . . After everything he'd done for her? How could she think, for even a second, that he'd use her, that he'd betray her to his father? He'd expected her to be upset when she learned the truth, but never once had he thought she might doubt his intentions or his integrity. The blow was a fatal wound dealt to his pride, one he wasn't sure he'd recover from anytime soon, not after everything he'd sacrificed for her. And he sure as hell wasn't about to stand there and defend himself when she'd already judged him guilty. He'd be damned if he was going to hand her his balls as well as his heart.

And what could he really tell her, anyway? Nothing. What Aiden had done, turning the flash drive over to the DA and the FBI, he couldn't tell her—he couldn't tell anyone. Not until this was over, and by then it would probably be too late. The damage was already done. The accusations were already made, the hurt and betrayal ran too deep. If Ryann truly loved him, she would have believed in him. Fuck, she could have at least given him a chance to explain instead of trying to run out on him. If he'd been five minutes later, he would have come home to find her gone.

Anger and betrayal surged anew and Aiden slammed his fist into the bag over and over, welcoming the pain as his bare knuckles connected with the leather, abrading—burning—any distraction to dull the pain in his chest.

Aiden heard the door open behind him and ignored the intrusion, too caught up in his own head to pay attention to the click of the door. He knew full well who was standing on the other side of it.

"If you don't give that shoulder a rest, it's going to be shot for your fight tomorrow." Nikko closed the door behind him. His sparring partner sauntered over and walked behind the bag, scooping up Aiden's gloves from the mat and tossing them at him. "Put these on."

Del Toro pulled off his shirt and tossed it on the metal chair in the corner. He didn't say anything else as he released the Velcro on his own gloves and slipped his hands inside the open mitts before fastening the straps. His friend moved into the center of the mats and raised his hands, positioning into a fighting stance. "I take it things didn't go well with Gingersnap."

"You think? I'd say that's an understatement." Aiden circled left and Del Toro countered the movement.

"I warned you she'd be pissed if she found out. You can hardly blame her. It had to be a hell of a shock, discovering your dad snuffed her pops." Nikko jabbed and Aiden deflected, ranging him with a left-handed punch that just fell short. Aiden was moderately ambidextrous, and since he'd injured his right shoulder, he'd been trying to strengthen his left-handed striking. But Nikko wasn't here to train—his body lacked its usual guarded tension. That determined glint in his steely eyes wasn't there.

Fuck . . . he wanted to talk. Well, Aiden had done all the chit-chatting he cared to do. He wanted to fight. With a quick feint to the right, Nikko ducked to the left, closing the range and Aiden connected a solid uppercut to his ribs.

Nikko grunted with the loss of air but used his momentum to send a spinning hook kick into Aiden's shoulder that could have just as easily been his head, had his friend meant business. The blow knocked Aiden out of range, and as he readied his stance again, Nikko was quick to get in his verbal jab. "I know you're pissed, man, but manhandling and scaring the hell out of her probably isn't winning you any points in the trust department. I'm just sayin'."

*Fuck this* . . . Aiden shot for Del Toro's waist and took the fighter to the mat. They grappled for several minutes, but Aiden was already exhausted from working out. Nikko was still fresh, giving him the advantage, and he got behind Aiden and slipped his forearm beneath Aiden's chin, locking him tight in a rear naked choke. Caught in the clinch and unable to speak, he had no choice but to listen to what his friend had to say, or tap—and there was no fucking way he was tapping.

"Have you even stopped to consider how things might look from her perspective?" Nikko growled next to his ear. "She hands you her father's evidence and you practically ghost on her. What's she supposed to think when you don't talk to her and she discovers who really killed her father? I don't know who's feeding her the intel, or if it even matters at this point, but you guys had a rocky start and trust issues are bound to come up. You're both going to have to cut each other a little slack."

Nikko released the choke hold and shoved Aiden away. Aiden was too exhausted to do anything other than roll on his back and suck air. He canted his head to the side and held Nikko's gaze, who was doing his own mat recovery.

"I don't know, man," Aiden panted. "I've never been in love before, what do I know about relationships?"

"Probably more than you think, and a hell of a lot more than I do. But even I can see that woman loves you, and if you let her go over a misunderstanding that you're too damn stubborn and prideful to work through, then you're a fool and you don't deserve her. Not once has a woman ever looked at me the way Ryann looks at you—like her sun rises and sets on you—like you're her whole world. Take my advice, a woman who looks at you like that is worth giving up everything for. Don't let her go, man. Some shit a guy just can't recover from, and losing the love of a good woman is one of those things. You have something special with her, Disco. Don't let your pride fuck it up."

# CHAPTER

After denying Aiden's request that Ryann let him in, he didn't return to their room again. She'd locked the bedroom door after he'd left the first time. Amid her heartbroken sobs, she heard the rhythmic echo of his heavy bag and the sounds of his paced breathing. He had been in there a good hour before she heard Nikko's voice, but she couldn't make out what he was saying between the dull thuds of their sparring and the whap of flesh slamming against the mats. A little while after that, she'd heard the metal chink of the doorknob's resistance, followed by the soft knock and Aiden's request she open the door.

She hadn't been ready to see him yet. Everything was too jumbled in her head. She had too many questions to sort out and doubts to work through. She could close her eyes and still see Aiden's bold, unwavering stare and the hard-core determination he displayed whenever he stepped into the cage to fight. It was a trait she admired in him—until that look had been turned on her last night.

He'd met her stare head-on—challenging and belligerent—but where was the guilt, the remorse for his betrayal? Hearing the truth from his lips, admitting he knew his father was responsible for her father's death, was a blow she hadn't been prepared for. His voice had been hard as steel and just as unbending. It hurt far worse than she'd ever imagined.

Even now, she fought against the ache in her heart as she remembered the accusations she hurled at him and his furious, indignant response. But he hadn't come out and denied any of it. He'd lawyered her, twisting her words around by asking *her* how *she* could believe such a thing. How had it all gone so wrong? Just when they were never closer to seeing Moralli and his father brought to justice, they were never closer to losing each other.

The rest of the night had dragged on. With the passing of each hour, more doubts infiltrated her mind. Her discovery of the truth had been such a shock that doubt and suspicions had been swiftly ushered in right on its heels. If she'd had more time to process everything before seeing Aiden, had the time to reason through her thoughts and suspicions, she could see there was a very real possibility that she was wrong. And then again maybe she wasn't, but she at least owed Aiden the opportunity to explain himself. She sure as hell wanted one for the strip club. But other than that, she had to admit that much of her assumptions had been based on circumstantial evidence, and just because it made sense to her didn't necessarily make it true. Maybe if they could just sit down and talk things through, they would find a common ground. Last night she hadn't been ready to do that, but this morning, she was ready to face him—to hear what he had to say.

She unlocked the bedroom door and slowly opened it, listening for voices but hearing only silence. Stepping out into the hallway, her bare feet padded against the cold marble as she went in search of Aiden. She checked the gym first, but it was empty. Turning back, she headed to the living room. A twinge of guilt pierced her heart at the sight of the wadded-up blanket and pillow lying on the vacant couch. She checked the dining room—empty. Her last stop was the kitchen. When she walked in and found the fridge door open, she breathed a sigh of relief. She wasn't too late. She could hear someone rustling around on the other side of it. Her pulse quickened with anxiety. She wasn't sure why she was so nervous—she'd never had trouble talking to Aiden before. In fact, just the opposite . . .

"Aiden?"

The rustling of glass jars stopped. When the door closed, it wasn't Aiden who stood up, and Ryann knew a moment of profound disappointment.

"Sorry, Gingersnap."

Any thoughts Nikko had were locked down tight on his ruggedly handsome face. Her cheeks heated with embarrassment at the thought of what he'd witnessed last light—of her behavior . . . Had she really called out for him to help her? *Aww God* . . . Pushing aside her shame, she nervously cleared her throat. "Have you umm . . . seen Aiden this morning?"

"He left."

Alarm sent her heart galloping in her chest. "He left? Why? Where? Do you know when he'll be back?"

"I don't. We're not exactly on the best of terms right now."

*Because of me* . . . "Can't you just ping him, or whatever it is you do to find him? I need to talk to him, Nikko."

"His GPS is off, which means wherever he is, he doesn't want to be found. You probably should have talked to him when you had the chance last night."

Well, that was incredibly unhelpful and opinionated. The inflection of frustration in his husky voice was her first hint that he might be pissed—at her. "You're right. Maybe I should have, but I was too upset to think straight. I was too caught up in my head. I needed some time to sort everything out."

"And Aiden is caught up in his. He's not in a good place right now. I wouldn't recommend talking to him until he cools off. He has a fight to focus on tonight, a fight to win. Let's just get through one thing at a time, huh?"

Maybe Nikko was right. She wouldn't bother him right now. She could wait until he got home.

But as the day went on, Aiden didn't come home. She tried calling him, she tried texting him. He wasn't responding to her, and with each passing hour that drew closer to his fight, the more anxious she became that he wasn't going to come back. Nikko hadn't heard from him, either, which was making the unflappable Nikko Del Toro nervous as hell. Not that he'd ever admit as much, but she could see it in the fine lines of tension bracketing his mouth, pulling his scar tight—the tension that radiated from him. His frequent upward glances at the clock served as a constant reminder it was getting close to the time they needed to leave for the Lion's Den. Where was Aiden?

"I'm heading down to the Den," Nikko announced, grabbing his jacket off the back of the chair and pulling it on. "If you see or hear from Aiden, let him know I'm already there and text me. If I see him first, I'll text you."

She nodded. It was too difficult to speak past the lump in her throat. He grabbed Aiden's gym bag from the floor and left, leaving Ryann alone to stew in her own worry and wallow in regret.

An hour later, Ryann's phone buzzed in her back pocket and she halted her pacing to grab it. She swiped her thumb over the screen and a text from Nikko popped up. *He's here. He's fine. Be home after the fight.*

Oh, thank God! Ryann plopped into her chair, slumping with exhaustion. She was too relieved to dwell on the fact that Aiden hadn't bothered to respond to her himself. She was just glad he was all right. Ryann couldn't let herself worry about the upcoming fight tonight. This was Aiden's career. She couldn't put herself through that kind of emotional torment every time he stepped into the cage. Everything would be fine, she told herself, despite the doubt pricking her conscience. She was just being overly sensitive, because she hadn't slept in thirty hours. Aiden would be home later and they'd talk about things then.

Ryann enjoyed approximately five minutes of rest before Aiden's landline rang. She startled at the shrillness, her heart immediately taking flight. She crossed the living room and answered his phone just as the answering machine was picking up. "Hello?" The desperate part of her hoped it was Aiden calling to make sure she was there. What she wasn't expecting to hear was a woman's clipped voice on the other end.

"Is Aiden there?"

She recognized that voice, or more the sour, impatient tone. "No, I'm sorry he's out for the evening. Can I take a message?"

"Ryann, this is Madeline. I really must speak with Aiden immediately."

So the woman did know who she was, and if she wasn't mistaken, there was a definite sense of urgency in her voice that made Ryann nervous. "Aiden isn't here. He has a fight tonight. You could try his cell," she offered lamely, not sure what else the woman expected her to do. But that odd niggling of unease now returned with a vengeance. Why would Aiden's mother be calling and demanding to speak with him?

"I have tried his cell—several times. He isn't taking my calls."

*He isn't taking my calls, either.*

"Ryann, I need you to get ahold of Aiden. I overheard a conversation between his father and one of his men this afternoon. Moralli and Bennett know he's been meeting with the DA and the FBI. The fight is a setup, Ryann. Moralli plans to have him killed so he won't be able to testify. You have to warn him before it's too late, before he gets in that ring tonight."

It took Ryann a moment to get her mind wrapped around what Madeline was telling her. Her heart plunged into her stomach, trepidation seizing her as dawning reality sent her mind into a full blown panic.

Madeline's call confirmed how wrong she was, how hurtful and foolish she'd been with her assumptions. Aiden was working with the police after all. He hadn't betrayed her. When she thought of all the things she'd accused him of, the shame of it nearly crippled her. Oh, God . . . how could she have misjudged him so horribly? How could she have turned against him so easily? She glanced at the clock and checked the time. Depending on how quickly those fights went tonight, Aiden could already be getting ready to get into the ring.

"This had gone too far . . . It was never supposed to get this out of hand."

"What wasn't? Madeline, talk to me. I need to know what's going on."

"I hired you to find Aiden for Moralli. You were supposed to bring my son home—that's all. He was never supposed to fall in love with you. Once he and Cynthia were wed, he would have become the new don. But then that chit ran away with another man and it all fell apart. Moralli's been forcing him to fight. This has to stop. I can't stand by any longer and watch those men destroy my son. Despite what Aiden believes, I do love him, Ryann. Please, tell him . . . tell him I'm sorry, and that I never meant for any of this to happen."

"I will. Madeline, I have to go."

"Please hurry," she urged.

Ryann hung up the phone and quickly dialed his number while she grabbed her purse, shoes, and coat, and ran out the door. When the call rolled over to voicemail, she muttered a curse and dialed Nikko. When his call switched to voice mail, she disconnected and shot him a quick text as she waited for the elevator to arrive. When the door opened, she stepped inside, hit the lobby button, and headed for the Lion's Den, praying to God she wasn't too late.

# CHAPTER

43

I'm worried about this fight."

Aiden locked eyes with his friend, who was busy securing his hand wraps. "What are you worried about? I got this."

"Your head isn't in this, man. You know it and I know it. And in about ten minutes that fighter out there is gonna know it and you're going to get your ass kicked. If you're worried about Gingersnap—"

"It's not Ryann."

Nikko chuffed a *don't lie to me* grunt.

Aiden vacillated on how much to tell his friend. Though he'd been careful to keep everything confidential up until this point, he didn't want Nikko getting caught off guard when the shit hit the fan tonight. Del Toro had some touchy triggers, and there was a good chance an FBI raid was going to set one of them off. The only peace of mind Aiden took solace in, his only anchor to sanity right now, was that Ryann was at home—safe. Through this all, his main goal had been to keep her out of it. She'd already been through so much with the death of her father. He wanted to spare her the ugliness of bringing his father and Moralli down. In some respects, he'd failed—miserably, actually—but at least she was safe. In that, he had succeeded.

He'd had another long and exhausting day with the feds. This time, he'd had to go to One Police Plaza. There had been issues with his recorded confession, more red tape to cut, and last-minute scrambling to get the warrants in place and make sure the cases were airtight for tonight's raid. They'd confiscated his phone as evidence, since it had photos of documents he'd taken at the firm.

He'd hoped to get out of there with enough time to get back to the penthouse and try to talk to Ryann again, but that hadn't happened. He prayed Nikko was right and she just needed some time to sort the truth from fiction in her head. Maybe tonight, after it was all over and he could finally tell her everything, maybe then she'd believe him and see that everything he'd done from the moment they'd returned to New York had been for her, because he loved her.

"Listen, man, there's something I gotta tell you—" But before Aiden could say anything more, there was a sharp rap on the door. It swung open, and Vincent Moralli strolled in with Frank Luciana on his heels. Moralli was wearing a tailored pinstripe suit, looking like he was ready to go to a gala instead of an underground fight club. What the fuck was he doing down here in the pit?

"Aiden, getting ready for your fight, I see. Good, good . . . It looks like I caught you just in time."

Apprehension needled up his spine. The arrogant glint in the bastard's eyes warned Aiden he was up to something. "About your fight tonight . . . There's been a change of plans."

Aiden cocked his brow, feigning nonchalance when every instinct inside him was clamoring to attack. In sixty seconds this could all be over. He could KO this piece of shit, drag him out the back door, and deliver him to the FBI himself. It was a temptation he was giving serious consideration to when Frank, Moralli's enforcer, slipped his right hand inside his jacket, no doubt resting his palm against the butt of his gun. Of course the bastard wouldn't be dumb enough to confront Aiden unarmed.

"What kind of change?" he asked, tempering his voice but unable to completely banish his loathing growl.

Moralli grinned like the Cheshire Cat. Lacing his fingers, he steepled his index fingers and brought them up to rest beneath his chin. "You are going to lose this fight."

Nikko swore at the same time Aiden snarled, "The fuck I am." He shot to his feet and saw Frank tense from the corner of his eye. "I don't dive, and that was never our agreement."

"I think you'll change your mind."

"Don't fucking count on it."

Moralli shrugged. "We'll see . . ."

It took every last bit of Aiden's frayed self-control to let that fucker walk out the door.

"What the hell was that about?"

"I don't know." Aiden began to pace, his mind racing with scenarios. He hadn't seen this change in the game coming. "How long ago did you talk to Ryann?"

"Half hour ago. I texted her to let her know you were here. I told her we'd be home after the fight."

"Did she respond?"

"Yeah, she's fine. Well, as fine as she can be. She's worried about you. I think she feels really bad about what happened last night."

Aiden exhaled a pent-up sigh. "So do I. I didn't handle that very well at all."

Nikko stood and clasped him on the shoulder. "Well, you can tell her that when you get home. Let's go get this over with, huh?"

The arena was packed. Stepping into the spotlight, Aiden couldn't see beyond the blinding glow beaming down on him. The noise was chaotic, the cheering, the booing . . . Aiden kept his gaze down, his focus centered. For the next five rounds nothing mattered but winning this fight. He would not cow to Vincent Moralli, not now—not ever. Soon this bastard would know that Aiden was not a man to be trifled with.

As he made his way to the ring, he refused to give Moralli the satisfaction of his gaze. When he won, and only then, would he look that bastard in the eye and claim his victory. *Lose this fight* . . . not a bloody chance in hell. The announcer called his name as he stepped onto the platform. But it wasn't Disco Stick that entered the cage tonight. He wasn't here to entertain, to thrill, or to wow. This was no show. He was here to fight—fight for his and Ryann's freedom. As he slammed the door of the octagon closed, it all came down to this moment—the moment where he put his faith and his life on the line for justice.

His opponent was already in the ring, pacing his corner like a caged animal. As Aiden stepped forward, he noticed there was no referee to call out the fight, and he had all of two seconds to digest the significance of that before the fighter charged him. Aiden sidestepped at the last minute and used his momentum to send a spinning round kick into the guy's side. The fighter hit the cage, and dug his fingers into the links, clinging to keep himself on his feet. Aiden closed in and the fighter exploded, sending a swinging back fist around that caught Aiden in the cheek. The blow rocked him, sending him stumbling back as the fighter moved in, raining haymakers down on him. Aiden weathered the storm of his fury and took some damage, waiting for the fighter to gas out—waiting for his opening. Aiden thought he heard a woman scream but it was too hard to distinguish cries from the cheers.

Aiden was a fighter known for his stand-up and his rock-solid jaw. It was his ability to take damage and keep fighting that made him such a dangerous competitor. This fighter was good, but Aiden had fought better in the CFA. He sparred with better every day he stepped into the ring with Nikko "the Bull" Del Toro to train. Nikko hit harder and moved faster. There was never a doubt in Aiden's mind that he was going to win this fight. It was only a matter of time before his opponent made a fatal mistake. The error occurred moments later when his opponent dropped his guard and Aiden countered with a one-two punch.

The first strike was to the gut and the second an uppercut to the jaw. The fighter flew back and hit the cage again, and this time Aiden followed, shooting for his hips. He took the guy to the mat and braced his hands on the fighter's biceps, holding his arms down as he hopped to his feet. Aiden rocked back and shoved his knee up, passing his guard and taking side control.

He dazed the fighter with a few well-placed elbows, and moved in for an Americana submission. Pinning him with his chest, Aiden swept his arm beneath his opponent's and grabbed his wrist, leveraging his elbow toward the mat. The fighter was locked up, all he needed to do was pull down and the guy would tap—or his arm would break, Aiden didn't care which one. The challenge with this fight was going to be making it last long enough for SWAT to move in, or so he thought, until Aiden glanced up at Moralli, pinning him with a *fuck you* glare and froze.

In that moment time seemed to stop. The cheers and screams of the crowd dimmed to white noise as Aiden's heart seized inside his chest. The terror lancing through his veins was like shards of glass. Paralyzing fear gripped him in its merciless, unrelenting grasp as his eyes met and locked on Ryann. *Oh, my God, how did she get here? Why would she have come?* She knew it wasn't safe, he'd told her she was in danger. What could possibly compel her to disregard his warning and enter the devil's lair?

Tears streamed down her cheeks. The desperation on her panic-stricken face gutted him. And there, sitting beside her was Vincent Moralli, wearing a smug, triumphant grin. His hand was clamped tightly on her arm, restraining her to the place of honor at the dais beside him. All at once the realization slammed into him with the force of a freight train, *Moralli knows . . . He knows what I've done and he was right. I'm going to lose this fight.* Aiden just prayed the FBI would get here in time to save Ryann before it was too late.

She was too late . . . too late to stop the fight. Moralli and his men had been waiting for her the moment she'd entered the Lion's Den. It was as if they knew she was coming. She hadn't made it fifty feet before his enforcer had descended on her. She'd never stood a chance of escape. Whether Madeline Kruze had set her up, or if she'd innocently played into her evil husband's hand, Ryann couldn't know. Not that it really mattered at this point. They were going to die, of that Ryann was certain. But first, Moralli was going to make sure Aiden suffered, and was going to force her to watch it.

*You should have become a rook, Ryann, but I think I'll enjoy you better as a pawn after all.* The bastard's taunting words played through her mind as she frantically tried to figure a way out of this, but her thoughts were a quagmire of desperation. She'd felt a flicker of hope, watching Aiden fight. The way he moved, the way he dominated his opponent, she'd had no doubt he was going to win, but then he'd stopped, seconds from a submission and with the flicker of his gaze in their direction, everything had changed.

The crowd gasped in surprise, and many booed, when Aiden released his hold on the fighter and rolled to his feet, letting his opponent up. "What the fuck are you doing?" she heard Nikko yelling from the sideline as he rushed the cage.

"Aiden, no!" she screamed. She didn't know whether he heard her or not, but when he cast her one final glance, her heart broke as she stared at the face of defeat. It was a look she'd never seen in her fighter before, and one that would haunt her for as long as she lived. Her only consolation was that wouldn't be very long.

When the fighter slammed his fist into Aiden's jaw, he didn't even try to block it. The blow knocked him back, but he refused to go down—stubborn male. A sob broke from her throat and she covered her face. She couldn't watch another moment of this brutal assault . . .

Vincent grabbed the back of her head, his hand fisting into her hair and yanking her head up. He leaned close, his hot breath like scalding pungent vapors against her cheek. "You're going to watch this, Ryann . . . You're going to see what happens to those who betray me."

The fighter hit Aiden again—and again—and again. Nausea gripped her as the thud of fists striking flesh and bone sent a surge of bile up the back of her throat, bitter and burning. He dropped to one knee, refusing to fall and refusing to fight. His guard was down, heavily muscled arms hanging loose at his sides, arms she would give anything to be in right now. *Oh, God . . .*

"Stop this," she sobbed. Vincent's grip on her hair tightened painfully and he yanked her head back again when she tried to look away. "He's going to kill him . . ."

"That's precisely the point, my dear."

Desperation clawed at her from the inside out. Her wild gaze searched for Nikko, but she couldn't find him in the frenzied crowd. The last time she'd seen him, he'd been climbing the cage, yelling at Aiden. Where was he? Aiden needed him!

Aiden staggered to his feet, but her relief was short-lived. The next three punches were a crippling combination of body shots—two in the ribs and one in the gut, each blow sending him stumbling back. "No . . ." she screamed, her throat raw, voice cracking. Aiden must have heard her because he glanced up, giving her a chance to survey the damage. There was a large gash over his left brow, blood running freely down the side of his face, and his bottom lip was split. His breathing was fast and labored. By the strain of his tightly drawn brows, she knew each breath must be torturously painful, yet his body refused to grant him any quarter, the demand for oxygen overruling all other needs.

Their eyes connected and locked for one brief second, right before his slid to Moralli. At the sight of her held tight in the monster's clutches, fire blazed in Aiden's amber eyes that returned to her with steely determination. There he was—there was her fighter with the heart to never give up. And for the briefest moment, a flicker of hope blossomed inside her chest. She mouthed the words *I love you* and laid her hand over her heart. If she never got the chance to actually say it again, at least he would die knowing she loved him.

His top lip curled in the faintest hint of a smile.

*Wham!* The fighter dealt Aiden a blow that dropped him to his knees. An arch of blood splattered across the mat. Time stopped, temporarily suspended by her horror as Aiden toppled forward. "Noooo!" she screamed, leaping to her feet, fighting to get out of Moralli's grasp. Out of the corner of her eye she saw Aiden's opponent drop on top of him, raining down brutal punishing blows. She struggled and flailed to break free. She had to get to him, she had to stop this. Movement to the left caught her eye and suddenly Nikko was behind them. He lunged for Moralli, who must have seen him, too, because he let go of her to fend off the attack.

"Run, Ryann! Get out of here!"

He didn't have to tell her twice. Ryann bolted from the balcony and ran down the stairs, weaving in and out, and pushing past spectators who were on their feet, screaming and cheering. They were so engrossed in the fight, no one had any idea they were witnessing a murder—or if they did, they didn't care. She hit the ground floor, but instead of running for the doors like Nikko instructed, she ran for the cage. If anyone saw her, they were either too curious or too shocked to stop her. She charged up to the platform and burst into the cage.

"Stop!" she screamed, running toward Aiden as the fighter knelt over him, hammering him with punches.

When neither of them responded, she acted in thoughtless desperation and threw herself on the fighter's back. Slipping her arm beneath his neck like she'd seen fighters do during countless YouTube videos, she yanked back with all her might. But the move wasn't as effective for her as it was for the fighters on TV. She wasn't sure if Aiden was conscious. God, she wasn't sure if he was even breathing! What if she was too late?

"Stop!" she screamed again, pummeling the fighter with her fists. His momentary surprise swiftly turned to anger. The growl curdling in his throat sounded more animal than man as he turned and swung his arm around, knocking her off his back. He was stronger than she'd realized. And when the fighter's fist connected with the side of her head, stars exploded behind her eyes and she went flying.

Ryann tumbled across the mat like a rag doll. As she rolled to a stop, the roar of Aiden's fury filled the cage, drowning out the crowd's macabre cheers. Amid the pain rocketing through her temple, relief crashed over her. He was still alive!

It took a moment for the spots dotting her vision to clear, but when they did, she couldn't believe the sheer impossibility of what she was seeing. Aiden had the fighter pinned to the mat and was hammering him with punches. And the brutality she saw burning in his eyes—the rage, the vengeance . . . He fought with a fierce mercilessness she hadn't thought him capable of. How was it possible? How was he still conscious, let alone fighting? Yet there he was, caught in the throes of raw, primal aggression.

The man beneath him wasn't moving. He'd gone flaccid several punches ago, but Aiden showed no signs of stopping. The bloodthirsty crowd went wild, cheering and screaming for Aiden to finish him, and she had no doubt that *was* exactly what he intended to do. She couldn't let him do it. She knew him too well, knew if he killed this man, it would haunt him the rest of his life. Aiden wasn't his father. He wasn't a vengeful, heartless monster. He wasn't a killer.

"Aiden . . ." she called for him, wincing when the movement made the pain knifing into her head worse. She must have been hit harder than she realized. Ryann tried to sit up, to get his attention, but the room began spinning. Her vision blurred, fading in and out. "Aiden!" she called louder, panic edging into her voice. She laid back down, trying to stop the tilting that was full on tumbling now. Closing her eyes, she pressed her hand to her temple.

Aiden called her name, followed by a foul curse. He sounded a million miles away, his voice tight with urgency. But she was too dizzy to answer him, nausea churning in her gut. A moment later, a strong pair of arms slipped beneath her, lifting her up and cradling her against a wall of solid muscle. She could feel the thunder of his heartbeat against her shoulder. Through the scent of clean male sweat, Ryann could smell Aiden's familiar spicy scent and let her body relax into him. The darkness hedging around her consciousness began invading her senses and pulling her under. She couldn't fight it anymore. She was so tired . . . Every beat of her heart was like a spike driving into her temple, the dizziness clawing at her. If she could just rest for a little while . . .

"Ryann?" The fear in Aiden's voice pulled at her, but the lure wasn't strong enough to get her to open her eyes.

Just as she was drifting off, a loud bang resonated inside her head, followed by the pounding of footsteps and a voice calling out, "This is the FBI! Nobody move!"

# CHAPTER

Ryann opened her eyes and quickly shut them again. The light streaming in through the window was bright enough to blind the Virgin Mary. And that pounding . . . God have mercy, someone needed to stop that hammering. There was movement on the bed beside her, and a moment later she heard the sharp rasp of scraping metal and then everything became wonderfully dimmed. When she felt the mattress cave to the added weight beside her hip, she ventured another attempt at opening her eyes.

"You're awake."

Aiden's deep, husky voice was like a soothing balm over the throbbing in her head. Lord, he was a blessed sight. Aside from a line of sutures above his left brow and a few bruises, he didn't seem much the worse for wear. She wished she could say the same for herself.

"Where am I?" she croaked, her throat dry and raspy.

"The penthouse. You took a bad blow to the head. You've been in and out for a couple of days. I don't know if you remember . . ."

"A little bit, but not very much. It's mostly a blur."

He nodded and reached up to tuck a strand of hair behind her ear. "The doctors said you have a bad concussion. It might be a while before—"

"Hey, Aiden, my cab is here. Tell Gingersnap I said—oh, hey, you're awake." Nikko popped his head in the doorway. Finding her conscious, he stepped inside. The strap of his CFA duffel was slung over his muscular shoulder, the overstuffed bag resting against his hip.

"You're leaving?" She tried to sit up, but a wave of dizziness crashed into her, making her stomach roll, churning in the tide of nausea.

Aiden reached for her shoulders, steadying her as he gently laid her back against the pillow. "Easy, sweetheart . . . don't move so fast."

"Where are you going, Nikko?"

"Back to Vegas. My flight leaves JFK in a few hours."

"But do you have to go so soon?"

"I've been gone for three weeks. As fun as this has been, I gotta get back to the real world sometime." He dropped his bag into the chair as he came around the side of the bed. "Listen, I'm not good at good-byes, so I'm just going to say see ya later. When you're up to it, you can text me your guacamole recipe, huh? Never know when I'm gonna need it."

Ryann laughed. "Sure thing. Now come over here and give me a hug."

Nikko hesitated a moment. The tension that came over him was almost imperceptible, but she knew him well, and the unease was undeniably there. He gave Aiden a questioning glance and the two exchanged a brief look she couldn't decipher before Aiden canted his head and moved back, making room for Nikko to approach.

Nikko bent down and carefully slipped his arms around her. By the stiffness of his embrace, she could tell he wasn't comfortable letting people get this close—physically or emotionally. But he'd helped save her life, so he was just going to have to endure a little gratitude. When he pulled back, she brushed her lips against his scarred cheek. He flinched. *Wow . . .* she thought sadly, *whoever hurt this man sure did one hell of a bang-up job.* "Have a safe flight back home, Nikko."

"Take it easy, Gingersnap, Aiden."

Nikko grabbed his bag off the chair and turned to leave.

"I'll walk you to the door," Aiden offered, following him out.

While Ryann waited for Aiden to return, she tested her equilibrium again by slowly sitting up. This time she was far more successful. The pounding in her head had dulled to an annoying throb. She needed to use the bathroom and figured a toothbrush and toothpaste might help her feel a little more human again. A shower might be nice, too. Ryann braced her hand against the nightstand and tried standing. After the initial wave of vertigo, it was manageable. She gingerly made her way to the dresser and stopped to grab one of Aiden's T-shirts from the second drawer. All her clothes were still packed in her suitcase somewhere. Wow . . . was it really just a few days ago that she'd been ready to run away from Aiden? Now, all she wanted was to crawl into his arms and hear him tell her he loved her—that everything was finally going to be okay.

She gingerly entered the bathroom, and after seeing to her personal needs and brushing her teeth, she actually felt half human again. So far so good . . . Shower next. She didn't dally, just a quick scrub and hair washing. After toweling off, she slipped into Aiden's T-shirt, not noticing which one she'd grabbed until after she'd put it on. Ryann grabbed the hem of the red shirt, stretching it out to get a better look at the icon, and smiled at seeing the yellow *I* against a black backdrop encased by orange swirls.

She shook her head, smiling to herself, making a mental note to remember to ask him about his penchant for superhero T-shirts. Though she couldn't deny Aiden was her Batman, her Superman, and her Green Lantern, he was absolutely and indisputably her Mr. Incredible. She was still smiling as she left the bathroom. She'd almost made it back to bed when a stern, masculine voice fractured the silence in the room.

"Hey, what are you doing?"

*Crap . . . busted.*

Aiden's scowl darkened as he strode into the bedroom.

"I had to use the bathroom, and I figured I might as well shower and brush my teeth while I was up."

"And how do you feel?"

His arched brow told her he knew exactly how she felt. "Like I was hit by a truck," she confessed. He closed the distance and took her into his arms, gently helping her back into bed.

"Yeah, well, that truck has been retired," he grumbled under his breath.

The longer she was awake, the more her memories were coming back in bits and pieces of what happened that night—some memories she wished would stay gone, others she would cherish the rest of her life, like the undeniable love and sacrifice Aiden had shown her in that cage when he'd selflessly handed himself over to a monster he could have easily defeated.

"Did you kill him—that fighter?"

Aiden shook his head. "I would have if you hadn't stopped me. God, Ryann, when that bastard hit you—" His voice broke, and it took him a moment before he could continue. "When you tumbled across that mat, I thought . . . I thought he'd killed you."

She reached for Aiden's hand and gave it a gentle squeeze. When those mesmerizing amber eyes shot up to lock on hers, Ryann's breath caught in her throat at the sight of the luminous sheen glassing them. Emotion clogged her throat when she tried to speak. She cleared it and attempted again. "I'm going to be fine, Aiden."

"I know you are—especially now."

"What do you mean?"

"I mean it's over, Ryann. You're free. I'm free—free from Moralli, free from my father, and your father will finally get the justice he deserves."

"Oh, Aiden . . ." The tears she'd been fighting to hold back broke free—tears of relief, tears of joy, tears of gratitude. Aiden truly had saved her life.

"Hey, shhh . . ." he whispered, reaching up to dry her cheeks with his thumbs. "It's okay. We don't have to talk about it now."

"It's not that," she sniffed, swiping at a wayward tear. "I never . . . I never got a chance to tell you how sorry I am for doubting you. How sorry I am for the things I said, and for pushing you away. Will you ever be able to forgive me?"

Aiden pulled her into his arms. After giving her a long hug, he leaned back and took her face in his hands. Those gorgeous amber eyes flecked with deep browns and gold dust searched hers, looking for something. And what she saw reflected in them touched her to her very soul. God help her, she was so hopelessly in love with this man . . .

He kissed her forehead before letting her go. She sat beside him, alternating between glancing at him and picking at a loose thread on the comforter. Still, it couldn't be this easy . . . How could he not be mad at her for mistrusting him?

"Sweetheart, there's nothing to forgive—nothing to apologize for. We've both said and done things we regret, things we'd do different if given the opportunity."

Wasn't that the truth? She gave him a sad, apologetic smile. "Wouldn't that be nice? No lies, no secrets, no manipulation . . ."

"No roofies . . ." he added, teasing her with a sexy, roguish grin.

A bubble of laughter broke free and she nudged his arm with her elbow.

"Ouch . . ." he chuckled, wincing as he rubbed his shoulder.

"Oh, my gosh! I'm so sorry. I forgot about your arm."

"It's fine. Really. It's just going to take a little time to heal, that's all."

"Sounds like that's true for a lot of things, huh? Wouldn't it be nice to have a second chance? To be able to start all over and do things right this time?"

His smile faltered, his expression growing serious. "It's funny you'd say that, because that's kinda what I need to talk to you about."

The sudden shift in Aiden's mood sent alarms sounding off inside her head. What was he going to say? Lord, she didn't think she could take any more bad news. Ryann waited in silence for him to continue, each passing second interminably painful.

"I have to go into witness protection, Ryann. I don't know for how long. I guess that depends on how long it takes for this to go to trial. But since I have to testify, the feds don't want to take any chances, and they're not giving me a choice in the matter. It's a part of my immunity deal. I know it's abrupt and the timing is terrible, but this is actually happening really fast and there are a lot of decisions that have to be made in the next few days."

"I see . . ." she said numbly, feeling like her world was about to come crashing in on her for the second time this week. Oh, God, what was she going to do? She couldn't lose him. Not again . . .

"So I was umm . . . wondering . . . would you like to be Mrs. Michael Fisher?"

*Huh? Who?* Ryann's heart stuttered and then kicked into a gallop, her mind grinding to a screeching halt before jumping tracks. "Aiden, are you . . . are you asking me to marry you? Because I was hit on the head pretty hard, and that is a horrible joke to play on a woman with a concussion."

The smile he gave her would have made her swoon if she wasn't already sitting down. Aiden turned to face her, slipped off the bed, then knelt on one knee. Forget the gallop—her heart was doing the forty-yard dash. Her breath caught in her throat when he took both of her hands in his and looked into her eyes . . .

*Oh, my God! He's going to propose!*

"Ryann Andrews, will you do me the honor of becoming my fake wife?"

*Wait. What? Fake wife?* Was he serious? Ryann didn't know what to say. She sat there in stunned silence, staring at him in utter shock. She'd been hoping . . . Aww hell, she didn't even want to think about what she'd been hoping he would say. Maybe she was being unreasonable, expecting too much from him too soon. She should just be glad he wasn't leaving her. Especially after—

"And then, when this is all over, I was kinda thinking you could be my real wife."

He bit his lip, trying to hold back his smile as he waited for her answer, but failed. That ass . . . He was teasing her! And then she realized, *Oh, my God, he is proposing! For real!*

His grin began to falter. "All right, Ryann, you haven't said anything yet. I'm starting to get a little nervous you're going to say—"

"Yes!" she blurted out. "Yes, I'll marry you! And I'll be your fake wife and we'll have a fake dog and a fake house! It's going to be the fresh start I was hoping for!" She threw herself into his arms and he caught her before tumbling back, landing on the floor.

He chuckled at her excitement and then rolled her beneath him, pinning her with his solid weight. Lord, she missed this . . . she missed being in his arms, missed their connection—a connection she was relieved to discover had not been destroyed by their mistakes, their doubts, and their fears.

Aiden captured her mouth in a soul-searing kiss . . . a kiss that branded him inside her heart from this day forward, until death do they part.

# EPILOGUE

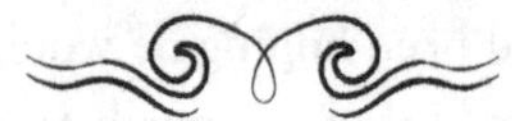

Ryann sat on the deck of their two-bedroom beach house, a few feet from the shore of Kauai, watching her "husband" learn how to surf. As she sipped her coffee, her hand absently glided back and forth over the slightly rounded curve of her belly. These past few months had been the happiest of her life. Never had she imagined such joy and contentment could be possible. But life would not remain on hold forever. Someday they would have to return to the real world again, and Aiden would be called to testify against his father and Vincent Moralli. But for now, they were enjoying their new home, starting over and forging a new life together. If there was one thing she'd learned since meeting Aiden, it was to embrace life and cherish each day for the blessing that it was, and not let the worries of tomorrow ruin the joy of today. With this man she'd found her heaven on earth, whether living on the beach of Kauai or amid the hustle and bustle of Vegas. As long as she and Aiden were together, her world was perfect.

When the wave Aiden was riding expired, she watched him take a dive headfirst into the ocean, and giggled. He was such a kid sometimes. Since he wasn't fighting, he'd needed another physical challenge and had taken up surfing. He was actually rather good at it. Occasionally, she'd ask him if he missed fighting, missed the CFA. He'd sacrificed so much for her; how could he not miss his friends, or at times yearn for his old life? But he never said anything to make her believe he wasn't happy or content. If she pressed him, he'd most often shrug noncommittally and tell her it was only temporary, and as long as they were together, that was all that really mattered. Maybe when this was all over he'd return to MMA.

When Aiden resurfaced, Tucker, their "real" Chesapeake Bay retriever, thought Aiden's splash meant surf time was over. The dog gave an excited *woof* and charged into the water after him.

She watched the two roughhouse in the breaking waves, smiling in utter contentment. She never dreamed life could be this good, this peaceful . . . As Aiden trudged out of the ocean, his board shorts sitting low on his waist, revealing those narrow hips and sculpted abs, she thought he looked like a water god. Sun shimmered on the droplets clinging to his sun-kissed skin. As he started up the beach, he shook his head, sending a spray of salty water everywhere.

Tucker followed suit, sending his dog spray all over Aiden. She laughed at the look on his face. He must have heard her, because he shot her a *think that's funny, do you?* glance. He shoved his hand into his pocket, sending the waistband of his shorts dangerously low. She froze, mug suspended halfway to her lips as she watched in ardent fascination, waiting for those shorts to slip lower. Just a liiittle lower . . . Damn.

He pulled a red rubber ball from his pocket and Tucker went wild, running in circles around Aiden and barking excitedly. Aiden gave the ball a hard throw and like a shot, Tucker bolted down the beach.

"That oughtta keep him occupied for a while."

Aiden climbed the stairs, giving her a totally drool-worthy show of hard-bodied, gorgeous male. "You know you love that dog," she teased, bridging the distance from her lips to the cup.

"Not a fraction of how much I love you."

He bent and brushed his lips over hers. Mmm . . . she loved the taste of his briny kiss when he came out of the water. The scent of the ocean air clinging to his skin . . .

"How are you feeling?" he asked, placing his hand over her belly and then kissing her again before she could respond. This time his lips lingered, tongue teasing the seam of hers until she granted him entrance and was rewarded with a kiss that sent shivers of delight into every nerve ending in her body. His hand slowly glided up, capturing the heavy weight of her sensitive breast through the thin cotton of his Superman T-shirt. She wore a pair of red matching panties that were already damp from the gorgeous show on the beach.

When his thumb teased over her nipple, she moaned, everything more heightened since her pregnancy. She was enjoying her body's changes, and so was Aiden. "I feel good . . ." she told him, answering his question when his mouth glided down the side of her neck.

A low growl of agreement rumbled in his throat. "You sure do." He slipped his hand inside her panties and discovered her secret.

"I've been watching you." She whispered the confession, then moaned when he slipped a finger deep inside her. Her core contracted around his offering, but she wanted more, needed more. Her pregnancy hormones were making her appetite for him insatiable, not that Aiden was complaining. It seemed neither one of them could get enough of the other these days.

His wicked, throaty chuckle rumbling against her ear was pure auditory sex. "You like to watch . . ." he teased, playfully nipping the sensitive flesh of her neck as he untied the string of his board shorts.

"Sometimes . . ." Her answer was breathless as she waited for him to tug them lower, past the outline of his straining erection to free that steely length of gorgeous male flesh. His mouth was hot on her neck. He put one hand between her legs; his other torturously teased her as his hand retreated to languorously slide over his chiseled abs and then back down to his cock. He gripped it through his shorts, and his touch was not as gentle as hers was, not adoring or worshipful. There was a primal roughness in the way he handled himself that was so erotic.

"Take them off . . ." The pressure inside her was building. The power Aiden commanded over her body never ceased to amaze her.

He lifted his head and arched his brow, a brow made all the more devilish by the scar slashed above it. "Out here?" He glanced behind him, checking to make sure they were alone. They lived on a private stretch of beach, but that didn't mean they still didn't get their share of wanderers passing through.

When she gave him a coy grin, he shrugged and stood to his full height. She should have known this man wouldn't have a modest bone in his body. Not that he needed one. Taking a step back so she could enjoy the show, he finished working his laces loose and let those blessed shorts fall to the ground. Her pulse quickened at the sight of him—like flesh-covered steel. Mercy, he was gorgeous . . .

"Take your panties off, Ryann."

"Here?" she squeaked, glancing left, then right. Now that they were talking about her, this exhibition was a whole other story. She, for one, *did* have a modest bone in her body—a lot of them, actually.

"Yes, Ryann, here." His husky, commanding voice was too seductive to resist.

She checked one last time to make sure the coast was clear and slipped off her panties.

"Come here, sweetheart."

He didn't need to ask her twice. In two seconds, she was out of that chair and in his arms. Aiden lifted her up, circling her legs around his waist as he backed her up against the patio door. She was already so hot, so close, it didn't take more than a few deep thrusts to send her spiraling over the edge. She shattered against him with a broken cry, and Aiden's harsh bark of release was right behind her.

As she slowly floated back down to earth, her high was crushed by the sound of a startled feminine gasp, followed by another. When she felt Aiden tense, she knew he heard it, too. Ryann lifted her head from his shoulder and found two joggers standing on the beach, mouths hanging open in shock as they stood there blatantly appreciating the bare backside of Ryann's husband.

"Oh, no . . ." she groaned, dropping her forehead back to his shoulder. He held her braced up against the glass. Thank God she was still wearing his T-shirt, but there was no help for him.

"Is it as bad as I think?" he asked, recovering his breath from coming so hard.

"Worse. It's Mrs. Kent and Mrs. Miller."

"Are they still there?" He couldn't move, not without giving them an even bigger show.

She lifted her head and peeked over his shoulder again, then ducked back down. "Yup. They're still there. They're staring at your ass."

Aiden groaned. "Well, I guess this is a good way to scare away the neighbors."

"Or maybe keep them coming back," she giggled.

"You're enjoying this, aren't you?" he accused.

"Maybe a little bit," she teased.

"We're going to hell for this," he grumbled.

"Oh, come on, now. It's not that bad. Besides, now they know what I already do."

"Oh, yeah, and what's that?" he asked.

"That my husband has the nicest ass on the island."

"You're funny."

She busted out laughing, unable to hold it in anymore. Perhaps her husband was more shy than she gave him credit for. "Don't tell me you're self-conscious. I'm sure this isn't the first time you've been caught in a compromising position."

"Maybe not for Disco, but that's not who I am anymore. The only woman I want admiring my ass is my wife."

"Aww . . . that's so sweet." She wrapped her arms around Aiden's neck and hugged him tight. After giving him a scorching kiss that would send any self-respecting woman running for the hills, she lifted her head and peeked over his shoulder again. "I think they're gone," she whispered.

"Yeah, but after that kiss, I'm just getting started," he growled, rocking his hips to prove his point.

"Maybe we should take this inside?"

"I like how you think." He kissed the tip of her nose and whispered, "I love you, Mrs. Fisher."

"And I love you, Mr. Fisher."

# ACKNOWLEDGMENTS

First and foremost, I want to thank God for blessing me with the opportunity to pursue my passion. Many thanks to my wonderful editors, Hai-Yen Mura and Melody Guy, and the amazing staff at Montlake for your dedication and commitment to Aiden and Ryann's story. To my agent, Nalini Akolekar, you've literally made my dreams come true overnight. I can never thank my fabulous critique group enough for all your hard work. Sally, Mikayla, Linda, John, and Lyanne, you make my stories shine, and I love you dearly! Last but certainly not least, I want to thank my wonderful family for your patience and continual support, for all the times you've heard "In a minute" or "Just a second" and patiently waited for me, knowing it was going to be another hour. I love you with all my heart!

# ABOUT THE AUTHOR

Melynda Price is a multipublished author of contemporary and paranormal romance. What Price enjoys most about writing is the chance to make her readers fall in love, over and over again. She cites the greatest challenge of writing is making the unbelievable believable, while taking her characters to the limit with stories full of passion and unique twists and turns. Salting stories with undertones of history whenever possible, Price adds immeasurable depth to amazingly well-crafted books. She currently lives in Northern Minnesota with her husband and two children, where she has plenty of snow-filled days to curl up in front of the fireplace with her Chihuahua and a hot cup of coffee to write.